MISCARRIAGES

MISCARRIAGES

A Novel by
Colin Heston

Special Australian Edition

HARROW AND HESTON
PUBLISHERS

Australia,
New York & Philadelphia

Library of Congress Control Number: 2019951094

ISBN: 978-0-911577-03-7

Harrow and Heston Publishers
Anglesea, Victoria, Australia. 3230.
Albany, New York
Philadelphia, Pennsylvania

www.harrowandheston.com

CONTENTS

1. The blackguard who drinks alone

I'm sitting here holding my Dad's hand. It's all rough and there's a big bump where he broke it punching his old man in the jaw, a story he loved to tell when he had a few in. Now it's limp. He's breathing in bits-and-pieces. His face is all bloated and dark purple like the cheap plonk he's been drinking. He's in a coma. They say he's going to kick it any day.

It's six in the morning and I'm supposed to be getting ready for school but I'm not going. My matric exams are coming up pretty soon, so I'm staying home to study. I'm the only one left with me dad. Mum took off a few years ago. She was fed up with his drinking, my auntie said. I can't blame her. But I didn't go. I liked it here because I could do anything I wanted, and nobody cared.

This isn't fun though. Watching my Dad die. They want me to blame him for it, I know they do. They reckon he's disgusting, and me—I dunno—they think I'm a poor little shit that's got to be saved from his Dad. They try to stroke my hair, even hug me. I push them away. They should mind their own business. The old pub was Dad's life. I don't blame him for that. The booze is killing him. So what? He had a lot of fun, and a lot of good mates. Cut short by the booze, but shit, anyone's life can be cut short, even mine, can't it? I've nearly been killed a couple of times just crossing the Melbourne Road.

Dad's wheezing now. I let go his hand. I think he's coming to. Dad? Dad? Are you in there, Dad?

*

I'm doing barman's work in the night cupboard, filling up the glasses on Mrs. Counter's tray for her customers in the Ladies Lounge, the Snake Pit as they call it. Mr. Counter will pay me good tonight. I'm going to live it up, have a few, then do that little

1

sheila I saw come in here with her old man last week. Saved up
and bought a new sports coat and pants. Can hardly wait.

A bloke comes up.

"Gimme a flask of Corio," he says.

I reach up to the shelf and dust one down.

"Five and ten," I says. He gives me a ten-shilling note. I ring up the
money and give him his change minus a shilling. He doesn't look at
it. I look back up at the shelf. There's a flask of Gilbey's gin there. I'm
going to swipe it for tonight. I dust off all the bottles and rearrange
them. Mr. Counter will be pleased. It might throw him off when he
counts the stock. He doesn't do it every day anyway.

*

Today I'm fourteen and I'm going to get screwed tonight. I'm in
the paddock behind the old pub. The back fence leans right over
like it'll fall on me. It stinks of piss and beer. It's getting dark and
there's a red glow all over the paddocks. The stubble of burnt
grass crunches under my feet. I squat, trying to hide in the giant
scotch thistles, bastards of things, without getting pricked. I'm in
my best clothes, white sports coat, navy pants, blue suede shoes.
Hair slicked back. My ass grazes a thistle as I drop down. The flask
of gin slips out of my pocket and clanks on a rock. It's the one I
stole last night.

It's dark. The cops cruise up and down, sitting in their car like
pervs at a keyhole. They shine a spotlight and it hits the old pub
fence. I freeze, scared shitless, not of the cops, but my old man if
he found out. Got no idea why they're cruising round here. The
pub's been closed for over three hours. All the drunks are well
gone. The spotlight strays by my hand that's gripping a rock to
keep me steady. I stop breathing, thinking they could hear me. It's
the Preacher! I think to myself. Then suddenly it's really dark.
The cop car drifts away. I struggle to stand up, my hand slips off
the rock, and I fall back into the thistles. I roll over on to my
elbow, right on the burnt grass so now I've got black all over the
sleeve of my white sports coat. Shit-head cops! I take a swig of
the gin. I have to force it down. How anyone can drink this stuff
I don't know. But I'm making myself do it. I'll get laid tonight no
matter what.

*

This crazy bitch, she says she's fourteen. I'd say she was thirteen at
the very most. She comes up to me out of nowhere just as I turn the
corner on Sparks Road. The church hall's lit up and the rest of my
gang's hanging around the door.

"Going to the flicks?" she asks.

It's Iris. I can barely make her out in the dark. She comes up real close, nose grazing my cheek.

"Dunno. What's on?"

"Dunno."

There's hardly anything of her, skinny as a rake, a little bulge at her breast, but a soft face, pale in the dark. She pushes her lips up to my ear. I imagine they're full, lush, like a rose sprayed with water.

"Let's go anyway," she whispers.

Blood rushes to my cheeks and elsewhere.

"Yair, OK."

I stick my arm around her waist and plant a kiss right where I think her lips are. She's on to me. We kiss like buggery. It's like kissing a serpent with a beautiful soft face. Her lips are wet and slippery. I'm half out of my mind.

The movies have started. We get to the church hall door and stop by the mums selling the tickets and the lollies. I buy a box of Jaffas. One of the mothers looks at me with a I-know-what you're-up-to look. I say, "Thank you Mrs. Lester," and take my change. We head straight for the middle of the fourth row from the back. That way, the sticky-beaks can't see us. The Movietone news is still running. I see the Beatles getting off a plane somewhere in America. Then we're into it.

She's got a hold of me. I pull back. Don't want to mess my underpants.

"Wanna swig?" I ask, sliding the bottle of gin out of my pocket.

"Nah, hate the stuff. What is it?

"Gin."

The movie's half way through. The lights go on while some kid's father puts on the second reel. We start eating our Jaffas. Iris drops one and it bounces like a ping-pong ball on the wooden floor. My mates look back to find me, grinning. They see I'm busy.

*

That was two years ago. Now I'm here with me Dad across the road from the old pub where he spent most of his life. We're in the old sleep-out on the back veranda that Dad added on to our commission house when I was little. I'm holding his hand trying to keep him going, jabbering to him, saying whatever comes into my head. I get up and go to the front room to look at the old pub, the walls, once red brick, painted a sickly cream, flaking away; the rusted gutters clinging to the veranda over a cracked concrete path; the big window with LADIES LOUNGE painted on it in fancy gold letters, the tall red chimneys, magpies perched on wires, white spots beneath.

They say the pub won't be there in a year or two. What will I do then? I'm only seventeen, well, nearly seventeen. I'm still at high school. My last year's about done. My mates around here think I'm crazy. They all got jobs a couple of years ago. My Dad always said I had to get a good education. He was telling me that right up until his coma. I should be studying right now, doing my one hour a day that I promised myself I'd do. Only I hate sitting in my bedroom at the desk he made me. I used to study right here where he's out to it, on the little cot. But Dad took it over when he got home from the pub and flopped down here after he'd had a piss in the toilet that was right next to the sleep-out. Anyway, I've read my economics, history and geography notebooks over and over, I know them off by heart. What else is there to do? What the hell are those smart kids at school doing when they're studying all day? Of course, there's English, but you can't really study that, can you Dad? You either can do it or you can't. And then there's my favourite subject Latin that I muck around with and I'm really good at, but none of the other kids at school know that, not even that I got my funny old Latin teacher to loan me a book that was what he called vulgar. I spent a lot of time copying out the whole book, all the rude words. A lot of fun that was, Dad. And you'd come up to me at my desk and say, "what the bloody hell are you doing all this time studying?" And I'd close the book and say, "nothing, Dad. Just my Latin."

Remember telling me about high school, Dad? I was in sixth grade and I asked you where was I going next, to the tech school like you did? And you went red in the face and said you'd go and talk to the teacher because he shouldn't be putting stupid ideas like that into my head. Next thing at school, my teacher, Snozzle we called him because of his big nose, draws two columns on the blackboard, one called "High School" the other "Tech School." He writes in the high school column, "4-6 years, then "Latin or French," and in the tech school, "4 years" and that's it.

"Raise your hands all those going to high school," he says.

I raised my hand along with one other kid.

"You going to do French or Latin?" he asks.

"Latin," I reply.

"Why not French?"

"My father said only the smart kids do Latin."

Snozzle wrinkled his nose a bit and the girls in the back row started giggling. "You'll all be going to girls' tech to learn how to cook," he told them.

And when I came home and told you what happened, remember what you did? You took me to Geelong and bought me a kitbag for when I went to high school. And I've still got it, Dad. It's right under my bed. I never take it to school though, because it's too big to fit in my locker.

Thanks to you Dad, I'm doing my matric exams in a few weeks, and then, like you wanted, I'm going to Teachers College next year. Yes, I know. Don't need matric to go to Teachers College, but I know you wanted me to do the whole six years and that's what I'm doing. I'll have lots of money, so my mates say. The Education Department pays us. Pretty good wicket, like you said Dad. I feel his hand twitch. His chest rises. He even licks his lips. I've made him happy, I have. I squeeze his hand and I'm sure I see his eyelids flutter just a little. "Don't worry, Dad, I love ya, truly I do."

*

They call the old pub the "blood house" but its official name is the Corio Shire Hotel, and I love the place. There's bloody fights on the street outside every Friday and Saturday nights. Only fist fights though. There's rules. No knives. No broken glasses. If ever that happens, the blokes grab the bastard and let the other bloke pummel him.

My Dad was easily the pub's best customer. He never liked me hanging around the place, but I did odd jobs for Mr. Counter, the publican. I ran errands, learned how to joke with the customers, and on race days carried bets to the back of the pub and placed them with Skeeter the bookie. I made some good dough, especially if I carried a bet that paid off. And Skeeter paid me as his spotter. I only had to tip him off a couple of times though. Mr. Counter had a deal with the cops.

Dad had his own place in the corner of what was called the "old bar" of the pub. He'd go on and on about how the old stone walls were a hundred years old. And he'd say how much better it was than the "new bar" that was built a few years ago showing off its u-shaped bar, with lots of space and fancy beer taps. The old bar was always crowded, shoulder-to-shoulder. Dad liked it. Reckoned he felt close to his mates that way, even though he always drank alone. And it was where most of the brawls broke out when a bloke's elbow spilled another bloke's beer. That's all it took. Mr. Counter's bouncer, Grecko, a champion heavyweight boxer, wouldn't stop the brawl. He'd just grab them all and push them out to the street. And all the blokes would cheer them on.

I kept out of Dad's way because he looked embarrassed when I showed up. But later, when things were not so good, he was happy to borrow a few bob from me.

*

I was thirteen when we moved into the commission house across the road from the pub. I took the bus to high school in Geelong every morning and it dropped me off at five o'clock every day in front of the pub. I was really scared. The tipsy blokes would come up to me and start chattering away about nothing. You couldn't be sure whether they were friendly or would hit you. And they'd breathe their fumes right in my face, grab my shirt or my loose tie, just as I was trying to cross the road. And the road was the Melbourne Road, a big strip of concrete with cars speeding up and down it all the time.

It took a few weeks before I was game enough to step into the pub. Then I nearly pissed myself! I put my foot on the old bluestone step, the greasy green and white striped canvas in the doorway rubbed my cheek, then a wall of stale beer and smoke hit me in the face. I turned and ran home straight across the Melbourne road, without looking, cars screeching to miss me.

The next day, though, I was back. This time I stepped past the old canvas and sidled up to the bar, but I slipped on the slime-covered floor and before I knew it, I'd called out "shit!" and all the blokes in the bar laughed at me. A bloke called out:

"You shouldn't be in 'ere ya little shit! Get the buggery out!"

Panicked, I ran out and across the road and nearly got run over again.

The next day I once more put my foot on the old bluestone step. It was about five o-clock. I heard the siren at the Ford factory. There'd soon be a crowd of blokes crossing the road and fronting up to the bar. I turned and saw them coming at me. I jumped away. I'll come back tomorrow, a Saturday, no school, and see it all up close.

*

Me mum, she was still home then, made me eat a German sausage sandwich with lots of butter. I loved those sandwiches, but all I could think of was getting across the road to see what was going on in the pub. I chomped down the sandwich and took off, mum calling out where was I going, but I was gone.

It was well after five and a hot night. The pub was packed, and it was hard to work my way through the big crowd outside. Being small, I slipped through the gaps between drinking schools and made it through the old bar entrance. Shit! The blood rushed to my face. I came out in a hot sweat; my ears went numb with the blokes yelling to each other. A bloke grabbed me by the arm.

"What ya bloody doing in 'ere?" he says with a big grin. He's a red-faced bloke dressed in oily overalls, no shirt or even singlet. I was scared shitless and couldn't talk. He didn't wait for me to answer. I pulled back, but couldn't see the doorway, only the windows and the iron bars that stopped drunks from falling through. Hot sweaty bodies closed in on me. I crawled along the filthy floor and bumped into a stool. A hand grabbed me by the hair and pulled me up. It was my Dad.

Remember that, Dad? And you know what you did? You grabbed me by the scruff of the neck and shoved me through the crowd and growled, "get back home and don't let me see you here again!" We got to the door and you gave me a push and I ran straight across the road. A car screeched. I was nearly run over again Dad! You must remember that. Nearly killed by my own father! Nah, Dad. No worries. I'm only joking. I'm squeezing the old man's hand. His knuckles are white, his fingers thin and bony. I lean over and look into his puffy face. His eyes are nearly closed, but there's a flicker. My nose is nearly touching his. It's OK Dad. You did a good job. Look at me. Going to Teachers' College next year. Just what you wanted. Pretty good deal, you always said, didn't you?

*

I've been moping round the house, stretching my legs, talking to myself all this time. It's kind of easier talking to myself than to Dad, because I don't know what he hears and I don't want to upset him. Who knows what's going on inside his head?

"You silly old bastard, look what you've done to yourself," I say, sitting in the old lounge chair beside his cot, grasping his hand in mine. Shit, you're drinking yourself to death all your mates reckon. I don't care what they say. I'll give you another glass of plonk if you wake up. You know who I saw yesterday? Yarra the chunderer. Remember him? They called him Yarra because his puke looked like the water in the Yarra. I was on this bottle drive, collecting beer bottles for the church. We went to his house. I didn't know it was his till I went around the back. There's a huge pile of empties stacked against the fence. A great find! And then I look across to the back door and he's sitting on the step. I go over to say hello. I couldn't believe it was him. You know how funny he is. I tell you Dad, I never saw such a sorry sight in my life. His eyes were all big and puffy and watery and red rimmed, just like a cocker spaniel's. Poor bugger. He looked at me. I pretended I never knew him. I didn't know what to say. He cadged a shilling off me. I couldn't say no, taking all his bottles away, you know. His little kid wanted to come with us. We couldn't let him of course. I thought he was going to cry, not the kid, Yarra himself. A grown man, for heaven's sake! What do you think Dad?"

Mum wouldn't go to the pub. I used to think it was because of Dad, but he said it was because she reckoned it was a disgusting place. Who knows? Like I said, my first time in the bar the smell of stale beer and sweat knocked me over. But now I don't even notice it. Of course, I'm not talking about the shit-house. If mum had seen it, she'd have wanted to move to a house a mile away!

Dad's coughing a bit. His eyes are half closed. I have to keep talking to him to keep him going. I'm starting to say the same stuff over and over. Dad, did you know I once sneaked in the pub after hours? Found an open window in one of the guest rooms and climbed through. I told mum I was at C of E boys club. A couple of years ago I suppose it was. It was creepy. I no sooner got in, I heard voices, loud voices and laughing and I peeked down the passage and you know what? There were cops boozing. Would you believe it? I got back out. I wasn't scared. I had to pee. I wanted to go bad, and I knew there was a toilet down the passage, but I wasn't game to go there. And to get to the shit-house out back— you must have done it a thousand times—to get there you had to walk down the side of the pub past the old cypress tree. As soon as I got that far I knew it was close because of the stink! Dad, I don't how you put up with it! It just stunk so awful, and every-thing round it and inside was all green and slimy. I stood up to the urinal, aimed high, but I couldn't go! It was awful! Thank goodness it was after hours and there was nobody there! I turned and ran back out. Forgot to button myself up even. I get to the cypress tree and there's a bloke there, drunk as a nut pissing full bore right under the tree, which happens to be right outside the pub kitchen. The cook's yelling at him and banging on the window. He turns full on to her and says, "sorry missus, didn't know ya wanted to see the bloody lot." I ran across the road and got home just in time. Nearly pissed my pants!

There's a little twitch at the corner of Dad's mouth. I'm sure he's trying to smile.

*

I'm in the bar, doing my job collecting empty glasses. I catch my foot in the lino that's worn through and turned up at the ends. I bang into a bloke's elbow and spill his beer. I'm scared shitless. My face turns red. "Gees. Sorry mate!" I say, "here, let me shout you another one."

I don't have the money but I know if I don't make the offer I'll get bashed up. He's a big brawny bloke with bare arms, bulging muscles, sun-burnt skin and wearing one of those white singlets that's gone yellow under the arms. He's looking down at me. I'm staring at his lips, waiting to be clobbered. I squeeze my way past his mates and make it to the bar. The barman looks down at me. He knows I'm in a spot. I shove the empties over to him, and push one forward and say, in a squeaky voice, "can you fill this one?" I nod towards the bloke. The barman, a good bloke if ever there was one, puts up two new glasses and fills them and pushes them across. The bloke pushes them back and gives me a fierce look. I'm done for, I reckon. He grabs my arm and I wince. Then just as quick, he lets go and roars laughing and his mates join in. He pats me on the head and says, "didn't I see you down at the old Clarendon pub?" I see my Dad out of the corner of my eye. He's staring straight ahead. Hope he's not listening.

"Me? Nah, never been there," I lie. I was there all right. It's the pub just across from the Geelong footy oval. He's lost interest though. He grabs his two free beers and he and his mates get down to it. I slink away. My Dad never said nothing.

*

Dad's breathing stops and starts again. I think he's going to kick it soon. I suppose someone should tell mum. She went and stayed with my auntie in Yarraville, Mr. Counter told me. She's been gone for a while now. She was only going to be there till she found a job then she'd get a place of her own. I don't know. I don't remember much about her to tell the truth. She never hardly spoke up, was always in the kitchen cooking. I'd light the stove for her each morning. She'd cut my lunch and I'd run off to school. She ought to know that Dad's going to kick it pretty soon. She probably does. Don't think she'd care, though. Not that Dad beat her up or anything. He wasn't that sort. He was, like they say over at the pub, a quiet drunk. Just sat on his stool in his corner and drank from nine when the pub opened till five minutes before it closed at six. Then he'd buy a flagon of plonk and take it home. And the next day he'd start all over again. Mum just stayed in the kitchen and cooked and didn't say nothing. Except on Thursdays, she'd run out of money and ask him how she was going to feed us. I was about eleven or twelve then, I think. Somehow, she always put something on the table. I was never hungry. She must have been a good Mum, I s'pose. Then one day, she just wasn't there. She'd gone. My Dad never told me nothing. I had to scrounge for myself. Lived on bread, butter and Vegemite. Good old Mr. Counter at the pub let me into the kitchen and the cook gave me leftovers, so I did all right. Then one day my auntie Connie showed up and tried to get me to go away with her. But I wouldn't. Dad just stood there, sipping his plonk, looked at her, like she was some kind of dog that strayed into the kitchen.

Dad? Are you in there, Dad? Are you all right? Take a deep breath, Dad. That'll make you feel better. Would you like a sip of plonk?

I'm feeling under his cot. There's always booze under there.

*

Hey Dad! Do you remember that night we were round at Millie's? Remember her? I bet you do. She really liked you, I know. She liked me too! A bit too much, to tell the truth. I could have done her, but you were there. Well, sort of. She tried to do me, but I just couldn't do it with someone three times my age. Anyway, she was yours, wasn't she? Don't think you're hearing this, are you, Dad? And just as well. I told my mates at school all about that night. They couldn't believe it. You couldn't drive, remember? I wanted to drive you. There were cars all down the street. Millie's place was right across from the police station. Unbelievable! I already knew Millie from the pub. I'd go into the Snake Pit, what they called the Ladies Lounge, and all the women would go crazy over me. I loved that. Trouble was they were ugly as shit and too old! Anyway, we get in there...

What's up Dad? Squeezing my fingers? You're in there, are you? Oh, that's right. She wanted you to be best man at her wedding! That was a riot! I left that out, didn't I? So, I'm in the Snake Pit and you walk in. And Millie latches on to you—hey Dad, do I see a little smile on your face? Are you coming good?— and she says, "I wantcha to be best man at me wedding tonight." And you look at her and say, "I'd be honoured, Millie me love." And she grabs your arm and drags you over to her table.

"You see here?" she says, pointing to an old leather case, "it's me going away case. Packed all ready for me honeymoon."

And you say, "shit Millie, that's great."

And she says, "don'tcha believe me? Here, look inside," and she opens the case and tips everything out!

She was really something, Dad, wasn't she?

So we get to her party that night. We go in the door and you trip over this drunk passed out in the hall, and you're lying on your back.

Millie calls out, "hey! Whatcha doing lookn up me dress?"

And you say, "gimme a beer, Millie."

"It's me wedding night," she says, "'and all you bloody think of is beer!"

You struggle up—I think I helped you—and you give her a peck on the cheek. Don't know how you could do it, Dad.

"Now can I get my beer?" you say.

"Somebody get me best man a beer," she yells, "and get me another brandy you pack of bastards!"

The smoke and the drunks are killing me. I grab myself a lemonade and take off out the back door. Then I'm gawking at the back yard. It's a circus. One of the cops from the police station across the road is driving round and round the rotary clothes line on his motorbike with a red-faced drunk sitting in the side-car singing Round and Round the Mulberry Bush and sucking on a bottle of plonk.

Remember that Dad? And they tie the bike to the clothes line and the cop revs up the bike and makes it go faster and faster. Crazy bastards! Then wham! The bike breaks free of the line and smashes into the fence and the silly buggers go flying in the air. Were you there for that, Dad? I saw you, I think. Millie was hanging all over you, crying because the bike ran over her veggie garden.

I did see you, Dad. I never let on to you, or anyone else, except my mates at school, that is. Can you hear me this time Dad? Squeeze my hand, Dad. That's right. I know you're in there. So I was there that time at Millie's. I was standing right there in the bedroom doorway. You and Millie were going at it. I dunno what I was thinking. It was a horrible sight, but it got me all worked up. The two of you were on the bed. You tore off her dress. You were starkers. And Dad, I hate to say it, but you were so drunk, you were dribbling all over her tits. And she was lolling around, her tongue hanging out of her mouth like a thirsty dog's. A shit-awful sight, I tell you! Oops, sorry Dad, didn't mean to swear, hope you're not upset. I mean it was so bad I couldn't look any more. I couldn't last it out to the end. It's my big regret. I never saw you finish her off. I had to go to the toilet, you know?

The ride home that night was pretty scary Dad. But then you probably can't remember. You and Mr. Counter were both drunk and I wanted to drive, and you wouldn't let me because I never had a license. We were going to get more beer, remember?

Mr. Counter drove all over the place and you egged him on, reckoned he was doing a great job! Shit, Dad. I was scared and I was huddled up in the back seat. Then there's this sudden swerve and screech and I look up and there's this lamp post coming at us. And Mr. Counter lets go the steering wheel and out comes this huge burp, and Dad you slide off the seat on to the floor. And there's a big jolt as the car hits the curb and bounces up on to the footpath. I feel like I'm floating and I see a shadow or something, arms flung up in the air and then there's a thump and I sees this bloke's face squashed against the windscreen, then slide back as the car stops, and the body rolls off. Shit, Dad. It was really awful. You were swearing and trying to kick open the door, and Mr. Counter was slumped over the steering wheel, snoring.

Someone peeks in and yells, "are you blokes all right?"

Dad, you were the most violent I ever saw. You kicked open the door and fell out and grumbled, "where's the bloody beer?"

I climbed out and a bloke tries to help me and I shake him off. Then I saw the body slumped across the gutter and the blood coming out of his mouth. He was one of the regulars from the pub. And he was drunk too of course. Did you know him Dad? I think you did. What happened about that, Dad? Do you know? Was it Mr. Counter's fault? Should have been. But nothing happened to him, did it?

*

I got knocked out this day over at the pub. It was just before mum walked out. I was helping out in the beer cellar and one of the extractors blew out of the barrel and banged me right between the eyes. I was walking round in a daze with blood coming down my face and someone called out for Mr. Counter. The cook cleaned me up then Mr. Counter brought me home. Mum opened the door and Mr. Counter handed me over and he hugged my mum and said, "he'll be OK." And mum just looked at me and I went straight to my room and went to bed. And as I lay down I tried to convince myself that they were just being very friendly and mum was thanking him for taking care of me. She asked him in. Do you think something was going on, Dad? Gees, Dad, did you know? Don't suppose you cared anyway. I know it's none of my business. But I can't help wondering.

I've got your hand, Dad. Do I feel you squeezing me again? I don't think so. You're too far gone, that's what I think. I found a little flask of brandy under the cot. Here, taste it. I put my finger into the bottle then tip it up. Brandy runs down my finger and I lick it off. Then I put my finger in Dad's mouth. I have to force it in. How's that Dad? Bring back old memories?

*

I know the quack can't do anything. He was useless yesterday, wasn't he, Dad? He might be able to make you more comfortable. I phoned him. He says he's coming. Just a minute till I have a sip of my cuppa tea. Here, try this. Found the eye dropper. Filled it with a bit of whiskey so I can slip it in your mouth. There, that good? Ok, Ok, not too much. That's right. Calmed you down, didn't it? I've got your hand again. You can still squeeze it, can't you?

When I was boiling the kettle I was thinking about Little Linda. Remember that time in the Snake Pit? Who could forget it? I was picking up glasses and I runs into this thing, woman or girl standing at the bar cupboard where they got their drinks for the Snake Pit. She's this short skinny little thing. Looks about the size of a kid in grade six except she's got this big swollen belly, pregnant like you wouldn't believe. And she's got this wrinkly face. You know Dad? And the wrinkles are full of dirt, something awful, Dad! She's got these thin glasses that's stuck together with sticky plaster. Everyone called her Little Linda because she was real little, not like her dad who they called Tank because he was the size of a tank and he barged around like one, and everyone was scared shitless of him.

Mr. Counter says, "what can I do for you, Linda my love?"

And she laughs and says, "don't come at that fuckn luv business with me! Gimme two whiskeys and a beer, and make it quick. I feel bloody crook."

"Shouldn't you be in the hospital?" says Mr. Counter.

"Go to the shit-house, you bastard!" she cackles.

"How long to go, Lin?"

"Shit, I dunno! The way I feel, it could be any minute. It's a fuckn nuisance. The sooner the better, that's what I say."

She gets her grog and off she goes to the Snake Pit.

I'm back in the bar collecting glasses when there's these terrible screams. I remember you sitting on your favourite stool in the corner, staring at your beer. But the screams even made you look up, and you say, "what the hell's that coming from the Snake Pit?"

I run around to the Snake Pit and there's Tank standing at the door, slapping and banging anyone that comes near the place. Mr. Counter comes up and yells, "Tank! What do you think you're doing?"

"Keep out of it Eddie, or you'll get it too. I warn youse all. No bastard's going in there while me daughter's like that."

"Like what? Oh no! You don't mean she's dropping it right in there, do you?"

And she has the baby right on that greasy lino floor in the Snake Pit. Could you believe it Dad? I sneaked in under Tank's arm, and there she was! And I saw it all! Wish I hadn't. It was disgusting! I could've thrown up. Nearly did.

And then, you remember this Dad? The next day, she shows up like nothing happened, asks for a beer and two whiskeys. She looks just the same, haggard and filthy. And she's got this old pram.

"The new one?" asks Mr. Counter, pointing at the pram.

"Yair. Struth! Am I glad it's there and not in me guts! Don't just stand there gawking! Get me drinks! I'm bloody crook!"

She downs the whiskeys and takes her beer and pram to the Snake Pit. I follow her in. The women in there, they all go up and gawk at the baby and it gets lifted out and passed round. It's making a feeble cry. I dunno, Dad. I felt sorry for it, I really did. But what can you do?

Dad? You OK? The whiskey help you? Yes, that's it. A bit of the old dog, right? You're smiling inside, aren't you? I know you are.

*

Dad, I've got to keep talking. I can't just sit here saying nothing, watching you die. Remember that New Year's Eve when the corpse got lost? After the six o'clock bell went and all the customers were gone, and the barmen were having an after-hours drinking session with Mr. Counter? There was this banging on the front door. Grecko the bouncer opens it. And that big round copper they call Dopey pushes past him half waddling, half running down the passage, his fat gut bouncing up and down over his belt.

"Quick, Eddie," he calls, "ring for an ambulance!"

"Why, what's the matter, been an accident?"

"There's a corpse out in the car park! Dead as a doornail he is! I'll have a whiskey while you're ringing the ambulance if you don't mind."

"You don't want an ambulance, you want a hearse!"

"No jokes you bastards, this is serious. Ring for that ambulance before I run you all in!"

"Hey, Grecko, ring for an ambulance will you? Dopey, you sure he's dead?"

"Of course. He's not breathing, I tell you. And he's as white as a ghost! And I reckon he's going stiff already! Another whiskey, make it double."

"Hey, Dopey, will I call the police as well?" jokes one of the blokes and Dopey spills some of the whiskey as his hand shakes bringing the glass up to his big huge mouth with its bulging lips.

"We better go out and have a look," somebody says.

"There's no need," says Dopey, "I've seen it. You all better stay away. You never know, might be foul play! I think I'll have a beer now if you don't mind. This sort of thing's a bit hard on the nerves you know."

Of course, Dopey never pays for nothing. He sips his beer and licks the foam from his lips, and everyone starts quaffing it down waiting for the ambulance.

"And how's your good wife, constable?" asks Mr. Counter.

"Huh, how should I know? Came home late the other night from the police boys club and just because I smelt of a bit of grog, she slapped me face and pissed off! I'll have another beer if you don't mind." Dopey holds out his glass.

"She's run out again?" asks Mr. Counter, amused.

"Yair."

"This must be about the fourth time in six months."

"I'm getting used to it. Getting to like it really. Married men don't get as much freedom as I do with her out of the way."

"I never thought of it like that," says Mr. Counter and the other blokes nod wisely.

"I'll have another beer, if you don't mind," says Dopey as he dabs his watery eyes with a hanky.

There's a banging on the front door and Grecko let's in the ambulance man. He's a little bloke all dressed in a grey dust coat like my fourth-grade teacher used to wear.

"Er... you got a corpse here I think?"

"That's what our constable here reports," Mr. Counter says. He's trying real hard not to grin. "It's out in the car park."

"That's right," says Dopey, being all official. "Come on and I'll show you."

Big Dopey waddles off, the ambulance man at his elbow, and the rest of us tag along.

"How do you know it was a corpse? I mean, how did you know it was dead?" asks the ambulance bloke.

"Now really sir. He's stiffer than a board. I've been a cop long enough to know whether a bloke's dead or not," says Dopey all put out. "It's just around here, beneath the cypress tree. You can see his boot sticking out just under that lower branch."

The ambulance bloke runs forward.

"Here! Over here!" cries Dopey.

It was very dark, Dad, don't you remember? We were all pretty much breathing down Dopey's neck and he yells at us, "orright! Orright! Keep back there! Wait till I turn on me torch!"

We're all sniggering and joking and Dopey flicks the torch on and then we see it! A shoe, a crumpled-up tie, and a bit of vomit.

"Ahem! Are you sure it was here?" asks the ambulance bloke, a big smirk on his face.

"It was here, I tell you! Somebody must have swiped it!"

"Now, really Dopey, who'd want to swipe a spew covered corpse?"

"But I tell you. The fuckn corpse was dead!"

"And how else could a corpse be?"

"Cut the fuckn jokes," Dopey whines, "this is serious!"

"I'll say it is," snarls the ambulance bloke. "It looks like you've got us out here on a wild goose chase. Somebody really sick might have needed us right now. I might have to report this, constable."

"But I tell you…"

Things didn't look too good. Then Mr. Counter steps in to save the day. Gees, what a good bloke Mr. Counter is, Dad, isn't he? I don't even have to ask you, Dad, do I? He's been your best mate forever.

"It looks to me," says Mr. Counter, "that this corpse was probably well and truly flaked with too much grog. Then it got up and walked away. Really flaked alkies often seem like they're dead you know."

"Yes, that's right Eddie. That's what happened," gabbles Dopey. "He's probably still around."

"What I want to know is who's going to pay for the ambulance? I'm not going away from here with fuckn nothing," complains the ambulance bloke.

Poor Dopey. He looks around us all, and we're sniggering and nudging each other. Then Mr. Counter takes Dopey aside and whispers to him, but we can hear it all.

"Look Dopey. There's still plenty of drunks staggering around the place. All we have to do is grab one, sock him one if he makes too much noise, and chuck him in the ambulance. And he pays the fee."

"Do you think it would work?"

"Of course! Come on." So Mr. Counter tells us to spread out and look for the corpse, and he goes off with Dopey and they pretty soon find a drunk staggering around and Mr. Counter says, "here's one Dopey. I'll grab him from behind and when he swings his arms, you step up to him, tell him he's drunk and disorderly, then thump him one. Got it?"

"Well…"

"Good. Let's go."

So they grabbed the bloke. He never knew what hit him, and they stuck him on a stretcher and chucked him in the ambulance.

Dopey calls out to the ambulance bloke, "we found him flaked out in the gutter. You better be careful with him. Drunks get wild when they wake up you know."

The ambulance bloke closes up the ambulance and locks it tight.

"Rightee-o" he says, "let's go inside and do the paperwork."

We all go back in the pub, and Mr. Counter lets them all have a few more beers until the ambulance driver gets tipsy, and then Dopey informs everyone that it's past closing time and they all have to leave or he'll book Mr. Counter for trading after hours!

*

Are you getting sick of me Dad? I'm doing all the talking I know, and I must be repeating myself. I wish you could talk to me Dad. There's probably lots I've left out. What about the other yarn about Dopey and his boss, the Preacher. They're a funny couple of cops, aren't they Dad?

The Preacher called himself an "individualist" whatever that was supposed to mean. I couldn't understand a word he said, could you? He always had a bible and read bits out to blokes he reckoned were too drunk. And he'd even give lectures in a booming voice, about duty to God, Queen, and the law. And he'd walk round the bar, slapping drinkers on the back, sometimes even buying someone a beer. And if a bloke wanted to buy him one back, he'd say, "fellow citizen, it's against the law to drink in uniform, but, I shall accept because it's necessary for a policeman to be on good terms with the populace." Then he'd take off his cap so he wouldn't be in full uniform. And he'd gulp down his beer, and slap his hand on the counter and announce, "well, I must away and do my duty."

This night, the Preacher came in and as the last customers were leaving the bar, he raised his right hand holding his bible above his head and said, "the peace of God be with you."

Remember that Dad? You were sitting on your stool, and you called out "Amen!" and then he and Dopey go around to the night cupboard for a few free drinks. And the Preacher says, "now, Dopey, my boy, how's the wife? Is she with you, or is she with you not?"

"She came back yesterday. I'll have another beer if you don't mind," he says to Mr. Counter.

"It is with great pleasure that I am pleased to hear it," says the Preacher, "I am glad that you are present here tonight Dopey. Your assistance will be essential."

"So, what's the trouble?"

"You know Fred's in hospital? Got run off the road on his motorbike."

"Yair."

"He is getting much better now that he is almost well, and being thirsty he requires something of the kind that you and I are drinking tonight. I consider it to be our duty as fellow policemen to see that this state of affairs is corrected."

"So, you think..."

"Do not interrupt. It is my personal and individual opinion that the far too officious staff of the hospital will not allow said refreshments on said premises. We shall thus be required to put into action a plan for smuggling in same. Do you understand sir?"

"Well, I s'pose so, but..."

"Good, then it is that we shall proceed. We'll do it tonight. I have already cased the joint, as the criminals say, and know exactly what we must do."

"But Preacher, my wife's home tonight, I promised her I'd go straight home. You know she's not there too often."

"Shame on you constable. Do you not recognize your duty to Queen and country when it is pointed out to you? The plan will not operate without you. It is beholden for you to come."

"I'll have another beer, if you don't mind," Dopey asks in his whiny voice. He makes this big sigh and his eyes go all watery. Gees, Dad, poor old Dopey, the poor bugger. And then Mr. Counter says, "inspector..."

And the Preacher bristles, "I am not an inspector, I am a first constable. We are the ones who do all the hard work."

"Oh, sorry, Reverend. I was just going to offer you a hand, then Dopey could go home to his missus."

"Well, of that I am unsure. It should be a member of Her Majesty's constabulary. But I suppose it could be done. I am not an unreasonable man. You are able in body, I presume?"

"Never been better."

The Preacher stands up straight, like he's king George.

"Then it is exactly correct," he says. "So shall it be. Peace be with you. Now we must fortify ourselves for the mission. I'll have a double whiskey as well as the beer this time."

Mr. Counter —what a good bloke he is, Dad—fills his glass, and Dopey pushes his forward too, and the Preacher gives him a really shitty look and says, "young man, you have had enough. Run along home to your wife immediately. You have an individual responsibility to her."

Gees, Dad, the two of them, they were a funny couple, weren't they? This big lanky Preacher, over six feet tall, and Dopey shorter and round like a giant pear. The Preacher looks down on him over his pointy nose that just about touches his chin. And Dopey doesn't say a word, he just kind of nods at Mr. Counter, and plods away.

"Well now Mr. Counter, are we ready?"

"What grog do you want for your mate? I'll get it while you fortify yourself," says Mr. Counter with a smirk.

"Oh. Let me see. Nothing much at all. What about, I should consider, a bottle of whiskey—Corio is fine, a bottle of brandy, a bottle of rum, and let me see. Yes, a bottle of port thrown in for good luck. Port is an excellent invalid's drink. It used to be drunk in the year of our Lord, you know."

You were there then, weren't you, Dad? It was the time when you were still doing a few odd jobs for Mr. Counter.

They sped off to the hospital in the police wagon, siren screaming.

"Well, what's your plan Reverend?" asks Mr. Counter.

"My good sir. It is that I have tried to smuggle these goods past the nurses at the entrance without success, and so I have been unable to do so. I have therefore surveyed the situation with the utmost scrutiny that a man in my position and individual responsibility is able to do, and have decided that you must climb up a large creeper that leads to the second-floor window where our beloved comrade lies. That is why I asked you to bring the string bag to carry the grog."

"Don't you think it's a bit early to do that yet? I mean, it's only eight o'clock. We should do it when nobody's around."

The Preacher looks at him for a moment and says, "you are correct. Good thinking. I like the way you plan the method and execution of your attack. We shall delay some hours. I have also just realized that this parcel of alcohol is too heavy on the long climb as we intend. Therefore, I suggest to you that you open the whiskey. We shall pull up here while I phone the station and tell them I'm on patrol." They pull up beside a telephone booth, but the Preacher stays in the wagon. They knock over the bottle of whiskey and then the Preacher advises the utmost caution and suggests a further delay until the very early hours of the morning. Then he opens the bottle of port.

"Now Reverend!" says Mr. Counter, "we should keep the port for a special occasion. You should have it after a meal or something."

"Again, you are exactly correct, Mr. Counter. So it shall be. We'll catch a meal to have with the port."

"We'll what?"

"We'll go rabbiting my boy. The spotlight on my police wagon is very excellent for night shooting. And I have a rifle, a shotgun and my police revolver if needed. Away! Away we shall go!"

The Preacher speeds off to the paddocks just outside of Bannockburn. He turns on to a dirt track, and then into a paddock full of rabbit burrows and mounds of dirt. And every bump they hit, the Preacher calls out, "may the Lord have mercy on our souls!" and Mr. Counter thanks him for it.

They took turns driving and shooting, both of them drunk as lords, too drunk to drive and they couldn't hold the spotlight still, let alone the gun, so they kept missing the rabbits, even with a shotgun! Then there's this huge thump.

"Shit! We've hit a kangaroo!" cries Mr. Counter.

"Rubbish, sir! We have merely run into a tree."

"Thank Christ for that!"

"I am pleased to hear you thank the Lord for small mercies, but really this must mean the end of our festivities here. We must make for the hospital immediately. Away!"

So they get back to town and they're getting close to the hospital when the Preacher stops the wagon right near a crossroads. They sit there until a car rolls through a stop sign. The Preacher darts out in front of him and the poor bloke smashes into the wagon. The Preacher gives him a lecture on individual responsibility and tells him he better have good insurance because he'll have to pay for the crumpled fender on the police wagon. He gives the bloke a ticket as well. And then they go off to the hospital.

"Now, in consequence, Mr. Counter, up you go!" The Preacher points to the creeper running up the wall.

"Who, me?"

"Well, of course. You could not expect me to do it. It is against the law, and I'm a uniformed policeman."

"Bugger you. I'm not going up there. I'll fall and kill myself. Besides, someone might see me."

"Who, the police?"

"Very funny reverend. But I'm not going up. And that's it."

"As an official member of the Victorian Police force thereby representative of the Queen, I hereby order you to do it."

"And I order you to go and get stuffed!"

"Mr. Counter. You are using indecent language. I've a good mind to book you. But I'll let you off only this once. Now, run along and do your job."

"It is not my job!" Mr. Counter goes to get out of the wagon, but he hears a click as the Preacher grips his arm. The Preacher has handcuffed him to the steering wheel!

"Now, sir, I must ask you to do as I tell you."

"Look, you stupid bastard, I'm not going up that wall for you or anyone else!"

"Then that settles it. I'll have to take you down to the station for questioning. I am charging you with being drunk and disorderly, and for using indecent language to a police officer, a senior constable no less."

"And stuff you again!"

"I am an officer of the law, in Her Majesty's service. I do not play games with law enforcement."

The Preacher drives off, Mr. Counter still cuffed to the steering wheel, they pull up at the police station, and the Preacher takes him in and locks him up! Next morning a cop comes and lets him out, and to this day, Dad, so Mr. Counter says, the Preacher's never said anything to him. Like it never happened!

I'm shutting up for a while, Dad. Going over my economics notes for the matric exams. I'll make another cup of tea.

*

Remember Swampy, Dad? Remember him? He was one of the funniest blokes, wasn't he? He always reminded me of Robert Menzies, you know? The prime minister? It was those big bushy eyebrows, that's what it was. He had a roll of fat under his chin too. And his voice, it was really deep and gruff.

Dad, I bet you remember this one. I know you seen it. I must have been about fourteen at the time, doing my job for Mr. Counter collecting all the empty glasses. Then I heard this loud bark. It was Swampy.

"Woof! Woof! Woof!" he yelps.

"Baa! Baa! Baa!" A little crumpled up bloke answers from over the other side of the bar.

"Woof! Ruff! Ruff! Woof! Haw! Haw!" barks Swampy.

"Go-on-ya bloody dag-arsed ewe!" calls the other bloke.

"Haw! Yer bloody mongrel dog-catcher!"

So, this crumpled up bloke, his head sunk into his shoulders, goes on bleating like a sheep, and he's wearing this tweed double breasted coat with the collar turned up over his ears. And get this Dad, when he talks, his tongue shoots out like a lizard's and licks the tip of his nose. You must have seen him Dad. He and Swampy were always fighting. Remember what happened, Dad? Yair, gees it was funny.

Yair, that's right, Dad. I see you're trying to smile.

One day, Swampy shows up at the pub riding his old draft horse, his mongrel dog in tow, the best shepherd dog in Victoria, he boasted. So he hitches his horse to the bike rack and gets stuck into the booze the rest of the afternoon. His dog follows him into the bar and sits by the door. Mr. Counter tells him, as he does every time, that the health inspector said no dogs allowed in the bar. Swampy orders the dog to go home. Instead, the dog wags its tail and goes over to Mr. Counter and licks his hand. Swampy curls his leg round the other, wipes his nose on his sleeve and yells at the dog some more and it just wags its tail harder. Mr. Counter gets sick of the dog slobbering on his hand, so he walks away, mumbling to Swampy something about he'll call the dog catcher. Swampy swallows his beer, slams the glass down and then gives his dog such a kick in the ribs it runs yelping straight out the door, its tail between its legs, like they say.

About an hour later, the dog catcher comes into the bar and stands at Swampy's elbow. He swills a beer down then nudges Swampy in the ribs and says, "Aye, y'own a mongrel with a black spot over its eye, cross between a collie and a foxie ?"

"Yair, so wot?"

"I just picked 'im up."

"Aye? Haw! Wot? Yer picked up me bloody dawg?"

"Yair."

"You bloody, haw, bloody dawg-catchn bastard!"

"What's the matter with you? I'm doin' the right bloody thing by tell'n ya."

"Haw! Shit! Who ya think y'are, ya crossbred bastard! Where's me bloody dawg? Aye? Aye?"

"Givvus another beer," says the catcher to Sugar, the head barman.

"Where's me bloody dawg?"

"Well," sniffs the catcher, as he licks the tip of his nose, "he's in at the council shelter. I took 'im in half an hour ago. Had no tag on him. Poor bloody dog was starving anyway."

"Shit! Haw! Haw!" cries Swampy as he gulps his beer, curls his leg, "you can just fuckn go and get 'im back."

"Get 'im yer bloody self."

"You get 'im. You took 'im!"

"He's your dog, you get 'im!"

"You bloody Haw! Haw! Shit-house thief!"

"I told yer, I done me duty. You can do wot ya bloody like."

The catcher walks round the other side of the bar and ignores Swampy who's swearing at him and making all kinds of weird noises.

After a few more beers, Swampy goes quiet. He says he's going for a piss, and goes out to the dog catcher's cart and grabs the dogs from the back of the truck and locks them in the cabin.

The dog catcher knows something's going on, so he runs out. Swampy's nowhere in sight because he's gone for a piss. The catcher opens the door of his truck, and the dogs leap out, baring their teeth and biting anything that moves and then they run in all directions. By this time, Swampy's back in the bar, boozing on.

Later, a bloke comes in and says, "hey, Swampy, yer 'orse is gone." Swampy lets go a huge donkey-like noise and he staggers out of the pub.

"Me bloody 'orse!" he croaks.

His dog is sitting on its haunches, whining, tied to the bike rack where his horse was.

"That fuckn shit of a dog catcher! He's pinched me bloody 'orse!"

Just then the dog cart pulls up, his horse peering out from the back of the truck. The catcher struts around the truck, twitching and licking his nose.

"This your 'orse ?"

"Yair. Wot you bloody doin' wiv it, you fuckn mongrel bastard dog catcher?"

"It was shitting on the footpath. Can't allow that, against health regewlations!"

"Haw! Haw! There's no fuckn footpath, yer shit! I want 'im back!"

"You can't 'ave 'im!"

"Haw! Gimme me 'orse!"

"Get stuffed!" The catcher's tongue darts out.

"Hey, Bessy!" drawls Swampy to his horse, "the bastard's locked yer in 'is cart. Why don'tcha kick yer way out luv?"

"You'll 'ave to come an' collect 'er at the shelter."

"Like buggery I will!"

Swampy picks up a stick and pokes Bessy. She's not too happy.

"Come on Bessy luv! You can make it!"

He pokes her some more, and she moves away but doesn't kick or anything. So he slides his arm through the rails and jabs the stick hard up her rear end. Poor old Bessy neighs as hard as she can, jumps and kicks, shaking the truck until the trailer gate pops open and she ends up on the road and gallops away up the Melbourne road as fast as she can go, with Swampy chasing her.

Ever since that day, Swampy's always barked at the catcher whenever he came in to the bar, and the catcher always bleated back.

2. Your path through the future and mine

Dad, I have to take a snooze. Been up with you all day and all night, you know. I don't mind. But I just can't stay awake any more. And I don't know if you're in there still, even if you're breathing, know what I mean? Are you there? I'm just going to sit back here in the old lounge chair I brought in. Gees, Dad, have to tell you, I'm running out of stuff to talk about. It's bloody hard. Wish you could talk, Dad. Really, I do. There's sweat or something on your forehead Dad. I'll get a damp cloth and pat you down. Don't know if it means anything. Are you hot or something? There's that white stuff getting stuck on your lips. Don't worry. I'll wipe it off.

*

I'm sort of snoozing in the old lounge chair, dreaming—Dad's breathing fast now—there's this girl, I can't get her out of my head. Can't be a dream, though, because I'm not asleep, least I don't think so. You know the one, Dad, the one I told you about. We went to the movies. I mean, she was, well I told you Dad, hotter than you could imagine. I just, I mean, it can't be OK, me thinking like this, sitting beside my Dad watching him die. And here I am getting all worked up, I'm going to have to run to the toilet. Shit, I could do it right here. I lean over the cot, rubbing myself on the edge, to see if Dad's still breathing. The little huffs and puffs remind me he's not dead yet. She's driving me crazy and she's not even here! I mean, it can't be right, can it? Dad? Dad! Dad!

*

I dunno what's going on Dad. You didn't always hit the booze, did you? I can remember you taking me to the Pivot phosphate company, I think it was. We all called it the Phossie like you did. I was really little, I know that. Mum was happier then I suppose, or am I just making it up? I don't know any more. Don't suppose it matters. I remember only bits of it. There was a huge shed with a mountain of fertilizer, you said it was. I could hardly breathe for

25

the stink that you said was sulphur. And there was this conveyor belt that went to the top of the mountain, that you built, you said. The blokes there, they all told me how smart you were Dad. Gees, Dad. How did you lose it all and end up over at the pub?

OK. I'll stop asking questions. I know it's not fair, cos I really know the answers, don't I? The way everyone looks at me when I go down to the shops or go over to the pub to pick up your booze. They even tell me I should get out of here and go live with my auntie Connie and me mum. What would I do? I'm still going to school so why should I leave you? I don't wag it much, except to earn a few bob on a good day at the pub. They tell me you're an alky. The grog got you and you lost your job at the phosphate company years ago. So what? None of their business. Mr. Counter took you on as a barman, they say. But I don't remember that. Never started going over there till I was a lot older. You were well and truly gone by then. I mean, you got too sick to do the bar work. You did odd jobs, and then Mr. Counter put his foot down and wouldn't give you work anymore. Something about when you were doing the paint jobs he caught you drinking metho. That's what burnt all your lips, Dad. That's why they're all red and swollen. You know that? Course you do. You couldn't help it, I know. We all know that. Can't blame you for that, can we? The grog got you and there's nothing anybody could do about it. If I was older I might have been able to get you off it. I suppose mum tried, and couldn't and that's why she left. Wish I knew what she was like. Can't remember much of her at all. Dad, me mouth's all dry. I'm getting sleepy again. I'm going to make a cuppa tea. Don't go away, now, will you? Stay there. Wish you could talk Dad. I do really.

*

I've been going over my history notebook, trying to get ready for the matric exam. But I don't know what I'm doing and can't concentrate because of Dad. He's breathing in fits and starts. He's going to die any minute. Dad, I can't hold your hand right now. Got a cuppa in me hands. While I was waiting for the kettle to boil I was thinking about what's going to happen to you Dad. And then I remembered the Salvoes. I don't know about them. They tried to help you, didn't they? That Captain Billington, he was always nagging you. I never liked him. He tried to grab me once. I kicked him in the shins and he never tried it again. I never told you of course.

I put my cuppa down and grab Dad's hand in both mine.

Remember Captain Billington, Dad? I feel a tiny squeeze from his hand. Or maybe I imagined it. He's still in there, I reckon, but not for long. Dad, I'm going to leave you for just a little while. It's Saturday night. The Salvoes will be at the pub in full swing, revving up *Onward Christian Soldiers*, your favourite. I remember last New Year's Eve you stood next to Billington and sang it so loud, and I couldn't believe you could do it. I never heard you speak in a loud voice ever, let alone sing. I never thought you had it in you. I'm going over there, Dad. I'll be back real quick, you won't know I was gone.

I let his hand go, and I run out quick, not looking back. He'll still be there when I get back. I just had to get out of there. Dunno why. I get these things into my head and I have to do them.

*

These Salvoes, they're a bunch of shits. They squeeze their way through the blokes in the bar, jingling their little box, selling their newspaper, putting on this fake smile, like they was Jesus himself. And they all look the same. Got these pale faces and bright red cheeks. And after they've done their rounds collecting money, they go outside and start singing hymns, trying to drown out the drunks' swearing.

"I wouldn't give you mob a bloody penny!" says a drunk, one of many.

"My Jesus loves you sir!"

"Y'know why? Yer shits! Stopped ten o'clock closing, now you're taking money off us that wanted it. Bastards!"

"Jesus loves you, my friend." The Salvo puts on this big smile like Jesus loves him more than the drunk.

"Huh. Wouldn't be bothered with your bull shit. You don't even know what you're preaching, do ya? Huh? What's God like more 'bout you than me? Huh? Why don't He stop wars, then?"

"Sir, join us in song, worship the Lord!"

"Ya don't fuckn know, do ya? All you mob want is our money to waste on those shit-house instruments of yours."

"Well, sir, come down to our citadel tomorrow and I'll try to help you."

"All you want to do is get me bloody money. Can't answer me questions, can you? You care as much for God as me fuckn ass!"

The blokes start sniggering and crowding round because they think the drunk's going to belt him one. Then up comes the biggest hypocrite of them all, the righteous Captain Billington. He's waving his stubby arms, and his navy Salvoes coat is too small to button up round his beer belly. He keeps coughing and his watery eyes look like they're going to pop out each time he coughs. He rubs his beer belly against the drunk.

"Who the fuck are you?" snarls the drunk.

"I, sir, am Captain Billington, the Salvation Army's leading member. Also the most broadminded. And you, bloody sir, are a blasphemous bastard."

"Whatdja say?"

"I said that you're a blasphemous bastard."

"Didja say you're broad-minded ?"

"Yair, I did."

"Then why don'tcha have a beer?"

"I have already bought myself and you one."

"Shit! You mean you booze up?"

"Only on special occasions, and this is one of them."

"Well, bottoms up mate and I'll buy you one!"

A bloke yells out, "A fuckn Salvo boozing! Didn't think I'd ever see the day!"

"Sir," says Billington as he slurps his beer, "you don't know what you fu—ahem—pardon, are talking about."

"Fuckn Christ!" mumbles the drunk.

"Blasphemous bastard!" proclaims Billington.

The bloke was about to hit him, but right then Billington plopped down on the ground.

"Shit! He's out to it!" A few of the blokes grab him under the arms and sit him down on the gutter at the edge of the Melbourne road, and he stays asleep sitting there.

Then comes the band.

"Onward...Chris...chun...sol...BOOM...djers...BOOM...March.. UMPAH...ing... BOOM....to war...!"

There's these two girls, shit, I imagine them out of their uniforms, pretty nice, banging on tambourines, a half-pissed bloke playing the accordion, and a little bloke humping the tuba. And this other kid, about my age, stands up real straight and belts out something on a cornet. And this drunk stands up on a beer box and starts conducting. All of a sudden, Captain Billington, rears up and taps the conductor on the shoulder then pushes him off the box.

"My dear friends," he says, "it is with great joy that I pass God's divine message to you this lovely evening!"

"Givvus anuver song! Anuver song!"

"Gentlemen! Brethren!"

"Yair! Anuver bloody song. Lesh sing the sholdjers one again!"

"Silence! Shut up you bastards!"

"Onward...Chris...chun...BOOM!...BOOM!...soldjers! Marching...UMPAH...to war!"

That's as far as Billington got. He slipped off the box and sat on the ground, looking down at his bare belly that had popped out over his belt. The band plays on, and Billington staggers up and starts to cross the road. There's cars coming, so I grab him and help him cross the road.

Dad, I'm gunna get the quack in again. I think you've kicked it. I can't see you breathing and your grip is kind of shallow. Hands still warm though. And now you've started to smell. Don't know what it is. It's not piss and shit. I don't know what to think. I'm going to get you another blanket to keep you warm. Dad I dunno what to do next. Can't you just keep going a bit longer? I'll get you a brandy. You always used to get that for mum when she had her fainting spells. Back in a jiffy.

*

I'm in the bar. It's about half past five, I think. I dunno. Haven't got me watch. There's no clock on the bar wall. Everyone's watching the new TV Mr. Counter put up. The Olympic games are on. Mr. Counter isn't too pleased with it but he can't take it down. "They watch the TV and don't drink their beer," he complains.

I start picking up glasses and bringing them to the bar. It's hard to get through the crush. Everyone's packed in to see the TV. It's the first TV most of us have seen. Sugar sees me and says, "g'day. How's your old man?"

"He's all right," I lie.

I'm in a kind of daze. I don't know what to do except what I'm doing, picking up glasses. I stay there until the 6 o'clock bell and the bar's empty. I go to leave with them all, but Mr. Counter grabs me and asks, "is your old man OK? I didn't think I'd see you here tonight. I heard he was pretty bad. On his last legs, they say."

I turn and look at him right in the face. "He's good," I say. "I got to get back to him. You want to come see him?"

"I'd like to young fella, but you know what it's like around here this time of night."

"Yair, OK. Might see you tomorrow if he's doing all right."

"Son, if there's anything I can do, just say so. Your dad was a great friend of mine and I want to make sure you do OK too."

"I know. Mr. Counter. I know. Thank you. I got to go now."

I was going to cry, that's why I had to get going quick. But I didn't go straight home. I walked around to the back fence where Skeeter used to take bets. And I had a piss in the old out-house, and I walked out into the bare paddock, scratching myself on those damn thistles. I peered at the horizon beyond the burnt fields, the red glow of the early summer sun. I wondered what was over there, remembering when I was a kid, about twelve I was, when I took off into this paddock and reckoned I was going away and never coming back. But I was too scared even to go as far as the next paddock. My hands in me pockets, I kept walking, and walking.

I must have gone a long way. By the time I got back home, I saw an ambulance and people going in and out of the house. I kept away and waited till the ambulance drove off and there was nobody left going in and out. I went into the house, and my Dad was gone. I hope they were good to you, Dad, I say, looking at his empty cot. And I went to my bedroom and I flopped down on me bed and I grabbed my pillow and I hugged it. And I slept.

I'm standing in the middle of the Melbourne Road, facing Melbourne. There's this big truck coming at me. I'm trying to get out of the way, but I can't. I'm rooted to the spot. I'm waving my arms, yelling at the top of my voice. But it just keeps coming at me. And just as it hits me, I wake up, all sweaty and gasping for breath. It's my nightmare I've had for as long as I can remember. I'd call out in the middle of the night, "It's coming at me Dad! It's coming at me!" And me Dad would be there shaking me and yelling at me, "wake up! Wake up! You're having a nightmare!" And I'd wake up and I'd turn over and go back to sleep. I must have been real little though. Dad wasn't into the booze then.

I roll out of bed with my pillow and drift out to me Dad's cot in the sleep-out and I plop down in the lounge chair. I don't know how long I sat there, hugging the pillow, dreaming, wondering what I was going to do. Then I get up and go across to the pub. I couldn't think of anything else to do. And I collect glasses for Mr. Counter, I laugh and joke with the customers and I pretend nothing's happened.

*

There was a big send-off for Dad. I knew there would be. Mr. Counter told me the funeral was set for three o'clock and most of the mourners took the day off work so they could pay their respects, as they put it. My auntie Connie had tried to get me to go with her and get all dressed up and sit in a black car but I wouldn't talk to her and I wouldn't even look at her. I hid away in the pub. It was the best place I knew to get away from her. She wouldn't dare come into the bar. All those blokes would scare the shit out of her.

Lots of blokes started to show up at the pub at half past nine, because they reckoned they needed an early start. I was amazed to see lots of them dressed up in black suits and ties. Shows just how much respect they had for dear old Dad. And I hung around, picking up glasses like I always did, listening to the blokes talk about him.

"G'day mate. Bad luck, wasn't it?"

"Could see it coming all the way, though, don'tcha think?"

"Yair. I tried to tell him. I tried."

"By Christ he drank some grog the last couple of years!"

"I'm buggered if I know why he did himself in. The grog just got him I suppose."

"It must have been something in his blood."

"Yair, too much blood in his alcohol stream."

"That's for sure."

Mr. Counter banged a glass on the old counter and stood up on the bar.

"Mates…" he says.

"Geddown ya mug!"

"Mates!" he cries, "listen you bastards!"

"Calls us bastards. Who the hell's he think he is?"

"Please! Quiet! He was a really good bloke!"

Someone shouts, "give him a go!" And I couldn't believe it, everyone went stone silent. Imagine it! The bar was always loud, always. The silence was, like I've heard them say, deafening. And at that very moment, I kind of grew up. "Now here's something important that's just happened," I thought. I was thinking to myself! For a moment, I felt I kind of knew who I was. I'm looking at all these blokes, and wondering what made them be here, what were their homes like, what were they trying to do in their lives.

The blokes around me are holding their glasses like there's going to be a toast or something. They're all looking like I never saw before. The silence, it's spooky. A restless quiet I'd call it. They're kind of looking into space, except there's no space in the bar. They're looking like they're trying to make out the shimmer of a rider in the distance like you see in the movies of the wild, wild west or something.

I give Mr. Counter a look. He sees me out of the corner of his eye. I know he thinks I'm going to cry or something. And I think I am too. My face is starting to flinch, I'm holding back a gush of tears. It's agony. It's been quiet for so long, or seems like it. And just as I was about to burst into tears, Mr. Counter saves me and he makes a loud cough and starts his speech.

"Ahem! Mates. It is now nearly three o'clock and the funeral is about to start. It's too late for us to get there now, but I know it for a fact our old mate Harry Henderson wouldn't have wanted us mucking round his grave, he'd be more than happy knowing we were in here having a few beers on his behalf. He was a great mate of mine, you know. He never did a bad turn to anyone and by Christ he could drink."

"Here! Here!"

"He had a great sense of humour and could take a joke. He was a top-notch bloke you know, and he never said a crook thing about anyone."

"Yer said that before, Eddie!"

"Yair. Finish it up, and let's get back to the booze. He was a good bloke, now he's six foot under pushing up daisies, so let's forget about it and have a few beers."

"Yair. Here! Here!"

"Okay fellers," says Mr. Counter, "here's to good old Harry and the next round is on me!"

And here I am, standing back, my tears all swallowed, and I start thinking again. What am I doing here? All these buggers in the bar, who cares about them? And why should they care about me? Course, right now they don't. Loud cheers fill the bar, and it's back to serious drinking. "The old pub's back to normal," I say to myself, then immediately wonder, "did I say that?" And I feel pleasantly lost in the noisy din, the arguments, the smell of cigarette smoke and sweating bodies, the warm and stuffy atmosphere, the jostling shoulders and elbows, the clinking of glasses and the steady beat of the cash register bell. Is this *me* thinking all this?

And outside, the air's full of the noises of life, the cars on the busy Melbourne road, the throbbing noise of the Ford factory, the shouts of workers as they make their way to the pub.

And across the road, there's builders' sheds beside my own house where the others have been demolished. Workmen are busy laying new foundations, and there's spectators gathered around, because they're going to build a new pub, the biggest for a hundred miles around, and one of which we'll be so proud.

*

I got drunk. Someone came to get me into the black car that followed the hearse, that pulled up outside of the pub. Buy a bloke comes up to me and says, "here young fella, a beer will help you get over it. Sorry about your old man." I look back at him. I was after all old enough, only a month short of seventeen, to have a few drinks, I thought. And I'd mucked around before. Wasn't like I didn't know what was going on. I had one beer and then I had a few more, and I wasn't sure what was happening to me. I started to gather up the glasses as usual, and somebody grabs my arm and says the hearse was here and asks didn't I want to say good-bye to my old man. So I go out with this bloke and I see my auntie Connie sitting in the car behind the hearse and I just stop dead in my tracks and shake my arm free.

"I want to stay with me Dad. He's not there, he's in the bar with his mates."

"But it's your father's funeral."

"His funeral's inside here. You're just getting rid of him at the cemetery. I'm not going."

And I turn around and go back in the bar and I collect more glasses and put them on the counter. And Mr. Counter comes over to me and he touches me lightly on the shoulder and hands me a beer and says, "we know how you feel, mate. Here, have another beer."

3. Where loves roses grow

That horrible day. The day my Dad was carted off to the cemetery with me auntie sitting up like a cockie in the back of the black limo.

Mr. Counter's at my side, and he hands me a beer. I walk back outside and watch the limo disappear up the Melbourne road and I down the beer in one big gulp. I push aside the greasy canvas hanging in the doorway and walk back into the bar. There's a bounce to my step. I bang the empty glass on the bar and yell at the barman, "gimme a whiskey," and he looks at Mr. Counter who nods. I grab it, and swill it down. "Gimme another," I yell. My voice, it was screeching like a cockie's. The blokes in the bar. They all was gone quiet. Mr. Counter mutters, "one more and that's it." I grab it and rush outside to see the hearse, but it's gone, and I picture it rolling over the flat hills, up past the burnt fields of thistles, going somewhere, I dunno where. They were going to stick my Dad in a hole. Bastards, that's what they were going to do. I go back in and I down the whiskey, neat again. Nearly choked, and the other blokes, they begin to laugh. And the hecklers start.

"Hey Eddie, give him another. Nah, give the little shit a brandy next. He's gotta learn the hard way."

I look at this bloke and I rush at him. He was a little bloke, pretty old. A few silvery whiskers sticking out of his cheeks. I grab him by the neck with my spare hand and I'm going to pummel him with my beer glass, right in his fuckn face, that's what I'll do. And he's coughing, dribbling beer and spit out of the corners of his mouth that's wide open, and I can see his rotten teeth.

"This fuckn glass is going right down your throat, ya cunt!"

I've got my arm up and the glass pointed right at him and it's coming down so hard it'll come out of the other side of his neck. Except that an iron clamp grabs my wrist and before I know it, I'm down on my knees and Grecko the bouncer's got my arm twisted up me back and I'm screaming in agony and there's real tears coming down my face.

Then the blokes turn on Grecko.

"Give him a go. He's just a kid."

"I'm no fuckn kid!" I call out in between sobs.

Mr. Counter comes up and takes the glass out of my hand.

"You need to sober up, son," he says quietly so the other blokes won't hear.

"I'm all right. I just need another beer to calm me down."

"Give him a drop a plonk like his dad used to drink. That'll fix him. Poor little bugger," some bloke says.

Mr. Counter looks at Grecko who loosens his grip just a little. I can stand up, and now I'm licking the tears round my lips, and trying to wipe them off my face with me free hand. Gees, I'm crying and all the bar's looking at me. Mr. Counter grips me on the shoulder and squeezes hard and I wince and nearly start crying again. It's the worst moment of my life. All these blokes looking on. And me crying, trying like hell to hold it back. A bloke comes over. It's Bossie, one of Dad's old drinking mates from before he got into the booze and started drinking by himself. Everyone said the grog had got him then. He hands me a glass of the red stuff. I look at Mr. Counter. He doesn't say nothing, just stares at me like there's a pimple on my nose or something. So I grab it and take a big mouthful. Me eyes tear up again, and my mouth and cheeks, I dunno, shrink or something, it was so bitter.

"Hey!" calls one of the blokes, "put some sugar in it for him."

Everyone laughs, so I down the rest of it and smack my lips.

"Not a bad drop," I says, "I can see why me Dad kept it under his bed."

I smiled and the rest of the blokes in the bar burst out laughing and then there was the loud din of the blokes talking and jabbering about nothing. I felt really like I was back home though I didn't really have a home as of now. But I just felt OK. Right in my place.

I looked at Mr. Counter and he smiled back. He gently patted me on the back and said, "all right. I can see you're going on a bender. Probably best to get it over with, and tomorrow we'll talk about what you're going to do with yourself. You better stay with the beer though, or you'll get real sick."

Mr. Counter handed me another beer and a fiver to spend the rest of the afternoon.

So, Dad. There you have it. That's how I ended up the day you left us. I knew you were going to kick it, I knew, OK? It's not your fault. You were just like the blokes in the bar said. You was got by the booze and there was nothing you could do about it. You did your best, Dad. I know. Don't feel like you could have done anything else. I knew what was coming and I was ready for it. I just had a few second thoughts or something. Don't know what it was. But Mr. Counter, your best mate, was right there for me. And the blokes in the bar, they were great too. We had a great time that day and well into the night. I nearly saw it through. I did pretty good.

*

I'm out to it on the bed in my clothes. I don't know where I am. I lick my lips, they're dry as a bone. I'm poking me finger into my mouth, scraping off the dried stuff caked to its roof. I don't know where I am because I can't bear to open my eyes. I feel the sun streaming in through the window like one of those laser beams in a Flash Gordon comic. I'm looking at my eyelids from the inside, they're bright red and I'm squeezing them tight. Someone's poking me in the ribs, poking real hard.

"Fuckn go away. Leave me alone!" I growl.

"Don't you swear like that to me, ya little bugger!"

"Who the hell are you?"

"I'm Abbie, and Mr. Counter said you have to get up and go to school."

I roll over to get away from the poking and fall off the other side of the bed.

"Ya silly little bugger. Whatchya trying to do? Get up and into the shower. There's a towel on the dresser. Now go on. Get!"

"Fuck you!"

She's pulling my hair. "Just cos you've got those lovely brown curls doesn't mean you can swear at me! Now get up or I'll get Grecko to come and throw you into a cold shower!"

I sit up and open my eyes a bit, shade them with my arm. The sun's glare is awful and me head's throbbing like I never knew. It's the maid or whatever they call them. She's got this dark oily skin and big round face and huge teeth. Gotta be an abo.

"Fuck you, you black bitch. You're not my mother!"

"Lucky for you I'm not. And I'm not a bitch either!"

She pulls me up by my hair and pushes a towel into my face. "Now get going. I'm telling Mr. Counter. I'm supposed to make the beds. I'm not your babysitter!"

"I'm not a baby!"

"Then don't act like it!"

I climb back on to the bed and lie flat on my belly. My head's going round and round, and the bed feels like it's going to tip me out. She pulls me over on to me back and slaps me face. Then she grabs me by the nose and pulls me up, helpless, out of the bedroom and down the passage to the shower.

"Now getcha self ready. Mr. Counter said you have to go to school."

She throws the towel in after me and slams the door shut. I take my clothes off and they stink of beer and smoke. I dare not look in the mirror. I showered until the hot water run cold. I put the towel around me and walk back to the room, carrying my clothes. "Hey Abbie," I call, "I can't wear these shitty clothes to school, so I'm not going."

She comes to the door and eyes me up and down. I give her a little smile. She's not that bad, too bad she's so old. She's got an armful of clothes.

"Mr. Counter sent Grecko over to your old house to get your clothes. He says you're staying here for a while."

"Yair? So who's he to tell me what to do?"

She chucks the clothes at me and I have to drop the towel to catch them.

"You better behave yourself," she says as she looks me up and down again. I stand there starkers, and she steps back real quick.

I got dressed, then sank back on the bed. My head ached like never before. I suppose it was my first real hangover. I put my head between me hands and rubbed me fingers through my hair. Shit! What the hell am I going to do, Dad? I got to talk to Mr. Counter. So I follow the smells of the kitchen, feeling like I'm going to throw up, and step out of the gloom of the passage into the kitchen, full of people working away and Mr. Counter's sitting at an old wooden table that had been scrubbed so much the top was furry.

"You've got time for some bacon—very good for you in your condition," he says without looking up, chewing on his own bacon and grinning at the same time.

"Time for what?" I says.

"Before the bus comes and you go to school."

"I'm not going to school."

"Yes you are. Your dad said so, because you're doing matric and going to Teachers College aren't you?"

"Everything's finished anyway."

"What do you mean? I saw all the kids going off to school this morning."

"I'm doing matric. The exams are in a couple of weeks. All we do is study. There's no classes. There's only a few of us anyway."

Abbie drops a plate of bacon and eggs on the table and pushes me on to a chair.

"I'll throw up if I eat eggs," I say.

"Then leave 'em. Now listen to Mr. Counter."

"All right. So here's the rub. You can stay here at the pub until you figure out what you want to do. If you don't want to go to Teachers College, that's up to you and your Dad. But you can't stay here unless you go and do those matric exams or whatever they're called."

"I want to stay in my old house where me and my Dad were."

"I know you do and so would I if I were in your shoes. But you can't. They're pulling the place down this week. Besides, it'll make it a lot harder to get over losing your dad if you stay there even one day more."

"I don't want to get over it." I'm chewing a really nice piece of bacon, having a lot of trouble listening to Mr. Counter.

"Yes, sure. But you have to stay here. You can study in that back bedroom we put you in last night. It's nice and quiet."

"I don't like it quiet."

"Yes, you do. You like it that way so you can have your talks with your dad."

"That's none of your business." I felt my ears go all red and my cheeks flushed. I swallowed me bacon, and sat, sullen.

"Agreed? You can go over there after you get back from school and clear out everything and bring what you want over here. I'll send Grecko over with you to help."

I stood up and grabbed my cup of tea, gulped it down and looked sideways at Mr. Counter and then looked right at Abbie. She was grinning and showing all her big teeth.

"And you can earn your keep by working around the pub and in the bar when you're not studying. Fair enough?" said Mr. Counter.

Well, what was I going to say? I love the pub life and yesterday, gees, I felt like I really belonged here. It did feel like home, and it was Dad's home most of his life anyway. So why not me too?

"Mr. Counter. Thanks, mate. But after yesterday…"

"Yesterday was a special day. We don't need to talk about it. Abbie put you to bed. You were out to it. But you were OK. Except

for the bloke you were going to smash in the face. But Grecko
and I talked with him. It's all OK."

"I really like working in the bar. Can't I just do that? Why bother
with school?"

"Because your dad wanted it. And so do I. Just do the exams
and everything will be all right."

"But I'm going to fail. They're not easy you know."

"You're a smart fella. I know you can do them."

I swallow really hard and rub the back of my neck. Truth is, I
was about to start sobbing again. "Seeyas," I mutter as I turn away
and run out straight to the loo way down the end of the passage
near my bedroom.

"Yair, my bedroom, Dad. Doing it all for you. Hope you're happy."

                                    *

"Stop muttering, laddie!"

"Stuff you, I'll talk to me Dad any time I want."

"Show consideration for others. And enough of that language."

"I have to go to the toilet."

"This way then."

He might as well handcuff me, the pommie bastard. Calls me
"laddie" all the time.

"This way and keep your eyes straight ahead, laddie. I'm on to
people like you."

I've been sitting in this tin-can church hall for a couple of hours
trying to do my Latin exam. I'm trying to translate this paragraph
from Ovid. I can't believe they chose this of all poems. I hate the
fuckn poetry, can't understand a word of it. Have to memorize the
translations then I just write them down in the exam. I'm staring
at this sentence:

*Odi concubitus, qui non utrumque resolvunt. Hoc est, cur pueri
tangar amore minus.*

Shit! Is it saying what I think it is? Struth! It's my last exam. I
have to give it a fair go. I thought I did pretty good in my English
exam. I wrote about my Dad kicking it. A real tear jerker and all
those sentences with very correct grammar that I learned from my
Latin. Why don't the shit-heads write like they talk? All the words
have to be exactly right and the verbs have to be in the right place
and match the subjects and on and on. By the time the words are
on the paper, who would want to read them, Dad?

"Dad?"

He's not answering. Probably into the plonk again, Bet they
have it in heaven too. Good old Dad will sniff it out if it's there.

"Laddie!"

There's a hand pulling my ear. I stand up to relieve the pulling and knock over my chair and make an awful noise. The other couple of kids, from the grammar school probably, keep writing away, don't even look up.

"This is your last warning. Now stop your muttering or you will be sent out. You hear me laddie?"

He let's go me ear and I pick up my chair and bang it down. I stare at the sentence. I know what it says. I'm going to translate it my way, so I write:

Simultaneous orgasms are best which is why I don't fuck young boys.

How's that Dad? Gees, dad, I dunno. It's what this bloke is saying, I know it, so why shouldn't I write it down just like we all talk?

*

You gotta understand, Dad. Those exams they nearly killed me. So when I ran into Iris just as I came out of the Baptist Hall, and I'd written "fuck" in my Ovid translation, I was kind of crazy. I stopped at the bottom step, almost bumping into her..

"Fancy seeing you here!"

She smiles and wiggles her little thin body.

"Whatcha doing here?" she says.

"Done me last exam."

"Exams in a church? What silly exam is that? You going to be a preacher?" She looks flabbergasted and she stands back eyeing me off, suspicious.

"Nah. Doing my matric exams. Me dad made me do them."

"Yair? So you do everything he tells you?"

"Yair, mostly." Fact is, I wanted her body right then and there. I was all worked up over that Latin exam, feeling crazy, and free, free of everything. Free as a bird, like they say.

"So wanna do something?" She comes up to me and I think of Ovid, the dirty old bastard. She strokes my hair – they all seem to like my hair – and then gives me a nice wet kiss on my cheek.

"Yair, let's go for a walk." I take her hand and look at her. She looks thirteen to me. Well, maybe fourteen.

"Where to?"

"We can have a look at the new houses," I say slyly.

"You mean all those commission houses like mine?"

"Yair, if that's what you live in."

I pull her along and we run down Spruhan avenue, then stop and kiss. Her sloppy kisses, they just drive me out of my mind.

Then she breaks away and I chase her. She runs into a house that's half finished, the roof is on and some of the walls, and half the floor is done. She leaps inside and lightly dances across the open beams in the floor and then leaps to what's probably the bedroom. I leap over several beams and fall gently into her. She grabs me and then we're at it. I never felt so free. We're down and we roll on the half-made floor, roll over loose nails and don't feel a thing. Everything in my life that's gone before, it's given up for a few seconds. "Ovid!" I call, "Ovid, you bastard, take this!"

We never had time to completely undress, so we're lying there half naked. And I'm exhausted. All that study and that three-hour exam, and now this. I'm completely fucked, lying flat out on my back. But she's not. She's running her hand through me hair. And I turn to her. She's lying on her side, her super short tartan dress bunched up above her hips and her panties completely gone I dunno where. She runs her hand down to my legs. They're bare, dunno where me pants are. I roll towards her and unbutton her little white blouse. And pretty soon we're both naked and this time we're at it again. Dad, I tell ya, you never told me how good this is. And to think that I once even was tempted to have a go at your Millie.

"Who's Ovid?" she asks.

"Never you mind." I rub my cheek on her belly so she can't see me grin.

"So why aren't you at school?" She grabs my hair and gives it a bit of a tug.

"Why aren't you?"

"I asked first."

"I'm a sixth former, that's why. I'm done with school as of today."

"Think you're smart, don'tcha?"

"Nah. I just did it because they all made me."

"Who did?"

"Me Dad."

"Who's he to tell ya what to do? And just because he says so, ya do it?"

"Well he can't now, but Mr. Counter does it for him."

"What are ya fuckn talking about?" Mister who?"

She pulls my head around by my hair and plops one of her wet kisses on me forehead. I roll back and then I start looking at her body all over again. Gees Dad, I'm out of control.

"You're so piss-weak you just do whatever your dad tells ya?"

"Mind your own fuckn business," I says, big smile, trying to be kind of dreamy like Dean Martin. I want more. I'm moving in on her again.

"So tell me," I grin and she grabs my hand and chews my fingers, "what about your mum and dad? I s'pose you asked them could you come here? Why aren't you in school?"

"None of your fuckn business either!"

"So now we're even!" She rolls me over and suddenly she's on top of me. And then we're into it yet again. Dad, what's she doing? Oh gees! Oh Dad!

*

She's asleep. I must have dozed off for a while, and I wake up with a shiver. A cool breeze has come in off the Corio bay. I get a familiar whiff of sulphur as it drifts in from the Phossie plant. I can't stop staring at her body. I force myself to look out through the open walls of the house and I see bare beams and half-finished roofs everywhere. I look up through the open roof and squint at the deep blue of the late November sky. I hear the distant banging of hammers and shouts of the builders as my eyes settle on her white, glistening body. She's gotta be more than fourteen. But her tits are small and I suppose still growing. I put my hands on them and rub each one gently. They're nice and firm. What more could a bloke ask for? Thank goodness I took the Latin exam, Dad, or I wouldn't have run into her! Dad, I know it was your doing. Thank you Dad! Thank you!

I must have rubbed her a bit hard. She wriggles then wakes up with a bit of a start.

"Shit!" she says. "What time is it?"

"Five o'clock. I better be going. Gotta work in the bar till six. What about you?"

"I'm staying here."

"What? You can't! What if someone comes? And it'll get cold."

"I can't go home."

"Why not?"

"None of your business. I'm never going back to that shit hole."

"But you can't stay here. If they find you they'll call the cops."

"Do what you like. I'm staying here."

I want to grab her and fling her over my shoulders and carry her away with me, just like that picture in my Latin book of the Romans carrying off the Sabine women.

"You're coming with me, then."

"We can go to your house?"

"No, there's workers in there, pulling it down."

"What for?"

"They're building a new pub. I'll think of something on the way. Come on!"

"Nah! I'm staying here."

I grab her and pull her close to me. We're still stark naked and I'm getting ready to go again. Oh God!! Then I feel her shivering. She's cold, I guess. But then she starts sobbing something awful.

"Gees, Iris, what's the matter?" I look around for my school pants and shirt. They're pretty filthy. Only ones I've got anyway. Now Iris is holding me tight, her fingernails digging in to my back. "Ouch, Iris, what's going on? It fuckn hurts!"

"Fuck you. You got what you want and now you're running off. Me mum said they all do that."

"Shit Iris, I want you to come with me." I kind of push her away and she clings even tighter. "Iris, let me go! I gotta go to work."

"Fuck off then!" She pushes me away and then drops down and curls up on the floor.

"Shit Iris. You're all fucked up. Come back with me. You can stay in my room."

"What room?"

"At the pub."

"They won't let me in there. I'm too young."

"They don't care. There's kids running around the Ladies Lounge all the time."

I pull up my pants and tuck in my shirt. I take her clothes to her and say, trying to be funny, "you want me to dress you?"

She throws her clothes back at me and calls me all the shits you ever heard of. She jumps across the beams to the corner of the room and squats down hugging her knees. I lean forward with her clothes and hold them out, just like I was feeding a croc at the zoo. I dunno what's going on Dad. I mean, we were going at it just a while ago. And now...

"Stop muttering," she growls, "who are you talking to?"

"You're the only one here."

"I'm not your dad, then," she says with a smirk. Baiting me I think she was. I squint at her. She's a lot older than she looks, I say to myself yet again.

"I wasn't talking to me dad. I told you, he's dead and gone."

"Yair, sure."

"Get your clothes and let's go." She squats down straddling the open beams and has a piss. I look away, can't bear to watch her. Gees, I dunno, Dad.

*

That fuckn dog. They called it Nipper. Mr. Counter kept it tied up on a ten-foot chain hooked on to the tap at the gully trap just outside the kitchen door. There was no one in the kitchen at half past five, peak hour in the bar. We'd come in the side gate. So we had to pass by Nipper, a vicious little shit of a thing, a foxy with a full tail. I tried to pat it and talk to it but it wouldn't stop yelping. And it bit at my pants and tore them with its razor teeth, but had to let go to bark. And it just wouldn't shut up. Then it runs up and down, straining at the end of the chain, getting it wrapped around me feet.

"Nipper, you little shit," I say trying to be nice, "shut the fuck up!"

It barked even more and rushed so fast to the end of the chain it was jerked back by the throat and launched into the air.

"Why don'tcha be nice to it?" says Iris. I was keeping her behind me so she wouldn't get bitten.

"I'm trying. What's it fuckn look like?"

Iris pulls me away and laughs. "You silly bugger," she says. Then she gets down on all fours and crawls up to the dog. Nipper stops in his tracks. I'm frozen shitless. I can see it all before me. The fuckn dog's going to leap at Iris and tear a piece of flesh right off her lovely little face.

"You silly bitch," I mutter, "get away for Christ sake. He'll bite your fuckn head off!"

Iris squats, just like when she had a piss at the Commission house. She puts her hand out and beckons with her fingers. Nipper's fucked up. He doesn't know what's going on. He starts walking around in circles. And the chain's getting all tangled up. And bugger me, he stops barking. He starts whimpering instead. Iris's fingers just touch the back of his neck and she manages to wiggle them into his fur. And now she's patting him with smooth slow strokes, starting at the top of his head, then right down his back.

"There, there Nipper," she says in her thin little voice, "we're going to be good friends, aren't we?"

I'm starting to edge back out of Nipper's range. I don't trust the little shit of a dog.

"Iris," I whisper, "we gotta get away from here. He'll turn on you, I tell ya."

She ignores me. She's got Nipper in her sights and she won't let go. Nipper whimpers more and more, then for shit sake, he starts to rub his head against Iris's leg and she responds by twiddling with his ear. I'm feeling fuckn jealous! I step back, a big step back, and I see Nipper's other ear twitch and I know he's watching me out of the corner of his eye.

"There, there," says Iris, "there's nothing to be upset about. We're friends you and me."

I take another step back, and Iris gives me a look, as if to say, "you fuckn idiot."

Then all hell breaks loose. Nipper jerks his head back then snaps at Iris's hand. She loses her balance and falls over backwards. Nipper grabs the closest thing to him, Iris's foot. And he won't let go, all the time snarling and baring his teeth. I grab Iris by her armpit and pull her away. Her sandshoe comes off in Nipper's teeth and he rushes in the other direction until the chain jerks him into the air by the neck. And the barking starts all over, Iris's shoe sits chomped up out of reach. I'm waiting for Iris to cuddle into me, make herself feel safe in my arms.

"You fuckn shit. Why didn't you stay still? You nearly got me bit!" she growls.

"You're the fuckn shit. Trying to show off. I told you the fuckn dog's mad."

"Now he's got me shoe, thanks to you!"

"Soon fix that!"

I step forward, right within Nipper's reach. The shoe's in easy reach, but I know if I put my hand down, the fuckn mad dog will bite it off.

"Here, Nipper, come here old fella," I call.

Nipper couldn't care less what I'm saying. He lunges at me and I'm ready. I give him my best kick in the ribs and he screams, yelping as the force of the kick sends him flying across the other side of the gulley trap. I grab the shoe and retreat to Iris.

"Your shoe!" I say, all proud of myself. She looks at me like I was her father or something.

"You didn't have to do that," she says, looking scared.

"I gotcha shoe. Fuck you."

She looks at me like she's going to slap me or something. She's a silly little fuckn bitch. This is all fucked up. "Come on, I'm taking you home. You can't stay here."

"You said I fuckn could!"

"That was before."

"Before what?"

"I have to work."

"You said that before."

"I know." My mouth is moving, saying things I don't want to say. "It's not gunna work out."

"Then why'd you bring me here?"

"Because I couldn't leave you in that half-built commission house, you silly shit."

"Me mum was right. You're sick of me. I don't need you anyway."

"All right then. Fuck off!"

Now she's crying. Works all the time. I look over at Nipper. He's eyeing me off, but he hasn't left off barking. If he could get loose, I know what he'd do. I stamp my foot at him and he goes nuts. The chain practically pulls his head off when he leaps at me. Iris is squatting down again. Like she's having a piss. Dad? Dad? Are you watching this? Was mum like this? I dunno what's going on.

Iris looks up, her lips twitching. "I'm going," she says.

"OK. Go then, fuck you."

"You don't have to talk like that. Just because I let you fuck me."

"Yair, right! You fucked *me*, that's what you did!"

Dad, I think I just said the wrong thing. Dad! Dad, are you there? I need you.

She's snivelling now. It's like she's been smacked by her old man and she's feeling like she did something bad. "I can't go home," she says and looks up at me. And now I'm going to pieces. Gees, Dad. What am I going to do? I don't really want her here all the time, but I do want her.

"Why can't you go home? You never told me yet."

"It's me dad."

"So what, he'll give you a back-hander?"

"Nope, probably not. Not at first."

"Then what's wrong then?"

"He'll fuck me…" There's that snivel again. I dunno what to say. I mean, she's got to be lying, hasn't she, Dad? I'm just frozen speechless. Don't know what to say.

"What about your mum?"

"She won't be home."

"So have you told her?"

"I don't have to."

"What the fuck are you saying? Course you have to."

"She watches us."

"Shit!"

"Yair. She watches us. While she prays to Jesus."

She snivels again and there's lots more tears. I grab her in my arms and she whimpers, just like Nipper. I give her a squeeze and she clings to me. I look across at Nipper, fucking stupid dog. I want to kick him really hard. I mean really hard. I'd like to kick every fuckn bark out of him. I take Iris's hand and pull her along to the kitchen door. We slip through the kitchen then run down the passage to my room. The noise of the bar fades as we slip inside. I give her my nicest sweetest kiss on her always wet lips. I take her gently to the bed and she plops down, sitting on the edge. She can see what I'm thinking and it's not good. Dad, I can't hide it. I just can't. And I can't help it.

"Got to go to work. They'll be running out of glasses. Mr. Counter will be cheesed off."

And I'm gone.

*

Iris fell back on the bed and rolled on to her side, facing the little window. The old blind was closed, a narrow rip down its middle letting in a red shaft of light from the setting sun. She rolled off the bed and stood at the window, peering through the rip. The curved silhouettes of the Quonset huts that housed all the New Aussies hovered over the dark outlines of drunks staggering around to piss at the back fence. She fell back on to the little narrow bed and hugged the pillow. It smelled of him.

"I could love you," she murmured, "but I could hate you too." She buried her face in the pillow, still snivelling. She dreamed of strolling in the bush, hand in hand, smelling the gum trees, frolicking in lush green grass by a billabong.

*

A huge roar rises up from the crowded bar. I'm trying to squeeze my way through the pack to bring in the dirty glasses. The barmen have run out of glasses. I'm holding handfuls of them above my head.

"Get 'em down, I can't see," someone yells above the roar. They're watching the Olympic games on the new TV that Mr. Counter put up specially for the Games. It was the first TV any of us had ever seen. I reached the counter, put down the glasses and struggled out to get more. Outside there was a bloke taking bets. They were all giving him money on John Landy to win the gold 1500. "Paying gold or nothing!" calls the bookie, and they can't give him their money quick enough.

"When's the race?" I ask the bloke next to me.

"Stuffed if I know."

I don't recognize the bookie. He's not Skeeter who I usually ran for back behind the fence near the dunny. He spies me looking at him.

"Piss off, sonny, you're too young to bet," he yells in between calling out, "Landy to win, c'mon, place your bets!"

"Two bob to place!"

"No, nothing doing. Win or nothing! It's five to one to win! Place your bets!"

"Two bob for him to lose," I says, without knowing what I'm doing. I don't even have two bob on me.

"Piss off you little shit," the bookie scowls, "go home to your mother."

My ears go red and me eyes are burning. I'm gonna blow. I leap over the blokes crowded around him and grab his nose. He's only a little bloke, and his nose is all puffy and red, not that different from my old man's.

"You leave my mother out of it!" I shout.

The bookie shrieks and grabs my wrist. He's got these big hands and in no time, I'm down on my knees, his hand bending back my wrist.

"Next time pick on someone your own size, sonny," and he knees me on the chin and I go sprawling backwards, and my face bangs against the blokes' legs and boots. They take no notice. I crawl away, and they're still betting like nothing happened. I stand up feeling stupid. Now I'm flushed all over and I'm going to rush back into the mob and have another go. I feel a bit of blood dripping off my chin and pull out my hanky to wipe it off. Then I see Grecko standing on the other side of the mob, his arms crossed. He's eyeing me off. I start collecting glasses.

I make my way back into the bar. There's a hush and low mutters all round.

"What's going on?" I ask a bloke.

"It's the Landy race."

And they're off! I turn to see where the bookie is, but he's nowhere in sight. The runners are all spread out, but Landy's keeping up. By now, though, we can all see that he's not going to win. Poor bastard. Everyone had a lot riding on him. The blokes in the bar start yelling.

"C'mon, ya tired shit! Run, you fuckn idiot!"

Poor bugger ran his heart out, but it wasn't good enough. The blokes start calling out for more drinks. I look for the bookie again.

He's gone. No wonder he wouldn't take bets on a place. Landy gets the bronze. Poor bugger.

The six o'clock bell goes and the barmen start filling up the glasses for the final swill. I'm running around grabbing up glasses. There's a lot of drunks staggering around outside. I'm laughing and joking with the barmen. I'm looking forward to a beer with them once we get the bar cleaned up and the last of the customers out the doors.

*

It's Saturday night and we're all sitting on the floor in the passage outside the old bar back door, leaning against the wall, legs stretched out in front of us, our beers sitting on the floor next to us. It's half past six and the cops have left already, each of them carrying a couple of bottles of beer under their arms. Mr. Counter is in his little office counting the money with Sugar, the head barman. We're talking about the race.

"Landy should have won."

"Bull shit. Never had a chance."

"*The Argus* put too much pressure on him."

"Either he could do it or he couldn't."

"Did ya have anything on him?"

"Yair, just a couple of bob."

"I tried to bet on him losing," I say, "but the fuckn bookie wouldn't take the bet."

"Watch your language, young fella!"

As if anybody cared. It was old Bulla talking – had a big name for himself because nobody ever heard him swear. A big bloke, as wide as he was tall and big beefy hands that made a beer glass look like a toy. He was the size a Mount Bulla, so that's what they called him.

"Get stuffed!" I say, a cheeky look at the other blokes.

"Hey Bulla, you gunna take that from a cheeky little kid?"

"I'm not a little kid," I says.

Bulla is the only one of us still standing. We all knew why. Because if he sat down on the floor he couldn't get up!

"You see this?" says Bulla, looking very serious, his eyes just little slits sitting behind a round puffy face. He puts the glass of beer to his lips and gulps the beer down, then holds out the glass. "Think of this as your neck," he says with a smirk. Then his fist starts to tighten around the slender little glass and you can see his face going red like he's trying to lift a big weight. His whole arm is shaking with the pressure, and we all start clapping, "Go! Go!

Go!" and he clenches his teeth and then, "Pop!" the glass shatters in his hand and bits fly across the room and he drops what's left of it on the floor.

We're all cheering.

"You beauty! G'donya mate! Give him another beer!"

There's blood on his hand, but he just licks it off. Mr. Counter comes out of his office. He's got a shitty on.

"You better clean it up. Then piss off home. No more free beer tonight." He looks across to me and calls me to his office. He sends Sugar out and pulls me in, closing the door.

"So, who you got in your room?"

"What do you mean?"

"The girl, I know you got her in your room."

"Girl in me room? Gees, wish I did!"

"Don't bull shit me. And did you do your matric exams?"

"Yair, I said I would."

"And did you pass?"

"I dunno. Did the best I could."

"And the girl?"

I look down, decide to come clean, almost. "I met her when I came out of the exam at the Baptist hall."

"And?"

"That's all."

"What's she doing in your room, then? I'm not running a brothel here, you know."

"It's just that…"

"What?"

"Well she didn't have anywhere else to go."

"What do you mean? Doesn't she live around here?"

"Yair, down on Spruhan Avenue, I think."

"So why isn't she there?"

"Because she hates her father and mother and they kicked her out."

"She can't stay here. If the cops found out they'd close me down."

"I'll take care of her."

"I bet you will."

"I don't mean like that."

"Oh sure. You've got yourself a nice little piece and you think that's perfect."

"I'll take care of her, I promise. I love her!"

"How old is she anyway?"

"Fifteen."

"She didn't look that old to me."

"You saw her?"

"Yes, when you were mucking around with Nipper outside the kitchen."

"Please, Mr. Counter, can't I keep her?"

"No, she's got to go. What if her parents come down here looking for her?"

"They won't. They don't care about her. Anyway, they probably both drink here. Could've been here even tonight."

"What's their name?"

"Dunno."

"What's her name?"

"Iris."

"Take her home. Now!"

"But Mr. Counter. Just tonight, Let her stay just tonight and I promise I'll take her home first thing tomorrow."

"And what about school? Doesn't she go to school?"

"It's Sunday tomorrow."

"She goes now! Go down to your room and take her out. Not through the front door, out the way you brought her in. I don't want to see her. She's never been here as far as I'm concerned."

"But…"

"No buts!"

I said nothing more. I was getting all worked up again. Dad! I dunno Dad. He's your best friend, and here I am seriously thinking of hitting him. And I know if I say anything more, he'll call me a little shit and kick me out along with Iris. And what the hell would I do then? I'd have to go to Teachers College or something, because I wouldn't have anywhere else to live. Dad! I need another beer. I'm starting to see why you hit the booze like you did.

The other barmen had left. Only Sugar stayed. He lived in anyway, had the room next to mine. We called him Sugar because he was diabetic. He gave me a smirk as I pushed my empty glass to him and he filled it up. I gulped it down and banged the empty glass on the counter. My fists were clenched tight, the nails digging into my palms. I was all set to knock that smirk off his face. But Mr. Counter was standing up close, watching my face, drumming his fingers on the counter.

"You better go," he says quietly, looking at Sugar. There were beads of sweat on Sugar's bald head and he stared right at me too. I don't think he liked me.

*

It's Monday, and it's my first real day at work. I suppose you'd call me the rouse-about. I spent all my time sweeping, wiping down counters and window sills, mopping up floors, chit-chatting the customers, gathering up the glasses and pouring a few beers when the lunch time crowd from Fords showed up.

The worst part of the job was cleaning the dunny. I had to fortify myself, like they say, with a couple of beers before I went out back and tried to clean the ramshackle piece of crap. It was beyond cleaning. I'd just hose it down with lots of water and sprinkle some horrible smelling disinfectant all over. And I did the same to the rotten old back fence with its green mould on it and stench from the piss of a thousand cocks.

This day there was this bunch of blokes squatting down behind the dunny. They were yelling and screaming then all of a sudden they'd jump up.

"Ya fuckn bastard!" yells one. He picks up something, I couldn't see what it was, a green lump of a thing and flings it out into the paddock and it caught on one of the big scotch thistles and hung there like a wet rag. The other blokes turn and laugh, except for one of them who screams and screeches at them.

"That's me fuckn favourite!" he screams, "ya fuckn bastards!"

So I go over, and there, sitting quietly are five big green frogs, I never saw any so big, sitting there very still.

"What the hell are you doing?" I ask.

"What's it fuckn look like?"

"Here, sonny, here's ten bob. Go and get us a few beers, and one for yourself."

"Give me your old glasses then."

I run off to the bar. I get up to the tap and start pouring and I see Sugar eyeing me off.

"Where you going with that?"

"The blokes out back want their glasses filled," I says, "what's it fuckn look like?"

"You cheeky little shit. Where's the money? Are you paying for it?"

"They gave me ten bob. Here, see?" I have to put the glasses down on the counter and stop pouring the beer while I reach into my pocket. "Satisfied now?"

I give him a smirk just like he smirks. He licks his lips. There's those beads of sweat coming out on his bald head again. He's a skinny narrow shit, even smaller than me. I turn to face the till and ring up the sale, but just as I do, Sugar snatches the note out of my hand.

"I'll do that," he says, "you're not ready to be handling the money."

"What do you mean?" My ears are already flaming red, I know it. I look at him and grin in a nasty way. I'm looking at his tie. Yair, that's right. He wears a tie all the time, even in the public bar. I grab his hand with the ten bob note and snatch it back. And then I grab him by his tie and pull it tight. His eyes start to go wide like they were going to pop out. And the sweat is really pouring out of his bare head and down his cheeks and into his eyes. I let him go and ring up the money in the till and scoop out the change. But he's still standing there, looking like he's choking to death. Then he starts swinging his arms around and yelling all kinds of nonsense. He swipes his arms across the bar counter and knocks all the glasses, the ones I just filled, right off the bar and they go smashing to the floor. I'm just standing, my mouth open, and I know I've got a silly grin on my face, but I can't help it. Grecko comes up out of nowhere and gathers Sugar into his arms. He looks across at me.

"Run to the kitchen and get a biscuit, some sugar or something."

I stand there, rooted to the spot. What the hell is he talking about, Dad?

"Go on, you little shit. He's having a fit!"

"So what?"

"So, if you don't move yourself I'll knock your fuckn head off. Now go! He's going into a coma."

Gees, Dad. I didn't know, did I? But Grecko looked like he was really going to do me in, so I took off like you wouldn't believe and came back with a biscuit. Sugar's down on the floor, his tongue rolling around in his mouth, spit and dribble all over the place. Grecko rams his fist in Sugar's mouth so he can't bite his tongue. Gees Dad! He looks like he's gunna kick it!

"The biscuit! Stick a bit in his mouth! Go on!"

I push nearly the whole biscuit into Sugar's mouth and Grecko cries out, "not the whole fuckn biscuit, you idiot, you'll choke the poor bugger!"

"Gees, Dad! I didn't know!"

"Gees who? Are you going off the deep end too, are you?"

I've got my finger wedged into Sugar's mouth, between his teeth, trying to scoop out some of the biscuit. I don't need to, though, because Sugar's coughing it all up. It's so disgusting I let go and jump back.

"You fuckn little weasel, you're a useless shit. That's what happens when you stay at school as long as you have," jokes Grecko.

Some of the bickie must have got down him because Sugar's gone quiet and he's not thrashing around anymore. Grecko takes his fist out of Sugar's mouth and he swallows a bit, and I hand over the few bits of biscuit I have left. He swallows that down too.

"He's gunna be OK," says Grecko as he lifts Sugar up onto his wobbly legs. Sugar leans against the bar and Grecko grabs a wet cloth from the sink under the bar counter to mop up the sweat on Sugar's face and bald head.

"I'm all right! I'm all right!" says Sugar, "leave me, I got work to do." He staggers off around the bar and starts to arrange the glasses and bottles. It's just then I remember the four beers I had to deliver round by the dunny. The blokes will be getting worked up. I pour the beers then off I go, proud of my being able to carry four glasses of beer without a tray and without spilling them.

I just turned the corner at the back fence on the track to the dunny, when one of the blokes nearly runs into me.

"Where the fuck have you been?"

"Sugar threw a fit. Grecko made me help."

The mention of Grecko slowed the bloke down. I think he would have hit me. "Gimme the beers," he says, and he takes two and turns back to his mates. They're still squatting behind the dunny. I get closer and see the frogs are still where they were when I left. I hand over the other beers and the bloke that gave me the ten-bob note says, "well, where's the change?" I had to feel around in me pockets because I couldn't remember what I did with it in all the mucking about with Sugar. "I've got it here some place."

"Come on! Come on! You little shit. I'm putting it all on Toes."

"Who?"

"Toes. The one on the left, taking big gulps of air. He's Toes. Can't you see how big his feet are?"

I find the money in the bottom of my pocket. I hand it to him and he looks it over. I'm not sure if it's all there.

"All right, I'm putting two bob on Toes," he calls, standing up to swill his beer, then back down to squat. There's a bunch of money sitting on the side. "Sonny, you can be the umpire When you call 'go!' we all set our jumpers to go for it."

This is fun. I could do with a beer myself. "On your marks!" I says, raising my hand like I've seen them do, "go!" and I drop me arm. Then I burst out laughing because nothing happens. The blokes are tickling the asses of the jumpers, but they take no notice. They're just sitting there like frogs, gulping a bit, but like they were stones.

I just can't help it. I lean down close within inches of Toes and in my loudest voice I yell, "go you bastards, go!" I saw him flinch and I swear his toes waggled a bit. The other blokes saw it too and they jumped up screaming, "asshole, you can't do that. It's against the rules!"

"What rules?" screams Toes's handler, "there aren't no rules. Anyway, he hasn't jumped!"

And then Toes jumped. He went a good couple of feet. Trouble was he didn't stop there. He kept going. His handler ran after him, struggling through the thistles, getting pricked right and left, falling over, screaming at the thistles calling them every shitty word you could think of. The other blokes started tickling their frogs' asses. One frog made a little step forward and that seemed to set the others off. They leaped in all directions and kept going. But the one that took the little step stayed put. His handler quickly claimed victory, saying that the frogs that didn't stay on the course were disqualified! He leaned over and grabbed the pile of money and took off around the dunny and back to the pub. The other blokes were still running in the thistles, getting pricked. I nearly felt sorry for them, because I've told you how I hate those damn prickles too. I squatted down and finished off their beers then quietly sneaked away to the pub to do my next jobs. If my job was going to be like this every day, it was going to be great! Couldn't beat it, could ya dad?

*

Dad I remember you liked the dago. The two of you joked all the time and you called him Spuds, because like lots of new Aussies from Italy, he had a market garden, growing veggies, and he'd bring spuds in to sell in the bar. I thought you were bar mates but you told me that you never bought him a drink and neither did he for you, because you always drank alone.

Swampy shows up this morning and has Spuds in tow. They were waiting at the door right on nine o'clock when we opened up the old bar. I was polishing the counter, trying to look busy, but the truth was I had a hangover from the night before, a biggest night of many nights before, because me and my school mates waited up all night for the blokes in the back room of the Addy to give us our matric results that would be in the newspaper next morning. All but one of us scraped through, and I was proud to introduce most of them to their first serious boozing session. We did a crawl of all the back doors of the pubs in Geelong. Them were the days, I tell you! But now I was paying for it. I was still half asleep and had a sledge hammer in my head. Nearly slept in, I did, and if it wasn't for Abbie I'd still be sound asleep in me room.

"G'day Swampy," I say, "how's the veggies going Spuds?"

"Don't-a say this is the little shit that was Harry's-a kid?" says Spuds like a real Aussie. He nudges Swampy with his elbow and grins at me. He's the only I-tie I know. Solid scrawny bloke, dark greasy looking skin, nearly as dark as an abo, and with lots of black hair. Wavy, a bit like mine, and combed right back, not like mine, because I always had a straight part on the left. He's got these big hands though, and real thick fingers, I suppose from all that digging in his veggie garden. He ruffles my hair with his big fingers.

"Get out you bastard," I cry.

"Haw, haw," growls Swampy, rubbing his stubbly cheek with the back of his grimy hand, "he's poor Harry's kid. Hey, you want a beer, kid? It's on us."

I'm about to say "you bet" when Mr. Counter comes out from behind the bar and gives me a look. "All right Swampy, none of that leading my men astray."

"Haw! Haw! We could use a bloke like him today. Canya rent him out? Haw! Haw!"

I'm thinking what the hell's going on. Rent me out? On a farm? Digging up potatoes?

Mr. Counter pours them a couple of beers. "He's pretty useless," he jokes, or at least I hope so.

"We'll whip him into shape for ya. Won't we Spuds?"

"Yair," he says with his big grin, and tries to ruffle my hair but I duck away.

"Fuck off, you bastards," I say with me own grin.

"Shit! Haw! Haw!" says Swampy, "the little bugger can swear too. That'll go a long way!"

I look at Mr. Counter. I don't really want to go with Swampy. I'm looking forward to the next few days. It's school holidays and Christmas has been and gone. I'm getting the hang of the bar and getting pretty good at pouring beers using the old taps, with just the right amount of head. And I can ring the money up at the old till and do the change quick as lightning. I reckon I'm faster than the other barmen now. A pot of beer is one-and-thruppence-happeny—I know, it's spelled all wrong, but it's how we say it, isn't it—so it takes a while to count out the change of a ten-bob note, even a two bob coin. New Year's Day is a few days away, and on that day I'll be eighteen so I'm looking forward to a big cele-bration, old enough to drink and drive! But I'm real busy working for Mr. Counter because the old pub's bursting at its seams with customers. Gees, they put away some grog! Please Mr. Counter, don't rent me out!

"I'll tell you what," says Mr. Counter, a bit of a smirk on his face, looking at me sideways, "you can have him after New Year's Day. I need him here up to then. Anyway, you two blokes aren't going anywhere but here the next few days, are you? It's New Years' after all."

"Haw! Haw!" Swampy licks his moustache and rubs his leg with his toe and leans all over the bar counter. "Whatcha think, Spuds old mate?"

"I think we oughta have another beer and-a think on it."

"Haw! Haw! Yair! Two more beers Eddie, old mate. And one for the young'n here," and he tries to grab me, but I duck out of his way.

"So who's paying for this round?" asks Mr. Counter.

"Shit! I forgot me wallet!" says Swampy.

"Poor bugger. He's got no money," says Spuds, "hey sonny, ya gonna pay for this-a round?"

"Get stuffed!" I grin.

"Eddie, for Christ sake, when ya gunna teach your barmen some manners? Haw! Haw!" And with that, Swampy plonks down a tenner. Mr. Counter grabs it up and rings up the beers. He looks to me and nods towards the new bar, "You better go across and get it ready to open. The beer pipes need flushing."

So I took off.

*

What happened to Iris? I know you're thinking I fucked her over. Well, I kind of did, but not like you think. I mean, she wanted me, didn't she? She came on to me and just got me at the right time. OK. Any time's the right time. Shit Dad. What was I going to do? I did the right thing, didn't I? Poor bitch she was in trouble with her old man, and what the hell, with her mum watching them. I dunno, Dad. I mean, I asked her back to my room at the pub, and she came there and what else could I do? I took care of her as best I could, didn't I? I even gave up my bed.

That night. I had a few grogs with the blokes after we finished up and the customers were gone and the cops had their fill too. We got into a drinking game and they all ganged up on me and

got me to mix my drinks, beer and red plonk and Corio whiskey.
We were sitting in the passageway, leaning against the wall, our
legs out straight like we always did. They're all half-pissed, and
I'm well and truly gone. I try to stand up so I can shout the
round—and it cost a lot because there was at least eight of us, so
that's eight shouts minimum for everyone to do his bit. I'm trying
to roll over and put my hands down to push myself up and one of
the blokes kicks my foot away from under me and I go ass-over-
tit on to the floor and the blokes are laughing their heads off, and
then I'm crawling to the little cupboard where I serve the beer for
the Snake Pit, and I dig my nails into the old wallpaper on the
wall and claw my way up.

"OK mateys. Watchya having?" I don't wait for an answer, I
just call out to whoever is behind the bar in the cupboard, I think
it was Sugar, "eight whiskeys and sixteen pots!"

"You're drunk you silly little bugger," says Sugar, treating me
like he was me big brother or something, his smirk bigger than
usual.

"Get stuffed Sugar, you skinny bald shit, or I'll ram a biscuit
down your throat."

"Yair, you and who else?"

I push myself away from the wall and take a step towards him.
He's holding a beer gun in his hand and he's got eight pots lined
up ready to fill them. He points the gun at me face and I go, "yair,
all right," and I point my finger in me wide open mouth, "fill 'er up
right here!" And Sugar's smirk changes into a big laugh and I can
see his yellow teeth.

"OK then. The customer's always right," says Sugar and he
lets fly with the gun and a big stream of beer hits me in the face
and then finds its way into my mouth. I can't swallow it quick
enough and it goes down the wrong way and I cough and choke
and stagger back to the wall, beer dripping all down my front.

"You fuckn cunt!" I scream, "gimme more!"

But Mr. Counter shows up out of his office from counting his
money and stands there, his hands on his hips, glaring at Sugar.

"For Christ sake, Sugar. He's just a kid," he says. And he looks
at all the other blokes who are in stitches, but then they see that
Mr. Counter is going to tell them to get the shit out. "All right
boys," he says, all formal, "beer's off. Get home to your wives
and kids. And Sugar, shut down the cupboard and clean the place
up." Mr. Counter turns to me. I'm stooped over like a chimp, and
I feel like my eyes are going to pop out of me face. "As for you,"

he says, "get the hell out of here." I'm trying to move me feet but they won't move. I lean against the wall with both hands and I'm stooped over, and then I'm barfing all over the old wall, and the vomit dribbles in big dollops down to the floor. I look around to Mr. Counter, nearly losing my balance and I've got a stupid grin on me face.

"You know where the bucket and mop are," he says, being too calm about it. "Clean it up." And he goes back in his office.

I wipe my mouth on the back of my bare arm and I stagger off towards the kitchen and out the door to the gully trap and the bucket and mop. Nipper starts sniping at me and I fall over and bang my elbow. Nipper's got my foot and I swear at him but can't shake it loose. I reach for the mop and I manage to stand up and I lift it up with both hands then jab it down hard right on Nipper's head. But he still won't let go. So I turn the mop upside down and this time jab the handle down hard into his ribs. Lucky for him I was so drunk because the handle wasn't on centre, otherwise I would have skewered him for sure. But it was enough to make him yelp and I got me foot loose and grabbed the bucket and hose to fill it with water. Nipper's going crazy and doing that high-pitched bark that drives everyone nuts. I get tangled up in Nipper's chain and I'm going around and round and don't know what I'm doing. I fall down, the bucket and mop with me and I'm all wet, lying on my back, Nipper on top a me. He's going for the juggler, I reckon. I'm slapping at his mouth and he's baring his teeth and his nose is nearly touching mine. I hear Dad telling me to get up, but I can't move and I see Nipper coming down on me. I'm going to have a big bite mark on my neck or face. I'm done for, I reckon. I close my eyes and clench my teeth, getting ready for the end and then all of a sudden, I feel someone grab my leg and I open my eyes just in time to see Nipper hanging upside down, Grecko holding him up by the tail. Nipper's so startled he's stopped barking for once. And I'm rolling away, spewing my guts out as Grecko's holding Nipper at arm's length while he unravels me from the chain. He gently drops Nipper down, and Nipper scurries away and tries to hide behind the gully trap. And I'm now sitting up, feeling sober almost, shaking like you wouldn't believe. Grecko picks up the bucket that's still half full of water and he sloshes it into my face.

"Fuck you!" I say, and he laughs.

"You better get yourself cleaned up. You can't get in bed with your pussy smelling and looking like that."

And it was then I remembered Iris was still in my room and that I promised Mr. Counter I'd get rid of her. Gees, Dad. I dunno. What am I going do?

"What did you say?" says Grecko looking at me like I was Nipper.

"Nothing. Just talking to myself."

"Tell you what. I'll clean up your spew and you get yourself into the bathroom and clean yourself up. You can't go to bed looking and smelling like that. You won't get no pussy." He grins. I look up at him.

"Grecko, me mate. You're a bloody good bloke, but I tell ya, there's no pussy in me room."

"Yair, yair. Now get to the bathroom."

I'm still looking up at him. I want to thank him for saving my life. I go to shake hands and he slaps my hand lightly and says, "go on! Get the hell out of here!"

I stagger into the bathroom and do what all the blokes say you have to do to sober up. Get into a cold shower with your clothes on. That's what they say, Dad, you said it yourself enough times, didn't you? So I did, and it made me as cold as buggery and I dashed out and hit my shins on the bath getting over the lip, and then I look all round and there's no towel, so I start rubbing myself down with my old pants but they had spew on them and were wet as well, so I got into a panic and rushed out of the bathroom and down the passage to my room and turned the handle only to find that it was locked and I never had a key because I never locked the door. I'm standing there naked, shivering like buggery when Sugar comes sauntering down to go to his room.

"What the hell are you doing!" he asks, his whole body shaking like mine, only he's laughing and I'm shivering.

I look at him and I can't say anything because I think I'm going to cry, that's what! Gees, Dad. I can't do that. They'll think I'm a little kid! And I'm so cold! And what will Iris say? Dad! Help me!

"You poor little bugger," says Sugar. Let me open it. And he uses his key to open my door. I didn't think to ask him how come he had a key, but I found out later that all the doors opened with the same key!

So he opened the door for me and he tried to peak in to see if it was true I had a sheila in there. But I was sober enough by now to bump him out of the way and push me way into my room and slam the door shut behind me. Then it was pitch black and I didn't want to turn on the light because I might wake Iris up. So I thought I'd get in my bed nice and gentle and snuggle up to her to get warm, so I did.

Only trouble was, she wasn't there. Then I saw that the torn blind was gone, and the window was open. She'd pissed off!

*

It's New Year's eve and I'm working in the night cupboard next to the old bar pouring the drinks for the Snake Pit. The hags there are enough to turn anybody off sex for life! Then Millie comes up. Yair, remember her Dad? I heard later that she went to your funeral. Can you believe that? You must have turned over in your grave, even if you had a hard-on as well! Gees, sorry Dad. I didn't mean that. Don't know what I'm thinking these days. I've had a few drinks, I admit. Yair, I know I'm not supposed to when I'm working.

"G'day darlin'," she says, giving me a sneaky look, "what's with your little friend?"

"You want a beer or what?" I ask, treating her like the silly bitch she was.

"You got what you wanted then you kicked her out!" she says, looking at me like she was my Latin teacher.

"A beer or what?"

"A beer and a lemon squash for me little friend." She tries to get up close to me. I pull back like any bloke would. She reeks of brandy. "You can sneak a little gin in the squash if you like. Me little friend would like that."

"The gin will cost you."

"Oh, you wouldn't do that to your little friend would ya?" She grins and licks the corners of her lips like she always does when she's either coming on to you or she's making trouble.

I put up the drinks and say, very business-like and ignoring her bullshit, "that's one and tuppence."

"You want me to tell her you spiked her drink for her?" Millie asks, full of mischief.

"I gave you what you asked for, Millie."

"Yair, and so did she, didn't she?" Millie grabs the drinks and swaggers off down the passage.

"Next please," and I go on filling glasses. I'm too busy doing my job, but in the back of my mind, I know what she's up to and I don't know what I'm going to do. I've been having such a good time in me job, been so busy too, working for Mr. Counter, and having a lot of fun drinking with me mates, I just never thought much about Iris because she up and pissed off. It wasn't my fault, was it? I did the right thing. I just didn't get around to bothering about her after that. I had too much drinking to do.

The six o'clock bell goes and the cops are helping clear the bar and settle themselves in for a drinking session to bring in the New Year. It's going be a great night! I can see Dopey across the other side of the bar, and the Preacher has just walked into the Snake Pit.

"Good evening Ladies!" he says, standing tall, his bible in hand raised above his head, "may the Lord be with you, and now get the buggery out of here!"

They all snarl at him and call him all the assholes they can think of and someone turns off the lights and it's pitch black for a few seconds, but they come on again.

"The Lord God has sent you a signal. Time to get out, or you will be stuck in the valley of the shadow of death!" He walks further into the Snake Pit and using his bible as a kind of fly swatter, shoos the women and their men out the door. I'm busy but I'm trying to see who my supposed little friend was, but I don't see anyone with Millie. And Millie grabs the Preacher by the balls and says, "see ya later darling" as he swats her hand, ever so lightly, with his bible.

"May God be with you my dear!"

*

About half a mile up the Melbourne road from the pub there was an old saw mill. They were pulling it down getting ready for the new double lane highway to come through. I used to visit it when I was little and me mum was still at home. She had a friend there who sometimes took care of me. I was scared shitless of the mill because of the whirring noise of the giant saws. I imagined falling into one and me being sawed in half. Just behind the mill there was an old shack that was hardly even a shack because they'd started to smash it down too, in fact it was a charred wreck because some delinquents (not me!) had set fire to it a few months ago. But like often happens, they'd put the fire out with a lot of water and some nice green grass had grown up in amongst the charred ruins. So when I woke up here, lying on the nice soft grass, I felt like I'd sort of come home, except that who was beside me was none other than Iris, asleep, curled up cuddling into my back. I had no idea how I got here because I got well and truly plastered that night, the night of New Year's Eve

I twist me head around to look at her. We're both naked under an old blanket that looked like it had come off my bed back at the pub. My head's pounding away at me and each time I turn it I think it's going to explode. I need a drink! A bloody Mary with a heavy drop of bitters the blokes at the pub reckon will fix it. The pain is really bad as I struggle to turn around and face her. I twiddle my finger lightly around one of her nipples and she doesn't budge. But I can't get up the energy to keep at it so I fall back and close my eyes waiting for the pounding to stop. My back's getting cold because the blanket isn't heavy enough to keep out the chill of the early morning. I can feel the dew on the grass beside me, and the chill coming up from the ground beneath, which is as hard as a rock. I start stroking the contours of her body, at first lightly, then followed by a tickle around her nipples. I don't know what it's doing to her, but I know I'm starting to feel it and the trouble is that my head's feeling it too and the throbbing ache is unbearable.

She's awake, I know, I can see her eyelids flinch. She's a pretty nice piece of work, I'm thinking to myself. Can't believe my luck having run into her outside the Baptist church after my Latin exam. I really like her thick blonde hair that's cut almost short enough to be a boy's. But it's kind of sexy when it resists my fingers as I run them through it, kind of like ruffling Nipper's fur. And her skin, it's got a gorgeous light tan, smooth and oily. I love to run my hand over it and rub my leg against hers. She's a doll, that what she is, Dad. If only you could see me now, Dad. But then again, maybe you can.

"This ground's getting hard," I whisper to her. But her eyes stay closed.

"Where the hell are we?" she says, still eyes closed.

"Open your eyes and you'll see."

"Shit no. It's too nice just snuggling here." She pulls the blanket around her and it slides off my back.

I start to get into her. To hell with my pounding head. I gotta do what I gotta do what I have to do what I wanna do what I...

"Hey, leave me alone. It's too early." She tries to push me away and I'm having none of it.

"Come on little nipper!" I cry, and I fling my head back and the pounding nearly knocks me out and she rubs her knee into my groin and I cry out "Oh God!! Oh Ovid!" and I jerk off all over her leg.

"Shit! You dirty bastard!" Iris cries, now her eyes are wide open.

I roll on to my back and my ears are all flushed. There's a stone digging into the bottom of my spine and I push myself up. The pounding has stopped and in its place I have a dull heavy ache just above my eyes.

"What the fuck are we doing here?" I look down at her.

"We ran away!"

"We what? Ran away from what?"

"We just ran away!"

"Why?"

"Don't you remember? Of course you don't. You was drunk as a shit and going on about your Dad. And I got sick of it and told you to shut the fuck up. And you started screaming at me and I started screaming back, and that bloke in the room next to yours started banging on the wall telling us to shut up."

"You were in my room?"

"Yair. I was."

"But how did you get there?"

"Sneaked in when you were all swilling it down celebrating New Year's Eve."

"Through my window? You sneaked in through my window?"

"Nah. Down that dark passage while you were all boozing. You remember the lights went out in the Snake Pit?"

"Yair."

"Well I popped out and down the passage to the bathroom, and then later to your room."

And now it all began to sink in. "So it was you with Millie?"

"Yair."

"How do you know her? She's a fuckn witch and the pub bike."

"Yair, I know. But she's me sister's best friend, and I don't care what you call her, she's me best friend too because when I have a fight with me Mum and Dad I go to her. And she understands."

"Shit! Sorry. Didn't mean to hurt your feelings. I've seen Millie do a few things. Once with my Dad."

"You're kidding?"

"It's true. I could have done her myself..."

"Just like me mum says. You're a fuckn animal like them all."

"Being an animal is fuckn good, as long as I don't get kicked around like Nipper."

"It's you does the kicking."

"Yair, I know. It's when I lose my temper."

"Yair, I know."

I'm on my knees now, kneeling over her. She looks into my face. Her lovely pale blue-grey eyes are so big but I just wonder what's behind them. I know what's behind mine, a horrible awful pain.

But hers? She didn't drink much, I don't think, though how would I know because I was plastered all the time. "You got a hangover like I have?" I ask.

"Nah. Not me. I don't drink much. Makes me sick."

"Well, I'll just have to make up for you and drink your share." I joke.

"Yair."

I look at her eyes again, trying to see what's behind them. They don't let me in. She doesn't smile much.

"Where did you go all that time anyway? You took off that night through my window. I was so relieved."

"You what? You wanted to get rid of me?"

"No, of course not. Mr. Counter told me you couldn't stay and I had to get rid of you that very night. And when I got into my room, half sobered up after a bit of a run-in with Mr. Counter, you were gone."

"Yair. I took off because I didn't want to be your sex slave."

"Fuckn what?"

"Your sex slave."

"What the fuck is that?"

"I stay locked in your room until you're ready and you come in full of booze and root me whenever you want. Me mum warned me about it lots of times."

"And your dad? Him fucking you and your mum looking on, and you're worried you're gunna be my sex slave? Shit!"

"I made that up."

"Made up what? About your mum or about your dad or all of it?" My ears are getting red, and she can see it.

"I was just trying to get you to let me stay with you. I didn't want to go home that night."

"Well, I wanted you to come home with me and you said no and then you said yes. What the fuck am I supposed to do?"

"And by the way. Where the hell were you all that time I was gone? You never even came looking for me, did you?"

"I had to work. I never had time. Mr. Counter worked me to death."

"Bull shit. You never even thought about me, did you? All you blokes want to do is booze, booze, booze. It's what me mum always said."

"I thought of you every night and every morning I woke up…"

"Yair, and taking care of things on your own. Men. You're a bunch of bastards."

"Your mum's filling your head with bull shit. Just because your old man's an asshole."

"He's not me father."

"But you said…"

"Yair well he's not."

"But you said he was doing you at home with your mum watching."

"Yair well I told you I was lying."

"Lying like how?"

"Me real father's dead, that's what."

"So who's the bloke at home you didn't want to go home to?"

"God killed me real father."

"You're a fuckn crazy bitch, Iris. What are you going on about?""

"I'm cold. We need to get out of here."

Iris stands up and looks around for her clothes. She's got the same ones she had after me Latin exam. I look for my pants and I see they're the same ones I had too, me old school pants, and I remember that I don't go to school anymore, and I have a job and I suddenly feel free, at least for a few seconds. Then I remember that I have to work today, New Year's Day, a big day at the pub. Mr. Counter will be looking for me. "What you gunna do?" I ask her.

"Go home, I s'pose."

"All right, then. See ya."

"That's it? No kiss good-bye?" she says, half grinning and I'm not sure if she's joking or not.

"Gees, Iris. What the hell!" And I lean over to her and awkwardly give her a peck on the cheek. She grabs me and gives me her unbelievable wet kiss and I just feel like collapsing, my legs buckle and she can see it. She smiles a big smile.

"See ya," she says, and runs off, picking her way through the charred ruins of the old shack.

"Hey, wait! I'll come with you!" I'm running, my head throbbing with every step, trying to miss the giant thistles and the charred ruins, but she keeps running. And I don't know what I'm doing, because I really like my job at the pub and drinking with the blokes. Dad! Are you there? I really need you. She stops at the edge of the Melbourne Road, and there's cars speeding past both ways, the dust flies up and gets in my mouth that was already dry. I pull up, out a breath. "Iris! Wait for me! I'm coming with you!"

She turns, her little skinny body, got no shape at all really, but it's the way she stands with her hands on her hips, smiling bigger than I ever saw her, and she's not puffing at all like me. She's

standing, her hips pushed forward. And she waits. I take her hand
and I wait for another one of those sloppy kisses, but she squeezes
my hand tight and drags me across the Melbourne road, a car
nearly hitting us as we dart across, the car horn blaring out and
the bloke behind the wheel screaming at us.

Now we're making our way down the newly paved footpath on
Spruhan Avenue. Most of the commission houses are finished on
this street. Some of them even have gardens and a bit of a lawn.

"Which one's yours?" I ask, and she let's go my hand and starts
to run again, and my head's throbbing like buggery. She's darting
around like a little kid. "Gees, Iris, me fuckn head's killing me."
I'm holding my head and I'm slouching along.

She stops in front of a commission house that must have been
one of the first to be built, because it looks all old and worn, and
there's massive weeds in the garden, well not really a garden
because I don't think anything had ever been planted, and of
course there's those damn thistles. There's weeds growing out of
the gutters, even the roof, and all along the front of the house—a
double fronted house too, done with that stuff, stucco they call it,
a dirty yellow—there's rows and rows of empty beer bottles
stacked up with a few whiskey and wine bottles poking out.
There's a broken front gate that's hanging off its hinge, all rusted.
She steps over it and I stop right at the gate. I'm wondering what
the hell I'm doing here.

"Well, are you coming in or aren't ya?"

"So whose empties are they?" I grin, pointing at the bottles.

"Me big sister and her mates."

"Nah, women couldn't drink that much beer!"

"I said her mates, and there's also me stepfather."

"Do I have to come in?"

"Well, why'd ya follow me here if you're not gunna come in?"

"Who's in there, then?"

"I dunno. Mightn't be anyone. It was New Year's Eve last night,
remember?"

"Oh, yair. Look Iris, I gotta go to work. I don't want to get fired
after just a few weeks on the job."

"You're fuckn scared to come in?"

"I'm already late. I'm s'posed to be getting the bars ready for
the big day today."

"You're piss-weak, aren't ya?"

Iris grabs my hand and pulls me over the gate. Just the light touch of her hand buggers me up. My knees are like jelly. She starts rubbing my cheek with her finger.

"What are you doing?"

"You've got charcoal on your cheeks."

I look down and I see I have charcoal all over myself. And so does she. "Shit, Iris, we look like tramps! I can't go in there looking like this!"

Iris looks across at the stacks of empties. "You think they'll notice?" And she tugs me some more and I give a little, but then I stop. Dad, thank you Dad. I've come to my senses.

"I'm not coming in Iris. I gotta go to work." I pull my hand away from hers.

"You don't care about the work. I know you blokes. All you care about is the boozing with your mates."

"Shit! Iris! That's not true!"

"Yair? So where were you all this time since we was outside the Baptist church? Bastard!"

She starts off down the drive nearly tripping on the long weeds, and just then the front door opens and a little filthy kid runs out followed by her mum chasing her. And I squint at her, because the sun's now really bright and it hurts my poor aching eyes to see, but there's no mistake Dad! It's Little Linda!

Iris has stopped, and comes back, standing next to the bottle stack. I look at her. She's nervous, licking her lips. I know she's wishing I wasn't here. Even though she made me come. Gees, Dad. Can you believe this?

Little Linda stops in her tracks too when she sees me. "What the shit are ya doing here?" she says. And she's right, what the fuck am I doing here? My place is at the old pub. This is foreign land to me, Dad. I'm like a fish out of water, like they say, Dad!

Anyway, I ignore Little Linda like she shouldn't be there and I turn to Iris and I say, "So this is your mum?" She bursts out laughing.

"Me mum? You're a fuckn hopeless bugger. Does she look old enough to be me mum? She's me sister, you dope."

My ears are getting red, and I'd really like to step over to those bottles and smash a few of them. "How am I s'posed to know? She looks old enough to be your grandma!" Gees. Dad. It just popped out! Little Linda would have thrown one of the bottles at me if she wasn't chasing her brat around. The little kid starts screaming for no reason, and Linda runs after her and grabs her and drags her inside. The kid's kicking and swearing at her until Linda pulls her inside and slams the door. I look back at Iris.

"I know her, she's at the pub all the time. And I saw her have that kid in the Snake Pit a few years ago. And I know her dad's called Tank, right? So he's your dad, then? The bastard that--"

"He's me step father, I s'pose. And Linda's me step-sister. And no, he didn't..."

"I'm going to the pub."

"Me mum's inside, I s'pose."

"I'll see ya."

I'm turning to leave, and Iris is standing there looking kind of lost. "You can come in and see me mum if you want," she says.

I stop, and my ears are still red. I can hear screaming coming from inside.

"Don't s'pose you know what time it is?" I ask.

"Nah."

"I better be going then."

Iris comes to me. I'm going to get one of her sloppy kisses, I know. I hope. She grabs one of my fingers and pulls me a little to her. And as I go to her she turns her back on me and pulls me behind her. We go around the back of the house and there's more stacks of empty beer bottles against the house and against the garage, and they even lie beside the few steps going up to the back door. "Come on," she says, and she pulls open the old screen door that squeaks and there doesn't seem to be a back door there at all. And then there's the smell of the kitchen and smoke. It's not like the smell in the old pub, the stale beer and smoke and decaying lino and wood of the bar counter. I like that smell. I suppose it's what you get used to. It smells like home to me. But this kitchen, it makes me want to throw up. And there's this old lady sitting at a green laminex table with chrome legs and chair to match. There's a big ashtray with mounds of butts and an open packet of Garrick cigarettes. And this old hag sits there, sipping a cup of tea, and drawing on her cigarette. She's not doing nothing else. Just sitting there and smoking, looking at nothing, except I suppose the old laminated tabletop. Her fingers are yellow from the nicotine, and even around her lips it's all yellow, and the deep lines in her face, all thin and wrinkles, loose skin hanging from her chin and cheeks, eyes set deep into dark holes, and a nose that's red where she keeps wiping it and wiping it with an old grey hanky. She doesn't even look up when we come in. And there's in the background the screams of the little kid and Linda chasing her around the house.

"This is me mum," says Iris.

"Hello Mrs…er," I mumble. For a moment, I think she's not going to move or say anything and I'm already thinking of leaving. Then she takes a big draw on her cigarette and turns her head, long strands of thin grey hair dangling across her shoulder and says, "leave me daughter alone and get the buggery out."

I should have left right then. But Iris was standing right there and was squeezing me hand really tight.

"Me mum's a silly bitch," says Iris, "that's her way of saying hello." But Iris is looking away out the smoky window while she's talking.

"Get me another cuppa tea," says the mum. And Iris tops up the old aluminium teapot from the kettle that's always sitting on the gas stove, then tops up her cup of tea. I'm saying to myself. This is the Iris that made fun of me because I did everything I was told. Shit, Dad! I dunno.

"So what's her name!" I say to Iris, "Missus what?"

Iris gives me a really dirty look. "It's not Missus anything. It's Flo."

"Flo?"

"Yair."

"How come I never see her at the pub? Little Linda's there every day almost."

"She doesn't drink. Hates it."

Flo blinks slowly and turns to look me straight in me eyes. I stare back at hers. They're grey the colour of her wispy hair. Her Garrick cigarette is hanging on her lip.

"Turn to Jesus, son," she says, "it's your only hope."

There's this silence, like we're frozen in time. My mouth is open and I can't think of anything to say. She's staring right at me and her face is dead and lifeless. I want to get up and run out of there but I see Iris shifting on her feet. I want to turn to her to see her face, but I'm glued to Flo. Then all of a sudden, Flo takes a big draw of her Garrick and starts this horrible racking cough, like a car that won't start. I jump back and knock over the chair and I see that she's got this silly grin on her face but it's hidden by her awful cough. Then she starts laughing and coughing, you can't tell which is which. Iris picks up the chair and starts banging Flo on the back.

"Shit, mum!" she says, "when are you gunna give up those death sticks?"

"Mind your own business," says Flo, "you're a daughter from hell, that's what you are!" She looks at me as though it's my fault. But Iris seems to have calmed her down, because her coughing stops and she settles back into her chair to stare at me again.

"Go to buggery, ya silly old bitch. You're the devil's mistress, that's what you are!" snarls Iris.

"Don't you dare speak to your mother like that, you little shit from hell!"

Flo starts her rasping cough again and reaches for the packet of Garricks. She stubs out her cigarette, only half smoked, and lights another one with the matches sitting on the table. Iris reaches forward and snatches the lighted match from her hand and smacks the cigarette away from her mouth.

"Ya little bugger!" growls Flo, "I never should of had ya! And you," she points her yellow finger at me, "get out of here and don't come back until you've gone to Jesus, ya little prick!"

I move towards the back door and it squeaks as I push it open.

"And I mean *little* prick," she says, coughing and laughing. And that makes my ears go red, and I feel my fists tighten. Dad, I don't want to do it, but she can't talk to me and Iris like that! I turn back and I hear the old wire door creak shut. Flo, she's stopped coughing. She knows I'm going to clobber her. It's like she wants me to do it. But Iris gets in the way.

"Don't you fuckn touch her!" she warns. I grab her by her skinny little arm and I'm going to push her away.

"Go on then!" says Flo, "show Iris your true colours."

Dad, I'm standing here, can't help myself. I'm going to clobber her. I know I shouldn't but I just can't take that sort of shit from anyone. I push Iris aside and she falls down, grabbing the chair she'd just picked up.

"Leave her alone, you bully. She's just a stupid old bitch!" pleads Iris.

And I'm there, grabbing Flo by the collar of her old cardigan that's got tea stains all down it.

"Go on, then, hit me! It's all you bastards know what to do!" she cries.

And I'm gunna hit her, I've got me fist up, clenched tight. And just as I'm about to do her, Little Linda rushes in chasing her little kid, and behind her is Tank. I stop like I'm in mid-flight and fall across the table, pushing myself away and then I'm out of that kitchen door like you wouldn't believe. Tank chases me, yelling that he'll break my neck, but he's too big and lumbering, can't catch a nimble bloke like me. And I run and I run, till I'm breathless. And I at last look around and he's gone. He's probably in there beating them all up.

I stand there, my hands on my hips, my head throbbing like buggery. I walk and I walk, not thinking where I'm going, till I find myself in the rubble of my old house, looking across the road at the old pub. There's a bulldozer cleaning up the block, pushing the rubble into a pile. I can see bits of the old cot Dad slept on and I pick my way through the rubble trying to figure out where the cot used to be, where I spent my time with him while we talked, right up to the end. Dad, I miss you, I really do. And now I don't know what's going on. But then I feel a dig in my ribs and for a moment I think it's Tank and I jump, scared shitless. But I feel that steady grip on my arm and I know it's not Tank. It's Grecko.

"What the hell are yer doing here?" he asks.

"I dunno."

"Mr. Counter sent me over. You should have been at work a couple of hours ago."

"Yair."

"Yair what?"

"I'm coming, I'm coming."

"Well you better hurry. Mr. Counter's waiting for you."

I pull my arm away from his grip.

"All right. I know."

We walk across the road and Mr. Counter's standing at the entrance to the old bar, the greasy canvas curtain still hanging there, still streaked with black grime of the workers. I feel the sun coming down on me. My head's exploding, my hangover's come back. I put my arm up to cover me eyes. I squint at Mr. Counter standing there. He's angry.

"Where the hell have you been?"

"I, I don't know."

"You look like a tramp. Soot all over your face, rips in your pants and shirt, black soot or whatever it is all over your clothes. And you're two hours late for work!"

"I'm sorry. I got stuck with my girlfriend and her silly bitch of a mother."

"With your girlfriend? That's your excuse?"

"I said, and her mother."

"And that's it? And that's how you got all that black over you? And tore up your clothes?"

"I said I'm sorry."

"Sorry? You don't even know what you've done. This is a real job I gave you. You turn up to work no matter what and on time, and looking respectable. What are my customers going think?"

"I'm sorry, Mr. Counter. It won't happen again, I promise."

"It better not. I know what you've been doing, don't think you can go on doing it."

"What do you mean? I'm not doing nothing wrong."

"Oh? It's that little piece a fluff that's got you in, and the grog too. I won't stand for your boozing all the time. That's what made you late, isn't it?"

"No, no. I'm not like that. Besides, it was New Year's Eve last night."

"That's no excuse for not showing up to work on time. You know full well that today is a big day for the pub."

"Yair. I'm really sorry, Mr. Counter. I dunno what's wrong with me."

"I do. You're getting like your Dad. You're hitting the booze too much. So lay off it."

"OK, no more booze."

"Now get in there and get yourself cleaned up. I'm docking you half a day's pay for this."

I'm looking down, can't look Mr. Counter in the face. Truth is, I haven't listened to hardly anything he's said, my head hurts so much, and I can't help thinking of Iris.

*

Iris sat in the kitchen staring at her mum. Tank came back puffing, out of breath and he was going do something, at least that's what Iris told me. And he looked around and the little kid is running around and round the kitchen table yelling and screaming and banging anything she could with an empty beer can – and they were big ones in those days. She rushes past Tank and bangs the can against Tank's shin. It was just what Tank wanted, an excuse to go at it. He lifted the little kid up first by one leg and he's got her hanging there like he caught a rabbit and was gunna gut it. Linda starts screaming for him to put her kid down and leave her alone. And Iris starts yelling too and grabs his arm trying to get him to let go. But he laughs crazily and lifts the poor little kid up high then turns her back up the right way and sets her down on the floor. The kid thinks this is great fun and asks for more. Tank then does his favourite trick. Using both hands, he grabs the her by the head and lifts her clean up above his head. Flo looks up but she says nothing, takes a draw of her Garrick. The kid starts to go red in the face and she's decided that she doesn't like this anymore. She starts wriggling but it means twisting her head on her neck that's taking all the weight of her body. Iris yells to Linda to save her kid before her neck snaps and her head comes off. Linda, though, has run away into the next room, crying like a little baby. Then Flo gets up, grabs her smokes and matches and walks out after her. "You're all fuckn mad," she mumbles.

Tank lowers the kid down and holds her until they're face-to-face. "Ya learnt your lesson, you little shit?" he says, pushing his nose against her nose, and that scares her more than anything. But what he doesn't realize is that the kid's feet are hanging down level with his balls. The kid starts kicking and screaming. Of course, she didn't know what was there. And all of a sudden, Tank drops the kid like a ton of bricks and yelps, holding himself and limping out the kitchen door. "You're fuckn shits all of you!" he cries.

Iris grabs up the little kid but she's already trying to copy Tank. She grabs Iris by the neck and tries to pick her up.

I could have guessed what she did next. Yair, Dad, that's right. Iris pulls her close and she slops one of her wet kisses right on her lips. Can you believe that? The little bugger giggles and so she gives her another and then guess what? The bugger bites Iris's lip, and Iris leaps back and she wants to slap her, but stops herself just in time and turns and runs out the kitchen door. That fuckn house. No wonder Iris won't live there. It's a fuckn zoo I tell you Dad. And I would have given that little kid a beating she'd remember. Dad, you remember the time you did it to me? I've still got the scar on me ass, I think. At least that's what Iris told me. But I never told her how I got it.

*

New Year's Day turned out to be a day to forget. My hangover stayed with me right through the day, but at about four o'clock, I couldn't stand it anymore so I sneaked a couple of beers out the back in the tap room. They were just enough to give me a bit of a buzz and lighten my head a bit. Every now and again one of the customers would want to buy me a drink and of course Mr. Counter had told me I wasn't allowed to drink on the job, so I always said no, except this day when my hangover was really getting to me. Now, I started having a few as I wandered around the bar gathering up glasses. And it wasn't long till I started having a sip of the dregs that were left in the glasses. You'd be surprised how much beer the drunks leave behind. So by closing time I was pretty well on, laughing and joking with the regulars who always stayed till the very last minute before closing. I was staying next to Grecko as we herded them out of the bar and they hit the street outside, and the cars were revving up as they all took off home or wherever they were going. We all came inside and lined up in our favourite place in the passageway leading to the Snake Pit, sitting on the floor leaning against the wall, ready for a few more sips. Trouble is, by this time I was pretty well on, plastered really, and when I get plastered, I get loud and my ears go red. Then Sugar clips my ear as he hands me a beer, the first of many, I hoped. Mr. Counter always turned on free beer for us barmen, and we knew we'd get a lot more because it was New Year's Day.

"What you think you're doing?" I say to Sugar.

"Take your fuckn beer and shut up if you know what's good for you," he says like he's joking, but I now he's not.

Just then, Mrs. Counter comes out of the Snake Pit. She's been tidying up the place, because. as Mr. Counter says, it's always the women that make the biggest mess. She gives Sugar a look, then looks down at me. I reckon she's staring at my red ears and I don't like it.

"I think the boy has had enough," she says. Sugar quickly passes out the beers he's got in his hands and goes back into Mr. Counter's office. The rest of the barmen start sniggering. They're waiting for me to lose my temper like I always do, and I can see Grecko getting up off the floor, just in case. But I've got my beer and I'm happy, and I look back up at Mrs. Counter, her little round face sitting on top of a big hanging bosom, her long skinny neck draped in a gold chain several times round. From where I'm sitting she looks like a rose that's lost its petals, sticking up out of a big round flower pot. So Dad, I'm trying to hold back a laugh and this big snort comes out of me and the blokes all look at me and they're not sure if it's a fart or what.

Mrs. Counter leans back on her heels, she's upset but she's trying to hold back a laugh too. I take a big sip of my beer, hoping it will help me and then I see out of the corner of my eye Grecko looking like he's coming over to me. I've got my hand to me nose, squeezing hard, hoping I can stop myself from doing it again. So now my whole face is red as well as my ears, and I'm looking around and everyone's laughing, so in the end, I down the rest of my beer while I'm still holding my nose. And I thump down the empty glass and let go my nose and look up at Mrs. Counter, a big grin on my face as I suck in a whole lot of air. Mrs. Counter, not to be outdone, leans right over and I press back against the wall. Her gold chains are touching my face and I'm scared her huge cow's tits will smother me! But a grin is stitched into my face and I can't move. She looks at me with her little beady eyes and says, "you're just a boy. Now go to your room!"

Of course, now my ears are on fire and the blokes are waiting to see if I'm going to hit her. But what I don't realize until it's too late is that I'm sitting there with my legs spread apart and she's standing between them. "Didn't you hear me?" she says, "go to your room!" But I'm frozen to the floor, both my hands pressing down hard. Then she puts one foot forward, a foot clad in an old sand-shoe, and steadying herself with a hand on her knee, slowly presses her foot down on me, right between my legs, and repeats, "just a boy." And then she pushes herself away from the wall and struts off to the kitchen. And I'm so embarrassed I just sit there, my gob hanging open like a panting dog. The blokes are all gaping at me and they start to laugh because without thinking about it, I've got my hand down there, cradling me cock and balls. "I think I need another drink," I say, and I manage to stand up and I reach out to collect the other blokes' glasses. I go to the cupboard to fill them and I'm expecting Mrs. Counter or Mr. Counter to come out and stop me. But they don't. "You better go to your room this minute," the blokes say, but they're joking and sniggering. I don't remember how it ended up, except that I woke up next morning in bed, Abbie shaking me to get me up in time for work. Dunno what I'd do without her, Dad.

4. While passion and pride are strong

I'm working in the old bar, wiping down the counter and this bloke comes in and he comes right up to me. He's this stocky bloke, muscly arms sticking through a dirty white singlet. He bangs money down on the counter and says, his head pushing forward like he's trying to scare me, "what's a young bloke like you doing pouring beer? You should be in the army fightn the fuckn commies."

"Didn't ya hear?" I say, and I feel a nudge from Sugar. He's trying to tell me something. "There's no national service any more. I don't have to go."

"You yellow little shit. What's wrong with young kids these days? They got no guts! Gimme a beer!"

"I'm not yellow" I bristle as I pour him a beer and push it slowly toward him.

"Then why aren't ya fuckn fightn, then?"

"Because I haven't been asked."

He takes a gulp of his beer, and I see four other blokes all looking a bit like him, coming up to the bar. This bloke, he's got hardly no hair except a bit of blonde curls growing out around his ears and a kind of light fuzz growing from the back of his neck to half way up his head. Then he's bald as a bandicoot and there's this big dint in his head right above his right eye that's looking sideways. And when he gulps his beer down, the dint comes to life and pulsates. He knows I'm staring at it, but he turns to his mates and says, "you all have pots?" and they all nod or grunt.

"Four more pots," he says, "and stop staring at me war wounds. I'm fuckn proud of them, proud I wasn't a fuckn coward like all you young blokes these days, not to mention your boss."

I'm busy pouring four beers at the tap. The beer is a bit lively so I'm waiting for a lot of the foam to settle down. Sugar comes up to me and whispers in my ear, "watch it. He's got a plate in his head. He's half fuckn mad."

Like I always do, I ignore Sugar, and I push the beers forward and say, "here you go. That's six and five-pence-ha'penny "

"Tell your boss that it's on the house, and if he doesn't like it, I'm paying him with this," and he hands me a white feather.

Dad. I bet you'd remember this bloke, because he had it in for you too, so the blokes in the bar said. He has a real fierce look about him and there was always a bit of dried spit in the corners of his mouth and when he smiles it isn't a smile, it's more like Nipper baring his teeth, and this bloke's teeth are sparkling white, the ones that's there, that is, with a lot of gaps and a big gold filling on the bottom. And when he talks he has this funny way of sliding his tongue to lick the corner of his gob. You had to keep clear of him because he couldn't talk without spraying his spit everywhere. They called him Bomber because he reckoned he was a pilot in World War 2, but none of us believed it. He was a Banana Bender after all, he couldn't fly a kite! That's what the blokes reckoned anyway.

I opened my big mouth and said, "so what's Mr. Counter done, then?

"He hasn't told ya? Course not. He's yellow, that's why. You see this? You see this hole in me fuckn head? I got that saving him and the rest of ya."

"I dunno what you're talking about."

"Like fuckn hell. Where's your boss? Go and ask him."

"Six and five-pence-ha'penny, please," I say.

"You see these four blokes drinking with me?"

"Yair, so what?"

"They're me brothers. We all went to the war. There was six of us, one never came back."

Immediately, the five a them go, "Shhhsh!" then raise their glasses all together and say, "to baby Ted!" and they down their beers.

This seemed to quiet them down, so I asked again for the money, "Six and five-pence-ha'penny."

"You know," says Bomber, "you'll get called up for Vietnam, I'm telling you."

"Nah. I'm always lucky. If they do a lottery call-up, I'll win. Anyway, I haven't registered. Never had time."

"You fuckn what? You never registered for the draft? You fuckn little yeller weasel." He reaches across the counter and grabs me by the collar. Fortunately, I'm not wearing a tie, much to Mr. Counter's disgust. "Fuckn little shits like you should have their balls cut off. That's what! Give us another round of pots and make it quick!"

I feel Sugar breathing over my shoulder. He's pulling at my shirt trying to move me away. But of course, I don't do what he wants.

"I can't give you more beer till you've paid for the first round. Mr. Counter wouldn't like it, you know."

"You know what? Fuck Eddie Counter that worm of a fuckn coward. Give him that fuckn feather and tell him we'll be back!"

They banged their empty glasses on the counter and marched out, Bomber yelling, "Left! Right! Left! Right!"

Yair, Dad. Poor Mr. Counter, he copped it. I went and gave him the feather and said it was Bomber who wouldn't pay for the beers. He took the feather and threw it in the bin. I lingered in his office, expecting Mr. Counter would tell me what had happened. But he just went on counting the day's take. I started to back out and just as I got near the door, he swivelled around on his stool and said, "he was after your Dad too. Your Dad had a really good job down at the Phossie, he was an engineer so he was in an essential trade that didn't have to go to war, and what he did for a lot of blokes was he signed them on so they wouldn't have to go to war too, and one of them was me."

I opened my mouth to ask what was so awful about helping your mates, but Mr. Counter cut me off and said, "now I've told you. I'm not talking about it ever again."

*

We were just closing up and all the drunks were pretty much gone. For some reason, the Preacher and Dopey never showed up, they must have had the day off. Easter was coming up. We were sitting in the passageway settling in to the grog and we just sucked down our first round when we heard this big smash and Nipper was yelping his head off. Mr. Counter comes out of his office and he's holding this white feather squashed up in his hand.

"It's Bomber and those bastard brothers of his," he mutters.

And we all look at each other and I'm wondering what's the big deal. But me mates, they're looking like there's a war about to start. Mr. Counter runs out the front door and Grecko follows, then the rest of my drinking mates struggle up and start running out. I get up to follow, but Bulla holds me back and says, "it's not your war, son. Better you stay here."

But I couldn't stay behind, could I Dad? It'd mean I was yellow. And I'm not a coward, Dad. So I downed me beer and I sneaked into the night cupboard and poured myself a whiskey and downed that too and in no time I was ready to get out there.

I ran out the front door and nearly tripped over Grecko rolling round in agony on the gravel. Bomber's blokes must have been waiting for him, because he had blood coming out of his nose and you could see bruises and cuts on his legs where they'd kicked him while he was down. Disgusting. Hitting a bloke while he was down, that was the worst. My mates were running around in all directions and Bomber and his brothers were armed with cricket bats and the broken stubs of beer glasses.

Bulla calls out to me. "Son! Get away.! Those glasses will cut you so bad you'll be ugly as shit the rest of your life. Run in and get Mrs. Counter to call the cops." And while he's yelling that, he's got this bloke by the scruff of the neck and he's banging him against the cream-colored wall of the pub. There's blood pouring down the bloke's head. One of his brothers comes up behind Bulla and gets in a whack on his shoulder with a cricket bat. Bulla has to let go and turn to face his enemy. I'm frozen, staring at the war, because that's what it was. Bulla yells at me, "ya heard what I said? Call the cops!" Bulla's getting out of breath. He's such a big bloke, but he's so top heavy that it's only a matter of time before he trips up and goes down, and once that happens, he won't be able to get up. I run over and I'm pleased with myself because I've still got my beer glass. I smash it against the pub wall and I'm left with a nice sharp base. I come up behind the bloke that's got Bulla cornered with the cricket bat and I ram the glass into the back a his head, or that's what I tried to do. He was moving a lot, so I it ended up missing most of his neck and slicing into the side of his head and then I see half his ear's hanging off.

"Fuckn assholes!" I scream.

"For Christ sake, boy!" yells Bulla, "call the cops!"

I look around for more victims. I grab the bloke's cricket bat and bash him again over the head, where he's trying to put his ear back together. He goes down like a sack of spuds.

"Watch out!" Bulla yells, and I turn around just in time to duck Bomber himself swinging at me with a broken glass. He's a short, stocky bloke, all muscle I can see, and I know immediately that I'm done for, so I fling the bat at him and make off inside the pub and lock the door behind me. I call out for Mrs. Counter, and she's running up from the kitchen. "Call the cops!" I yell.

"I already did!" she says, her head sticking out further like a stalk than ever before. "Is Mr. Counter all right?"

"I dunno. It's pretty fierce out there." And we hear a lot of glass smashing and loud bangs as rocks are tossed through the windows. And I run into the old bar and see this bloke banging at the big plate glass window with a cricket bat, but the bat's bouncing off it. I'm looking for something heavy I can take back out with me. Then Sugar appears out of the office. He's got an iron bar. Mr. Counter always kept it in there because it was where they counted the day's takings.

"You looking for this?" he says with his familiar smirk. "You know I can't go out there. I'd like to, but I can't. I've called the cops a lot of times. They're not answering. The bastards have gone off for Easter is my bet."

"Thanks Sugar. Just what I wanted. The bastards aren't getting away with this!"

I run out the front door again, banging it shut behind me. There's a few blokes lying on the ground, moaning. I can't tell whether they're my blokes or not. But Grecko is starting to get up, so I go over and give him a hand, not that I'm hardly any use to such a big bloke. He sees the iron bar in me hand. "You better give me that," he says.

But I skip past him because I see the Bomber bastard and I'm going to be the one that gets him. "I got no beef against ya," Bomber says, "you was hardly born when the war was on. It's the yellow bastard that didn't go that we're giving it to. And that bastard was Counter."

"And my Dad," I say, though I shouldn't have.

"And who might that be?" asks Bomber, walking up to me, still carrying a broken beer glass and his cricket bat.

"Mr. Counter's best mate, Harry Henderson."

"Yair, I know that yellow bastard. I'll get him too. Where the fuck is he? I s'pose he's hiding out somewhere."

"He's dead," I say.

"Well, fuckn good riddance. Saves me having to help him on his way."

"Fuckn asshole!" I scream.

I can't believe it but Bomber, the stupid bastard, turns his back on me and goes after someone else. I'm looking for Mr. Counter but can't find him anywhere. I'm after blood, so I start to run after Bomber. Grecko sees what I'm up to and he starts after me. But I got a head start so he won't reach me in time. And I'm right up behind Bomber and I'm about to swing the iron bar at the back of his head, when one of his brothers calls out, "behind ya! Behind ya!" Bomber tries to stop in his tracks and turns around just as I'm swinging the iron bar at his head. He puts his arm up, the one with the glass, to fend off me strike, but the bar is way too heavy for him and smashes into his arm. The broken glass drops to the ground and Bomber screams out in agony. I've busted the bastard's arm and it hangs limply as he holds it against his body. I'm about to finish him off, when Grecko grabs my swinging arm—gees, he's done that so often to me – and he says, "better leave it. Don't want to kill him now do we?" He calmly releases the bar from my grip and I'm all worked up, my ears throbbing and my mouth's dry. Grecko holds me tight. "Better go inside and have a beer," he says as he pushes me a little towards the pub entrance. I look up and I see broken windows everywhere and Bomber's brothers are helping each other get back into their big truck. Bomber's sitting in the front seat holding his arm. One of his brothers starts up the old truck with a crank handle, then climbs in the truck and they drive off. Our blokes start to file into the pub, but we still haven't found Mr. Counter. Mrs. Counter has come to the front and she's asking where he is. So we all fan out looking for him. We're all scared of what we might find. I walk around the back of the pub, and I see that just about all the windows have been broken, including mine in me bedroom. And I keep on walking and get to the dunny and I hear someone moaning. There's nobody in the dunny, gees, you'd have to be in bad shape to hide in there, and then I see Mr. Counter lying in the green grass behind the dunny. He's got some blood on his face, but otherwise he looks OK.

"Are you all right Mr. Counter?" I go over and help him up. He looks real upset, but except for a few scratches on his face that look worse than they really are, I'm guessing that he's OK.

"I think I'm OK. I don't know how I ended up here."

"Yair, dunno what could of happened. We gave them what-o anyway, Mr. Counter."

"You did?"

"Yair. Gave them a good hiding."

"Didn't the cops come, then?"

"Nah. Who needs the cops anyway?"

I'm feeling good with myself. I played my part and I know the blokes won't call me "son" any more, and Mrs. Counter better not call me "boy" either.

*

Mr. Counter's called me into his office. It's lunch time so I know there's something up. I wonder what it could be, because I've been doing my job pretty good. Been doing just what the other full-time barmen do, work hard all day then get plastered at night. And on my day off which was Mondays, I go off into town and get plastered there too at the Criterion pub near the Kardinia Park footy oval, my favourite pub where I used to hang out with me Dad when I was a kid and followed the footy. So I wonder what could be up. Mrs. Counter's been kind of hovering over me too, giving me looks when we're sitting in the passage boozing on after we've finished up. I go into his office and Mr. Counter's sitting there counting out his money like he always is. I stand there waiting for him to finish. He doesn't tell me to sit. There isn't anywhere anyway because he's sitting on the only stool in the office.

"You wanted to see me Mr. Counter?"

"Yes. Be with you in a tick. It was your day off yesterday, you remember that?"

"Course I do. So what?" Something's up I know, because my ears are getting red already.

"A mate of mine is the licensee at the Criterion."

"Yair?"

"Yes. He says you had to be thrown out of the pub and that from now on you're barred from going there."

"Shit! What for? I didn't do nothing!"

"Yes, no doubt. So why would he bar you then?"

"I don't remember nothing." And that was the truth.

"I'm not surprised, you were so drunk, as I heard it."

"Well I had a few."

"Yes. Well it was a few too many."

"Why, what'd I do?"

"You got into a big brawl, that's what, and it was you who started it."

"Not me. I just do what me Dad used to do. I sit in the corner and drink on me own and mind my own business."

"Not this time. Though you really were doing what your Dad did, you were drinking plonk."

"Yair, I remember that bit."

"And whiskey."

"Yair."

"And beer chasers."

"Yair. So? I paid for it all didn't I? Can't I have a few drinks on me own?"

"Not if you're starting to go the way your old man did."

"Well I'm not. I know what I'm doing."

"I don't think you do. You beat up an old pensioner just because he said you shouldn't be drinking the whiskey with beer chasers."

"Nah, not me. I just scared him a little bit, that's all."

"No. You beat him up really bad and he's now in hospital. You should be ashamed of yourself."

"Mr. Counter. I don't remember doing that. Mr. Counter, that's not me. You know me. I wouldn't beat up a poor defenceless old man."

"Well you did. I couldn't believe it either, but my mate says you really did, and I believe him. He's got no reason to make it up."

"I don't remember." I'm starting to plead.

"Well you did. And I feel a bit responsible for you because I haven't stopped you from getting on the booze. And it's all you do. I pay you a good wage and you just spend it all on booze. You're going to finish up like your old man. You've got to stop."

"I'm sorry, Mr. Counter. I promise it won't happen again."

"I know what blokes like you are like. I watched this happen to your dad. The grog's got you and I have to do something about it."

"Gees, Mr. Counter. I'm all right. I can knock it off."

"Your dad used to say that all the time and he ended up on the metho. Even you'd remember that."

I stood there, my face red, ears throbbing. My mind was blank. I didn't want to think about it. I remembered my Dad. I'd promised myself lots of times I'd never end up like he did. I just stood there, looking at the floor, feeling like a little kid being yelled at by his teacher.

Mr. Counter swivelled around on his stool. Then he said, "here's what I'm going to do. From now on I'm only giving you a few bob a week to buy a few smokes and things. The rest of your wages I'm putting in a bank account that you can't get at. And when the time comes you want some money to spend on something important, you'll have to come to me to get it. Understand?"

I kept looking at the floor and I shifted from one foot to the other. I hadn't felt like this since high school, which wasn't that long ago anyway.

"You understand?" says Mr. Counter again.

"It's not fair. I did the right thing by you. When Bomber's blokes were going to do you in, I saved you. And this is what I get for saving your life?" I couldn't believe I said all that.

"And I'm saving your life right now. I'm stopping you from going down your father's track. You don't want to end up like him, do you?"

I looked up from the floor, my ears redder than ever, me mouth as dry as it was the night I beat the shit out of Bomber.

"Who are you to talk, you bastard? You're the one that helped Dad on his way. It was your booze he drank and you gave it to him."

"I made a mistake. And I'm not going to make it twice."

"You're a… a hypocrite!"

"Maybe so. Say what you like. But I'm doing what I'm doing."

"Fuckn asshole!"

"Get back to work."

"Get stuffed!"

I turn to leave, and then Mr. Counter says, "oh and by the way. I think you need to get away from the pub life for a while, so I've loaned you out to Swampy for the next couple of weeks, like we agreed a few months ago."

I stopped in my tracks. "You can't do that!"

"I just did. Swampy's coming in this afternoon. And after he's had a few beers, he and Spuds will take you back with them. You can stay there if you want, or he said he'd bring you back here to sleep in your own bed. Up to you, but it'd be easier for you to stay out there. He's got a sister, you know."

"Yair. Old enough to be my grandmother. I'm not staying out there with that filthy old bastard."

"Please yourself. But you'll have to be out there at five every morning. That's when these farmers start their day."

"I'm not going."

"We'll see about that."

*

Swampy and Spuds showed up and I was behind the bar washing up glasses.

"Haw! Haw!" laughs Swampy, "gimme a couple of beers, nah, make it three, one for yourself."

I look around and pour three beers and then I walk around to the other side of the bar. Mr. Counter had a rule that if you ever felt you had to accept a customer's offer of a beer, you had to go around the other side of the bar, so it looked like you weren't drinking on the job. We raise our glasses together and cry, "bottoms up!" I take a big sip. I'd been longing for a drop all day, especially after my run-in with Mr. Counter.

"So you-a come-a with us?" asks Spuds.

"That's what Mr. Counter said."

"Haw! Haw!" laughs Swampy, "the kid's got the sulks!"

"I fuckn don't, and I'm not a kid."

"After the next-a few weeks, ya won't-a be," says Spuds.

"Anyway. I'm not going. He can't make me."

"But we can," grins Spuds. He chuckles away and Swampy slaps him on the back.

"We can, we can!" crows Swampy, and with that he orders a round of whiskeys and beer chasers. Sugar's serving, and I'm expecting him to refuse to serve a drink for me. But he goes right on filling them all up. And when he's done, Swampy puts up the dough, but Sugar pushes it back and says, "nah. This one's on the house."

"Haw! Haw!" says Swampy and he picks up his whiskey and cries, "dags up!" and downs the whiskey, bangs the empty glass on the counter, then downs in one gulp the beer chaser. I have no choice, not that I was even bothering to think about it. I follow suit with Spuds and we down ours too.

"We better go," says Spuds with a grin, "we got all them sheep to round up and dag."

"Can't," says Swampy. "Haw! Haw! It's blowing a gale outside. Can't dag sheep in wind like this. Have to wait for the wind to die down."

"Mr. Sugar!" calls Spuds, "another round!" He pushes forward a crumpled ten-bob note.

"Coming up!" and he refills the glasses and pushes the money back to Spuds. "On the house. Compliments of Mr. Counter."

"Dags up!" we all cry and soon the whole bar is watching us.

The wind gets stronger, and we can hear it whistling through the old cypress tree and rattling the old iron roof. Spuds walks outside and comes back again, a silly grin on his face. "Fuckn wind!"

And so, the afternoon passed, with many "dags up" toasts and Sugar pushing back the money and refilling the glasses. It must have taken a couple of hours or more. I can't remember much of what happened after that. They tell me I was drunk out of me mind, staggering round the bar, trying to shake blokes's hands, telling them what a good bloke Mr. Counter was, and chattering away till Grecko had to grab me and tell me to stop yapping because I might say something that would upset someone. Then Swampy, hardly able to stand up straight himself, anyway he couldn't stand up straight when he was sober, staggers outside, the comes back waving his arms, steps up to the bar and stands on the only stool in the whole bar, Spuds holding him so he doesn't fall and announces, "haw! Haw! The wind has ceased. We are free to go!"

Dad, I wish you'd been with us. Swampy was in his element. The three of us stagger out and pile into Spuds' old truck. But the wind's blowing like buggery, and I keep slipping on the step up to the back of the truck. Spuds gives me a whopping lift and I land in a truck full of potatoes, onions and fertilizer. Swampy slips off the front seat on to the floor as Spuds revs up the old ute, and guns her round in a mad U-turn and up the Melbourne Road. I thrash around throwing onions at anything we pass, but pretty soon I snuggle in amongst the veggies, and I'm sound a sleep

5. Drums of all that's right and wrong

I'm half out to it, lying in the back of the ute. The spuds are digging into me and the onions pong something awful. My tongue's nearly stuck to the top a me mouth. I need a drink.

"Hey you bastards! Where's the booze?" I yell as I struggle off the truck. We're parked outside an old ramshackle shed, half covered with rusty corrugated iron and rotten wood planks. It's big, though, and I can hear the bleating of sheep so I suppose it's a shearing shed or something. I dunno. I wander in where there's a tractor parked inside and there's Swampy and Spuds sitting on a bale a straw drinking plonk. There's a bunch of sheep penned up over in the corner and they're bleating away like they were crying for their mothers.

"Haw! Haw! Ya know how to shear a sheep?" asks Swampy.

"I need a drink, ya bastard." And I see a flagon of red sitting there. I go to pick it up and fall ass-over-tit. I'm still boozed up.

"Haw! Haw! How ya gunna hold the sheep while you're pissed as a cricket?" laughs Swampy.

"Yair. Sober up, ya silly bastardo," says Spuds, as he hands me an old tin mug.

I grab the mug and crawl to the flagon and pour myself a drink. Right there, Dad flashes into my head. It's what he drank the last few years of his life. My hand starts to shake as I pour. The flagon is nearly full so it's pretty heavy.

"Poor bugger's got-a the shakes," says Spuds.

Swampy stirs off his bale and starts to dance, if that's what you could call it. And then he's singing "Old Adelooooine! Old Adelooooine!" and makes like he's dancing with her. I'm squatting on me haunches sipping away and my mouth's feeling better already. I stand up and I'm dancing with him. Spuds tries to pull me back down, but I shake him off. "Old Adelooine," I cry, spit and dribble flying out of my mouth. I go to grab Swampy like I'm his dance partner and he yells, "ya fuckn poofda! Get the fuck away from me!" He swings a wild punch that just grazes my chin. And my knees buckle as if he'd hit me and as I go down, I hear a faint woman's voice.

"What's going on in here?"

I'm on all fours, looking over to the bright outdoors. There's a silhouette of someone standing there, and I feel Swampy plop down beside me. He wants to ride me like I was a horse!

"Get the fuck off me!" I yell.

"Haw! Haw! Watch ya fuckn language in front of moi sister!" Swampy chortles.

His sister prances across the barn. She's wearing jodhpurs, big brown leather boots and she's got a riding whip. She gets within arm's length and she starts whipping Swampy like buggery. He pretends to be hurt, cries out "Waah! Waah! Haw! Haw!" and tries to shield the lashes with his arm. But she's not stopping, and she sees me gawking at her and she starts after me and I get up and run away across to the sheep. But I'm staggering and she catches me and starts whipping me too.

"Who's this little bastard?" she yells, "what are you doing bringing a young boy on the farm? And what are you doing giving him booze? He's just a kid."

This is too much for me and I stop right at the little fence holding the sheep in and I turn to her and I say, "I'm eighteen, ya silly fuckn bitch!"

Gees, Dad. I was half pissed, so I didn't know what I was saying. She rears back, hands on hips, and I'm squinting, staring at her little eyes tucked down behind her cheeks. They're as black as buggery and her face is white as a pommie's back side.

"Get out of here young man! Get out of here this minute. This is no place for a boy like you!"

She starts her whipping again and I'm taking lashes over me arms and me back as I turn and jump over the railing into the sheep. They start wailing and bleating like I was going to slaughter them. They rush in all directions and knock over the railings and then they run off all over the barn. Swampy and Spuds suddenly sober up and start running trying to round them up, but it's hopeless. And big sister chases Swampy and Spuds and lays some pretty good strokes on. I find my way back to the flagon and take a deep swig and pretty soon I'm rolling around on the straw, having a good laugh at the silly bastards running around in circles, big sister chasing them and the sheep gone off into the paddocks. Spuds, though, managed to grab one and bring her down. And by this time, big sister has pissed off back to the farm house.

*

Holding a sheep isn't easy. I got my left hand under its chin and I'm pushing it up while I'm grabbing it around the waist and pulling it into me knees. Swampy's going "Haw! Haw!" and rubbing his big moustache with his bony fingers. But the wriggly bastard thing is struggling like I'm going to slit its throat. I lean over and I look into its grey eyes and it doesn't look anything like it's alive, its face says nothing to me. I mean, it's a thing, you know? Dad? Did you ever do this? Shit! The fuckn thing just kicked me in the shins.

Spuds is dancing around clapping his hands, yelling, "Go! Go! Pull! Pull! Ya silly bugger!" So I give it a yank and it gives a huge kick with its back legs and I lose my balance and fall backwards but I don't let go so the stupid thing rolls twisting on top of me, and I lose my grip and it flips around and its horrible mouth bangs into mine and I smell its horrible rotten breath and Swampy and Spuds are dancing around laughing their heads off, and then the stinking thing leaps off me and runs straight into Swampy and trips him up and it bleats and takes off out of the shed and into the paddock. And the other sheep that's corralled in the corner getting ready for shearing, they all go crazy and they rush at the railing and knock the rest of it down and they all take off into the paddock too, knocking Spuds and Swampy over as they're laughing their heads off, and then Spuds scrambles up and goes for another flagon of red.

"Fuckn-a shit-a!" he yells, "let's get-a the rifle and we'll kill these bastardi, that will-a teach 'em!"

"Haw Haw, like hell ya will! Don't want to bloody their wool, ya dope. You better get back to your veggies and leave the sheep to me. Gimme a drink!"

"Me too!" I says as I stagger over and put my hand out.

"You-a haven't earned it," grins Spuds.

"Get stuffed," I says, "look at me poor legs, all scratched and bloodied by that shit of a sheep."

Swampy comes over to me. He's rubbing his moustache and he's looking kind of funny. "I'm taking ya back to the pub. You've done enough damage for today."

And I think right then he's going to touch me or something. But he doesn't. He puts out a tin cup and Spuds fills it and then he hands it to me.

"You've been a fuckn good sport. I'm taking ya back to Eddie. He needs ya more than me."

I down the cup of plonk in one gulp. I don't even know what time it is. I don't want to go back now because I'm having such a good time.

"But ya better sober up first. Haw! Haw!"

And I says, "yair, gimme another plonk."

Spuds tops up my cup and he looks at Swampy and then to me. "Hey, I need-a some help digging up me spuds. What about coming with-a me and you can sober up while we work."

"Haw! Haw!" goes Swampy. "Take me truck then. I have to tell me sister we can't dag the sheep today. She's gunna be shitty. Haw! Haw!" And he starts rubbing his leg with his other, and stroking his moustache and twisting around into all kinds of contortions. As far as I'm concerned, I don't care. I got me grog, the plonk's keeping me going, so I can dig a few spuds.

Spuds shepherds me into Swampy's ute. Swampy goes over to talk to the sheep hoping they'll come back, but they've run off far away across the paddock. Spuds revs the ute and red dust flies out the back as we zoom across the paddocks along an old track. I'm trying not to slip off the seat, because I'm pretty well gone, and the track's got furrows in it as deep as the Werribee gorge.

"Where the fuck are we going?" I mutter and just then we come over a rise, and I see this beautiful green paddock running all the way down, and there's rows and rows of veggies, green as green, and the rows are straighter than a horse's dick.

"Gees! This is yours?"

"Yair. Not too bad-a for a Dago, *non e vero?*"

"Fuckn what? Speak Australian, bugger ya!"

"Stuff you! I am-a for Christ-a-sake-a," and he crosses himself and I can't help staring at him. It's the first time I ever sat close to someone who did that.

"You're a fuckn mick?" I ask in disbelief.

"What ya expect? I'm a Dago, for Christ-a-sake-a," and he crosses himself again just as we go over a big bump that causes him to nearly poke his eye out. We pull up half way down the paddock and he goes to get out.

"Did ya bring the grog?" I ask, seriously.

"Nah, got me own. Come on, the spuds are right-a here and they gotta be dug up or they'll be no good in a couple-a days."

"I need a drink first."

"Yair, of course. I tell ya, I got something-a special. It's in-a me little tool shed over there."

Spuds runs over and comes back with a shovel and a greasy looking bottle that was once a lemonade bottle and it's got this murky looking stuff in it.

"What the fuck is that?" I ask, swaying a bit and eyeing off the shovel. I'm not really up to digging.

"It's-a my brother's grappa. He makes it himself up at-a Mildura where they grow all the grapes. It's the fuckn best, I tell ya. Here, take a swig."

I'm always game when it comes to trying out grog. I grab the bottle and pop it straight in me mouth and take a big swig like it was any old plonk. And it tastes really like strong wine, and then I swallow it and shit! It's like I imagine it must be like drinking metho! I drop the bottle and the grappa starts pouring out of it and Spuds starts yelling and screaming like it was liquid gold running out all over his potato patch.

"Affunculo! Ya useless little piece of-a shit!" he screams and he grabs up the bottle that's half empty. He looks at me and I know he wants to beat the shit out of me.

"Gees, I'm sorry. It was fuckn good stuff. I just wasn't expecting it to burn me guts out." Spuds is hugging the bottle to his chest with both arms. Gees! Dad! Is that stuff so good? "Shit, Spuds. I'm sorry. Come on, I'll dig up all your spuds for ya."

I grab the shovel and I ram it into the ground, but the ground's hard and cracked because there hasn't been much rain for a while. I stand on the shovel trying to jiggle it down, and then I step off and pull on the handle to dig up a shovel full of potatoes and dirt, except that the ground's so hard I have to really force the handle down, and then there's a loud "crack" and the handle of the shovel snaps and I fall down on top of it. Shit, Dad. Maybe Swampy's right. I'm fuckn useless out here. I look over at Spuds who hasn't seen what happened. He's too busy sipping at his grappa and muttering away to himself in Dago. I stagger over to him and ask for a swig. He looks up, and hands me the bottle. I take it, and with me other hand I give him the handle of the shovel. He takes it and then looks at me and at the grappa. If he socks me one, the grappa will go to the ground and there'll be none left. So he stands there looking at the handle, trying not to smack me with it. I'm about to take a swig, but as it just gets to me mouth I can't do it, because I burst out laughing. I hand him back the bottle and he drops the handle and grasps the bottle in both hands and hugs it to his chest again. And then I see him shaking all over and I think he's crying, but it can't be true because he's a real tough bloke. But I'm having a laughing fit and then he bursts out laughing too and takes a swig. He hands me the bottle and I have another swig and this time I'm ready for it, and now I really like the stuff. Only thing is that I felt like the blood was running out of me head, it was so strong. I hand him back the bottle and I start yelping and dancing around and pretty soon we're both so drunk we can't stand up and we're rolling around in the potato patch every now and then trying to pull them up by hand, but it's impossible.

The sun has dipped below the rise and the sky is red. I'm listening to the veggies talk to each other, their leaves are rustling, I put my ear to the ground and I can hear it murmur. I'm fuckn paralytic.

*

This big fat koala's sitting on my chest, and it's pushing the air out of my lungs and I can't breathe. Dad! Help! It's a monster and it's suffocating me to death. Dad, how'd I end up like this? It's huge head's in my face and its paws are grabbing my ears and shaking my head so hard it will rip my ears off. Dad! Help me! Please Dad! I'm going to die! Die I tell you! And the monster animal pulls me head up and I open my eyes and it's Mr. Counter leaning over me and I feel the damp of the leaves around me. I'm still in the potato patch. I look around for Spuds, but he's gone and so is Swampy's ute. Mr. Counter's holding the empty grappa bottle.

"You been drinking this?" he asks the obvious.

"Yair, I s'pose so."

"You stupid little bugger. You're getting more like your father every day."

"Shit. It's not my fault Mr. Counter. You made me go with Swampy. I just did what you told me."

"I thought you'd handle yourself better than this. Getting drunk on Dago grappa. That stuff's like metho, you know. It's dangerous."

"I didn't know."

Mr. Counter's pulling at my old school shirt, trying to get me to sit up.

"Look at you. You're a disgusting mess."

"Shit, Mr. Counter. It's not my fault. Those blokes are crazy!"

"That's what they say about you!"

"And Swampy's sister, she's just as mad!"

I struggle to get up, and with Mr. Counter's hand under my arm, I manage to get nearly upright. He let's go of me and picks up the handle of the shovel.

"I see you've been working," he says.

"Yair. I don't think I'm cut out to be a roustabout on a farm. And I hate sheep anyway."

"Well, it was worth a try."

"I just want to work at the pub and be your best barman, Mr. Counter."

Mr. Counter looks at me. He's such a good bloke and he was such a good mate to me Dad. I don't know what I'd do without him. I'd do anything for him, I would. He's smiling.

"Come on," he says, and he gives me a nice tap on the shoulder, "let's get back to the pub. There's a lot to do."

We walk to his new Humber and he drives as slow as a tractor over the great holes and furrows in the track, and at long last on to the Melbourne Road. I'm already looking forward to cleaning the bar counter, pouring the beers with just the right amount of head, having a few beers with the mates after closing time. And how good it'll be to get in my own soft bed.

*

I've been trying out all the booze. Went back to the gin. It was the first booze I ever drank, out there in the paddock among the thistles. Seems like years ago. But it's awful, I have to admit. I tried it like the women do in the Snake Pit, having a gin squash, but it's so sweet with the lemon cordial and then the lemonade as well, I just couldn't drink much of it because it filled me guts up. Besides, gin stinks even in squash so I wouldn't get away with drinking it during the day while I was working. So I tried the vodka. And holy shit, that was the drink for me! When nobody was looking I first tried it neat, and I nearly choked like the day I drank Spuds's grappa. But I got it down and phew! What a hit! At first I tried it in lemon squash, but the stuff filled up me guts and I couldn't drink enough of it to keep me buzzing all day. Then a woman comes up and orders a vodka tonic, and I reckoned I'd try that. And it worked! I could drink as much as I wanted all day and soon I managed to pretty much fill the glass half vodka and half tonic, and the best thing was the vodka didn't smell like gin did. So I'd just keep telling people that I loved the tonic water and it was good for my digestion.

Then after closing time when we had our few drinks and the mates told stories and we sucked down the beers, on my shout— although it was really Mr. Counter that gave us all our beer free —I'd sneak a couple of whiskeys behind the bar while I was filling the glasses. Sugar, though, he was watching me like a hawk. He never liked me. He was jealous because Mr. Counter treated me like one of his family, and Sugar was just another barman. I couldn't help that, Dad, now could I? But he liked scotch and didn't really drink much beer because he said it had too much sugar, so I'd pour him a couple of scotches and while I was doing it, I'd turn my back and take a quick swig out of the bottle.

By the time all the blokes went home, I was blotto as usual and I'd wander into the kitchen and look through the fridge for something to eat, but really, I wasn't ever much hungry, so I'd chew a piece of bread and have a glass (well a few glasses) of plonk to go with it and then I'd stagger down the passage and flop on my bed. And I'd feel around under me bed for the bottle of plonk I kept there, yair, just like me dear old Dad, and have a few swigs before I dropped off.

I don't know how long all this went on for. They were my happiest times for a long while until I started to notice that the blokes would look at me and say nothing but I knew there was something wrong. I thought this was because I had the shakes a bit, especially in the morning when I sat down for breakfast in the kitchen and Abbie would plonk down a plate of bacon and eggs and I'd try to scoop up the bacon with my fork but me hand shook too much, so I'd just end up eating the toast and that was all. Once I got a few grogs into me, though, the shakes went away, and I was right as rain. So then I started sneaking a small flask of scotch and kept it in my room and as soon as I woke up, I'd take a swig or two and that steadied me down so I never had the shakes in the kitchen and Abbie stopped looking at me like I was a criminal. But I could never swallow those eggs. She'd keep making them in all different ways. But they just turned me off. And she'd stand there with her hands on her hips, big toothy grin telling me I had to eat them because I needed to keep up my strength.

*

This day I'm serving the Snake Pit and Little Linda shows up and she's chasing her little brat kid around the Lounge and finally catches her and drags her up to the bar.

"Whiskey and beer," she says as usual.

"G'day, Linda," I says.

"Where ya fuckn been?" she asks.

"Here, of course. Where d'you fuckn think?"

"Don't ya like Iris any more or what, ya bastard?"

"Course I like her. I been busy working me fuckn ass off in the pub."

"And ya had no fuckn time to come and see her?"

"Why couldn't she come and see me?"

"Because I dunno where she is, that's why."

"What do you fuckn mean?"

"She's gone again. Hurry with the scotch, will ya? I'm fuckn sick."

"Shit and hell! When?"

"The drinks, ya bastard. Get the fuckn drinks."

The kid brat pulls away from her hand and starts running and screaming up and down the passage. I get the drinks and she grabs them off me.

"That's one-and-thruppence."

"Fuck you! I'm broke."

She walks away and I'm left standing there so I have to feel around in my pocket for the money and make up the till, because if I don't Sugar, when he does the money tonight, will find out the till is short. But I'm shaking too. I reach for my tonic water and it steadies me. God in hell! Iris, Dad. I forgot all about her. Well, didn't really forget, always I'm thinking of her when I'm down there in my bedroom on me own, getting into the plonk wishing I was with her, you know what I mean Dad? I suppose this happened to you too? I just can't seem to get myself to leave this place and the booze.

Little Linda. She buggered up my day, and I had to hit the booze more than usual. Sugar was watching me like never before, and I had a good idea that Mr. Counter was too. So after closing time, instead of staying with the mates for our usual few beers, I went down to my room to have a drink on my own. Even then, though, I was having trouble walking a straight line, but the blokes wouldn't be able to see me because the passage was so dark. And when I opened the door to my bedroom and the sun pierced me eyes like a frigging dagger slicing through the slit in the blind, I put up my hands to shade them and then I saw lying on my bed, little Iris all curled up and there were tears on her cheeks, those lovely white cheeks.

I close the door softly behind me, but I'm so unsteady it bangs shut and Iris wakes up. She doesn't do more than just open her eyes. I'm down on my knees and I'm nuzzling my nose into her face. I'm looking already for one of her wet kisses. But she just lies there and curls up even tighter in a ball.

"Gees Iris! What the hell? Are you all right?"

"Bugger you," she says in a little mousey voice.

"Gees, Iris! What'd I do?"

"You're a fuckn hopeless shit."

"What'd I do?"

"And you're a fuckn drunk."

"I'm fuckn not!"

She sits on the edge of the bed. She's looking down at me. And I know she wants to ruffle me hair. But she's not. And I'm waiting for one of her wet kisses. But her lips are dry and she's licking them. My knees are getting sore from kneeling and I'm having trouble staying up straight anyway. I try to grab her hands but she pulls them away. She didn't say it, but I know what she's saying. "Don't touch me." Shit Dad. What have I done? All I done really is have a few drinks. That's all. And every bloke does it, all me mates in the bar. They all have their few beers. That's all. Yair, Dad. And if our women would have a few beers that would make it a lot easier.

"You're talking to your father again, you fuckn weirdo," she says.

"Shut the fuck up." I'm getting angry, my ears are red and I think I'm falling sideways.

"Stand up ya fuckn drunk. You can't can ya?"

I grab the bed and I push myself up and I fall over on to the bed and I knock her backwards and end up lying across her lap.

"Get off, you're hurting me." She's going to howl, I know she is. I'm feeling around under my bed for a drop a plonk.

"Get off me!" she cries and then I find the plonk and I pull it out and I sit up all proud.

"There, you see, I found it! We're set for the night. Here, I've got a spare glass somewhere in the drawer."

I try to stand up and fall back on the bed. Iris dodges me and stands up, her back against the torn blind. She's got her hands on her hips and she looks like Swampy's sister. I think I'm stuffed. She doesn't have a whip, though, so I'm lying on the bed on my back, holding the bottle of plonk on my chest. I'm trying to pour a glass but I can't get the bottle to go to the glass. She sniffs and snivels and then she takes a step forward, and Dad, I knew I was in for it. She grabs the bottle of plonk out of me hand and throws it against the wall and it bounces off, and sprays plonk all over everything, me included. I'm madly thinking that I must look like

I just came out of the Nile the day it ran red. Then she sits on top of me and for a fleeting moment my body says, "this is going to be good" except she doesn't stop there. She leans back and grabs me dick and everything. Gees Dad! Is this what they do when they get mad? My ears aren't red any more. I'm getting ready for one of the best. But then she squeezes and squeezes and before I know it I'm calling out, "Stop! Stop! What the fuck are you doing?" And she leans back on to her hand and puts even more weight on me and I'm doing all I can not to scream. "Fuckn shit and hell, Iris. I might have been a bastard, but this, this... aahhh!" I cry and I try to roll away from under her, but I'm too drunk to do it. She lets go a little and I'm lying there, I can't talk. I might even throw up with her sitting on me guts. What a mess it would make. Then she leans forward and I think she's going to kiss me. I see her lips are really nice and wet like they always were. "Yair, Iris," I say, "that's the girl." She gets even closer and pushes her nose against mine.

"You know what?" she says.

I don't want to answer. I'm waiting for her kiss. I move my lips like I was saying "what."

"I'm pregnant."

So now, you got to understand, Dad. I heard the words but I didn't have a clue what they meant. I mean it was just like someone told me I forgot their birthday or that they had the mumps or something. So I say, "gees, I'm sorry."

"Did ya fuckn hear what I said, ya dopey fuckn drunk?"

"Yair. You're pregnant. So that's all right, isn't it?"

She lets go of me dick and gets off me. Trouble is, even in my drunken state, I've got a hard on and of course she knows it. She looks down at it.

"Your brains are swollen again," she says.

And I'm about to laugh but I see she's not laughing.

"I'm pregnant, don't you understand? And you did it."

So now it's beginning to sink in. Even though she raped me—that's what she really did—she's blaming me.

"Me? What about your old man? You said he does you all the time."

"I told you. I made that up."

"Then who else, then?"

"You're the only one. I thought I loved you."

She sits on the edge of the bed again and puts her hand into my hair and it calms me down a lot.

"So, you can get rid of it, can't you?"

"What a shit you are," she says, and gets up and walks to the door.

"Where you going?"

"Don't know. I'm not going back home."

"That's what you said last time." I think I'm sobering up.

"Yair. But I mean it this time. If I went home Tank would beat me senseless and try to knock it out of me belly."

"He's that kind of bastard?"

"Yair."

"Me drinking mates talk. They know where you can get fixed. Their sheilas do it all the time."

"I'm not doing that."

"Why not?"

"You're a real fuckn dumb shit, that's what you are. Didn't you learn anything besides Latin at high school?"

"Thanks. I'm only trying to help."

"And what about you?"

"What about me?"

"You're its father, ya fuckn drunken wombat!"

"Well, what do ya want to do then?"

"What do *you* want to do?"

"Fuck you right now," me body says, but I lie there looking her up and down. Those white cheeks, the red sloppy lips. I can't stop drooling.

"Well? What do you want to do about it?" she nags. "What?"

"I don't know. I mean it's yours, isn't it?"

"So... It's nothing to do with you? You'll just keep on drinking with your mates and forget all about me, so you don't fuckn care what I do?"

"No, I won't, I mean, course I care, but I'm not giving up drinking with me mates, if that's what you mean."

"I'm three months, you know."

"Yair? It's been that long since I did me Latin exam?"

"Shit. That's what you remember, is it?"

"No, course not. That time in the commission house. Oh, gees, it was the best." And now I'm going off again and I want to get into her. So I start to sit up and get a bit closer to her.

"Fuckn stay right there," she says, sounding like Swampy's sister again.

"Gees, Iris. I'll marry you if that would fix things. Is that what you want?"

Dad, you gotta listen to me. She stood there staring at me like I had said something really awful, the worst. And I haven't a clue what I said, not really. I said it hoping it would make her feel better, but I meant it too. I mean "meant it" without a clue of what it meant. Gees. Dad. I'm all fucked up.

I start looking around the room. I pick up my old towel and try to wipe off the red splashes of plonk on the walls and closets. She follows me with her eyes as I move around the room, and I gradually inch closer to her. I wipe her eyes with the clean tip of the towel. And I see the water in her eyes, and gees, Dad, tears start pushing at the back of my eyes as well. It just all of a sudden happened. And Iris sees the tears, and she raises her finger and lightly touches the corner of me eye and follows a tear down the side of my nose. I drop the towel and I gently slide my arms around her and we draw close. And at last she plonks one of her sloppy kisses on me dry lips. And I think everything's back to what they were after my Latin exam. To my amazement, I pick her up in my arms and gently place her on the bed. And I lie down beside her and we cuddle together and even though I'm ready to do her over and over again, we fall asleep in each other's arms.

*

Gees Dad. I have to be honest. When I woke up, I was kind of hoping she'd be gone like last time. But she wasn't. She was right there, her lily-white eyelids closed tight, her eyes rolling around behind them. Dreaming of me, I hope. My hand's shaking a lot, but I try hard to lightly run my fingers through her cropped hair that I've always loved, and gradually down her neck. I plant a kiss on her eyelid, and I see a flicker of her mouth. She's in there, Dad. I know what it's like, don't I?

Iris opens her eyes and I see that she's kind of shocked to find me there, staring into her gorgeous blue-grey eyes. Not that different, I say to myself, to the colour of Swampy's sheep. But hers are full of life. She sighs and stretches out her arms and I lean into her hoping she'll pull me in. And she does. But I'm shaking like buggery and she pushes me back. I start feeling around under the bed for a bottle of booze. Should be some scotch there somewhere. It always stops the shakes. Then out of the blue, she says with a cheeky grin,

"I'm going to call it Ovid."

At last, I find a little flask of scotch and I have to hold it with two hands to steady myself so I can get it up to my mouth. I'm not listening to her.

"Did you hear me? Ya bastard, all you think of is your booze. Me mum's been right all along."

"Gees! Hang on! I'm just trying to steady myself. I'm just trying to calm myself down. I mean, you scared the shit out of me getting pregnant."

"What a shit you are! I'm getting out of here."

"What'd I do now? I can't help it if you got yourself pregnant!"

"You're a useless asshole, that's what you are. I'm leaving and I never want to see you again!"

"Iris! For Christ sake! You're going off your rocker!"

And she runs to the door and just as she grabs the doorknob, it flies open and there's Abbie standing there her mouth gaping open. I'm sitting on the edge of the bed, no pants on, holding a flask of whiskey over my crown jewels.

"What the hell's going on here?" she says, trying to sound real bossy, but she's holding back a laugh, putting her hand up to her big white teeth.

Iris looks like a little primary school kid next to her and she backs away like her teacher had just told her to 'sit down right this minute.' So she sits down on the edge of the bed right next to me.

The scotch is working its magic and my hands are getting steady.

"Abbie, this is my girlfriend Iris," I say, waiting for Abbie to say something, but she doesn't, and then I blurt out, "we're getting married."

I feel Iris stiffen up and she puts her hand on me leg and digs her nails right into me.

"Really?" smiles Abbie like she's going along with a fairy tale, "and when are you going to get up and get ready for work?"

"Get stuffed. You're not my mother."

"Thank goodness. But Mrs. Counter asked me to watch out for you, and that's what I'm doing even if it's not my job."

"Pleased to meet you," says Iris and she holds out her hand.

"Hello love. Welcome to the pub. Now tell your silly boyfriend here to get himself cleaned up. She looks me up and down. "He looks like a… don't know what."

She backs out of the room and pulls the door slowly shut. I take another swig of the scotch and drain the bottle, and slide it under the bed.

"It's a him?" I say, making like everything's back the way they were. She's starting to snivel and sob. "Gees, Iris love," I say, putting my arm around her and giving her a little hug, "don't cry. Everything's going to be all right."

"Why did you tell her we're getting married?

"Gees, I thought that's what you wanted."

"Marry a drunken bastard like you?"

"I'm not a drunk. I'm just having fun at the pub with me mates."

"Yair. OK. That's what all me mum's blokes told her, and my sister's too."

"So, what do you want to do then?" I'm getting angry. I feel the blood in my ears and I start to finger them.

"I don't know! I don't know!" She sobs and she puts her arms around my neck and cries into my chest that's all sweaty and smelly. And then she keeps rubbing her lovely white cheek against my chest that's tight and smooth as well, and her cropped hair is tickling my tits. I put my arms around her too, the least I could do, Dad. And we sit there, rocking backwards and forwards. And after a long time when her sobs have stopped, I ask, "are we gunna get married then?"

"I don't know, I really don't," she whimpers.

"Well I'll marry you, if you want. I don't care."

"You don't care? Shit! You bastard!"

"I didn't mean it like that."

"Like what?"

"Like that."

"It's your drinking, you know that."

I look down at her belly.

"You could get rid of it you know."

"You mean *we,* don't you?"

She looks at me like I'm a criminal.

"Shit, Iris. What are you talking about?"

"I told you. Tank will beat it out of me."

"I'm not Tank, for Christ sake."

"Yair. But I don't know how to do it either."

"I could talk to me mates. There's places you can go. They talk about it all the time."

"Yair, but then everyone would know."

"Nah. They keep it quiet. Because you're not supposed to do it, are you?"

"I don't know."

"I could ask Mrs. Counter. The trouble is she doesn't like me."

"Why don't you ask Mr. Counter then?"

"Because he told me I had to get rid of you. Remember?"

"But that was before."

"Shit, Iris. I got to get cleaned up and get to the bar. Sugar will be knocking at the door any minute."

"So you're just leaving me here, then, just like last time"?

"Shit, Iris. What the hell can I do? I got to go to work. And if we're going to have a baby, we need money, don't we?"

"All right. Go then. I don't know what I'm going to do all day in here."

"Maybe you could help Abbie or something."

"Bugger off then!"

I grab my towel and I'm about to open the door when I see the handle turn. I grab it and pull it open, and there, sure enough is Sugar. He's smirking away, and he's got his eyebrows in that frown of his like they nearly meet each other at his nose and I find myself staring at them. I'm sure he plucks them and trims them too.

"Fuck off, Sugar!" I scowl and wrap the towel around my waist. He stares at the towel and sticks his tongue out to wet his lips.

"Mr. Counter wants to see you right away."

"I'm having a shower." I push past him and walk none too steady down to the bathroom.

"I know what you're doing, you smart ass," he calls.

Then I remember I never shut the bedroom door. I turn back and start running. Sugar thinks I'm after him and when I get close, I stamp my foot and go like I'm about to punch him. He steps back and bangs his head against the wall, and I brush past him saying, "gees, I forgot me underpants."

*

I'm in the shower and I'm thinking what I'm going to do. I'll tell Mr. Counter that Iris and me are getting married and I want my money that I've earned fair and square and can we stay in the pub. Maybe Iris could do some work for Mrs. Counter or something. I'm standing there, letting the water run over my throbbing head and down over my face. I need another drink. There's a bang on the door and someone comes in. I must have forgot to lock it. But I can see through the old plastic shower curtain that it's Sugar.

"Get going you little fuck! Eddie's got a big shitty on you," he says.

"Get the fuck out of here you asshole!"

"Well, don't say I never told you."

I cup my hands and fill them with water, toss back the curtain and throw it on his bald head.

"Fuck off!" I say.

"You bastard. You'll be sorry for all this. You're getting too big for your frigging boots."

"You want fuckn more? Get the fuck out!" He stands there staring at the shower curtain. "You hear me? Fuck off!"

*

Gees, Dad. Flo and Tank, are they really married? Shit! Will me and Iris be like that when we're old like they are? Gees, Dad, I never thought about getting married. Sweet Iris, Dad, she made it look like we had to and that was that, don't you think? And I didn't think much of it. For Christ sake, the people that come into the pub that's supposed to be married. If they can do it, so can we, don't you think? I just never thought about it. It's like having a birthday or something. It's just something that happens. It comes along and you have a big party, and then you wait for the next one. Right?

I was trying to figure out who was who in that hell-house anyway. Iris, she lies half the damned time about who's who and who does what. Linda's supposed to be her big sister, but is she a half-sister or what? And she really looks like Iris's little sister, and that's weird because Iris is little herself. And whose kid is the brat? Can you imagine Tank and Flo going at it? Shit and hell! He's so big and Flo's tiny. It's the smoking, that's what Iris says. She smokes and doesn't eat much. She lives on toast and Vegemite. And she's got no money because the Seventh Day Adventists took it all, that's what Iris said. Anyway, Flo never had any money. Iris says she grew up in a traveling circus and her bedroom was an open trailer with a mattress plonked down in it. I don't believe that, do you Dad? Shit. Iris keeps telling me stuff, I wish she wouldn't.

*

Flo was lying on her water bed flat on her back, drawing on her cigarette, looking up at the ceiling. She knew every little crack and smudge on that ceiling, she'd been on her back so much in this room. The daddy longlegs left their marks all over and so did the flies, little black spots of crap. She heard the kitchen screen door open and slam shut so she rolled over and stubbed out her Garrick. Tank was on his way. She heard the fridge door open and slam shut. He was getting a beer. And now he was pacing up and down the kitchen while he drank it. The house was quiet. Linda and the brat must have gone to the pub. She lit another cigarette and drew deeply. Death sticks Iris called them. What did she know? The sin of her life was such a weight and Iris was the sin she had hidden from the church. They would kick her out if they knew.

But that wouldn't be so bad, except that Jesus surely knew. Of course, Tank was her partner in sin. He stopped beating her long ago and the truth is she missed it. She deserved it, that's what. When he beat her it made it easier to live with herself. But now, every time she saw Iris, the heavy weight fell on her back like a huge stone crushing the life out of her. Tank came to the bedroom door.

"I'll throttle that little shit when I catch him, I tell ya," he growled.

Flo lay there expressionless. She closed her eyes and said a prayer. "Dear Jesus, I know that what I've done is too bad to be forgiven," she said, her lips moving without noise, "take me, Jesus, I'm ready!"

Now Tank paced up and down the bedroom, sipping his beer.

"You hear me Flo? Ya silly old bitch!" he said.

Flo remained motionless except for her lips.

"I'll yank his fuckn head off and then I'll deal with Iris, the little whore!"

Flo flinched. She took a draw of her Garrick and began to cough, but managed to speak. "Don't you fuckn touch her," she said, her face still flat and expressionless, "you and me made her like that, it's not her fault."

"She's a silly little fuckn bitch."

"Jesus told me she's pure, pure as snow."

"Yair? While she's fuckn that little prick?"

"Because we made her like it."

"Your stupid fuckn minister's feeding you bullshit."

"I never told him nothing. I only told Jesus."

"You always was a stupid bitch."

"You must have been stupid to marry me then."

"Fuck you."

Flo rolled over to stub out her cigarette and added it to the mound of buts in the ashtray. She sat on the edge of the bed and looked at Tank who stopped his pacing and stood there, draining the last drop of beer from the bottle.

"Go on," said Flo, "hit me with the bottle like you always do."

"You'd like that, wouldn't ya? So you could call the cops."

"Go on then."

Flo brushed past him and went to the bathroom. She looked briefly in the mirror, then walked to the kitchen where Tank was getting another beer. "I'm going to church, "she said, "and so should you."

"This is my church," said Tank, raising the bottle to his lips. It was Saturday. He was going to the pub. And if he caught that little bastard he would break his fuckn neck.

*

Mr. Counter put me on pie duty. He had a not-so-friendly talk with me. I didn't make it to the bar until nearly eleven o'clock. I only ate a round of toast for breakfast and left most of that anyway, even though Abbie had made eggs for me as usual. She wasn't too pleased this morning. And she kept giving me looks like I should talk with her in private or something. I didn't, though, because I was scared what I might say. Then Mr. Counter came into the kitchen and he stood at the old table and Mrs. Counter came up and stood next to him. Abbie took my plate away and put some fresh toast with the eggs I left, and then she gave me a look again, and took the plate away and left the kitchen.

"This is my last warning, to you," said Mr. Counter. His missus was standing there with her hands on her huge hips. "I've done everything and more to help you get over your Dad's passing. Now you have to help yourself. This is your last chance."

"Mr. Counter. I'm sorry. I'll give up the booze. But I want my money."

"You what?"

"My money that you said you put away for me. I need it."

"What for? More grog?"

"Young man…" began Mrs. Counter.

"It's something urgent. I can't tell you what."

"Well, the answer's no. Not until you show me that you can give up the grog."

"But I need the dough now."

"It can't be that urgent. Go on the wagon for the rest of the week and we can then talk about you getting more of your money."

I'm sitting there sullen, and scratching at the table top. "Mr. Counter, please. It's really important."

"How important?" asks Mrs. Counter.

"Well, I can't tell you. I really can't."

"Are you in trouble?" asks Mr. Counter.

"Nah, I wouldn't say that. But a mate of mine needs help urgently." I surprised myself saying this.

"Well, tell us what it is."

"I can't. I promised I wouldn't say. He's an old mate. I have to help him."

"How much do you need?" asks Mr. Counter.

"All my money."

"It's not much anyway, because you haven't been doing your work properly, have you?"

I'd said enough. Didn't want to risk saying any more or I might bugger myself up. I just sat there, head throbbing in my hands.

"Well, let's see how you do today and then we'll talk again tonight. I'm putting you on pie duty this morning. You can run the pie shop yourself. All right?"

"OK Mr. Counter."

So here I am now, putting the pies in the warmer and they smell really mouth-watering, and I'm wanting to eat one, but the shakes have come back and I'm having trouble handling the pies and pasties, my hands banging against the warmer and burning me. The pie shop is at the back of the new bar, so I have to sneak out and into the storeroom behind. There's boxes and boxes of booze and I find a case of whiskey flasks, rip it open and grab a flask and pull at the cap, which is hard because of my shakes. But I get it off and take a few quick swigs, then I'm right as rain, and I do my job in the pie shop, no worries.

*

There's this hell of a noise and I know it's the brat right away. She comes running into the pie shop and little Linda's chasing after her. She grabs her and lifts her up on to the counter.

"She wants a sausage roll," she says.

"Roll! Roll!" the brat screams.

I get her a sausage roll and she snatches it out of my hand before I can put it in a bag. Linda grabs the brat and walks off carrying her on her hip.

"Hey! You forgot to pay," I yell.

"No, I didn't," she yells.

"Fuckn bitch!" I yell. My ears are red and I'm off after her, I'm going to squeeze the money out of her. I don't want to, but I haven't got any money of my own anymore, so I can't make it up to the till. Sugar will find out tonight that it's short and he'll tell Mr. Counter I've been fingering the till.

Linda stops and turns as the brat squirms free of her clutches and runs away. "You better watch yourself," she says, "me old man's after you, says he'll break your fuckn neck. And he's on his way to do it, right now."

I stop in my tracks. I grab a stray beer glass and run out of the pie shop and into the storeroom. If he comes after me, I can smash the glass and cut him with it. There's a trap door down to the beer cellar where all the barrels of beer are hooked up to the pipes going to the bars. I grab a flask of whiskey and down I go. It's cold down there, so I don't know how long I can stay put.

Not very long. What am I fuckn doing? I climb back out of the cellar and back to the pie shop. It's time for me to close it down anyway. And then I hear a lot of shouting and this time I'm sure Tank is coming for me, so I start for the storeroom, but this time Sugar's standing there waiting for me, a big smirk on his face, practically undressed, and he's got only his underpants on and nothing else. He locks the storeroom door and just stands there smirking. Me, I'm clueless.

"What the fuck are you doing here?" I ask, breathless, looking to the door expecting Tank to smash his way in any minute.

"What are *you* doing here is more like it," he says with a grin.

"Tank's coming to kill me, that's why. I have to get away."

"He's not coming. I told Grecko to watch out for him."

Sugar comes up to me and stands up close. He's got this horrible sweet breath like he's been eating Steamrollers for breakfast. And I look at his eyebrows again, they're plucked for sure.

"You're not having a fit again are you?"

"Not that kind of fit," he says, and he licks his creepy mouth like he was a kid licking an ice-cream.

I step away and he follows me until I'm up against a stack of beer boxes, my back arched over and he's up against me. I'm still clutching the beer glass.

"What the fuck are you doing?" I say, "you're breaking my back, for Christ sake."

He doesn't say nothing but he steps back a little, and then I see it plain and clear. Dumb bastard you are, I say to myself. Dad, if you could have seen us right then. I suppose it was funny. But real quick I smash the glass on the edge of a barrel, my ears are red and I'm ready to let him have it. I push him away and I swipe the glass across his body aiming for one thing, a thin stalk like a carrot, not much bigger than Nipper's. I miss my mark and the glass gets caught in his pants and he's panicking so I jab the glass into his crown jewels and he yells and there's blood seeping through his underpants. I'm about to finish him off with a jab to the face when the storeroom door bursts open and in comes Tank with Grecko hard on his heels. They both stop in their tracks when they see us, but Grecko quickly grabs the glass from my hand, and Tank, he's just standing there, puffing and panting trying to decide which one of us to hit first.

"He's a fuckn poofda!" I yell, pointing at Sugar, "a fuckn stinking poofda!"

Sugar starts moaning and drops to the floor. There's blood trickling down his legs. Grecko's holding me back with one hand. Then Tank starts forward and Grecko stiffens. But instead a going after me, Tank looks at Sugar and laughs, "I always fuckn thought you were, ya little fuckn shit!" He turns around and goes off laughing his head off. Grecko gives me a shove towards the door and says, "better call an ambulance." I look down at Sugar and there's blood everywhere. He's dropped to his knees, about to pass out.

*

With Sugar out of the way for a while, my life was a bit easier. I was expecting to get a visit from the cops because the job I did on Sugar was pretty horrendous. He had to have a lot of surgery to get fixed, it was touch and go and he nearly died. But the cops never came and nobody ever said anything to me. I don't know if Mr. Counter will have Sugar back, now that everybody knows he's a poofda. There'll be blokes going after him as soon as they get a bit of grog in them. Trouble was, Mr. Counter blamed me for it all, even though it was not my fault, was it Dad? He said I had a bad temper and it would get me into big trouble if I didn't do something about it and that it was made worse by me being on the booze all the time, so I better show him I could give it up or he would fire me. And there was no way he'd give me any of my money until I showed him I was on the wagon, and he didn't care what I wanted the money for, I wasn't going to get it.

"Mr. Counter," I pleaded, "if I don't have my morning grog, I can't work properly. I have the shakes so bad, I can't pour a beer."

"Yes, I know. And you'll steal the booze from me so you can keep drinking even when you don't have any money. And I've seen you drinking the dregs from the beer glasses."

"Gees, Mr. Counter, don't embarrass me, I can't help it."

"You've turned into your father," he says, looking at me and looking really sad.

For the first time since that day Dad died, there's water coming to my eyes and I'm going to cry. I gulp a few times and my face is all red from my embarrassment.

"Mr. Counter, you don't know what trouble I'm trying to fix. I really do need the money."

"Then go on the wagon."

"I've tried, you know that. I can't, and do me job at the same time."

"Is Iris still living in your room?"

The question came like a bolt of lightning.

"How'd you know?"

"Abbie hinted to the missus, and when I saw Tank after you, I put two and two together."

"Unless she's gone off again, she's still in my room," I confessed.

"Maybe she can help you get on the wagon."

"She mightn't be there. I don't know where she is half the time."

"The only way to fix you is to lock yourself in your room and not come out till it's over."

"How long will it take?"

"A few days."

"I, I don't know, Mr. Counter."

"It's easier if you have someone with you."

"Maybe Abbie could?"

"She's got work to do... Iris... you need Iris."

*

Iris was still there! She was still lying on my bed, all curled up. She looked so beautiful, I stripped off and slid into bed beside her. She turned and faced away from me and I cuddled into her, snuggling me nose into the back of her neck, rubbing it into her hair. And then I started to shake. Not just my hands, but my whole body. I felt under the bed for my flask but couldn't find it. I leaned over to look and there was nothing there. And the shakes were so bad I fell out of bed. I went through all my drawers but there was nothing there either. My room was bare. And I'm hugging myself shivering and shaking and Iris opens an eye and then the other. She starts to laugh.

"Ya silly bugger, get back in here," she says.

"It's not funny!" And I'm trying to put some clothes on to get warm.

"Come on. Get in and I'll keep ya warm,"

And the tears just gushed up and burst out of me, I couldn't hold them back no more. I collapsed into bed and the shakes got me in convulsions and Iris, my dear little Iris, tries to hold me as tight as she can and I'm trying not to hurt her with me convulsions. She lies on top-a me and her weight is nearly enough to hold me down and she fights to keep there and I gradually feel the warmth of her sweet little body coming through to me and I'm trying to stop my arms from flailing around and she's dodging them and she's trying to plant a sloppy kiss on my cheek but my head's whizzing side to side and my nose bangs her lips but she doesn't stop trying to kiss me because she knows that's what I love most. Gees, Dad, I love her so much, is this how it was with you and mum? Iris stays there still, and slowly my body gives in, tired and aching, my arms and legs at last slowing down and going limp. Sleep was coming, thank God Dad, and Iris was just lying there on top of me and I'm getting warm and I'm waiting for sleep.

I saw a movie once about a bloke with the DT's. He thought there were spiders crawling all over him and he yelled and screamed and thrashed about like he was crazy, trying to brush the spiders away. Didn't happen to me. How could it, when I had the most beautiful girl in the world lying on top of me? I had a kind of nightmare though. It started out like my usual one where I'm on the Melbourne Road, but this time instead of standing there waiting for the truck to run me over, I was lying across the road, don't know how I got there like that, but I was lying there and I look up and see a big truck, Bomber's truck it was I reckon, boring down the Melbourne Road coming right at me. I'm trying desperately to get up and run away, but there's this big weight on me that keeps pressing me into the concrete pavement. "It's coming at me, mum! It's coming at me!" And I see my mum way across the side of the road standing there and she's calling out to me but I can't understand what she's saying. And the truck's almost on me, I can hear its old engine roaring, and I'm calling out, "Mum! Mum! Come and get me!" And then me Dad pushes past her and he's coming but he falls down and can't get up and he's crawling but not to me. He's getting off the road. "Dad! Dad! I'm over here!" but it's too late, the truck's right on me and I see Bomber's face staring at me through the dirty windshield, his glaring white teeth bared like a Tasmanian devil. And then all of a sudden, I feel someone grab my leg and fling me across the road and the truck just evaporates. And I see Sugar standing over me, his big smirk as usual. I'm staring at him, I don't know what to say. Shit, Dad. What have I done? Did he die? My eyes jerk open and I look for Iris. She's not on top of me and I can't see her anywhere. I feel like I'm done for. Without her, I feel like nothing. I curl up and try to sleep but I can't. I want Iris. And I feel like shit. Need a drink. But I can't get out of bed, and I feel under the bed but there's nothing. My mind's gone bung. I'm thinking it's the end. I scream into the old blanket I'm holding over my head.

It makes me feel a bit better, so I go on screaming until I'm hoarse. And then at last sleep comes.

*

The window's open and Iris is gone again. My door opens and in comes Abbie with a glass of soda water and an aspirin.

"And how are we this morning?" she says, a bigger than usual smile on her face.

"What time is it?"

"What day is it? You mean."

She hands me the soda water and aspro and I take them like I'm her patient.

"Where's Iris?"

"Who knows? She was here yesterday, when I came in."

"Yesterday? You mean…?"

"Yep. You've been out to it for a couple of days and your little Iris stayed with you all that time."

"Gees, Abbie. Do you know where she is then?"

"Nope. She keeps to herself. Comes and goes through the window. I brought her some breakfast yesterday, though, and she ate it. She's a good little girl. You're very lucky to have her."

"Yair. I know. You got something a bit stronger to go with the soda water?"

"Now! Now! Don't muck things up after all you've been through. You're on the wagon now. You know what Mr. Counter said."

I'm sitting up, my legs pulled up under my chin and I'm holding them tight.

"Abbie?" I say.

"Yair?" she answers and bustles around the room like she's doing the dusting.

"Do you know people…?"

"What people?"

"That can fix up a girl."

"Talk straight, ya little bugger. What are you asking?"

"Iris is pregnant and we don't know what to do, and please don't tell Mr. Counter."

It just all blurted out and I'm hiding my face behind me knees. Iris saved me the last couple of days and now I've gone and told Abbie, the biggest loud mouth in the pub. Abbie moves to the door.

"Don't go! Don't go! And please don't tell anyone, especially Mr. Counter."

"Why not? He might be able to help you."

"Do you know anyone?"

"Mr. Counter told me you were getting married, that's what you told him, isn't it?"

"Yair, I did. But I didn't know what I was saying and I don't know if Iris wants to, although I think she does, but we don't know what to do, Abbie."

"Then I don't know what fix you're asking me about."

"Abbie, please. You do. You know what I'm talking about."

"Well me answer is I don't. But I know someone who does."

"You do? Who?"

"Well, I don't know if she's the right person. She's not, er, she's…"

"Yair? What? Who? Gees, Abbie, say it."

"Well she's had a lot of experience with getting fixed. You know her, she's in the Snake Pit all the time."

"Gees, Abbie. You mean Millie?"

"Yair. Everyone knows it."

"But me Dad…"

"Yair. And everyone else."

"Gees, I don't know, Abbie."

"You should tell Mr. Counter. You should."

"I just can't. And please, don't tell anyone."

"The poor little kid. You need to take care of her, you poor thing."

"I will, I really will. I just need a drink."

"That's the last thing you need!"

And Abbie left.

*

Sitting in a bedroom that's not much bigger than a prison cell, with no booze, what's a bloke to do? Gees, Dad, I could really do with a drink. I'm getting a pretty good idea of what you went through. And without Iris to take care of me, what can I do? I suppose I could go and find her but I'm scared her old man will beat me up.

Then there's a faint knock on my door and I jump up and open it. It's Mrs. Counter, her boobs hanging like a bull's balls, but she's smiling and I think that maybe she does like me. She holds out a big parcel and I take it.

"Young man," she says, "It's time you looked the part, so I got you some new clothes. There's some Fletcher Jones pants and a couple of nice white shirts for you to wear in the bar. Them old school clothes are fit for the bin. We can't have our barmen looking like runaways, now can we?"

"Gees, thanks Mrs. Counter. I can't wait to try them on."

"That's a good lad. Very good to see you smiling again. You must be feeling better?"

"Yair, Mrs. Counter. Thanks a lot for asking."

I'm wishing she'd go away and I'm holding the door ready to close it.

"Well, keep it up. Mr. Counter has been very worried about you."

"I will Mrs. Counter, thank you."

She stepped away and I shut the door as quick as I could. I threw the parcel on the bed and then I noticed there was a box in the corner. I suppose it must have been sitting there for who knows how long. Grecko must have left it there when he brought my stuff over from the old house. I rummage through the box and find my old exercise books with my class notes in them, and I pull them out and I start ripping out all the notes till there's a big pile on the floor and I thumb through the pages that's left in the books and there's a lot of them. I search around for a pen or pencil and find a ball point pen and I lie down on my bed, flat on me belly, the pillow under my chin and I start writing:

Dear sweet, gorgeous Iris.

I want you, I want you.

Please come back and we'll make everything right.

I love you I love you.

Please come to me.

I need you I need you.

I can't wait for your wet kisses.

They're all I live for.

Please, please come back.

I had to stop right there. I was getting worked up and my hands were starting to shake again. I look under the bed, but of course any booze that was there was long gone. I rolled off the bed and I ripped out the page and threw it on the pile. Then just as quick, I grabbed it back and put it under my pillow. I opened the parcel of clothes and tried on the Fletchers and shirt. They fitted me OK, so I rushed out of the room because I couldn't take staying there a moment longer and went down to the kitchen for some breakfast. And everybody was being so nice to me, I felt like I was some kind of horrible person that everyone had been told they had to be nice to. Abbie even put her arm around me and showed me to a seat at the old table, and she set up a boiled egg in an egg cup and some overdone toast how I like it. Everyone was making themselves busy pretending they wasn't taking any notice of me. So I cracked open the egg and cut off its head just like I used to when I was little and me mum cooked googie eggs for me. And I covered it in salt and spooned it into my mouth, managing to control my shakes to just a little tremor.

I showed up at the old bar and Mr. Counter gave me my jobs to do, and so my day on the wagon at work began, and it went on and on like it would never end, and there was someone right beside me, spying on me all the time. They weren't going to let me have one sip of booze. It was driving me mad. I asked Mr. Counter if I could have some time off to go and find Iris and he said no of course because he didn't trust me to stay on the wagon.

*

Saturday came and I was doing my forced labour and I heard a familiar voice coming from the Snake Pit. I sneaked up there and sure enough, it was Millie holding court and hanging all over some bloke. She was plastered as usual, but then you couldn't really tell if she was drunk or sober. I was hoping Iris would be with her, but she wasn't.

"G'day Millie," I said.

"Well if it isn't me former husband's little kid all grown up!" she joked.

"Yair, Millie. Have ya seen Iris?"

"Why would I?"

"I just thought you might."

"Why? Have you been a bastard to her again?"

"Fuck no, Millie. I love her."

"Ya do, do ya?"

"You know where she is?"

"Me glass is empty. Get me another one, will ya? Gin and tonic and make it a double."

The fuckn bitch, she knows something. I take her glass and make her another gin and tonic. Mr. Counter is standing at the door of the old bar watching me like a hawk. "She's pissed as usual," I say to him. He walks back to the Snake Pit with me.

"Millie," he says, "I think you've had enough today. This one is on the house, so drink it up and go home."

"Eddie, me old mate. Don't ya like me anymore?" She leans over to the bloke she's with and strokes his leg and squeezes his thigh. He's about as drunk as she is.

"Now Millie. Do the right thing. All right?"

"Yair, all right. Are ya taking care of me boy here?" she says, nodding to me.

"I'm not your boy," I complain. And Mr. Counter nudges me.

"He's doing all right. Now off you go home."

Millie downs the gin and tonic and tramps off, her bloke trailing after her. I follow them to the door and I get a glimpse of Iris across the road. I grab Millie and say, "Millie, is that Iris over there? She's with you, is she?"

"Yair, she is. Wouldn't come in though. Says she hates the booze. She always was a strange little thing."

"I'm coming with you," I say, but I feel the grip of Mr. Counter's hand on my arm.

"She says she doesn't want anything to do with ya cos you're a drunk like your old man," says Millie.

"I'm not! I'm not! I'm on the wagon."

"Yair, that's what they all say."

"No! No! It's not like that!"

"You'll fall off it and it's a long way down, that's what I told Iris."

I shake my arm away from Mr. Counter. "You fuckn bitch! Who are you to talk? Stay away from Iris, get it?"

"Shit Eddie, this kid's just like his father, ain't he?"

"I'm not! I'm fuckn not like him!"

Mr. Counter grabbed my arm again. I was angry. Angry at myself. How could I say that about me Dad? What's happened to me? "Millie, please. I have to see her," I pleaded.

Millie bangs her bloke in the back and says, "Come on! Let's get away from here," then turns to me and says, "she'll come and see you when she's ready."

"What does that mean, you stupid fuckn bitch?"

"Easy, son, easy," mutters Mr. Counter.

Millie staggers off with her bloke and they make their way across the Melbourne road, the cars screeching and swerving to miss them. I put my arm up to shade my eyes from the sun, but I can't see Iris. She's gone.

*

I know I said that the day my Dad died was the worst day of my life. But I didn't know then what was gunna happen. This horrible day was the worst day, the day Iris came back.

I was sitting in my bedroom writing in one of my notebooks when there was a tap on the window and I peeped through the rip in the blind and there was Iris. I threw the window open and pulled her in and we fell down heavy on to my bed and before you knew it we was going at it, like never before, even better than the first time across from the Baptist church, it was that good. At

least I thought so. I was completely out of my mind and she was
on top of me dropping those lovely wet kisses all over me, and I
mean all over me. My eyes are shut tight and she kisses them
both. Oh gees! This is the best! Worth waiting for, and me sober
too! Shit! Oh Ovid you beauty! I'm in Heaven, that's what it is.
She does something and I open my eyes and she's on top, sitting
back and her hair has grown a fair bit and I realize how much I
missed running my fingers through her stubble. But it's not short
any more. I put my hands to her breast and they're gorgeously
curved and firm and, gees, they're a lot bigger! I try to reach the
nipples with me tongue but she's too heavy and I can't get my
head up high enough. She's looking at me with those sheepy eyes
of hers, and I'm wondering what's there. She's looking serious, not
like she's going at it like Ovid says they do. But it's working on
me, and she knows it. God! Ovid you bastard! Oh gees! And I
make a super human effort to lift me head up to kiss her nipples
but she stays back, taunting me I think. I give up and drop back
on to the pillow and that's when I saw it.

And she saw me looking too. We stop. We look and stare at
each other.

"Well, whatcha looking at?" she says, no smile, nothing.

"Your belly. It's getting bigger."

"Shit, ya bastard. Are ya telling me I'm getting fat?"

"You know what I mean."

"I'm well past three months, you know."

"Yair. What's happening then?"

"You're not going to be a father," she says, leaning down,
touching the tip of me nose with her tongue.

"So we're not getting married then?"

"God in hell! Is that what you want? You don't want me fixed
up? Millie told me that's what you wanted."

"I never told Millie anything. She's a stupid fuckn liar."

"Someone did then, because that's what she told me you wanted."

"But you're not fixed up, then? It's still in there?"

"Yair. But not for long."

"Are you really going to do it?"

"Do what?"

"You know what. Get rid of it."

"Millie said they can put me in gaol if I do."

"Then what are you up to?"

"Like you care, you're just a fuckn drunk."

"Shit, Iris! Don't you know? I'm on the wagon. Haven't touched a drop for a whole week!"

"Yair? Well, I'm getting rid of it."

"I'm getting all me money from Mr. Counter tomorrow. You can move in with me here, Mr. and Mrs. Counter said it would be OK."

"How nice of them."

"Shit Iris, they've been really good to me."

"Well where was they when you were having those DTs?"

"Shit, Iris. You were here! You saved me!"

"They didn't like me here then, and that fuckn Sugar, the twisted bastard, he hated me."

"I suppose you heard. Him and me had a big row. I cut him pretty bad."

"Yair, I heard. Me old man told me. He thinks you're all right, now."

"Yair? So he didn't beat the kid out of you?"

"Nah. Reckons you're all right because he saw you beat up that poofda Sugar."

"Then we're gunna get married?"

"Shit, what is it with you? I told you I'm getting rid of it."

"I can pay for the doctor when I get me money."

"You stupid shit. Doctors won't do it. They go to gaol if they do, Millie told me. I'm too far gone, don't you see? Are you that fuckn stupid?"

I felt my ears get red. Boy I needed a drink right then! "I'm not stupid, Iris. I love you, unless you think that's why I'm stupid."

"I already got it fixed, anyway."

"But it's still in there."

"Not for long."

"Now I am stupid. What have you gone and done then?"

"Millie gave me a special potion to drink. She swears by it. She's done it stacks of times."

"Shit, Iris. Are you sure she knows what she's doing?"

"She has to, don't you think?"

"She's fucked half the pub's customers, I know that."

"Well you think she could do that without getting pregnant all the time?"

"Shit, Iris. Are you sure it's safe? What did she give you?"

"Some stuff she mixes up from a jar she keeps in the top cupboard of her kitchen. Tastes like rotten carrots. She made it into soup. Wasn't too bad with a lot of salt."

"So, when did you take it?"

"Just before I came here. I wanted to see you before it dropped, just in case something…"

"Iris! Something could go wrong?"

"Course it could. That's what Millie said. She warned me not to take it if I didn't think I could go through with it."

"Can't you change your mind?"

"Too late for that. Anyway, there's no other way. Like me mum says. We're both too young to have kids."

"We are not. I've got a steady job now, and I'm on the wagon."

"And where are we going to live and raise the kid? In this shit of a place? Stuck in this fuckn prison cell?"

"We can save up and go somewhere else."

"Like where? Line up for a commission house?"

"We could live with your mum."

"And you'll become a Seventh Day Adventist?"

"If it takes that, yes, Iris. I'd do it for ya."

"And what about me fuckn asshole step father?"

"You said he likes me."

"Yair, likes ya like everyone else he likes, which means he can beat you whenever he wants to."

I grab Iris and hug her to me and I roll over so she's on her back, and I kneel astride her, me crown jewels just tickling her belly at the hairline.

"I love ya, Iris. I'll do anything for you."

"Yair, I can see that."

"I mean it, Iris. I do!"

"Well, there's one thing you can do."

"Yair?"

"I'm staying here till it drops and you can call the doctor just before it does, just so they can't say I killed it."

"When's it going to drop?"

"Twenty-four hours, Millie said."

"Gees, Iris. I'll be here. I'll be with you all the way."

"Won't you have to work?"

"It's Sunday tomorrow. And I'm finished in the pub for today. I don't drink with the mates after hours any more. I'd fall off the wagon as quick as a wink if I did."

"You're a sweetie, you know that? I love you too, you know."

Gees, that was the first time she ever said she loved me and if I wasn't already on my knees I'd have fallen on them. I'm looking at her and she knows what I want. I climb off her and lay down beside her, pressing into her, caressing her hips, fingering her longish hair, wishing it was short. We weren't frantic any more. It was a long, juicy drawn out affair after which we gently fell asleep in each other's arms.

*

"Sweetheart," she says.

"Yair?"

"I'm feeling sick. Could you get me a glass of water?"

I jump out of bed, grab a towel around me and head for the bathroom with the old glass I keep under the bed.

I get back and she's clutching at her belly and she's breathing fast, almost puffing. I switch on the light and we're both blinded and then I look down and I see a pool of bright red blood on the bed. She's looking white as white. I'm about to lose it.

"Shit, Iris. I better call for the quack. Are you all right?"

"I'm OK I think. Just a bit of wind."

She's dreamy kind of, her eyes more like Swampy's sheep. It's scaring me to buggery.

"There's blood all around you," I say, "can't you feel it?"

"Gees, I thought I wet the bed or something."

"I'm getting the quack."

"Please don't leave me. I'll be all right. A little bit of blood is normal, that's what Millie said."

"Millie, the fuckn bitch. What would she know?"

"She's done it. Never had any problems," she said.

I'm sitting there and the bloody patch is getting bigger and bigger. I don't know how to ring the doctor because I've never done it before and I don't even know how to look up the number. I know there's a phone book in the old bar that we loan out to the customers. But it will take me ages to look it up and then choose which one. So there was nothing for it but to get Mrs. Counter. Only I didn't know what time it was, because I don't have a watch. I get up to go and knock on their door. But Iris grabs a hold of me hand and pulls it hard.

"I'm scared, I'm scared. Please don't leave me."

This scares me all the more and I shake her off and rush out the door and down the other end of the passage and knock on Mr. and Mrs. Counter's door. I'm knocking so hard the door's shaking on its hinges. I give up and turn the knob and its open so I rush in. Mrs. Counter screams and Mr. Counter pulls out a cricket bat from under his bed.

"Mrs. Counter! It's me! Come quick! Iris is sick. She needs a doctor. She's bleeding to death."

"What? What's wrong? Who?"

"Iris. She's bleeding to death, I tell you."

"You better go and look," Mr. Counter says to his missus.

Mrs. Counter struggles out of bed, she's so top heavy it's really hard for her to do it in a hurry. "Call doctor Staples, he's the only one that'll come at this hour," she says.

I'm running back to me room, worried sick that Iris will be dead already. I get there and she's crying in pain and sobbing and she's as white as a ghost.

"Don't worry, love, the doc's coming, and Mrs. Counter's on her way." And she sure is. She barges in and she pretty much fills the room. She pulls me away from Iris who doesn't want to let go of my hand.

"All right luv, "she says, "let him go so I can get a close look at you. Is what's happened what I think has happened?" Iris doesn't answer. She's nearly out to it.

"Yair, I think so," I say, looking at Iris, hoping she'll forgive me. "Millie gave her some medicine which is supposed to fix her problem."

"Oh my God in Heaven!" she calls out when she pulls back the blanket and sees the blood and the big swollen belly above it. "That dreadful Millie! Why didn't you come to me? Oh Father which art in Heaven," she looks up, "please for Heaven's sake save her!"

I'm standing in the corner, speechless, frozen with fear and trembling. Mrs. Counter looks down and places her hand on Iris's belly. "Are you in pain, luv?" she asks. Iris shakes her head a little. But her eyes are staring into space.

"What are we going to do?" I ask Mrs. Counter, "can't we stop her bleeding?"

"I don't know. Get me some towels from the linen closet at the end of the hall. I'll try to block it up. But we need the doctor really quick. "Eddie! Eddie! Quick! This is an emergency," she bellows, "call the ambulance! She's bleeding to death!"

I arrive with the towels.

"And you!" she says to me, "make yourself useful and get to the kitchen and bring back a dish of cold water and a small cloth. She's burning up."

So I do what I'm told and I'm on my way to the kitchen when there's a loud banging at the front door so I rush there and let them in. It's the ambulance bloke, the same one I recognize that came that night we had a dead body in the car park. I pull him inside

and he and his mate run down the dark passage to me bedroom.
I'm just about to slam the door shut when I see the quack pulling
up. Gees, thank goodness for that. I stand there yelling, "Hurry
up doc, she's bleeding to death!"

He hurries over, not fast enough in my opinion, and shakes me
hand, "How do you do," young man, "I'm doctor Staples."

"This way doc. Please save her!"

"Calm down. Everything's going to be all right, you'll see. It's
probably a simple matter of a little bit of bleeding. It often looks
worse than it is."

We get into the little room and immediately the doc orders
everyone out except the one ambulance bloke who has all the
badges sewn on his sleeve. But I say, "I'm not going out, doc. I
love her and I will not leave her."

"You two are married, then?" he asks while he's scanning the
length of Iris's body, stripped right down.

"Not yet but we will be," I say, kind of angry.

He stands up, he's all of six feet and lean, grey hair what's left
of it. He ought to be retired, I think to myself.

"Only next of kin can be here. Was that her parents that were
here just then?"

"No."

"Then please leave so I can get on treating your girlfriend."

"I'm not going."

Iris seems to hear. She feebly raises her hand and calls for me.
"Ovid," she calls, "Ovid," and there's a faint smile on her face. I
push forward and grab her hand.

"That's your name?" asks the doc, incredulous.

"No. It's a little joke we have between us."

The quack rummages through his little case and retrieves a
syringe and a vial of something. He prepares the injection and
then jams it into her arm. She doesn't feel it at all.

"What's that for?" I ask, trying to be as big a nuisance as I can
to keep him on his toes. He and the ambulance bloke talk some
medical mumbo jumbo.

"She's going into shock. The injection will calm her down."

But all of a sudden, Iris's whole body stiffens and she lets out
an awful scream like she'd been stabbed or something. The doc
looks down and we all see some movement in her belly. She lets
go me hand and starts clawing at it and the doc starts to feel
around there as well. He looks serious.

"She needs a blood transfusion."

"That's OK," I say, "she can have some of mine."

The quack smiles and says, "it's not that simple."

"But she's dying doc, isn't she?"

"If we get her to the hospital in time and they have the right blood there, we may save her."

The ambulance bloke has gone out and I can hear him talking to Mr. Counter. He comes back and looks at the doc and nods. The quack pulls out a pair of forceps from his bag. He looks at them, then at Iris. Then at me.

"I know you love her, but what I have to do next you don't want to see. So please leave me alone so I can get on with saving your girlfriend's life."

My ears are the reddest they've ever been, I bet. I really want to punch the pompous bastard on the nose. But I clench both my fists and back out like I'm backing away from a big red kangaroo. And the doc closes the door behind me.

I hear screams and other gurgling noises through the door. I want to go in, but Mrs. Counter is standing in the way. And I can't push past her, can I? Soon the ambulance blokes are back with the stretcher and they knock on the door. We wait.

"What's he doing in there?" I ask the ambulance bloke.

"I think he's trying to extract the fetus," he says like he's the doc's apprentice.

"Extract the what?"

"He means the baby," says Mrs. Counter.

"You mean it might be a baby?"

"Well what else would it be, a joey?" says the bloke.

I grab him by his sleeve that's got all the badges and pull him up to me and say, "you fuckn asshole! I ought to knock your fuckn teeth in."

Mr. Counter comes over and he puts his arm around my shoulder. "Take it easy," he says, "we know you're sick with worry. It'll be all right. We just have to hope and pray the doc can work his magic."

With that, the door opens and the doc steps out. He beats out some instructions to the ambulance blokes and they go in and quickly have Iris on their stretcher and they're wheeling her away down the passage. I start to follow them.

"You can't go, I'm sorry," says the quack, "you're not immediate family so you won't be allowed to travel with her or sit with her in the emergency room."

"But I'm all she's got, don't you understand?"

"I do. But the rules are there for a purpose. You can't be with her."

"And what about the, uh, fetus thing, baby or whatever it's called. What about it?"

I look down and see the doc has something wrapped up in a blood-stained towel.

"I'm afraid it didn't make it."

"And Iris?"

"If we can get enough blood into her in time and there's no infection."

"If I'm not with her, she'll die, you know. She's got nothing else to live for, you fuckn bastards."

Mr. Counter draws the doc aside. They talk a bit and then the doc says, "all right, if you hurry up and catch the blokes before they leave you can ride in the ambulance. But I can't be responsible for what happens once you get to the hospital. They have their rules."

I ran down the passageway and out the front door, leaving it open and just made it to the ambulance. They said I couldn't go with them and I told them the doc said it was all right.

"You're holding us up. Wasting minutes that could mean the difference between life or death," they said.

"Open the fuckn door or I'll pull you outa that fuckn wagon and drive her there myself!" I screamed.

The doc came to the door and told them to let me in. So they did.

And I wish I'd never gone.

*

"In an old bark hut, in an old bark hut," I'm singing softly to Iris, holding her limp hand, the ambulance bloke with the badges staring at me. "When you get better, you know what Iris, me luv? I was thinking. We could go off to Swampy's and we could build ourselves a bark hut and live in the woods together, just you and me. And we could have a little veggie garden and a road side stand and sell the veggies and we'd have enough money to live in the bush, just you and I, you and me, and to hell with the rest of them. Bugger the old pub. I know you must hate it, and now, I think I've fallen out of love with it. The whole fuckn lot is rotten. I have to get away from it. If I stay there, I'll die pretty quick, just like me Dad. It's a death house, Iris, don't you think? Gees, Iris, you're going to be all right, aren't you? I couldn't make it without you."

I can hear the siren and the ambulance sways a bit. We must be getting close to Geelong.

"What time is it?" I ask.

"About five," says Badges.

"Five what?"

"Morning, you silly bastard, what do you think?"

"We got far to go?"

"Five minutes." Badges acts like he's taking Iris's pulse. Mister importance, that's what he is. "They won't let you in, you know."

"How d'you know that?"

"Because I've been doing this a long time and I can tell you, the hospital has its rules and it doesn't change them for anyone."

"Yair, I bet they jump if a doctor tells them to."

Badges leans forward and looks hard into Iris's white face. Her cheeks are even sunk in, her eyes, gees, I can't bear to look at them.

"She'll make it," says Badges.

Maybe he's a good bloke after all.

"Yair. Thanks. She's a great fighter."

*

They wouldn't let me go with her. I was going to hit the bastard that grabbed me and pushed me down into the waiting room seat. But when I fell into the seat, my body just wouldn't do anything more. I just flopped down, and leaned forward, my head in me hands. The waiting room was full of people and there was a big circular desk in the middle of it and this bitch of a matron was strutting around like she was Queen Elizabeth. The place smelled like a morgue, sprayed with some insecticide and the chair I was sitting on had that greasy feeling, just like everything in the old pub. I crossed my arms and I leaned back, exhausted, and I fell asleep.

*

Somebody's got me by the scruff of the neck, shaking me so hard my head's going to fall off. It's got to be one of my dreams. I'm waiting for the truck to come and run me down. But the shaking's getting worse, and I'm trying to open my eyes but they won't and I'm trying to breathe but I can't. This must be what it's like to die, I think. Then I'm pushed back into the chair and I bang my elbow and I think I'm yelling, then I wake up, my eyes are hurting in the florescent lights. I'm still in the waiting room, and there's this big hulk standing over me. I blink some more, and for Christ sake, it's Tank.

"You fuckn little shit," he mutters, "wake up! Whatcha done to me little girl?"

"Fuck you!" was all I could think of to say. I feel someone sitting next to me and then I smell the smoke. It's Flo. They're both here! Iris must have died, then, I think. "Is, is she all right?" I ask Flo. She's sitting there, puffing on her Garrick, staring into space like always. "Flo?"

"It's up to Jesus," she says, hardly moving her lips.

"Don't listen to the stupid bitch," growls Tank.

"Yair, don't listen," says Flo, "because what I tell you is what this big shit doesn't want anyone to know."

"Fuckn shut up, bitch!" Tank's got his fist clenched and he's shaking it in front of Flo's nose.

"How'd you know Iris was here?" I ask, ignoring the bullshit.

"Millie, that filthy bitch, she told me," said Tank.

"I'm gunna kill her when I get a hold of that fuckn piece of shit. It's all her fault," I say, looking up at Tank.

"Yair, I know," Tank growls again.

"How'd you find out?"

Tank looks me straight in the eye. "I was paying her a visit," he grins, licking his lips. "She told me Iris paid her a visit and I wasn't paying much attention, because I gave up on Iris a long time ago. She was going the same way as Millie as far as I could see."

Flo looks up at Tank and then to me. "He'll rot in hell for what he's done," she says, "the devil's waiting for him and he'll gobble him up and spit out his innards."

"Yair, that's right, and you along with me. Truth is you're to blame for all this fuckn mess. You're the one that fuckn did it. She should never have been born."

I go to stand up, I don't know what the shit they're talking about, but Tank pushes me back.

"Go on then, tell him," says Flo.

"Fuck you!" yells Tank and he heads out the door, the matron just starting to come out from behind her desk to give him a dressing down.

"I'm going to the toilet," I say to Flo and I go to get up. She grabs my hand.

"I'm tellingya because Jesus told me I have to. You and Iris..."

"Me and Iris what?" I ask, belligerently. "What did he mean that Iris shouldn't have been born? Did you try to get rid of her?" My ears were getting red, I really had to go to the toilet.

"Nah. We made her, we didn't try to get rid of her. Though we should have."

"So, he really is her dad, then?"

"Yair, but…"

"But what? You're not her mother?"

"I am her mother and I deserve it!"

Flo was getting all worked up. She stubbed out her Garrick and lit another. That was the other thing about this waiting room. There were ashtrays full of cigarette butts everywhere.

"I'm going to the toilet. I don't know what you mean that you deserved to be Iris's mother."

"You have to know this," she says, pulling me back, "only Jesus knows it… and Tank of course…"

"Flo, for Christ sake, knows what? What in hell does fuckn Jesus know?"

"Talking like that about Jesus won't help you. Take it back!" growls Flo.

"Gees, Flo, I'm sorry. But for Christ sake, tell me want I have to know."

"Me and Tank--"

"Yair? What?"

"We're brother and sister."

*

The matron's coming towards us. Flo gets up and leaves. Who knows why. I still haven't been to the toilet and I'm getting jumpy. I could really do with a drink. The matron's looking serious.

"Are you Iris's relative?" she asks."

"Yair. I'm her brother. That's her mum just leaving. How is she?"

"She's still in critical condition. We're moving her to Royal Melbourne Hospital where they have more facilities."

"I'll go with her then."

"You cannot. No room in the special ambulance, besides it's against the rules."

"Thank you, Matron, bitch." I go to walk out but she steps in front of me. She can't believe I called her a bitch. She pulls a notepad from her white starched tunic.

"You won't get anywhere talking like that, young man." I want to grab her tunic and rip it off her. I step up close and push my face right in front of hers. We're about the same height.

"Is she gunna make it then?" I say, like it's all her fault that Iris is dying. She steps back, scared shitless.

"She's lost a lot of blood. It will take time. It's impossible to tell." I step up close again. So am I going with her or not?

"Is there a phone number where I can phone you?"

"Don't have a phone."

She looks lost for words, then pulls out a pencil. "You can phone this number to find out where she is and her condition." She writes the number on her notepad and hands it to me and I take it, crumple it up and stuff it in my pocket. She goes on, "I need some details about her. Do you know whether she has any health insurance?"

"What's that?" I ask. She looks at me like I'm rubbish, and that's how I feel too.

"The hospital bill's going to be quite expensive."

"Yair. You need her mum for that."

*

I left that hospital with its filthy waiting room and walked out past the old brick veneer hospital entrance and around the corner to the alley. I stood in the middle of the road and had a good, long piss as I looked up at the soft light of a full moon glistening on the T and G tower. I walked and I walked enjoying the heavy odour of bitumen as it cooled in the night air. I must have walked for a couple of hours or more, because when I finally came to my senses, I found myself standing at the side door of the Criterion Pub. I knocked a sharp short knock and a little latch opened up.

"Yair? Whatcha want?" comes a gravelly voice through the latch.

"You got a cuppa tea?"

"You're fuckn joking, right? You're at a pub, you silly bastard."

"Yair, I know. I'm an old customer. Used to buy a lot of me after hours booze here."

"Yair? Yair, I think I remember you. Last time you was here you was on a bender of all benders, right?"

"Yair, probably."

"You want a flask a whiskey then? Corio, you liked, didn't you?"

"Maybe"

"Maybe? What the fuck do you want?"

"I said I just want a cuppa tea."

"For Christ sake. What do you think this is a fuckn restaurant? We don't do tea you fuckn idiot. Are you a poofda or something?"

"Fuck you!" I say, and I walk off.

*

I walked all the way from the Criterion to Norlane, about five or six miles. I walked along the road a lot of the way, ignoring the few speeding cars and trucks zooming by, they could have run me down and I wouldn't have cared. Well, that's the way I felt. I suppose I would have jumped out of the way if a car had come at me, just like in my nightmare. Can't say I walked all that fast, because I was in a kind of daze. I stopped on the top of the Separation Street bridge and peered down at the railway lines and I wondered where they all went. Well, no I didn't. I just stared at them, watched a train come and go, a freight train pull into the wheat silos. I looked across at the old Telegraph pub, made my way towards it, but turned at the last minute and kept on going to the Ford factory, lingering at the dump where I used to play when I was little, then up the hill to where my old house was on North Shore road, right beside Fords and across from the pub. And I found myself standing in the debris that was my old house, still in piles, waiting for a front-end loader to come and take it away. But I never looked it over. Just stood in it all, like I was standing in the shallows of the beach, the soggy seaweed swishing around my legs, down on Corio Bay. There was nothing to do but to let it just ebb away from around my feet. I nudged an old wine bottle out of the way as I turned to look across the Melbourne road at the pub. It was right then that the pub dawned on me in a whole new light, like someone inside me let go a blind and it zapped right up behind my eyes. I saw the pub like I'd never seen it before. The sun had risen and I felt its heat already. The old pub shimmered behind the heat of the fresh bitumen of the Melbourne Road, the yellow of the painted stone dissolving into the air above. The grubby men, stick-figures clinging to their beers, lounging about in sweat-soaked singlets. And that deep blue sky, an enormous chasm that swallowed the pub and all its entrails, enveloped me and I felt myself carried forward, out of the ruins of my house, across the road, past the pub and its magpies perched on its chimneys, and I looked down on the Quonset huts and the barbed wire fence that enclosed them, and they grew bigger and the fence loomed higher until I felt myself fall so fast that I screamed, "Save me! Save me!"

*

And saved I was. Spuds was standing over me, looking down, offering his hand to pull me up. I was lying on my back, thrashing about, trying to fly or something who knows what. I don't know how I got here. But I was very happy to grab his hand and he pulled me up.

"What are ya doing-a here ya silly bugger? Ya been in-a the slaughter yards? You've got blood all down ya."

"What, Spuds, what?" I look down me and he's right. There's blood all over my shirt and new Fletchers that Mrs. Counter gave me.

"Did ya get pissed down at-a the meat-a packing plant? I've done that a few times. They're half crazy-a down there."

"Yair, maybe I did." Truth is, I couldn't remember anything at all. I felt dizzy. I grabbed a hold of Spuds to steady myself.

"Looks-a like ya need a sip of me grappa, mate," says Spuds as he tries to steady me.

"Nah, I'm on the wagon. I'm all fuckd up."

"Yair, rightee-o. If you are, then you-a come to the right place because this is the fuckn mad-house, mate, *sens altro*."

I looked around and saw that I was standing outside the main gate to the New Aussies hostel. There were people bustling about and talking in all sorts of strange languages. They were all so busy.

"This is where you live?" I ask.

"For the moment," answers Spuds. "You want-a come in for a drink?"

"Nah. I really am on the wagon. I got to get back to the pub. Got work to do."

"Yair, I betcha do."

"Thanks for the help."

"Are you OK? You're looking-a bit-a wobbly on your legs. Sure ya don't want a grappa?"

I wasn't sure at all. I put out my hand, to shake, and Spuds took it in his rough hand, squeezed it tight.

"Don't forget-a your kitbag," he said, with a grin, "it's got blood all over it too. You must have a horse's prick in it." But I didn't laugh like I might have done before. Embarrassed, he dropped my hand and walked away without another word. I looked across to the pub, and I saw the old dunny leaning over ready to fall down on itself any day. There were tears in my eyes. I was thinking about Iris and me growing veggies on Spuds' plot, and us living in a bark hut. I backed away and it was all I could do to drag my legs to stagger across the burnt paddock, now with patches of green from the Easter rains, scraping past the thistles, and up to my bedroom window, always open, threw in my kitbag and climbed in just like Iris used to.

Abbie had made the bed with fresh sheets and cleaned the place up a lot. You wouldn't know anything had happened. And that made me cry. It was as though Iris was dead, as though she'd never lived, as though it were all a dream. And I sat on the edge of the bed, just like I had done with Iris, and I put my head in my hands and I sobbed, sobbed just like she used to.

I awoke lying on my belly, the tears still on my cheeks. I buried my head in the pillow, wanting to stay asleep. But the spell was broken and I rolled off the bed and stood, wiping my tears with my sleeve. I looked around me and knew that I was at an end. The room was my cell, the pub my prison.

6. From your red lips warm and wet

I never saw Millie after she left the pub that time, with that pathetic bloke in tow. At least that's what I told the Preacher when he came snooping around. Some bloke found her beaten and strangled to death lying on her bed on filthy sheets, dried black blood all over, and a beer bottle shoved up her you-know-what.

Mr. Counter came over and called me out of the bar. We went out back to the tap room were the Preacher was waiting. He had a fresh beer in his hand and took a sip, licking the foam from his lips with great satisfaction. I'm all dressed up in my uniform, just like Mr. Counter wanted, nicely pressed Fletchers that Mrs. Counter had ironed, and nice shirt with a thin tie.

"Young man," says the Preacher, looking down at me over his long nose, "I want you to be honest and tell me exactly what happened."

"What happened when?" I ask, belligerent as usual.

"Millie. You heard about her?"

"Nah, but I hope it's bad."

"She was found lying in her filthy bed, beaten and strangled..."

"Fuckn great!"

"...and a beer bottle shoved up her vaginal orifice."

"Even fuckn better!" I say with a scowl and a smirk.

"This is no joke young man. This is an individual woman's life that's been violently and indeed consequentially taken away by a murderer doing the devil's work!"

"Hooray for the devil!" I laugh, putting my hands on my hips.

Mr. Counter steps close to me and gives me a nudge. "Take it easy, son," he whispers.

"Young man, this is no laughing matter. It is the devil's work and I very much hope he is not in consequence working through you!"

"Me? Doing the devil's work? That's a good one. The fuckn devil has done me over, I can tell you that."

132

"You were heard threatening to kill Millie." The Preacher leans forward imposing his great height over me.

"Bull shit! I never did that! Who's telling you that?"

"You were overheard in the waiting room at Geelong Hospital."

"It's bull shit. I never said that. They're fuckn lying."

"Young man. It is no secret that you have a violent temper. Where did you go after you left the hospital that night?"

"I bet I know who killed her."

"That's not what I asked you. Where were you after you left the hospital?"

"I walked all around Geelong and then I walked home."

"Your walked all the way from Geelong to Norlane?"

"Yes. I was upset and angry. I wanted to think things over."

"Can any person verify that you were with them on your walk?"

"I walked on my own. I wanted to think. I was confused."

"Confused? So, you do not know exactly where you went?"

"I remember being at the Criterion pub at opening time that morning."

"You walked all around Geelong that night?"

"I suppose I must have."

"And did you booze on at the Criterion?"

"I don't drink."

The Preacher looks at Mr. Counter who says, "that's right, officer. He's on the wagon."

"Then you walked all the way to Norlane from the Criterion?"

"Yes. All the way."

"And you went nowhere else of consequence?"

"Nowhere else."

"Are you sure?"

"Well, I think I remember mucking around a bit on the site of me old house that's been pulled down."

"And nowhere else of consequence?"

"Nowhere."

"Are you sure?"

"Well, I might have gone someplace else, but I might not."

"Young man, this is unusual and of consequence. Is it not that you went somewhere else or is it so?"

"I was confused and I woke up having this dream or maybe it wasn't a dream, and I was lying on my back when Spuds helped me up and I looked around and I was outside the Migrant Hostel."

"At the back of the pub?"

"Yair. Spuds helped me up and we talked a bit and then I came straight back to the pub and I think I even got into me bedroom through the back window."

"And the kitbag?"

"What about it?"

"You had it all the time?"

"I don't know."

"Thank you young man. Do not leave town, as I may need to speak to you again. Did you get all that Dopey?"

Dopey, sitting on a beer barrel across the other side of the tap room, has been furiously taking notes.

"Yes sir, got it all. Anything else sir?"

"Yes. Get off your ass."

With difficulty, Dopey slid off the barrel and as he did so, he dropped his notebook and pencil. I darted down and picked them up for him, because there was no way he could do it himself with his belly getting bigger and bigger every time I saw him.

"It is that I thank you on Dopey's behalf and also in my capacity as one of the Queen's constabulary," pronounced the Preacher.

"No worries," I said.

The cops helped themselves to another beer and left.

On our way back to the bar, Mr. Counter touched me on the arm. "You know who killed her?" he asked.

"Yair, for sure."

"Who then?"

"I'm not saying because he did me a great service and saved me the bother."

"Did you go there, then?"

"Where?"

"That night, to Millie's."

"Don't think so. I don't know."

*

Abbie was very happy these days. Every morning I got up on the dot of seven and was in the kitchen by 7.30, eating her eggs and bacon and munching the burnt toast. Then I sat and drank a couple of cups of tea and smoked a Craven 'A'. That's right, after all that boozing, I never had a cigarette. But now, still on the wagon, I'd taken up the smokes.

Mr. Counter was happy too. It seemed like I had fulfilled his dream, or something like that. He had saved me from my father's destiny, and that was enough for him. And something else he did was to move me across to work in the New Bar, away from the

Old Bar that served the Snake Pit, so I wouldn't have to worry about seeing Tank, Linda or the rest of them.

As for me, I was lost. For a few days after they took Iris to Melbourne, I carried around the crumpled piece of paper that had the number for me to phone. I'd roll it around in my hand, and put it back in my pocket. Pretty soon the numbers that the stuck-up matron had written down would be illegible. Nobody in the pub, all my old drinking mates, Mr. and Mrs. Counter and the rest, none of them asked me about Iris.

I began to spend a lot of time in "cell 4" as I called my bedroom, just lying on my bed, and moping around the room.

*

This old quack's sitting at his desk, his fluffy grey hair sticking up from a long head that's got too many brains crammed inside it. He doesn't even look up when I come in—too busy writing something. It's a long narrow office with a window at the end that's really bright and I'm squinting to see the quack at all.

"Clothes off," he says without looking up.

"What'd you say?"

"I said take off your clothes, and show some respect. I'm Doctor Robinson."

"Pleased to meet you, doctor. So I take them all off?"

"That's what I said."

There aren't many clothes to take off and they're pretty smelly as well. With Dad just dying and me only now getting settled into the pub, I don't know who's going to wash my clothes. And I don't really want to take off me underpants because they could be really filthy.

"Me underpants too?"

"Yes. And it's *my* not *me*. You need to speak properly if you're going to be a teacher."

"Fuck you, you stuck-up pommie bastard," I'm thinking. But I drop them anyway and I'm thinking if I stink, it'll serve him right.

He keeps writing away and I'm standing there, feeling stupid. I give a little cough. Maybe he's forgotten I'm even there! But doesn't even look like getting up out of his chair. I'm dazzled by the light streaming in through the window so I close me eyes and I start to day-dream. It was only a week or so after I did me Latin exam, so you can guess where the dreaming took me. Yair, Ovid of course, and then I'm doing Iris all over again! And shit! You know what that means! I'm trying not to think of her, but me body won't listen. I'm looking down there, and sure enough, there's action. Shit! The quack'll think I'm a poofda or something.

"Er, doctor, sir?" I ask.

"Yes," he says without looking up.

"I have to go to the toilet."

"It's in there. And do a specimen for me while you're there. Take a jar from my desk." He points to a bunch of little vegemite jars.

I prance over to his desk, trying not to let him see what's going on, trying to approach his desk ass-first. Don't know if he saw anything, but he didn't look up.

"Mr. Henderson, I have a tight schedule, We need to get on with the exam."

"Be there in a jiffy," I say, my voice kind of faint and shaky. I turn on a tap and run a bit of water, make a bit of noise.

"Mr. Henderson? Get out here please."

"OK. I'm coming. Took me a while to get it flowing if you see what I mean."

I come out, all red and embarrassed, carrying the little jar filled to the brim and I offer it to him, spilling some of it as I extend my hand.

"What happened to the lid?" the quack asks, really annoyed, "go back and pour some out and put the lid on."

I'm happy to turn my back on him and gain a bit more time, and by the time I've done what he asked, I'm pretty much back to normal and I stand there, starkers, before him. He looks me up and down, then runs his hands down me sides, then says, "turn around, son." I turn around and he runs his hands over me shoulders then down me sides again. "OK. Turn around again," he says, then as soon as I'm facing him, his fingers feel around me balls and I jump a bit because I'm still a bit sensitive there, but at least I knew what to expect because me mates who'd already been in, told me that's what he did. "Look away and cough please," he says. And I do, and he says, "again," and I do. He goes back to his desk and starts writing again. "You can get dressed," he says, without looking up, "you're in good shape."

I don't know what that's supposed to mean, and what feeling me up has to do with teaching little kids. Yair, that's right. Just before me Latin exam I put in my application to Geelong Teachers College just in case I changed my mind and decided to go. I never went because I was supposed to show up first of February and I forgot to, or to put it another way, I was too busy getting into the booze. But you wouldn't believe what happened.

*

It was Sunday and I was in cell 4 thinking of going to church because I was all depressed and fingering the piece a paper with the number that now I could hardly read. I decided to copy the number on to another piece of paper, so I rummaged through my kitbag in the corner of the room looking for an exercise book with a blank page. I pulled one out and flipped through the pages and out fell an envelope addressed to me. It was from Melbourne University. Grecko must have grabbed it with a lot of other stuff lying around the old house. I turned it over in my hand. The address on the envelope was written in very small and neat handwriting sloping backwards, blue ink and made with a fountain pen. I wrote down the Iris phone number on the back of the envelope. It was a long-distance number and I didn't know how to do a long-distance phone call, and I was too embarrassed to ask Mr. Counter how to do it, and as well, it would cost a lot more money.

I opened the letter and inside was a brief hand-written note that said:

Dear Mr. Henderson

I read with interest your translation of Ovid in the recent matric Latin exam. Your paper displayed a raw talent quite exceptional for one so young. It seems that you have not applied for admission to Melbourne University but instead applied to Geelong Teachers College. I think your talents will be wasted there, so please come by and see me when you are in Melbourne next. I may be able to arrange for you to begin studies here, possibly even with a scholarship.

Sincerely,

Professor Claude Pulcher

Chair, Department of Classics and Antiquity

University of Melbourne

*

I was wiping down the bar when all of a sudden, a big hand grabbed mine. I looked up and it was Tank. He was wearing his big slouch hat and had it pulled down nearly over his eyes. He leaned over and muttered, "I know what you fuckn did and don't you forget it."

My ears went red and I felt my cheeks burn. I ducked down so I could look at him straight in the eye, under the brim of his hat.

"And I know what *you* did, so now we're mates, aren't we?" I reply.

"What do ya mean? You little shit!"

"I'm not little. And you know what I mean."

He reaches over to grab my collar, but I was ready for it and ducked away.

"You was there, weren't you?"

"There where?"

"Don't be a fuckn smart-ass, you little shit. Just because you went to school too long."

"I don't know what you're fuckn talking about."

"Yair you do. You was there. I saw you."

"You were fuckn drunk. You wouldn't know what you saw."

"How do you know I was drunk?"

"You're always fuckn drunk, you fuckn dummy bastard."

"I'll break your fuckn neck you little shit."

"The cops were here, you know."

"So, what?"

"I could have told them"

"Tell 'em what?"

"That you were there. That's what you told me, isn't it?"

"You've killed me daughter and now you've killed me favourite root. You're a real asshole. And now you're trying to pin it all on me."

"Yair, well, I know about your daughter, you filthy fuckn piece of scum."

"What's that? Yer mean Iris?"

"Yair. She's a freak, isn't she? Her mum and dad, you're brother and sister, you disgusting piece of shit."

"Fuckn Flo, that bitch. She told you?"

"Yair. At the hospital. So fuck off and leave me alone."

"She's not a freak."

"Not to me she isn't. But Flo thinks she is because the two of you conceived her in sin so there's no hope for her. She deserves to die, that's what Flo thinks."

"You talk too much, you fuckn asshole."

"Yair. I do, but not to the cops. As for you. You've been beating the shit out of both of them, haven't you? Ever since Iris was born. You're a fuckn bully, and frankly, you're a piece of the devil's asshole, that's what."

"Where'd yer learn all that fancy talk? Been going to church with Flo?"

"Fuck off and keep your mouth shut, and so will I."

"I didn't kill her."

"And neither did I."

"So who did then?

"I don't care. Whoever it was deserves a medal. She killed Iris."

"Yair, I suppose you're right."

We look at each other and suddenly discover that we're mates. I reach for a glass and pour Tank a beer. And I see out of the corner of my eye Mr. Counter watching us. He calls out, "that's all right. Go around the bar and have one with him. It's on the house."

"But I'm on the wagon, Mr. Counter."

"Oh yes, I forgot. Then have a dry ginger."

I go around and Tank and me lean our elbows on the counter and we clink our glasses. "To the fuckn good bastard that did her in," I say, and we both say "Cheers!" Tank downs the beer then bangs the glass on the bar. "You're all right, mate," he says. And for the first time ever, I see him smile.

*

Flo lit up a Garrick while she stood across from the post office waiting for the Benders bus back home. Her eyes were red and watering from the coughing fit she'd just got over. It was so bad, people came up and asked her if she was all right. She'd had one in the Deacon's office as well. He just sat there and looked at her as though she was scratching her ass and he was annoyed having to wait till she finished. The Deacon was a stern man, tall even sitting on his chair, a mop of silvery hair well oiled, combed back without a part, and a well-scrubbed pink complexion.

"Have a seat Mrs. Devlin. I expect you're here for the usual thing. We've been through this many times. You must bring your husband to church. There is little I can do without my getting to know him. You have to help him find Jesus. You know that."

"Deacon, I'm not here about me husband."

The Deacon sits up straight. "No kidding?" he says, surprised.

"I gave up on him years ago. You know that too."

"Then why are you here?"

"Does there have to be a reason?" Flo searches for a window to look out of.

"You are not well, Mrs. Devlin, I can see that."

"I never slept all last night. Don't know when I last slept. I want to die, I think."

"Mrs. Devlin, you must not talk like that! Jesus is with you. Jesus is always with you. Dying is not of your choosing. It is up to God."

Flo looked over his shoulder at a photo on the mantelpiece above the fireplace. It was a group of happy smiling people all arranged around the Deacon standing tall and imposing. The photo had been touched up with colour to make the grass look green and the sky blue and all the people have pink faces.

"I pray to Jesus all the time. It's all I do except take abuse from my husband. But instead of comforting me, Jesus has forsaken me. He has taken my daughter from me."

"You have a daughter? You never told me that before."

"There's a lot I haven't told you, Deacon."

"Then tell me about her. How old is she?"

"She was seventeen, and she'd been kissed too much."

"And what has happened?"

Flo stood up suddenly and fell against the Deacon's desk. There was an awful wheezing sound as she tried in vain to find her voice. The Deacon pushed himself back from the desk.

"Mrs. Devlin! Are you all right? What has happened?"

"I can't tell you, except that she's dead, I know it. And it's all my fault."

"What do you mean? Where is she?"

"With Jesus by now."

"She died?"

"I killed her, that's what. I killed her."

"Mrs. Devlin, I can't believe that you'd do such a thing. But in any case, we must pray to God for salvation.

The Deacon came quickly around his desk, took Flo tightly by the arm, pulled her down to her knees beside him and they knelt together as he prayed:

"Heavenly Father, hear our pleas for forgiveness. Your world is so vast we tiny inhabitants cannot comprehend your great design. Have pity on Mrs. Devlin who comes to you with an open heart. She has stayed with Jesus all her suffering life. If it is her time to go, please let her know that her daughter sits with your Son in Heaven, awaiting the happy reconciliation with her mother. For Thine is the kingdom, the power and the glory. Amen."

Flo remained there, her hands clasped together, her grey head bent down, sobs choking her rasping throat. The Deacon stood and tried with difficulty to pull Flo up. But she remained there, coughing and sobbing.

"Mrs. Devlin. Are you all right? Shall I call a doctor?"

Flo coughed more and lost her balance, falling backwards on to the carpeted floor and she lay there, choking.

The Deacon rushed to the door and called out to his secretary. "Phone an ambulance! Mrs. Devlin's having a fit. I think she's choking." He turned back, leaned over to peer into Flo's face. It was grey, gaunt, her eyes red and glazed over. He pulled at her arms to get her sitting. She pointed to her hand bag that had fallen to the floor. He handed it to her and steadied her while she opened it. She grasped her green packet of Garricks and with a shaking hand managed to pull out a cigarette.

"Mrs. Devlin. For God's sake—excuse me Lord—you can't have a smoke now. You'll kill yourself." The words came out too soon as he realized that it was exactly what she was trying to do.

"Take me Jesus, take me," she said weakly.

The Deacon snatched the cigarettes from her. "Mrs. Devlin! Shame on you! How dare you tempt Jesus like that! It's a grave sin for you to smoke cigarettes in your condition!"

And with that, Flo shook her head in a spasm and blinked her eyes. She had awoken as if from a terrible nightmare. She snatched back her cigarettes, put them in her handbag and struggled to stand. The Deacon helped her up, but it was now with a feeling of distaste, even disgust. "You seem to have recovered," he said, almost disappointed. She took out a cigarette, struck a match and lit up right in front of him.

"Thanks a lot, Deacon. God has heard us both and I know Jesus is beside me still."

"Cancel the ambulance!" called the Deacon.

*

It was Sunday and I was in the old bar polishing up the glasses and trying to clean the mould from the lino counter top. I was into cleaning stuff. It made me feel a lot better. Mr. Counter was tinkering with the old cash register. One of the keys was jammed.

"Looks like Sugar's coming back," he said.

"Yair? He's all right, then?"

"I think so. Depends on how he holds up. He's got a walking stick now, you know."

"Yair. It's too bad." But I didn't feel all that sorry. He deserved what he got. And besides, now that everyone knew what he was like, he wasn't going to last long in the pub. Somebody else will do him over and the next time will be his last.

"Mr. Counter?" I said.

"Yes, Chooka, what?"

They called me Chooka now because these letters kept coming and they had my name on them, James Henderson. At first it was just "Hens" but then some of the smart bastards started saying I wasn't a hen but a chook, and so it stuck.

"Can I make a long-distance call? I've got this number they said to call to find out if Iris was OK."

"You mean, you haven't called yet?"

"I just couldn't get myself to do it. Might be bad news."

"Chooka, my boy. You have to learn to face up to bad news. Be a man, young fella!"

"Gees, Mr. Counter. Leave me alone, will you?"

"Use the phone in my office and I'll deduct the cost from your next pay packet."

"So, how do I do it?"

"You just dial zero and the operator comes on and you tell her what number you want in Melbourne."

Mr. Counter led the way into his little office. "By the way, Chooka," he said, "there's another letter here from the Education Department. They're coming every couple of weeks. Are they still trying to get you to go to Teachers College?"

"Yair," I lied, "but I'm not going."

*

That night I heard noises coming from the room next to mine. Sugar was back. I knew, then, it was time for me to go. I dragged the old kit bag from under my bed. It was squashed flat, but would do. I tried to clean the dried blood off it, then I put my exercise books inside and a few clothes. In the morning, Abbie knocked on my door as usual but I was already dressed. I'd showered early to avoid running into Sugar.

"Morning, Abbie," I said with a smile.

"My! Aren't we bright and early this morning," she laughed.

"Yair. I'm leaving today."

"What? Mr. Counter didn't say anything."

"He doesn't know yet."

"Has something happened with Iris?" she asked, trying not to pry.

"Not exactly. I'm going to find her."

"So she's OK then?"

"I don't know."

"So, she's out of hospital?"

"I don't know, Abbie. I phoned yesterday but couldn't get any answers. They'd never heard of her at the Royal Melbourne Hospital."

"So where are you going then?"

"To Melbourne to find her."

She looked at me, very serious. "I've never been there," she said with a frown, "but I've heard it's a very big place."

"Yair. But I've got to find her."

"I knowya do luv. And I wish you all the best of luck."

"I'll miss your bacon and eggs."

"Come on then, I'll cook up the best ones you've ever had."

She gave me a big hug and then stood back, holding my shoulders in her big hands and giving me her huge toothy smile. It was the charge I needed to face the world, least of all Mr. Counter.

*

"You can't be serious," he said.

"I have to do it, Mr. Counter."

"But you could have warned me."

"I only decided last night when I heard Sugar was back."

"But you don't know where she is. She could even be back home here."

"I'd have heard if she was back here. Tank would have told me."

"Are you sure you want to take all your money with you?"

"Yair. I want it all. Just in case."

"Well, it's your money. Come into the office and I'll make out a check."

"Mr. Counter, it has to be cash."

"But you might get robbed."

"What bank will cash a check from a homeless bloke like me?"

"You're not homeless. You've got a home here, you know that."

"I'm talking about Melbourne."

"Well, all right. But there's one condition."

"Yair, what's that?"

"That you go and look up your mum."

"No way."

"Then I'm not giving it to you."

"I'll do without it. I've got other money anyway."

"Bull shit."

"I mean it, Mr. Counter."

Mr. Counter looked away. He was upset I could see it. Gees. After all he's done for me, I felt like an asshole. He looked past me to the door and I turned to see who was there. It was Mrs. Counter.

"You're an ungrateful little bugger, aren't you?" she said, her hands on her hips like always, and boobs kind of pointing at me like she was about to stab me with them.

"I want to do this on my own," I said.

"So what's going to see your mum got to do with that?" she says. "Your mum was good to you. It was your dad that made her life so miserable that she left. You know that, or if you don't you've had your head in the sand all along."

My ears were red already and me fist was clenched. I gritted my teeth trying to keep it all in. I looked at Mrs. Counter, then to Mr. Counter.

"Yair, well. You had a little bit to do with that, didn't you, Mr. Counter?" I bit my lip as soon as I said it. Mrs. Counter turned and left without a word.

"You don't know what you're saying, son," says Mr. Counter,. "Here's your money." He hands me an envelope fat with cash. "All your money's there and there's an extra tenner for good luck and a note that has your mum's address in Yarraville."

"Gees, Mr. Counter. I didn't mean to…"

"There's lots you didn't mean to do," says Mr. Counter, his mouth pulled tight like he'd just sucked a lemon. "I keep hoping that one day you'll come to your senses. Your father was a good bloke till the grog got him. And you can't blame your mum for any of that."

"I'm sorry Mr. Counter, I know you've been good to me and one day I'll make it up to you."

"There's nothing to make up. All I've done was for your dad, my best mate."

"I will, I promise."

"It's best not to make promises, ever. It's inevitable they'll be broken."

"Not for me."

"Yes, you." He held out his hand and I took it. His grip was tight and I know mine was limp. Truth is I hadn't shaken hands with someone older than me hardly ever before. I opened my kit bag and dropped the money in it. "How are you getting to Melbourne?" he asks.

"I'm taking the train."

"I'll drive you to the North Shore Station, then."

"Nah, don't bother. I got plenty of time. I'll walk."

"And those letters that keep coming from the Education Department. Will I throw them out?"

"Shit no! Just keep them and one day I'll come back and pick them up."

"And when will that be?"

"Who knows? But please don't destroy them."

"I might mail them to your mum, then," he says with a glint in his eye.

*

I never went to the North Shore station. I took the bus into Geelong and went to the Bank of New South Wales where Mr. Counter had opened up my bank account a while ago when he was keeping my money from me. I had six checks to deposit. Every two weeks the Education Department sent me a check for fourteen pounds and eleven pence. I don't know why they're doing it. There must have been some kind of mix-up and they think I'm going to Geelong Teachers College and nobody's told them I didn't show up. Either that or they must want me really badly, and that's not likely, is it, given what I wrote on my Latin exam, although I did pass all my other subjects. Yair, that was a turn-up. Me and me mates got drunk that night when we waited at the Geelong Addy office for the results.

The Geelong Station was a bit scary. It had those imposing brick walls and arches, and wide embellished eaves hanging out over the platform, very Victorian, as they say, and hell, Queen Victoria was scary enough, wasn't she? And there were people running around all over the place, all busy going wherever they were going. I admit that all those people, although they were taking no notice of me, made me feel like I was no-one, like I was all alone and nobody cared about me. I thought I was used to crowds, given that the old pub at peak hour was so crowded you couldn't move without rubbing against someone. But here, it was different. There were many more people but they couldn't give a shit about you because they were hell bent on going someplace, who knows where. I nearly turned around and caught the bus back to the old pub. My old room didn't seem so bad now. And everyone knew me at the pub. I pulled out the envelope from the professor. There was a garbage can on the station platform and I went to throw it in. And I would have too, except that I bumped into this gorgeous woman dressed in a mini-skirt.

"Gees, sorry!" I say, pocketing my envelope. My ears are already red, but I'm not angry at all.

"Oh! No worries," she says, and reaches in front of me to toss in an apple core.

I'm standing there, speechless. She's carrying this leather satchel, a deep brown and all polished up. Her nails are lightly painted and she's wearing a light shade of pink lipstick that matches her nails. I never saw any girl like this before. When she said "worries" her pale pink lips came together, ready for kissing. Her eyes were unbelievably dark, painted with eye shadow and her lashes, they were so long. And her deep ebony hair, mounds of it, long and fashioned to just touch her shoulders, shifting gracefully as she turned her head and caught the light breeze of an approaching train. Only trouble is, she's a lot older than me. Must be at least thirty or even a bit more.

The train pulls in and I'm still standing there, rooted to the spot.

"Are you going to Melbourne?" she asks.

I make a small, pathetic little step towards the train. My mouth is frozen shut.

"Come on!" she says, and holds the carriage door open for me. I'm thinking, what the hell. I'm supposed to be holding the door open for her, aren't I?

We climb into the carriage. It's an old steam train. Can't believe they're still running them. I sit there, got my old kit bag on the floor between my legs. Another bloke gets in, he's a few years older than me, I'm guessing. He gives her the up and down too. He's wearing these old looking jeans, and t-shirt. Me, I'm wearing my usual—my old school pants and shirt. I left behind all the new shirts and Fletchers that Mrs. Counter bought me. I wanted a new start.

*

"I'm Katherine Hardy," she says, and holds out her hand. The bloke next to me grabs it. I'm rummaging around in my kit bag looking for one of me exercise books that I can pretend to read.

"G'day," he says with a big grin, "I'm Paul Grimes, pleased to meet you Kate—is that right? You look like a Kate."

She lightly licks her lips. "Not sure what a Kate looks like, but anyway, you got it right," she says with an amazing smile that just transforms her whole face. "I expect you're on your way to Uni?"

"Yes. I travel up most days. Mum and Dad wanted me to live in a College, but I like Geelong better and most of my friends are here. What about you? You look like you're a tutor or something at the Uni."

"You got that right too. You must have ESP!"

"What department are you in?" he asks, but she has already turned to me. I'm flipping the pages of my exercise book. She holds out her hand to me.

"I'm Kate, and you are?"

"Jimmy." I take her hand and squeeze it much too hard and she winces. I was trying to make up for my limp handshake.

"And are you going to uni too?"

"Yair. Going to meet with some Professor of Classics about my Matric Latin exam."

"Oh, so you're not a student there yet?"

"He wants me to be, but I haven't made up my mind."

I turn back to leafing through my exercise book. I'm comparing her to Iris. They're on opposite poles, they are. Iris, small, skinny, lithe, mischievous. This Kate, she's firm solid but not fat, and I'm guessing a little taller than me. The mini skirt she's wearing shows off legs with curves like the Great Ocean Road. In spite of myself I admit that she's incredible, and I'm on fire. I feel my cheeks redden, and I'm for the first time imagining doing someone other than Iris.

The uni student pokes out his hand at me. "I'm Paul," he says, "if you like I'll show you around the uni when we get in."

I don't like this bloke. He reminds me of the toffs in the saloon bar where they pay more for their beer just to show off how good they are.

"I'm Jimmy, but me mates call me Chooka," I say, not looking straight at him as I squeeze his hand softly. He and Kate give each other a look. They think my nickname is a joke.

"So what high school did you go to?" he asks.

"Geelong High," I say, "what about you?"

"Geelong Grammar," he says, and immediately he appears to me to have grown six inches with an overbearing look. I should have known. His blonde hair was combed most carefully, a perfect right side part, and flattened down with oil. I hadn't noticed it before, but now I could smell the hair oil and whatever else it was he'd put on himself.

"Oh yair? You're the first grammar school bloke I've met. What was it like out there?" Blokes in the pub had talked about it, stuck in the middle of nowhere on the edge of Corio Bay, half way to Melbourne. Mr. Counter used to go rabbiting and mushroom picking out there.

Kate's eyes flash and her long lashes send me a signal. Or at least that's what I hoped. Dad, I thought I didn't need you anymore, but I'd really like to know if you ever knew a woman like this one?

"Well now, Jimmy," she says with a grin and a glance across to Paul, "or should I call you Chooka?"

"Nah. Jimmy's OK," I say, not sure whether they're making fun of me or not, and I've got my head buried in my exercise book, "but I like James the best.

"Then James, I'm very pleased to meet you and maybe if you decide to go to uni you can stop by and see me. I may be able to help you settle in."

Paul shifts in his seat. "Oh, what do you tutor in?" he asks.

Without looking at him, and looking right into my eyes, she says, "psychopathology."

"Oh! Interesting," says Paul, "I'm doing an LLB."

"What's that?" I ask, then feel stupid yet again.

"It's law."

"What year are you in?" asks Kate.

"This is my third year, so I've done most of my subjects. Even did Latin," he says with a grin, turning to me.

"You have to do Latin to do law?"

"Everyone who does arts has to do a language, don't you know?"

I can feel Kate looking at me, so I finally raise my head from my exercise book.

"So where's your office, then," I blurt out.

"It's in the old arts building. Probably right by your professor's office. What's his name?"

I rummage through my kit bag for the envelope. "Wait a minute. Can't remember. He's chair of the classics and antiquity department, I think."

"Oh, that's Claude. Claude Pulcher. You'll like him, and I can tell he'll like you too."

"You think so?"

"Oh, absolutely. But please do drop in and see me once you've met up with Claude. My office is in the same building on the opposite side. It's only temporary. Next year they're opening the new psychology building on the other side of the uni and all the psych tutors are moving there."

"Gee thanks."

I go back to leafing through my exercise book. But I see out of the corner of my eye Paul leafing through a big fat book he's carrying. The spine says, *Cases and Materials in Criminal Law and Procedure* and the author's someone called Chappell. I know he's also eyeing me off. I feel under scrutiny like never before. Like traveling with your mother.

*

I found Geelong Station scary enough, but Flinders Street station was so overwhelming I wanted to run away and hide somewhere. To make things worse, Paul was trying to help me. "Watch your bag" he says, and I clutch it like I'd never done before. "Watch out for pick-pockets!" And I'm trying to keep hold of my bag, thinking of the big wad of money I've got in my bag. I'm a bit vague on how we got to Uni. I think it was a tram up Swanston Street. Kate had gone off shopping on her way to uni, so left us at the station, I think Flinders street. Paul, very nice, showed me the way, even insisted on paying for my tram ride.

I don't know quite what I was expecting the uni to look like. Getting there had already rattled me. Paul took me to the Law building which was scary enough, but then he pointed out the old arts building with its big imposing tower. And all that yellow sand stone, I didn't like it at all.

"Are you going back to Geelong today?" Paul asked.

"No, I don't think so."

"Oh, so where are you staying?"

"Er, I've got relatives in Yarraville."

"Oh, that's not too bad. We pretty much passed it on the train this morning."

We had stopped under the arches, called "The Cloisters" he said. They reminded me of the Geelong Station. "This is the Law School where I spend most of my time." He pointed across the green grass of the quadrangle. "You see that clock tower? That's the Old Arts building where you'll find your professor."

After a few mistakes, I found my way into the Old arts building and walked round and round the passageways trying to find Professor Pulcher's office. I opened one door and was horrified to find myself looking into a huge lecture theatre crammed full of students and a lecturer way down the bottom. There was nothing to like about this place. Nothing! I stepped back and ran down the stairs, reaching the bottom, then turning right looking for an exit, and there right in front of me was a door —all the doors were always closed—that said *Department of Classics and Antiquity*, so of course, that was where I had to go.

But I didn't. There's no way I'd stay here. What kind of people work and study in a place like this? All stuffed shirts and shit-heads prancing around like they were royalty. They'd even made the doors hard to pull or push open, it was like they didn't want you there. Not like the pub where everyone was welcome. I lunged at the door and nearly knocked someone over as I rushed out and immediately glimpsed a splash of green grass. It was the only thing in the whole university so far that attracted me. And there I went, and I lay down on the cool grass, on my belly, my arm over my kit bag, the other cradling my face. And my Dad spoke to me, "what kind of people lived and worked in the old Pub?"

"Shut up, you old bastard!" I said.

*

I must have fallen asleep because next thing I felt was this foot pushing down on my bum. I rolled over and opened my eyes, my arm held up trying to keep the bright sky at arm's length. But I immediately knew who it was. Those legs I had studied all the way from Geelong.

"I thought it was you," she said, "I'd recognize that kit bag anywhere. There must be something very important in it, you're clinging to it for dear life."

"It's got all my life in it," I said, trying to smile.

"So did you call on your professor Pulcher?" asked Kate.

"No. I couldn't find his office," I said lamely.

Kate squatted down beside me. She laughed and tossed back her head, her deep ebony hair flowing round her shoulders. "Well, it's a bit late now to find him anyway. Are you staying here, then? It'll get a bit cold here after the sun goes down and that won't be long."

"I should get going. I'm supposed to go to my auntie's house in Yarraville," I lied.

"You'll have to go back to Flinders Street station."

"Yair, that's what Paul said." I sat up, grabbing my kit bag. My eyes were on her legs. "But I have to visit a friend of mine who's in the Royal Melbourne Hospital. Don't suppose you know where that is?"

"You see that tall building over there?" She points across the lawn in the direction of what I now know was the new Baillieu library. "That's it. Just five minutes' walk."

I was kind of caught off guard. I hadn't really decided whether I wanted to go there or not, because, well, it was Iris and I was scared to find out what happened. I didn't know what to do because I couldn't go back to the pub, now I'd come this far and I didn't want to go to Yarraville, did I, Dad? I pulled my legs up and leaned forward, my head between my knees.

"James," said Kate, as she gently placed her fingers under my chin to which my head all on its own, responded, and I found myself staring at those voluptuous pink lips pursed together making a faint smile. "You are a very handsome boy, you know."

I blinked several times. No-one, including Iris had ever said anything like that to me. My mouth moved, but I was unable to speak. Had anyone else called me a boy, I would have clobbered them. But with Kate it was so very different. The sun had gone down behind the hospital and a long shadow crept over the lawn. My whole body shivered. She grasped my hand that was still holding the handle of my kit bag.

"I think you'd better come home with me,' she said, "you don't have anywhere to go, do you?"

"I'm not going back to Geelong," I said.

"Nor am I. I only go down there to visit my parents every now and again. I have a little place in Parkville."

"Where's that?"

"Actually, it's not far from the Royal Melbourne Hospital." Kate stood up, grabbing my hand, pulling me up. She was surprisingly strong and I easily complied.

*

The Royal Melbourne Hospital was about as scary as the uni. It was like they didn't want you there too and the doctors and secretaries or whatever they were, maybe nurses or something, treated you like they was doing you a big favour matrons strutted around like cockatoos on heat.

It had taken me a couple of weeks to get up the courage to go there. In the end, it was Kate who made me do it, but that was after we had got to know each other. She could see I was out of control. From the lawn in front of the Cloisters she guided me to her little flat tucked away in a big block of flats on Royal Parade. Right from that very first night she started in on me. As soon as we got inside her flat, she had me on her bed, all my clothes ripped off, and going at it. She kept telling me what a wonderful boy I was. And I loved her for it. We'd take a break at the local pub for a few beers, come home and she'd cook spaghetti, something I'd never heard of, let alone eaten. And pretty soon she had me cooking it. Then it was to bed again, until morning, and I'd get up and cook eggs on toast, make a pot of tea, and she'd kiss me good-bye and I'd go back to bed, then I'd shower, go out for a counter lunch at the local pub and do the shopping for dinner. Within days, she had trained me. And I was happy, waiting for her to come home from work, and we'd start all over again. Dad, if you're in Heaven, I hope it's like this!

After a couple of weeks, though, when I'd go back to bed after she left, I started thinking of Iris again. I even walked down to the hospital after my counter lunch, but I wasn't game enough to go in the door. It was so big, and there was glass everywhere, and people, really important looking people rushing in and out. So that night, after we'd been at it as usual, and I'm lying back dragging on my Craven A, she's running her fingers over my belly, and says, "have you been to the hospital?"

"You mean the Royal Melbourne?"

"Yair. I went down there today."

"To look for your friend?"

I never told her who it was.

"Sort of. I got down there, but I didn't go in."

"I go there occasionally. Dr. Franks sometimes has lectures there and I have to be there to help get the students into the right room."

"He's probably not there anymore, anyway. I should have gone sooner, I know."

"What happened, may I ask?"

"He was beaten up pretty badly in a bar brawl. This bloke in the bar thought he was a homo and socked him one right on the jaw, then the rest of the bar just pummelled the poor bastard senseless."

"You're best friends with a poofda?" she says, incredulous.

"Yair, why not?" I say, and for the first time I feel like I'm speaking up for myself like we were equals.

"I'm very proud of you," she says, and she starts in on me, her hand moving down my belly.

"So where should I go to find out if he's been there?"

"Would you like me to come with you?"

"Nah, it's something I have to do by myself. I just need to get in the door and find the right person to ask."

"You just go right in the main doors and follow the signs to Reception. Go there and give them the name of your friend and tell them when you think he was admitted."

Her hand has found the right place, and I'm ready to go. But would you believe it? I'm thinking of Iris, Iris all the way.

*

This old lady, her face all wrinkled and powder plastered all over her, a thin line of bright red lipstick smudged a bit at the corners, her silver hair puffed all up like fairy floss, is looking at me from behind her big desk. She's smiling really nice at me and I give her my best smile back.

"Iris is her name, and she was brought here from Geelong hospital about three weeks ago," I say. "She's my sister and I'm worried about her. Is she OK?"

"What's her last name, dear?"

"Devlin. Iris Devlin."

"That's quite some time ago. I don't think she would still be here."

"I just want to know if she's all right. She was nearly dying when they sent her here."

"That's Devlin, D-E-V-L-I-N?" she asks.

"Yair. That's right. She'd lost a lot of blood."

She starts flipping through a huge book that's got lists and lists of names.

"Was it exactly three weeks ago? It would help me if I had an actual date, love," she says looking at me with a glint in her eye.

"I'm not sure, but I think it might have been exactly three weeks, or maybe one day less, because she came here late in the night so she might have got here after midnight."

"Well, I don't think she's in this hospital. There's no one of that name registered. So that means she either was discharged or..."

The nice old thing, she looks up at me, her mouth hanging open.

"Or what?" I ask.

"Just a minute. She might have been sent back to the Geelong hospital."

"You know she was actually brought here then?" I phoned up weeks ago and they said she never came here. But I know she did."

"Are you sure?"

"Yair. I watched the ambulance leave the hospital and they said she was going to Royal Melbourne, and they wouldn't let me ride in the ambulance."

"You know, Mr. Devlin, sometimes when it's a matter of life or death, the ambulance gets diverted to another hospital. Have you tried Prince Alfred?"

"Where's that?"

"It's over in St. Kilda. You could go there. But makes sure you phone first."

*

Living in Heaven with Kate, I'd lost track of time. I wasn't sure what day it was, but I soon found out it was Friday. I'd gone straight from the hospital to the grocery shop and bought up spaghetti and stuff to make a big pot of Bolognese for Kate when she got home. I had decided to tell her all about Iris. I had also decided that Iris had probably kicked it, and the very nice old lady at the hospital didn't want to tell me. But Kate didn't show up at her usual time and the spaghetti sat there, getting cold. I opened a beer and quaffed it down. I lit up a smoke and fingered the Craven 'A' packet, took a deep drag. I opened another beer, then found myself rummaging through Kate's cupboards looking for booze, stronger booze. And I had another beer.

I know what you're thinking. He's fallen off the wagon. That's not quite right. The fact is, I'd been having a few beers with Kate ever since that first unbelievable night. I never got drunk (not drunk like at the old pub) at all when I was with her, and I never felt like I couldn't stop. So now, I'm at the crossroads. I was just about to open another beer when the door flew open and in walked Kate followed closely by Paul Grimes.

"G'day, Chooka!" says Grimes, and he puts his hand out. I shake it, but I'm annoyed. Kate never called me Chooka, and I don't like this bastard calling me that. It's my pub name.

"G'day yourself," I say, slapping his hand away.

"Now Sweetie," says Kate, and she comes up and lightly pecks me on my cheek that's bright red already. She sees all the cupboards open. "Don't tell me. You've been searching for the hard stuff."

I pull her roughly to me and plant a big kiss on her marvellous voluptuous lips. "You're a better substitute," I say, one eye on Grimes. He's standing back, trying not to look.

"So what's going on?" I ask.

"I have to go visit my parents in Geelong. My mum is sick. Paul happened to drive up today, so I'm hitching a lift with him. We thought you might like to come along and visit your mates at the old pub. Just for the weekend."

I push away. Buggered if I knew what to do. I thought I had left it all behind now that I'd found Kate, and she's trying to get me to go back to it all. I'm not game.

"Nah. Don't think so. Nice of you blokes to ask me. But I've had enough of the old pub."

"Why's that?" asks Paul.

"It's a long story," says Kate.

"Hey, you can stay with me and my parents," says Grimes.

"Gees, that's nice of you. But I think I might drop in and visit my auntie. I haven't seen her in several years."

"Really?" says Kate, "are you sure you want to do that?" She's acting like a psychologist or something.

"No, I'm not. But it was a good thought, wasn't it?" I tried to joke.

"Where does she live?" asks Kate.

"I told you. Yarraville."

"I can drop you off, then," says Grimes, "no worries. It's right on the way."

"Thanks, but no thanks. I need to think about it."

"I'm sorry we have to leave you," says Kate as she playfully runs her fingers through my hair. "Maybe you should have a haircut and shave while I'm gone," she jokes.

"Ha! Ha!"

"Well," says Grimes, "we should be going, it's Friday afternoon and the traffic's going to be heavy."

"Yair, that's OK. You blokes get going. I'll be all right."

When they get to the door, Kate turns and comes back to me. She gives me a light kiss, then presses a piece of paper into my hand. "I got that professor Pulcher's phone number for you. It's his direct line. Phone him. It's not too late."

She runs to the door and calls out over her shoulder, "be a good boy, now! And it would be a good idea if you had a haircut and shave before you go to meet Doctor Pulcher."

"Yes, mum," I say.

"And buy some new pants and shirt. You look like a tramp."

*

Gees, Iris, what can I tell you? I don't know where you are, but I'll find you one day. And when I do, we'll have such a great time, because I've learnt everything from Kate. Oh, sorry, I shouldn't have told you about her, should I? It's just something that happened. I didn't have anywhere to go. Anyway, she's too old for me. She could be my mother, for Christ sake. And lately she's been acting like she was.

It's Monday morning and I've been lying in bed all weekend, just smoking my Craven 'A's and feeling sorry for myself. I thought Kate would be back Sunday, but she didn't show up. She's probably fucking that stuck-up asshole Grimes. I felt under the bed, a funny feeling, like I was looking for a bottle of plonk, but I wasn't. I told myself after Kate left that I wasn't going to fall off the wagon, and I haven't. I didn't go outside the flat once all weekend. I'm feeling around for my old kit bag and some money. I'm going out for a haircut and a shave. I have to get cleaned up for Dr. Pulcher. Kate's right about that. It's an opportunity I can't pass up, can I, Iris? You'd understand, wouldn't you? No, I suppose not. I don't think that you even finished Form 2 at high school. And I don't remember you ever being at Geelong High. Where else could you have gone? Maybe to the Flinders Girls School? Gees, Iris, I don't know anything about you.

You know what? I've hardly touched any of my money all this time. Lived off Kate. She pretty much pays for everything. Amazing, don't you think? But who knows how long she'll keep me here. Her going off with Grimes, and all that mother talk. I think she's getting ready to kick me out. I'll have to start thinking up things to do with her. But I can't think of anything she wouldn't have already. I tell you, she knows everything. And seems like she's done everything. Maybe Grimes knows stuff I don't know, stuff he learnt in Grammar school. Yes, I know what you're thinking Iris, my love. Your guess is as good as mine.

Don't worry Iris. I'll come and get you at Alfred Hospital soon as I can. I got to go and see this professor. It's my only chance. Besides, Kate will cross her legs on me if she gets home and I haven't phoned the bloke. Gees, Iris. Sorry. I keep forgetting. But I tell you, Iris. You're the only one for me, I know.

And you, Dad, for Christ sake, shut up.

*

I'm in this flat on Beaconsfield Parade, right down from a big old pub. I'm dying to go there, but I'm not game. Professor Pulcher's letting me stay here for a while until I find my own place. He's a really good bloke, and I think he's going to get me a scholarship. Kate didn't want me to leave her, believe it or not. It took a couple of weeks for her to let me go and she kept saying nasty things about Dr. Pulcher, none of it true, as far as I could see.

The very first day I met him, he came right out of his office and welcomed me, even though the secretary woman or whoever she was, had told me he wasn't available. Only thing was, I pegged him right away as a pommie. He had this funny English accent and a high-pitched voice, a bit like Mickey Mouse, and he had one of those speech defects, I think you call it a lisp. And he was wearing this dark grey suit pulled tight and buttoned with just one button, and a tartan vest underneath. And he had this thing—I found out later from Kate, it was called a cravat—

bunched around his neck. Gees, Iris, imagine him showing up at the old pub! They'd tear him to pieces.

He ushered me into his office and sat me down on a low chair with curvaceous legs and a very soft, embroidered, fanciest chair I'd ever seen. He went to a cupboard wedged in the middle of a wall of books and took out a bottle of something and two tiny glasses. I never saw any so small, and I worked in a pub, for Christ sake. He brought them over to a matching curvaceous coffee table and sat down on the chair beside me.

"Sherry?" he asked, his lisping lips fluttering like the waves at Eastern Beach.

"Thank you," I replied, "is it sweet or dry?" I knew all about sherry because we had a customer in the Snake Pit who drank nothing but dry sherry. Mr. Counter told me it was very high in alcohol content.

"It's sweet. I hope that's all right? It's all I have at the moment. I asked Ruth to get some in, but she hasn't had a chance. We've been very busy preparing for the incoming class."

"Thank you. That's good," I said.

Dr. Pulcher sat back, raised his glass and said, "cheers" and I followed and took the tiniest of sips. Dad was into this in his last days. I'd rather not drink it. But little sips were what you were supposed to take, anyway. "Welcome James," he said, "I have been looking forward to meeting you."

"Gees, Professor Pulcher, thanks for inviting me and for your letter. I was all set to go to Teachers College."

"Well, I'm glad you thought it over. I don't mind telling you that I was most amused by your forthright translation of Ovid."

"Gees, thanks Dr. Pulcher. I was getting pretty tired and I kind of lost my temper with him."

"That's perfectly fine. It shows you were personally engaged with that marvellous poet. It wasn't just an examination exercise for you. It was personal. You put yourself right into the works. I could see it in other parts of your translation too. You are a courageous young man. You took a great risk doing what you did on your exam. My congratulations and I hope we can move forward and make a great classics scholar of you."

I shifted uncomfortably in my chair. I didn't have any idea what a great classics scholar does. If he meant that I would spend the rest of my life sitting at a desk translating Ovid, fucking hell! Iris! Can you imagine that? Shit! What a boring life! "Gees, Dr. Pulcher, I, I don't know what to say."

"Say nothing, James, say nothing. Oh, it's OK calling you James, I take it?"

"Oh, well some people call me, I mean, yes, everyone calls me James. I like that better than Jimmy. There's too many Jimmies, aren't there?"

"Indeed, there are, but only one James Henderson," he smiled a big, big smile, his lips stretching from ear to ear. Iris, he looked so funny I nearly burst out laughing. But I managed to keep my mouth shut and so there was an awkward silence, or at least it seemed so.

"So now, to business," he said as he returned to his desk, carefully straightening his wavy hair in the full-length mirror across the room that was behind my shoulder. He was very proud of his hair, dark brown, thick and wavy, starting well down his forehead, combed back with a part dead centre of his scalp, streaks of grey here and there. He rummaged around his desk and finally called out to his secretary through the open door.

"Ruth! Do you have that admission form please? Ruth?"

There was a rustling noise from outside and a muffled "just a minute" and I was feeling like I should do something, so I started to get up but Dr. Pulcher put his hand on my shoulder and said, "stay there James, Ruth will bring the form any minute." Right then, I opened my mouth and I knew I was going to say something stupid, but my mouth wouldn't stop.

"Dr. Pulcher, do you mind if I ask you a question?"

"Of course not. Fire away."

"You're a doctor, right?"

"That's what they call me."

"So why don't you work in a hospital or something?"

"Well, I'm a different kind of doctor," he says, his mouth flinching, I know he was holding back a laugh, "in academics, the best students go on to a post graduate degree past their B.A. and get their doctorate, called a Ph.D."

"P-H what?"

"It stands for Doctor of Philosophy."

"Yair?"

"Yes, only mine is in classics. Other people can get them in science, education, economics and so on."

"Gees, Doctor Pulcher, I feel stupid. I should have known that. I'm sorry."

"It's nothing. Once you get enrolled here, you'll quickly learn the ropes. I can see you're not stupid at all. You're a very bright young man." He put his hand on my shoulder again, and this time squeezed it very gently.

"Thanks Doctor Pulcher. I don't know what to say."

"Say nothing. Just promise me that you will put all your time and work into your studies."

"I will, I promise."

Ruth showed up at last with a very long form. She handed it to me and I looked at it dumbfounded. I could fill in maybe a couple of questions—my first and last name, although I wasn't sure what a Christian name was. Dr. Pulcher leaned down and took the form. "You know what?" he said, "I think it would be best if I filled in some of it with you, especially the subjects you will do for your first year—there's not a lot of choice anyway—and then Ruth can help you fill in the administrative questions, especially those that help to decide whether you qualify for a scholarship."

"What do I have to do for that?" I asked.

"Basically nothing. Just give Ruth some family details and how much money you have."

"That's easy," I said, "none on both counts."

"What do you mean?" He gives Ruth a look.

"Well I don't have any money, or at least none to speak of. I was working in a pub till a few weeks ago and that doesn't pay much. My mum took off somewhere and I don't know where she is and my father died last year. So I'm on my own."

"OK. That's good news, I mean, not good of course for you, but it will make it easier to justify a late scholarship for you."

"Gee, thanks Dr. Pulcher."

"Ruth, besides Latin 1 and English 1, he'll have to sign up for a history or economics class and a science, perhaps psychology. I think they have to do four subjects the first year, is that right?"

"Yes, Dr. Pulcher. Don't worry, I'll help him get everything set up and I'll walk him over to the registrar. There is one thing, though," she turns to me, "if you're on your own, do you have a place to stay?"

My ears went red and she looked at me as though she was trying to tell me something but didn't want to say it. "I'm staying with a friend for a few weeks, but I have to move out soon." Ruth looks over to Professor Pulcher.

"Ruth, could he get into one of the colleges on campus?"

"There's no way. You know how it goes. They're filled up long before the year starts with kids from the private schools."

"Of course, you're right. You know what?" he says, "I have a small flat in St. Kilda, or South Melbourne it is really. You're welcome to stay there until you find a place of your own."

"Gee, Dr. Pulcher, you're so kind. I don't know how to thank you enough."

"Well it's just a small place. And I'm afraid not especially handy to the university. You're welcome to stay as long as it takes you to get settled into the university. I'll drop by from time to time to make sure everything is OK."

"Gee, thanks Dr. Pulcher. Will I be in your Latin class?"

"No, I lecture only to advanced students. But who knows, you may be an advanced student very soon. I will make sure you get a really good tutor and I will also work with you from time to time. I try to keep up with all the students in our department."

"You must be really busy, Dr. Pulcher. Thanks again."

"Come into my office," says Ruth, "and we'll fill in the form and get you registered so you will be able to attend classes. They've been going now for a couple of weeks already."

"Excellent," says Dr. Pulcher, "and when that's done, come back to me and I'll arrange for you to move into the flat."

Ruth reminded me a bit of Mrs. Counter. She was a pretty scary lady, taller than me, and top-heavy just like Mrs. Counter. We filled in the form, or at least she did, and she got me enrolled in four classes, so now I was all of a sudden, a uni student. Gees, Dad. You must be rolling around laughing your head off.

*

Fact is, I had a lot of mates at high school and could have gone on with most of them to Teachers College. But here I am, sitting alone in a little flat owned by this big-time professor. Maybe I should phone up my old mates and they could come up to Melbourne for the weekend or something. I mean, what am I supposed to do all on my own, especially as now I've left Kate, and Grimes doesn't seem to want to know me. I told him he could stay with me any time he wanted to. The flat is small, but it's close to all the action (or so they say) in St. Kilda. I haven't even walked down there yet. In fact, I haven't left the flat except to go to the little milk bar on the corner and get something to eat. And I haven't even been back to the uni and I have to buy the books that are on the lists Ruth got for me for each subject. It's too much. And I have to go to the classes and find the lecture halls and there's these tutors I'm supposed to meet and go to their little rooms and act like I'm all smart and clever.

There's a knock on the door. It's Grimes.

"G'day, Chooka. Don't s'pose you have room for the night?"

"Shit, Grimesy, I never thought you'd show up. Come right in."

"Thanks. All right if I stay for a few nights? I know I won't be as entertaining as Kate," he says with a big grin, "but I'll try hard," he joked.

"Yair, I bet you could." And we laugh together.

"I have an early crim tute in the morning."

"Crim? What?"

"Criminal law tutorial."

"I s'pose I have a tute tomorrow too. I haven't got around to finding out where and when they are."

Grimes starts to unpack his bag. "You know," he says, "you should make sure you go to the tutes. Pulcher will be looking to see whether you show up. And he could do you in easily. You don't want to get on the wrong side of him."

"He seems like a good bloke," I say, "and he's been great to me. Got me a scholarship and everything."

"He did that?" asked Grimes incredulously.

"Yair. He did. And he's letting me have this flat until I get somewhere of my own."

"Why didn't they put you in a college?"

"They said there wasn't room. The private school kids get first dibs."

"Yes, of course. I forgot that. I could have got in last year. Sorry they wouldn't let you in. It's not right.

"No worries. I'm much happier being on my own. I don't think I'd fit in too well in one of those colleges, whatever they are."

"You're probably right."

"So why didn't you go into a college, then?"

"I just liked all my old mates in Geelong. I played footy with them every week, and we went to the pub together. I'd miss all that if I was in a college. And besides in a college you can't pick your friends. You're stuck with whoever happens to be there."

"My thoughts exactly." I was beginning to think that Grimesy wasn't a bad bloke after all.

"What have you got lined up for me tonight?" he asks with a grin.

"Let's go down to the pub," I say, "and I'll shout, but you have to promise me you'll take me shopping to the uni bookstore tomorrow. I couldn't even find the place today."

"Deal!"

*

Caesar's *The Gallic Wars Book 1* was the topic of the tutorial. Thanks to Grimesy, I'd bought my books and he'd shown me where the tute was going to be. He's a good bloke. Not like the others.

I pulled open the door and nearly collapsed in fear and trembling. There were just eight or nine students sitting around in a horseshoe on old wooden chairs and the tutor at the end sitting in the gap. I took a dislike to him before I even sat down on the one chair that was left. They all looked at me as though I was late, and I wasn't. I thought I was early, but I suppose not.

"Salve!" he says.

And I say, "G'day."

"Et tu es?"

"What?" The bastard was trying to make me look a fool, that's what. I plopped down on the chair and the other students started to snigger. Bastards all of them too.

"Et tu es?"

"Ego Brutus, ille est qui." I answered with a sneer.

"Very funny. You must be Mr. Henderson?"

"Ego sum, quis podex," I muttered, and couldn't help a big grin. A couple of the other students gaped at me. I looked the tutor in the eye and I could see he didn't know what to say. These stuck-up bastards, they think they're so fuckn good. And who would wear a corduroy jacket with the leather sewn into the elbows, but a poofda of the highest order.

"Thank you, Mr. Henderson. We do not use vulgarities in this tutorial. If you want to indulge, Dr. Pulcher holds a small seminar on *latina vulgaris* every month in his home."

He shifts in his chair and crosses his legs. They're long and spindly. He's wearing Fletchers for sure, with big cuffs at the bottom. And I bet they're worn shiny in the ass. He's even paler than Grimesy, his hair a sandy white but clipped to a crew cut that definitely doesn't match his corduroy jacket. He doesn't look much older than me. He makes a small cough.

"Now that we are all here. Let me introduce myself. I am Gregory Lepidus, your tutor for this year in Latin 1. We meet in this room every week at this time. I know some of you have only now just been enrolled, so you have missed three weeks. See me at the end of the tute and I will help you catch up. Now, I hope you all studied the first book of Caesar's great classic. Let us begin with the very first, and perhaps the most famous, sentence. We will go around clockwise, starting on my left. First read the Latin, then translate the sentence."

I look around and they're all hunched up poring over their little books. Me, I don't have to because I've learnt the translation off by heart, although I didn't have to do much because I learnt some of this in high school. It's too easy.

"Gallia est omnis divisa in partes tres…"

The tutor interrupts. "Before you go on, translate just those seven words."

"Gaul is divided into three parts," says this student obediently. She's a little thing with curly blonde hair. I imagine it cropped like Iris's.

"Indeed!" he says, "what do those words tell us about Caesar?"

Nobody answers, so he decides to pick on someone. It's the bloke next to me. He's sweating like buggery, I can smell it.

Just then, the door opens behind me and I twist around and see that it's Dr. Pulcher.

"Don't mind me," he says, "I'm just visiting."

The bloke next to me just about faints.

"Well?" says the tutor. He's a bit red in the face himself.

"Excuse me," I say, "but what the hell are we supposed to say about seven words? If we want to know about Caesar, what about the time he was Nicomedes' bum boy? Didn't *futuatque cum ad summum Caesar* ?" The tutor was struck dumb and the other students just stared at me like I was crazy. Dr. Pulcher sat stock still, his rippling lips fighting a smile. The tutor wasn't too pleased. And he poured out a whole lot of Latin, none of which I could understand. My spoken Latin was confined to swearing, but I think that this was what he was saying:

"Mr. Henderson, that is the most disgusting thing ever said in any tutorial I have supervised. For your information, it is only speculation that Caesar had any sexual relationship with Nicomedes, though it is true that he slept with many women, some of them the wives of his friends and colleagues. But all of that is irrelevant to today's text. We are here concerned with the brilliance and clarity of Caesar's writing, of which these seven words are a prime example. I would appreciate it, Mr. Henderson, if you would confine your interventions to the topic under discussion, not to fanciful digressions to your own obsessions."

"Futete!" I muttered. And I got up to leave. I never saw a bloke so red in the face. I thought his round cheeks were going to burst.

"One moment, now" called Dr. Pulcher.

I stopped, half standing, half sitting. To be honest, I didn't know what I was doing. If I'd been in the pub, I would have grabbed the shit-head tutor and bashed his head in. The tutor squirmed in his seat. The others were agog, staring down at their books, trying not to laugh.

"Mr. Henderson, thank you for your interesting digression and providing us with practice in using Latin profanities. Mr. Lepidus is following the lesson plans agreed upon by our classics committee. If you are interested in Caesar's fascinating sex life, that's fine. And in my small seminar on *Latina vulgaris*, we do look closely at that and the many other sexual activities—perhaps depravities, more accurately," a smile broke through his fluttering lips, "indulged in by our Roman and Greek ancestors. But now is not the time. Do please sit down. Mr. Lepidus is a foremost authority on Julius Caesar. You can learn a lot from him."

I wanted to get out of there. All the other students were gawking at me. I'd fucked up, that's what. And I couldn't believe I did it all in front of Dr. Pulcher. I stood, frozen in motion. The tutor decided to move on.

"Let's continue with the translation," he said, and nodded to the student to complete the first sentence. She droned on. Obviously, she had studied the stuff all night.

"...*quarum unam incolunt Belgae, aliam Aquitani, tertiam qui ipsorum lingua Celtae...*"

Dr. Pulcher quietly left the room, but I'm sure he winked at me ever so slightly as he passed. I sat back in my chair and started fingering the first page and counting up the sentences to figure out what one I'd have to do. I think I was sweating more than the bloke next to me. But I wasn't wearing hair oil. It made my hair go flat, and I liked my waves too much.

*

Flo started going to the pub with Tank. They even went with Little Linda and put up with her little savage brat running around. And Flo kept up her chain smoking, and only drank lemon squash, no booze. It was enough for her to get some sugar, that's what they said in the Snake Pit. I know all this because I asked my mate Grimesy to drop in at the pub on his way back to Geelong one weekend. He had started to stay with me for most of the weekdays now, and then go home weekends. I hadn't told Dr. Pulcher who dropped by and saw some of Grimesy's stuff.

"You have a visitor?" he asked.

"Just a friend from Geelong who drives up most days."

"Oh, were you friends before uni?"

"No. We met on the train. He's helped me find my way round the uni a lot."

"What is he studying?"

"He's third year law, I think."

"Well, that's nice. You understand that you can't have a permanent other person staying with you here. The local ordinance doesn't allow it."

"Oh, yes. Dr. Pulcher. And I promise I'll find somewhere of my own pretty soon. I just haven't had time trying to catch up with all the classes I missed."

"Of course, James, no problem. You can stay here for as long as it takes you."

"Gee, thanks Dr. Pulcher. And, I, I'm sorry I blurted out those things in Mr. Lepidus's tute. It was my first tute ever. I didn't know what I was doing."

"I'm sure he understands, I know I do." He came over to me and gave me a kind of hug. "Is there anything you need? Is everything going OK?"

"Yes, thank you. I'm catching up with my work and I hope I can come to your special seminar next week, if that's OK."

"Of course. You can get my address from Ruth. As a matter of fact, though, I was thinking that I could maybe hold it here, as it's more convenient for students. My place is way out past Eltham."

"Gees, I dunno where that is."

"Well, no worries. I'll see you next week, then."

*

I met Grimesy as planned in the student union cafeteria. The coffee had a taste all of its own, which I didn't mind, except that it didn't taste like any coffee I ever had. But it was cheap, even cheaper than tea. I was trying to finish off a lab report for psych one when I found Grimesy at my elbow.

"Late with your lab report, huh?" he says with a grin.

"Yair, fuckn thing. I dunno what I'm doing. The lecturer, he's a fuckn Nazi, that's what he is."

"Oh, you've got Knappenberger?"

"Yair."

I reach under the table and pull up my kitbag. "So, did you get them?" I asked.

"Yes. Your Mr. Counter had lots of questions, though. He didn't want to give them up, but I finally convinced him I was on the up and up. I told him that I stayed with you occasionally and he seemed to like that, although there was this bald-headed bloke who was listening in, he had this smirk on his face that I didn't like."

"Did he have a walking stick?"

"Yes. Greasy bastard if ever there was one."

"Yair. That's Sugar. He has fits. I beat him up once."

"You did? What for?"

"Let's just say that he got on my nerves."

"O.K. so here's the letters."

"Great. Let's go to the pub and I'll buy you a beer and lunch as well."

"I've got a criminal procedure tute. Gotta go."

"OK. Thanks again. See you tonight?"

"Maybe. Depends if Kate invites me in—you know what I mean."

"Sure. But remember, I'm on tomorrow."

"Fair enough. Aren't you going to ask me about Iris?"

My heart sank. How could I have forgotten? It was the main reason I asked him to drop in at the pub.

"Shit! Don't know what's wrong with me. Did you find out anything?"

"Mr. Counter said he had no news. He was real surprised, because he said he expected you to have found her by now and that's why you went to Melbourne. Is that right?"

"Mostly."

"He took me into the Snake Pit—a horrible place—and he talked with a big bloke, scary as hell, who was her father, I think."

"Yair, Tank, the bastard."

"And he was with this woman, Flo, I think it was, who just sat there staring into space, puffing on a cigarette. Said absolutely nothing."

"That's Flo."

"Was she her mother?"

"That's her. And why are you saying 'was,' like Iris was dead?"

"Shit, Chooka, I didn't mean to imply that."

"Yair I know. I'm beginning to think she is."

"When are you going to check out the Alfred Hospital?"

"As soon as I'm caught up with all this work. I didn't know being a uni student was so much hard work. Tending bar was much easier."

"No doubt. I'll see you around."

I tucked the letters in my kitbag and scribbled in the discussion part of the lab report.

*

By the time I made it to Kate's flat, I was out of breath. I ran full steam from Knappenberger's office that was way over the other side of the uni. The fuckn Nazi bastard. He sent me this letter that ordered me to show up in his office to discuss my lab report. I showed up, kitbag in hand because I was on my way to Kate's. He's this pudgy old bloke with pasty, dirty white skin, looking like he's on the verge of a heart attack. He's got these tiny little glasses sitting at the end of his nose, and he's slumped back in his big chair, smoking a pipe, sucking on it, then chewing it. What the hell!

"Mr. Henderson?" he says, through his teeth.

I'm standing kind of at attention in front of his desk. Reminded me of high school when that pommie bastard called me up ready to give me the cuts.

"Yair," I say, my ears all red.

"Sit down."

I sit down. We're face to face. He picks up my lab report, which I recognize from the coffee stains on the cover. He throws it across his desk and I catch it as it falls off the edge. He's got more to say.

"This is drivel. It is the worst lab report I have ever had the misfortune to read." He's got a thick German accent that I can barely understand.

"You didn't like it?" I say, mischievously.

"You think you are funny. It is not funny. It is disgusting. What high school did you attend?"

"Geelong High."

"You should not be here."

"I could try to rewrite it…"

"It iss not fixable. It iss beyond anything. I do not know how you got into this university. You do not belong here. Now get out off my office!"

It was all I could do not to lunge across his fuckn desk and ram those pip-squeak glasses down his fuckn throat. But I didn't. Kate would be proud of me. She'd shown me how to get control of myself, to make my body do what I (and she) wanted. I rose slowly from my chair and I gently placed my lab report on his desk. Then I snapped to attention and gave him a "Seig Heil" and left, slamming the door behind me.

Except that I left my kitbag behind. I went to open the door but thought that maybe I should knock first. Hearing no answer, I carefully turned the handle and slipped inside. He was still sitting there, slumped in his chair looking like he'd kicked it. I tip toed to the desk and grabbed my kitbag. He just stared at me, the pipe hanging from his teeth. Maybe he really is dead, I thought. Now that would be a good one.

*

I had to wait for Kate to show up, and I forgot to bring some beer, I'd come here in such a rush. So I sat at her kitchen table doing the translation for my next Latin tute. It was almost dark by the time she got in.

I met her at the door and planted full kisses on those wonderful lips. But she held her head back and pushed me away.

"What's going on?" I asked, my body raging for more.

"I just had a big argument over you," she said.

"Me? Not with Grimesy?"

"Oh no, he's great, you know that."

I took her hand by the fingers, long and adventurous, and led her into the bedroom. She complied, hanging back just a little to make me pull harder. We fell on to the bed, and I got started.

"So, who?" I said, with difficulty.

"That prick Lepidus, your Latin tutor."

"Oh, shit! You didn't?"

"I did."

"That corduroy cunt. I give him hell in the tutes."

"I know and that's what we were arguing about."

"So, who cares? He's just a stupid pommie bastard."

"I think he's jealous," she says with a grin.

"Jealous? Of me with you? But how would he know you and me are doing each other?" By now I've got most of her clothes off, and I've shed mine long ago."

"It's not me," she says, rolling away, exposing my body fully on heat, "it's Dr. Pulcher!" She tosses her head back and laughs, her mouth so wide open I want to fill it to the brim.

"No shit! That's really funny."

But now I'm on top of her and we're rolling around, she on top of me. No more talking. No more laughing. Just the two of us, completely bound together.

*

We lay on our backs drawing on our smokes. Kate was a bit annoyed I hadn't brought any beer. She always liked to suck down a beer after we exhausted ourselves. But I had a good excuse. I told her about my meeting with Knappenberger and she laughed.

"They'll be knocking on my door to arrest you," she said.

"What for?"

"Well if he's really dead, it'll be manslaughter or maybe even murder," she joked.

"He's not dead. That's the way he looks all the time, the fucking creep."

"Tut! Tut! Mind that language. You know what I told you. You swear too much."

"Too fuckn bad."

"No, really. I mean it. People get upset, especially if they don't know you."

"They should be broad minded like all the people I know back home."

"You mean the old pub."

"Yair."

"But there's a time and place for everything," she says, taking a big drag on her smoke, then blowing it out over my bare belly, blowing hard enough to tickle my mound of hair down there, my prick feeling like it's about to jump out of the jungle.

"You're right." And I'm on to her.

But she holds back. "You know, she says, "I promised Grimesy last night that I'd talk to you."

"About what?"

"Iris. He told me all about it. You have to get past it. You have to find out what happened to her."

"He shouldn't have told you."

"Hey, the three of us, we're all great lovers, aren't we? Isn't that what we agreed? There's no secrets."

"He hasn't told me what you're like in bed with him," I say, a devilish grin, and my fingers creeping to places she taught me.

"Well, that's a bit different. Besides, we don't have to talk about that. We find that out when we're in bed with each other. So what about it?"

"What?"

"Iris. Promise me you'll go to the Alfred tomorrow."

"I'll promise only after we're done. You have to make it worth my while."

"It's for your own good."

"Yair, I know. And so are you."

*

You wouldn't believe it. I phoned up the Alfred Hospital and asked them if Iris was there and they said someone called Iris had been there, but they weren't sure what happened to her. They remembered her because her card didn't have her last name on it, so they'd made one up. They called her Iris Grey. I knew right away that it had to be her. It was the colour of her eyes, and those of Swampy's sheep.

They told me it was an easy walk to The Alfred. I just needed to walk across Albert Park from my flat. So I grabbed my kitbag and walked out to Beaconsfield Parade—just in time to see Dr. Pulcher pull up in his red mini minor.

"James," he said, "looks like you are on your way out."

"Yes, Dr. Pulcher. I'm on my way to the Alfred hospital to see my sister."

"Oh. I hope it's not too serious."

"No. Just a little accident she had. Do you want to come in?"

"Well, I wanted to arrange a time for my *Latina Vulgaris* seminar."

"OK. That should be fun," I said, "come inside and I'll get you a beer or something. Don't have any sherry, I'm sorry."

To tell you the truth, he didn't look like Dr. Pulcher. I was used to him being all buttoned up with his suit and vest, open collar and cravat. Instead, he was in very short shorts like the footballers wear, and they were really tight, and a thin sleeveless t-shirt that was as tight as skin. It was a cool day. He must have been cold.

"Yes," he said, seeing I was eyeing him off, "the jolly forecast said a hot day, but as usual in Melbourne you never know what it's going to be like."

I turned and we went into the flat. I did have some whiskey, or at least, Grimesy did. He was partial to the stuff.

"Would you like a glass of scotch?"

"That would be excellent. And Johnny Walker too, I see."

"Well, a mate of mine brought it. I only drink beer myself," I lied. "I don't have any ice, I'm sorry."

"No problem James. I prefer it that way."

I handed him the scotch and I opened a bottle of beer for myself. We clinked glasses and we stood there in the middle of the room looking at each other. His lips were fluttering again. Things were a bit awkward. He downed the scotch in one gulp, and I'd made him a big one too, then he grabbed my arm, the one without the beer of course, and gently pulled me towards him.

"You know, James," he said, "when I read your exam that time, on Ovid, I knew we would be kindred spirits. It was the kind of translation I'd often thought of writing but wasn't game."

"Gees, thanks Dr. Pulcher." I took a nervous sip of my beer, "but I think you already told me that a couple of times."

"Well, that's because I really mean it. And your comments in Lepidus's class were hilarious." He slid his hand from my arm to the side of my belly and started rubbing it.

"Gees, I think I really upset him. I shouldn't have done it, but I can't help myself."

"I can see that," he said, "yes I can see it." And now he was stroking me more, his hand moving downwards, following Kate's path. I moved quickly away to the kitchen and he followed.

"Let's have another drink." I poured him another scotch.

"Salut!" he said and downed the scotch. "I'll have another," he said.

So I gave him the bottle. He took a big swig and slammed it down on the kitchen counter. I took a swig of my beer, a pretty big swig, because it had at last dawned on me what was going on. Dr. Pulcher came up close, his fluttering lips forming words I didn't want to hear. He stroked the side of my face, caressed me down below, and to my horror, my body started thinking he was Kate! I'd beaten Sugar up for less than this.

"Dr. Pulcher!" I muttered, "Please!"

"Let's go to the bedroom," he said as he grabbed me and licked his rippling lips

"Gees, the bed's not made," was all I could say.

*

I showed Grimesy the almost empty bottle of scotch and told him about Pulcher. Because of Kate, there were no secrets between us.

"Shit!" said Grimesy with a big grin, "you've turned into a frigging male prostitute!"

"Yair, well. I thought you were a homo when I first met you," I said.

"Shit, Chooka. How could you think that?"

"It's obvious. Didn't the blokes in the bar at the old pub call out 'poofda' when you walked in?"

"They did look at me funny. I was scared most of the time."

"Grammar school boys all look like homos to us," I said with a grin.

"But no more," said Grimesy with satisfaction.

"I'm not a homo, fuck you!" I complained.

"Of course, you're not. You're just earning a decent living. So, what are you going to do?"

"It was only one time, and fuckn awful. I can't stand his breath. It smells like old socks. What can I do?"

"You could get out of his flat for a start."

"Yair, but where will I go? Kate doesn't want me there all the time—and nor do you, naturally."

"You're right, there," said Grimesy with satisfaction.

"Besides, if I say 'no' I'll never pass Latin and I'll be done for."

"Are you going to tell Kate?"

"Shit no! And don't you tell her either! She'd tell me to fuck off if she knew."

"Yes, you're right. Then I'd have her all to myself," he mused, teasing me.

"Asshole. You know you could never satisfy her. She'd dump you too."

"I suppose you're right."

"Then you're going to service your good professor?"

"Trouble is, I'm scared I'll pummel him to death."

"But you don't mind the sex?" says Grimesy, teasing again.

"Smart ass! Don't be an asshole."

"You'd really beat him up?"

"I've done it before." I looked at Grimesy hard.

Grimesy frowned. "You don't seem like that kind of person," he said, pensively.

*

Thank God for Kate, that's all I can say. She had a relative, her auntie, I think, at Prince Alfred hospital who agreed to help me out. She was a nurse and a real nice one at that, but pretty old, probably should have been retired. She used to work the emergency room, said Kate, but it got too much for her so now she works on helping out with lost files and other kinds of stuff that go wrong in the huge place with lots of patients and nurses and doctors strutting around the place. It took me a while to find her office, but I eventually found it, tucked away in the basement, right next to the morgue.

"G'day. I'm James," I said poking my head in the door.

"G'day James," she said with a big smile. She was one of those people who's smiling all the time, no matter what. I liked her a lot right away. "I'm Frieda. Kate's told me all about you."

"Everything?" I said with a grin.

"Well, not quite, I'm sure," she laughed. "Now let's get down to it."

"So you've found her?" I asked.

"I'm afraid not. It just gets more mysterious the more I look into it."

"But she was here, though, right?"

"Right, it seems she was, under the name of Iris Grey, but you know that already. Now the trail's run cold. If she were in this building, I'd have found her by now. I've searched all the usual places and nothing. I even asked my friend next door who is the admitting officer for the morgue if she remembered anyone of Iris's description coming in, but she didn't. And there was nothing in her records either. I phoned the Geelong Hospital and there was no record of Iris's parents being there the night she was admitted. There were medical procedures for which her parents' signature would be required. There would be a record of that if either of them were there."

"But I was there on that night and I talked with them right there."

"As I said, strange."

"But her last name is Devlin, right? They had that down, didn't they?"

"No. Her card was blank on that score. It simply read, 'Iris' and that was it. It was the name that the ambulance driver had put down in the log."

"Didn't anyone check with the record of births and deaths somewhere?"

"That's kept in the Victorian Archives on Collins Street. They won't give out information over the phone and we don't have staff to run around Melbourne looking for a name."

"Wouldn't she have been born at Geelong hospital? It's the only one in Geelong."

"I asked them that too. There was no record of her birth at the hospital. They estimated she was between 15 and 17 years old. They looked over all the records covering those years. Nothing."

"She was born somewhere else then?"

"I'd say so."

I sat down on an old wooden chair by Frieda's little desk, hoping in a silly way that if I stayed there long enough Frieda would suddenly find something out. "I don't know what to do next. I've got to find her." Unbelievably, there were tears in my eyes, tears that I didn't think I had in me anymore.

"You need to go to the Victorian Archives. That's the only way you will find out who she really is."

Iris, you could really help me here, my love, love of my life, I thought to myself. Where the hell are you? And now, a question I'd never thought of before, who the hell are you? I looked away, and dear old Frieda—I felt I'd known her forever—came around and put one hand on my shoulder.

"Here's a copy of her file," she said, "at least you have that." She handed me a one page photocopy, you know, the old white on black copy on real thin paper. "It doesn't say much, but it does say when she was admitted at least. The mystery is that the discharge date isn't filled in. It's as if she just disappeared."

"Run away!" I said, "that's what she did! That's what she always did and I bet she slipped through the window of her ward.!"

"Well, she probably couldn't have done that because hardly any of them open. If she did run away, then she would have to steal someone's clothes and simply walk out the front door."

I sprang up, excited by my discovery. To my amazement, I gently gave Frieda a little kiss on her wrinkly old cheek and said, "thanks luv! You're the best!"

"Good luck!" she called, touching her cheek.

I bounded out of the Alfred and headed straight for the Victorian Archives on Collins Street. A kind of frenzy came over me. I spent three days searching the registry of births for 1935 through 1945. I missed all my lectures and tutorials. I never went back to the flat. I just found some doorway where I could sleep, wake up, get a cup of tea first thing, and then back to work. By the third day the stuffy officials were getting suspicious. They looked at me like I was mad. And maybe I was. I certainly must have smelled something awful. But I was determined to find out who Iris was, or I should say, is. In the end, at closing time, an important looking bloke came up to me and told me I could not come back any more. He made the mistake of grabbing my hand while I was turning the crank in the microfilm machine. I tensed up, and he immediately got the message and let go. He's lucky I didn't clock him one. But thanks to Kate, I held it back. It was then that I finally came to my senses. There was only one possible conclusion: that Iris hadn't been born! At least not officially.

It was getting dark outside, the sky bearing down, dense, wet Melbourne clouds. I was last out the door and the official loudly locked it after me. I tried to pull my old school blazer around my shoulders to keep out the chill. I'd slept in it the last three nights.

I slid down the wall, in the corner of the doorway, squatting, feeling like a beggar. I wasn't sure I could make the walk across Albert Park to the flat. A light drizzle set in. Cars were honking, splashing through puddles, sending up sheets of water that landed on the old white tiles of the entrance. Gees Iris, I don't know why I'm doing this. I could just as easily forget all about you. I'm having a good time at uni and I can't imagine you being there with me. I don't know how you'd fit in. But I just can't feel right without you and I know I should have tried harder to be with you after you got sick. But truly, the bastards wouldn't let me get near you and besides I only found out all about your shit-head mother and father after you were taken into Geelong hospital and then sent away without me. Tank and Flo. What shits they've been to you. I'm going to keep talking to you, Iris, and maybe if I talk enough you'll talk to me too and tell me where you are.

7. Family lies and family cant

Eddie Counter had never taken a day off since he became licensee of the Corio Shire pub in 1952. He was proud of the work he had done to build the business, not that there was any shortage of customers. Sundays were the only days he could take off, but there was so much to do checking the inventory, cleaning the beer pipes, patching up the old building that was crumbling away, keeping up with the accounts.

He would leave Sugar to look after the pub while he was in Melbourne for the day. Since Jimmy had left, he had become more and more dependent on Sugar who was a loyal employee and he had gradually groomed him to take over much of the day to day running of the pub, especially the counting of the day's takings and watching over the accounts. The truth was that he felt responsible for Sugar's dreadful beating suffered at the hands of Jimmy and kicked himself for not anticipating the whole awful business. It happened because he was trying to do the right thing by his old mate, by looking after his son, or more accurately "their" son as he thought of it.

So, Saturday night after all the barmen left, he and Sugar had a long talk, interspersed with a few whiskeys, about Sugar's promotion. He would take over all the management of the barmen, dealing with their usual squabbles and complaints, watch over the inventory and the quick hands of the barmen to cut down on pilfering, do the daily balance of the cash registers, and supervise the cleaning of the pub by the women. In return Mr. Counter increased his weekly pay by ten pounds, a big raise that Sugar definitely appreciated. Further, Mr. Counter would not charge anything for his meals or his room. He would live in the pub for free. Mrs. Counter had complained that this was far too generous, but Eddie had insisted. It was the least he could do to make up for the lasting damage Jimmy had done to the poor wretch. He still needed his walking stick and likely would have it the rest of his life.

He kissed his wife lightly on the cheek, shook hands with Sugar and said good bye. This seemed very much overdone since he was only driving up to Melbourne for the day. It was not as if he were going away for a long time. Or at least he hoped it would be only for the day, but he did not know where Jimmy was and was taking a punt on visiting his mother in Yarraville, hoping that Jimmy had looked her up and stayed in touch at least with her. Jimmy had filled him with such disappointment. He had heard nothing of him since he left so abruptly. That bloke Paul Grimes had dropped by, a grammar school kid of all things, but had revealed nothing of Jimmy's doings, except that he was "doing great" at the uni, which he took with a grain of salt. All the bloke would talk about was where Iris was, and nobody knew, not even her parents when he got them in to talk with Grimes. And he had to move mountains to get Tank and Flo to show up at the pub together to talk to Grimes who had no idea what had gone on, as far as he could make out.

Grimes asked for any letters for Jimmy and he handed them over with some hesitation. And now, after a couple more letters had arrived the Education Department, they suddenly stopped and were followed by a registered letter. He opened it and found a summons for Jimmy to appear before a magistrate on account of fraudulent cashing of checks. He opened the other letters and found checks made out to James Henderson. The little bugger had cashed them, but had not shown up at Teachers College and it had taken them all this time to find this out! He would have to fix it. After all, someone there had buggered things up, so they should be more than happy to make the problem go away. It would require a personal visit to the Education Department in Melbourne. "Someone has to talk some sense into him," he said to his wife, "or he's going to end up in gaol."

*

Mr. Counter rolled up in front of the little cream painted terrace house, single story, black wrought iron fence, corrugated iron roof painted dark red, front windows filled with white lace curtains. It was a modest house, not much wider than the length of his new Humber now carefully parked in front. There were empty blocks on both sides, barren blocks, full of grey rocky outcrops, ubiquitous scotch thistles, and, he would bet, full of rabbits and enough tiger snakes to eat them. He sat in the car, unsure, even nervous. The fact was, he didn't know what reception he would get. Her sister held tight with the secret, a secret that had been carried to Harry's grave. Young Jimmy, when he made that crack in front of his wife had come closer to the truth than he knew. But he didn't know. He couldn't know. Harry didn't know either. Or if he did, he never showed it or wouldn't admit it. Or maybe he didn't want to know. In any event, there was no way to really know, and in the long run it didn't make a lot of difference since he had been as good a Dad to young Jimmy as was Harry, which admittedly wasn't saying much.

He gathered up a couple of bottles of beer and a bottle of Crème de Menthe and walked quickly up to the front door, bending under an English drizzle that swept through the vacant blocks keeping the rabbits in their burrows. He had no time to ring the door bell, because it suddenly opened, and Connie stepped out, a frilly apron fluttering in the cold breeze, her face long and serious.

"Well, g'day Connie," he said and stepped up to give her a little peck on her cold cheek.

"You'd better get going," she said. "Vi"s not feeling too good."

"Gees, it's the first day I've taken off since I took over the pub, and I've come here to see you two."

"That's a big fib, Eddie and you know it," she said, a faint smile appearing at the corners of her mouth, a thin mouth, an unhappy mouth.

"Come on, we haven't had a proper talk for years and it's time we did. You wouldn't even stop to talk the day of Harry's funeral."

"There was no talking to be done. You'd best go."

"I need to talk to Violet. It's about young Jimmy."

"Who else would it be about? That little bugger has caused so much trouble for everyone around him."

"I know, I know, and I can tell you, he's caused me a lot more trouble than anyone else."

"That's your fault. You've turned him into an alcoholic like his no-hoper father."

"Christ, Connie, stop it! Please, let me come in and we can have a drink and try to sort things out."

"She doesn't want to talk. You stole her son and her husband. She's got nothing."

"She's got me."

"Yair, a lot of use you are."

"She could have had me fair and square, and she chose not to. You know that."

Connie crossed her arms and took a step toward him. "Get the shit out of it," she snarled. Eddie stepped to the side and said, "I'm going in." He elbowed his way past her and barged through the door.

The kitchen was all the way at the back of the long passage. There was a light on, so Eddie made for it, chased by Connie, the corners of her mouth turned down so far, her cheeks hung almost to her chin.

He strode into the kitchen and placed the bottles of beer and Creme de Menthe on the table. It was an old wooden table, oval, polished and stained in a dark cherry, covered by a creamy white lace tablecloth. Violet sat at the end, sipping a cup of tea. Eddie leaned over and gave her a light kiss on her cheek, a cheek the same colour as her sister's, but full, more nourished, even youthful.

"So you've finally come," she mumbled.

"I had to. It's Jimmy…"

"So now you can leave." She took a sip of her tea. Her sister went to the oven and peeped in.

"It's hot in here," Eddie said, staring at the oven.

"The scones will be done in a few more minutes," said Connie, "shall I make another pot of tea?"

"He's not staying," answered Vi.

"I am, and look, I brought you your favourite, Creme de Menthe. Remember how you used to go for that when we were…"

"Courting," said Vi.

"Yes, right," said Eddie as he sat down on a chair across from her.

"What's he done now?" she asked.

"Well, I don't know yet," said Eddie.

"Then why are you here?"

"Because I thought you might know where he was…"

"How would I know? He hates me and my sister like we were the worst witches in the world."

"…because I gave him your address and told him to come visit you. In fact, I hoped he might stay with you while he was at uni."

"What? He's at uni?"

"That's right. Seems he got accepted at Melbourne uni. He started a few weeks ago."

"I don't believe it. Are you sure?"

"Yes. One of his mates, a grammar school kid, dropped in at the pub and told me he's doing great."

"I don't believe it, Eddie. You'd believe anything, wouldn't you, Eddie? Anything Jimmy told you, you'd believe."

Eddie had just about enough of this abuse. He gritted his teeth and muttered, "that's because he's my son, and I love him, just as I loved his father."

There was a crash. Connie dropped the tray of scones as she took them out of the oven. "Oh, shit! Look what you made me do!" she cried.

"What are you talking about?" cried Vi. "You killed his father with the booze, and then you started little Jimmy on the same path. Do you call that love?"

"You up and left them both to fend for themselves. The boy was only twelve. I gave him the support of a father when his father could not."

"That's right, his father."

"Except that you know the truth, Vi. Jimmy's mine, I know it."

"Rubbish. He's an alcoholic like his dad, and you helped them both on their way."

"Jimmy's not an alcoholic. In fact, he's on the wagon. He's been a teetotaller for several weeks, I know for sure, because I sat with him through the DTs."

"Scone anyone?" asks Connie.

"He's my son, and you are his mother. Now act like it," lectured Eddie, shocked at his aggressive tone.

"He doesn't look like you," she sneered.

"He looks like you, though, and not at all like your former husband, bless him."

Connie plunks down a scone plastered with butter in front of him. Eddie reaches for the Crème de menthe and unscrews the top. "You got any liqueur glasses?" he asks, "this is better than tea."

"Anyway, Jimmy hasn't been here. He'll never forgive me for walking out. I know that. But I had no choice. I couldn't live with the two of them and watch his father drink himself to death and his son go the same way. A woman and mother can only stand so much."

"You can't blame her, Eddie, you really can't. You must see that," said Connie.

"I'm not blaming anyone. What's done is done. I'm trying to get you two to help me take care of my, our, son. All is not lost, though it's possible he may be a bit lost, and that's not unusual for young blokes these days."

"All right Eddie," said Vi with a sigh, "then why are you here? What has brought this on? If Jimmy's at uni, isn't that good news? He's gone further than any of us expected."

"I was hoping he may have contacted you. I'm worried about him on several counts. First, he's a hot headed little bugger with a violent temper. I got him out of a couple of tight spots at the pub when he bashed a couple of blokes up. I'm worried he may have too much freedom at the uni. He's not really old enough to go there, in my opinion. He would have been better off at Teachers College, where he should have gone, by the way, as they were paying him the studentship money every couple of weeks. But he took the money and didn't show up. And that's the second problem. I opened a registered letter he received accusing him of fraudulent cashing of the checks. He could go to gaol for that, you know. So, I have to track him down and sort it out. There's a lot of other stuff I could tell you about, but that's enough. If he stayed with you, he would at least have some adult supervision and hopefully guidance at times when he was on the edge, which is often, drink or no drink."

Silence overtook the kitchen. Connie put down the glasses and Eddie filled them with the bright green liqueur. The perfume filled the kitchen, floating on the hot air of the oven. All three grabbed their glass and took a large sip.

"Once I find him, can I tell him that you would love to have him stay with you for as long as he goes to the uni?"

The sisters looked at each other, and nodded.

"Thank you, girls. I know it's a big commitment. The only trouble is that first I have to track him down, and second, I have to convince him to stay with you. And third, I have to find someone in the education department so I can make the fraud accusation go away. And there, I thought that maybe you, Connie, might be able help, since you work for the education department, don't you?"

"Eddie, I can't do that. I'm in teacher placement, anyway, not the bursary department or whatever it's called."

"Maybe you can suggest someone I can call on?"

"Let me think about it."

"And while you're thinking, I need one more favour. Can I stay here the night? Then I can get started at the university first thing, and if all goes well, I can drop Jimmy off here."

"Eddie, it's so good of you to want to do all this. But don't you see? He will refuse to come here. What uni student would want to live with his mother and her sister?"

"I know, I know. But I have to try. Even if he stayed with you for a few weeks, it would be better than nothing."

*

Sugar hung up the phone, a satisfied look on his face. He had received instructions on opening up the pub on Monday morning, the barmen's shifts, till drawers checked and inserted. Everything he already knew, but he listened dutifully to Mr. Counter. Mrs. Counter had poked her head in the little office and asked him if everything was all right for the morning. Of course, it was. Though he hadn't told Eddie, or anyone else, that he suspected someone was using Chooka's old room. Even though Chooka (thankfully) made it very clear he was gone for good, it seems that Abbie went in there every morning after he left, and lately could be heard talking. For a while, Sugar just thought that it was Abbie pretending Chooka was still there because she loved the spoiled young brute, and Sugar couldn't stand it. But a couple of nights recently he thought he heard a window open.

Monday morning came and he positioned himself in charge of the old bar and serving the Snake Pit out the back door. The usual characters showed up, though he did miss Millie. It was too bad what happened to her and the bastard who did it, undoubtedly that shit Chooka, should get what was coming to him. Unfortunately, when Sugar talked with the Preacher the other night, they had come to a bit of a dead end. Tank was seen visiting Millie's about the time the cops think she was killed. Tank had tried to shove it off on to Chooka who everyone knew had threatened to kill Millie that night when he was in the hospital waiting room. But there was no evidence to prove otherwise, and anyway, Spuds had spoken up saying that he was with Chooka that night at the migrant hostel.

Then in comes Little Linda and her brat.

"The usual, Sugar, and make it quick!"

"O.K. Linda, me luv, anything for you," says Sugar.

Sugar hands her the beer and whiskey chaser and then says to the brat, "you want a lemon squash?"

Linda is already on her way to the Snake Pit, but to everyone's surprise, the brat stops and looks up at Sugar.

"What's that for," she asks, pointing to Sugar's walking stick.

"It's for beating cheeky little girls," Sugar says as he hands the brat a small lemon squash.

"Where's Chooka? I want him to give it to me," says the brat with a pout.

"You want the lemon squash or not, you little shit?"

The brat snatches the glass from his hand and gulps down the drink.

"I know where he is anyway," she says.

"What do you mean? He doesn't work here anymore."

"I know where he i-s, I know where he i-is-," she sings.

"Yair? Where?"

"I saw him at Millie's." She runs off down the passage to the Snake Pit.

"When?" Sugar calls after her. But there's no answer.

Sugar grabbed his walking stick and limped down to the office to phone the Preacher.

*

After several phone calls to the university, Eddie determined that Jimmy had indeed registered as a student, but his whereabouts as far as the university was concerned were unknown. When he arrived at the Registrar's office at the university they did tell him the subjects Jimmy was enrolled in, so that he could meet up with him by going along to one of the tutorials or lectures. That would have been a bit too much even for Mr. Counter who, although he had been educated as far as fourth form and had done a couple of years at the Gordon Technical College, was as overwhelmed by the university as was his "son" Jimmy.

He had more luck with the Education Department, thanks to Connie's efforts. She gave him specific instructions on how to get to the Department and who to ask for. When he produced a handful of uncashed checks and the registered letter threatening prosecution, he was quickly ushered into a tiny office shared by two people who were poring over stacks of papers. A withered little man looked out at him over tiny round spectacles.

"Please be seated Mr. Counter. I understand you have some money for us?"

"Yes. There's been a bit of a misunderstanding. My son, I mean my adopted son, is going through a difficult period, and he, er, forgot to show up at Teachers' College."

"I'm sorry to hear that. He must be a troubled boy. Usually they are breaking their necks to get to Teachers' College, they have such a marvellous time," the withered man smiled, a glint in his eye.

"So I've heard. Anyway, I wanted to express how sorry I am for this mess-up and that I didn't know he had cashed some of the checks. If I can make it up to you blokes in any way to avoid any more trouble, that would be best for us all, I should think."

"What is your line of work, Mr. Counter?"

"I'm a publican."

"I see. And what is James doing now?"

"Well, he was working in my pub for a while, but now he's at the uni."

"He chose that instead of Teachers' College?"

"Seems like it."

"He must be very bright, then."

"Don't know about that. He hasn't been acting like it lately."

The clerk made some calculations on a sheet of paper and then turned it around so Mr. Counter could read it.

"He owes the Education Department fifty-four pounds, eleven shillings and sixpence."

"Then I'd like to pay you that amount, and a bit more to cover processing costs perhaps, and then you would not proceed with the prosecution?"

The clerk did not look up, but remained staring at the sheet of paper with the amount on it.

"I don't think it would be right to charge you a processing fee. The mistake was as much our fault as his. We obviously should have known much sooner that he did not attend Teachers' College."

"Very good, then," smiled Eddie as he pulled out his check book."

"Ah, cash would be more suitable. Easier to process," muttered the clerk, still looking down at his paper."

"Of course." Eddie was well prepared for it. He produced a large roll of bills, many crumpled and damp from beer, and counted out fifty-five pounds. "This should do it then?"

"Excellent, Mr. Counter. That will be fine."

"Do I get a receipt?"

"If you want one, but I assure you it is not necessary."

"OK, then. And if you're down Geelong any time, please drop in and see me at the Corio Shire Hotel and I'll make you most welcome."

"Good day to you sir."

*

Dopey and the Preacher showed up at closing time, as usual. The Preacher left Dopey to round up the drunks and get them out of the pub, while he went and talked to Sugar.

"So, the boss isn't back yet, I presume in consequence?" he asked.

"Not yet," smiled Sugar, "I'm expecting him late tonight. He had business in Melbourne."

"Aiding and abetting that pugilistic delinquent son of his, I presume in consequence?"

"I couldn't tell you that. He was visiting his old girlfriend, and the little pugilist's mother."

"He knows where that son of the devil is, then?"

"Don't think so. Nobody does. He was going to bring him back with him, if he found him at his mother's place. But he wasn't expecting to."

Mrs. Counter appeared in the passageway. "He's on his way home now. He didn't manage to find Jimmy. But he did find out that Jimmy is registered at Melbourne University."

"That is information, I do regard seriously, and find it of much consequence," said the Preacher.

"You'll follow up that lead, then?" asked Sugar, that smirk well and truly back on his face.

"Taking care and following exact procedure, it is that I have already done so."

"You'll wait till Eddie gets here, then?"

"Is it possible that events suggest that Tank and Flo are in the Snake Pit?"

"It's possible, but they aren't. Neither is Linda, if that's who you want to see," said Sugar.

"Then after we have taken care of victuals and sustenance — I'll have a small beer if you don't mind and none for Dopey who has to make an arrest tonight—we shall proceed to our destination and wrap up the case."

"You mean you've solved the murder?"

"Of which are you referring, Mr. Sugar?"

"Millie's, you silly bastard, there's only one, isn't there?"

"I am not at liberty to discuss such police business in detail, sir. Now if you don't mind, fill up my glass."

*

I took the long way back to the flat. If Iris had run away, where would she go? She'd be homeless, so I decided that she'd be doing what I've been doing this last couple of nights. Sleeping in doorways or under bridges. I walked all around the shops and streets of Melbourne, looking in every doorway, but found her nowhere. I went under Swanston Street bridge, and looked in all the nooks and crannies at Flinders Street Station, and found lots of homeless blokes, but no women among them. Not one. When I asked if they'd seen Iris, they looked at me like I was an idiot. Exhausted, I finally staggered into my flat, only to find Kate and Grimesy there, waiting for me.

"Where the hell have you been?" asked Kate, "we've been worried sick about you. Frieda said you'd rushed out like a mad dog."

"I've been in the archives of births and deaths, that's where."

"For three days straight?" asked Grimesy, incredulous.

"Yair. Couldn't be bothered coming all the way back here to sleep, so I slept in a doorway somewhere in Collins Street."

"You're nuts," said Kate, "and that's a professional diagnosis!"

"Yair, funny." I pushed past them to the bedroom.

"What did you find out?" they asked in unison.

James could not answer. He was asleep.

8. With a little slit in the tail

When I awoke, Kate was still there, asleep on the sofa. Grimesy had gone. She looked up and said, "you look like shit. Get into the shower and have a shave for God's sake." She turned over and buried her face in the sofa. I did what I was told.

Shaved and showered, I emerged from the bathroom, naked, standing before Kate stretched out on the couch. She rolled over and reached out her hand, running her fingers in circles around what was now a throbbing piece of meat. Down I went, and when it was done, she sat up and sat astride me. It reminded me of Iris and I was embarrassed, but it brought me to my senses.

"We have to have a talk," she said, leaning forward, her nose touching mine, her eyes seeing through me.

"A professional talk?" I said, joking, but scared she was going to tell me we were through.

"More or less. I don't want to act like your mother, but..."

"I have no mother," I interjected.

"So you've told me. I'm going to have to play that role, then, and you know what that means, don't you?"

"What exactly?" I asked.

"Mothers aren't supposed to sleep with their sons," she said with a superior smile.

"You're not my mother, thank goodness."

"But for the moment I am," she said as she got off me and started to dress, "and you need to get some clothes on too. We can't have a mother and son talk while we're naked."

I don't often burst out laughing, unless I'm drunk, but I did then. The whole idea of me sitting naked with my mother just seemed hilarious. But I did what I was told.

"If we're going to keep seeing each other, there's got to be one rule," she said.

"Oh hell! A fuckn rule."

"Yes. And there's only one."

"Which is?"

"You go to all your lectures and tutes and keep up with your work."

"And if I don't?"

"We're through."

I went to the fridge and pulled out a beer. "You want one?" I asked, but she shook her head.

"No thanks, and neither do you. It's too early. Put it back."

I did what I was told, yet again. "Shit, you really mean it," I said.

"I do. And what's more, Grimesy agrees. You probably haven't noticed, but Paul does really well in his subjects. He's going to be a top lawyer one day. You could do the same if you put your mind to it."

"What's Grimesy got to fuckn do with it? The fuckn stuck-up grammar school boy."

"I don't think you mean that. He's a good mate to you, he's shown you the ropes right from the first day we met on the train. And he didn't mind me taking you on."

My cheeks and ears were bright red, I was sure. She was right. I didn't mean it. I looked at her, a silly grin on my face, stuck for words. "We've got a good thing going," I said.

"We do. We're a great threesome. I'd hate for you to mess it up."

She held out her arms and I walked into them and she embraced me. I felt wanted and realized that it was what I had been looking for all this time. It was what I had gotten, raw and unsullied, from Iris.

*

The other students in my Latin tutorial were much better than me. It was a real struggle for me to translate the sentence when it came to my turn. I had to memorize the translations before the tute, and the trouble was that Lepidus would sometimes make a student do an extra sentence, so I had to count forward again to the sentence that would be mine. I found the work, though, satisfying, in a way quite like the satisfaction I had when poring through all the archives for those manic three days. I had thought it was because I was doing the work to find Iris, but now I wondered if it was the work itself that gave such satisfaction.

I slaved away and attended my lectures and tutes, and wonderful Kate continued the regular trysts with Grimesy and me. I had only one problem and that was professor Pulcher. Every now and then, unannounced, he would show up at the flat, and I would have to accommodate him. I even asked Kate for her advice, half

scared that she would say that there was no way she'd share me
with a poofda like Pulcher. But she didn't. She just looked at me
and said, "sometimes we have to do nasty things to preserve our
good life," then added with a mischievous smile, "and even those
nasty things can have a pleasant benefit." When I asked her what
she meant, she replied with a knowing smile, "there are no bad
orgasms, are there?"

*

There were six of us, including Dr. Pulcher and even Lepidus my
tutor, sitting in a circle on the floor of my flat. I felt really stupid,
dressed in a sheet that was supposed to be a toga, nothing on
underneath. I even shaved off some of the hair from my forehead
to depict Caesar's baldness. Caesar, of course, was my character,
I worshipped him for his lasciviousness. Dr. Pulcher was himself,
more or less, dressed as Nicomedes, which made me his bum boy.
Lepidus had put together a gladiator's outfit complete with a
helmet that covered his entire head, and tight leather pants and a
kind of leather brassiere around his well-tanned very hairy chest.
The rest were girls, none of them especially pretty, all wearing
wispy dresses tied loosely under their breasts, flowers in their
hair, a couple combed long and hanging, the others coiffed up,
trying to mimic the pictures we'd all seen in our *Latin for Today*
books in high school. They did say who they were, one of them
Livia, but to be honest, I didn't pay much attention. I never found
the Roman women of much interest. And then there was Grimesy
who had pleaded with me to let him come, and I was surprised
when Dr. Pulcher agreed without any argument whatsoever.
Grimesy had, of course, taken Latin 1 a couple of years ago, so
he knew Lepidus, though had not actually met Dr. Pulcher. He
came as the lawyer Cicero, of course, who else? And he too had
one of my sheets wrapped loosely around him. His role, though,
was to remain in the kitchen supplying us with booze whenever
it was needed.
      We were playing spin the bottle. Dr. Pulcher would spin it, then
whoever it pointed to, had to write a vulgar Latin expression on
a flash card. The bottle was spun again, and whoever it pointed
to had to translate the expression. If either got it wrong,
misspelling or miss-translation, they had to remove a piece of
clothing. The very first spin, the bottle came to rest aimed at me,
who else? This is what I wrote:
      edicaba ego vos et irrumaba

"I knew you'd pick that one," laughed Lepidus. "Who knows where it is from?" he asked. Dr. Pulcher put up his hand, grinning. "You don't count," laughed Lepidus.

Dr. Pulcher spun the bottle, and it stopped in front of a wispy girl, who was very quiet in our tute, but she always got her translations exactly right. She was Lepidus's favourite, without a doubt.

"It's the first line in Catullus 16," she said, embarrassed, looking down. "It says, 'I will sodomize you and you can suck me off'."

"Brava!" cried Dr. Pulcher, "perfect!"

"But," she said, looking up and staring at me, "he didn't write it properly. It's edicabo, not edicaba. The same for irrumaba."

Everyone yelled "Oooooo!" or something like that and they pointed at me, chanting, "Toga off! Toga off!"

Grimesy came out of the kitchen and primed everyone's drink and then he joined in, "Toga off! Toga off!"

I was about to drop my toga when there was a huge crash. In that instant, a large body clad in a copper's uniform hurtled through the door, landing in the middle of our circle, bits of the door flying as far as the kitchen. The girls screamed and ran into the kitchen. They could not run out the door because framed in the doorway was the tall silhouette of none other than The Preacher, holding his bible in one hand, and a large envelope in the other. Peeping around the silhouette was a small hairy fellow with a rough beard, holding up a camera which flashed several times. I looked down at the floor and saw Dopey rolling around, trying to stand up, looking very pleased with himself.

The Preacher held up his bible and pronounced, "you have sinned against the Lord who is my shepherd at this moment in history, a moment of consequence."

Dr. Pulcher, stripped down to his now familiar tight footy shorts, stepped into the kitchen, which by now was getting pretty crowded. "What is the meaning of this, officer? You have interrupted a Latin seminar of the University of Melbourne, and I am Professor Pulcher, chair of Classics and Antiquity."

Dopey, trying to extricate himself from the tattered remains of the door, managed to stand upright and his huge rotund body now filled half the flat. The photographer sneaked past The Preacher and peeped around Dopey's huge frame. More flashes lit up the room.

"It is that I have here, as her Majesty's messenger and the voice of the Lord our God, a warrant for the arrest of one, James

Henderson. As senior constable of the Victorian Police Force, I request that such person step forward."

I was rooted to the spot, standing there starkers, having dropped the toga when Dopey came flying through the door.

"I repeat, on behalf of the Queen, would the so-named person please step forward?"

Dopey, always trying to be helpful, pointed at me and said, "there he is constable, sir!"

The Preacher ignored him. "For the last time, I request one James Henderson to step forward."

The photographer had sneaked further into the flat, leaving a small opening beside The Preacher's long legs where I could slip through if I were quick enough. I lunged for the gap, but at that moment, Dopey raised his fat arm to indicate who I was to the Preacher, thinking that the Preacher had not heard him the first time. "That's him, there, that's Chooka," he said. And before I knew it, he had his big beefy hand on my neck and I was done for.

"What is the warrant for?" asked Dr. Pulcher.

"It is that it is no business of yours, sir, and who may you be, in consequence?"

"I already told you, officer. You are interrupting an important Melbourne University seminar."

The Preacher pointedly looked around the flat. "So I see," he said, holding up his bible, "and so does the Lord."

I finally found my voice. "So what's the charge, Preacher?" I asked.

"You know what it is," said Dopey.

"It is my official duty as Her Majesty's servant, to arrest you for the murder of one Millicent Flattery on Sunday, February 10, 1957.

"Fuckn shit!" I cried, "That fuckn Tank, the bastard!"

"Watch your language, young man, in front of these girls," admonished the Preacher.

"Fuck you!" I yelled, trying to pull Dopey's hand from my neck.

"And get some clothes on. I can't arrest you dressed like that, in front of the Almighty! And you!" he pointed to Dopey, "get the names and addresses of the people in this den of iniquity!"

Dopey's grip on my neck slackened. I was able to twist around just in time to see Grimesy pulling his toga tight around his whole body, stretch his neck like a swan's, and announce:

"Hold on there. No one here is under arrest or suspicion that I have heard, that is except James, here. The police have no right to collect the names and addresses of any of the rest of us."

Dopey did not quite hear Grimesy. He was too preoccupied rummaging around in his many pockets looking for his notebook and pencil.

"And who, in the Lord's name, might you be, sir?" demanded The Preacher.

"Paul Grimes, third year law student, and doing my articles with Laub, Sampson and Grimshaw."

"I demand your name and address Mr. Grimes."

"I just told you, pretty much."

The other students started to mutter to each other, the girls to giggle. The photographer's camera flashed again.

"Are you a police photographer?" asks Grimesy.

"I am John Ferret, the official photographer for the Geelong Advertiser."

"Hand over the film. You have no permission to publish any of our photos in the Addy or anywhere else."

"Not a chance," says Ferret.

"Then I'll have to take it off you," says Grimesy.

"Are you threatening me?"

"With a law suit if you don't give it up."

"Now, in the name of the Queen, I demand that you cease and desist from this threatening behaviour," interjects The Preacher, directing his remarks to no one in particular. At this moment, though, Lepidus, of all people, the bloke I'd thought was completely spineless, jumps forward and snatches the camera out of Ferret's hands and quickly retreats to the kitchen behind our combined naked bodies. He pulls the film out of the camera and throws it across the room. Ferret, a bloke with a bushy beard and a massive crop of prematurely grey, unkempt hair, pleads for his camera and Grimesy gives it to him. Dr. Pulcher has disappeared underneath the kitchen counter. The girls are still giggling and Dopey gives up looking for his notebook and instead produces a pair of handcuffs.

The Preacher gives me a bang on the backside with his bible. "Get dressed," he says, "do not embarrass the Lord our God any longer."

9. Home of the mug

The front page of the Addy carried this article which I clipped and keep pinned to my wall:

UNI STUDENT ARRESTED FOR BLOODY NORLANE MURDER

Melbourne, March 31. Melbourne University student and former Norlane resident, James Henderson was arrested yesterday by police who tracked him down to his hideout in a flat on Beaconsfield Parade, St. Kilda. He is charged with the bloody murder on February 10, 1957 of Millicent Flattery of 25 North Shore Road, Norlane, whose beaten and defiled body was found on blood soaked sheets in her house on Monday morning by her neighbour who rang the police. Flattery was a well-known customer of the Corio Shire Hotel and was long suspected, though never charged, by police of selling her services to willing customers. Henderson, who has a history of violent outbursts, according to police, had been under surveillance for some time as the prime suspect, but could not be arrested because they had no witness who could place him at the scene of the crime. Two days ago, a witness finally stepped forward and told police that she had seen Henderson enter and leave the Flattery residence, and that he was covered in blood when he left. Police would not reveal the name of the witness. If found guilty, say police, he will face the death penalty. Henderson is being held in the Geelong Police lockup awaiting a remand hearing that will be presided over by J.P. Grace McShearn, of Manifold Heights.

*

Flo was sitting at the kitchen table chain-smoking as usual, staring at the kettle, when Tank burst in waving the paper.

"Did ya see this piece of shit?" he yelled. "They've arrested Chooka for murdering that fuckn prostitute bitch!"

"Well, he did it, didn't he?" answered Flo, still staring at the kettle, waiting for it to boil.

"No, he didn't! I fuckn know!"

"Why, because you did it?"

"Shit and fuck, Flo. Is that what you think of me, you fuckn old bag?"

"Well, you had a lot of practice beating me and Linda up, didn't you?"

"I was just keeping you in line. You don't know what a real beating's like, I tell you."

The kettle boiled and Flo stirred from her chair. She filled the teapot and sat back, waiting for it to draw. "Are you going do anything to help the little shit that raped our daughter, get off the hook then?"

"He never raped her, Flo. Get that into your stupid fuckn head, for Christ sake."

"He fuckn did. He filled her up then killed her to get rid of it."

"Shit, Flo. He didn't kill her. She went and did it all on her own. It was Millie that did it, if you want to blame someone. She deserved what she fuckn got, that's what."

"You was there, wasn't ya?"

"There? There fuckn where?"

"At Millie's. Must have been you. You're there a lot of the time, I know."

"Bullshit! It's your fuckn imagination, you silly old bitch."

Flo pours the tea, carefully holding the strainer over an old china cup, stained dark brown inside from years of use. "You want a cuppa tea?" she asks, not looking up.

"Fuck you!" says Tank and he strides out the door, waving the paper. At that moment, the brat runs in from the other room screaming, "I want me mother, where's me fuckn mother?"

Flo reaches out and grabs the kid by her arm and shakes her hard, pulling her close to her chair. "Don't you talk like that around me, you hear? I know the devil's got your tongue, but if you don't stop it, he'll make you bite your tongue off. You hear?"

Flo takes a sip of her tea, then drags the brat by the arm into her bedroom where she retrieves her bible. "Sit on the bed," she says, then starts reading:

"But the fearful, and unbelieving, and the abominable, and murderers, and whoremongers, and sorcerers, and idolaters, and all liars, shall have their part in the lake which burneth with fire and brimstone: which is the second death."

The brat squeals, "Yaaah! Yaaah!" and jumps off the bed, slaps the bible out of Flo's hand, rushes into the kitchen and knocks the cup of tea to the floor, where it shatters and tea splatters everywhere. Her mum, Little Linda, Flo's step daughter, is nowhere to be found.

*

When Linda showed up at the Snake Pit without her little brat, people noticed. And when she stopped drinking the hard stuff and quietly sipped a few beers, sitting in a corner all by herself, people noticed that too. Mrs. Counter, whose job it was to keep things under control in the Snake Pit, sat down beside her, leaned lightly on the rickety tin table and said, "Linda, luv, what's the matter?"

"Nothing's the matter except that me best friend's been murdered," Linda cried, tears in her eyes.

"I knew you and Millie were tight. But you know they've charged Chooka with the murder?"

"Yair, I know. It wasn't him, though, I'm sure. But it doesn't matter now. I'm going to have to make up for it."

"How do you mean, Linda?"

"Me little girl, brat that youse all call her, she fingered Chooka."

"I heard as much."

"But there's something you don't know."

"What?"

"Well, I might as well tell you because everyone'll find out soon."

"Yair?"

"Millie's left everything to me."

"What?

"Her house and everything, she's left to me."

"How do you know that?"

"Because we was best friends, that's why, and, well, you must know this, I was kind of her apprentice. I filled in for her when she was over booked, if you see what I mean."

"And that's where brat came from?"

"That's none of your business, is it?"

"Oh, no. I'm sorry. But I thought Millie lived from hand to mouth."

"She bought her Commission house. I bet you didn't know that!"

"I don't believe it!"

"Youse didn't know her like I did."

"That I'm sure of."

"She saved her pennies and I helped her when I could too."

"Linda, I never thought..."

"Yair, I know. I'm moving in there soon."

"But has the will, did she have a will that said you were going to get everything?"

"That's what her lawyer told me."

"She had a lawyer?"

"She had just about everyone you could imagine, wouldn't you reckon?" Linda cracked a little smile.

"I suppose so."

"Anyway, I gotta go. Checking out the house this morning."

*

Linda walked down North Shore road, free of the brat, looking to enter Millie's house, *her* house now, feeling like she was starting a new life. She would re-arrange some of the furniture, buy new beds for both bedrooms, get rid of all the bedding and start afresh. She hadn't dared go there until now, was frightened of seeing the bloody sheets they wrote about in the Addy. She and Millie had had their ups and downs, more downs than ups. That was because Linda was sure that Millie was her mum, though Millie would never admit it. And if you looked at it that way, Linda was the one, the only one, that Millie had spared, saved from the carrot juice. But the bone of contention was deeper than that. Linda would never give up nagging Millie as to who her father was. She suspected that it was Tank, since he was her best customer. But in their terrible screaming matches, Millie never once admitted any of this. As far as she was concerned, Linda was a "business partner" and nothing else.

As she turned the key in the front door, a door bearing the dints from the kicks of many men's' boots, she stopped. Listened. She heard a faint rustling noise and it was coming from Millie's bedroom. "Who's there?" she called. She stepped into the passage and heard the rustling again, then the noise of a window opening. She knew immediately who it was. "Iris! Iris, is that you? Don't run off, it's me, Linda, your big sister." The noise stopped. Linda hurried to the bedroom. It had no door. It was torn off long ago.

"You're not me fuckn sister," came the tense, thin voice.

"Iris?" Linda reached the doorway and saw Iris, standing by the window. "God in hell! You're not fuckn dead!"

"What's it fuckn look like?" says Iris, tense and hostile.

"What are you doing in here? Where's the sheets?"

"I got rid of them."

"Yer haven't been sleeping in here, have you?"

"On and off."

"Oh, Iris, I'm so glad you're OK." Linda rushed forward, arms outstretched. Iris stood, sullen. Allowed Linda to hug her, but she remained motionless.

"You're so like Flo," said Linda as she let go her hug. "So like her."

"Yair, well it's not my fault, is it?" Iris moves towards the window.

"If you're leaving, you can go out the fuckn door, you silly bugger," cries Linda, "But I don't want you to go."

"I gotta go. Gotta meet Chooka."

"Yair? I know he's been looking for you."

"Yair, well he didn't look too far, did he?"

"He went to Melbourne to find you"

"Yair? I didn't know that. But I gotta go."

"You know where he is?"

"He's at the pub, where he always is, isn't he?"

"So you haven't heard?"

"What?"

"The Preacher arrested him for murdering Millie. He's in gaol."

"Oh fuckn shit! Why'd he do that?"

"Because he blamed Millie for your death—we all thought you was dead."

Iris came back from the window. "Shit, Linda. What am I going to do?"

"Well, the first thing you should do is get yourself cleaned up and you can stay here for as long as you like. It will take me a while to get the place straightened up."

"I knew Chooka would do something like this. His temper, it was fuckn awful," said Iris.

"But he didn't do it. You should go see him right now."

"If not Chooka, who?"

"Who? Oh, but surely you can already guess."

"Yair. Tank, our dear old dad."

*

There was a timid knock at the door to Mr. Counter's office and when he spun around on his stool, Mr. Counter saw Abbie nervously standing at the door,.

"Abbie, come right in. Is there a problem or something?"

"I'm sorry to trouble you Mr. Counter, but I wasn't sure what to do."

"Do what? I'm a bit busy, trying to catch up on everything I missed by being away."

"Well, I think there's someone, er, well, we probably can guess who it is, sneaking into Jimmy's room."

"You mean…"

"I s'pose so, don't you think? It wouldn't be just anyone, would it?"

"Through the window?"

"Yes, Mr. Counter. I locked it, but whoever it is knows how to slip the catch."

"So, you think it could be Iris?"

"Has to be, don't you think? We all thought she was dead or something."

"And the bed is slept in?"

"Yair, and it's made up nicely each morning. That's what Iris used to do when she stayed there."

"The paper says they arrested Chooka for the murder," said Mr. Counter.

"Yair, but he didn't do it. He's such a nice boy. That silly cop doesn't know his ass from his elbow," Abbie said.

"Yes, but I'm not that sure about Chooka. He has a really bad temper. And that night of the miscarriage, it was a terrible night, he was capable of anything."

"I hope you don't mind my saying, Mr. Counter, but I hope you didn't say that to the cops."

"Of course not. But who could deny his bad temper? He showed it lots of times, and in public too. We've got Sugar limping around to show for it."

"I have to finish my cleaning, Mr. Counter."

"Yes. Thank you, Abbie, for letting me know. I'll keep a look-out for Iris. We all will."

10. The gaol of my boyhood

"I'm going to plead guilty," I said, looking Mr. Counter straight in the eye. The lawyer he brought along answered, "no you're not!"

"But you said you didn't do it," said Mr. Counter.

"No, I said I didn't know if I did it or not, there's a difference, Mr. Counter."

"You've only been at uni a few weeks and you're already sounding like a smart ass," said Mr. Counter. He was not happy.

"You understand," the lawyer said, "that you could get the death penalty for this?"

"So what? Iris is dead, so what's left?"

"You're not thinking straight," said Mr. Counter, "anyway, she's not dead."

"Then where is she, then? If she's not dead, she's run away and I'll never see her again. I searched for her everywhere. She doesn't exist."

"She what?' asked the lawyer, obviously thinking I had gone a bit loco.

"I searched all the government archives. There's no record of her birth or death in Victoria."

Mr. Counter made a little cough. "I wasn't going to tell you this, because I was hoping Iris would show up here and tell you what's been going on."

"Yair? Go on then. I can take it."

"She's been sleeping in your room at the pub."

"Fuckn hell!" I muttered to myself. I couldn't believe my ears. "She's what?"

"Abbie is convinced she's been getting into your room, her usual way through the window, and sleeping there off and on."

"For how long?"

"Nearly a week. Abbie didn't say when she first noticed it."

I put my head between my hands and tried to think. I needed Grimesy or Kate here to tell me what was going on, what to do.

We all fell silent. I could feel the heat coming out of Mr. Counter's ears. He'd come here to help me, got me a lawyer and everything, and I was acting like a shit-head. Mr. Counter coughed again.

"Mr. Counter. I'm sorry, I'm being a bastard. Thanks for all you're doing..."

"There's a bit more," he said.

"About Iris?"

"No. I went looking for you. I went to see your mum on the off-chance you'd gone there to stay while you settled in at uni." Mr. Counter gave the lawyer a look, and the lawyer excused himself and left.

"So, this is between you and me?" I asked.

"Yes. If I don't tell you now, there may be no other chance, and the crazy way you're thinking you could damage yourself and those who love you in ways we can't imagine."

"Only Iris loves me. Who else? Nobody."

"There's me," said Mr. Counter slowly, "there's me."

"Gees, Mr. Counter, I meant like love-love, you know?"

"Yes, I know. And there's your mum."

"Bitch. She ran out on me and my Dad."

"That was a long time ago. You could have gone with her, she wanted you to, you remember that, I hope."

"Yes. I do. I was sitting in the kitchen doing an exercise in my *Latin For Today* book. She used to help me with it. I looked up to ask her to hear my vocab, and there she was, standing in the doorway, her bag packed, and auntie Connie hanging around behind her like a bad smell. Mum was crying and she had dark rings around her eyes, they looked like they were bruises. But my Dad swore he never touched her, and I believed him."

"She didn't just up and leave. She'd talked about it for weeks, even months. It was when your Dad was starting in on the metho. There was no money to feed you, pay for your school stuff. I tried to help her as best I could. She just felt used up and it broke her heart when you wouldn't go with her. And..."

"Then she should have stayed, shouldn't she?"

"She couldn't stand watching you turn into him."

"A fuckn alky?"

"Well, we know now that you very nearly did, didn't you? And your mum heard all about your drinking after your dad died, and she blamed it on me for taking you in."

"Gees, Mr. Counter, that's not fair." Silence, and then I said, "what were you going to say before?"

"Well, your mum and I, we had an argument when I went to see her. As I said, she blamed me. But there's more to tell."

"Yes, I know. You had the hots for her and you probably had an affair, that's why you got angry with me when I kind of said so in front of Mrs. Counter that time."

"That's not quite right. I did have the hots for her, and we should have got married years ago. Your mum liked both of us, your dad and me, but I know she loved me more."

"So she married him, and you kept chasing her?"

"No. But we were together right up to her wedding, in fact she was pregnant before the wedding, which is the reason she rushed into getting married."

"So why did she choose him?"

"To this day I don't really know. All I can say is that at the time I didn't have a job to speak of. I was doing odd jobs, and your Dad he had a really good job down at the Phosphate plant. So I s'pose that's why she chose him."

"Gees, Mr. Counter. I don't understand you people. So why did you marry Mrs. Counter then?"

"Because I wanted to get married and have a family and she came along and looked just the right one that could have lots of kids."

"She doesn't look like that now."

"Nah. She'd had an abortion one time and something went wrong, so she couldn't have any more. I was fucked, as you like to say."

"So mum got married and had me, so end of story?"

"Not quite." Mr. Counter shifted in his seat. The copper outside the door peered in, sick of waiting for us to finish. There were no windows in the room. Just a table and a couple of chairs for visitors. I wasn't even handcuffed.

"So, what? What is it that you don't want to tell me?"

"That's just it. I do want to tell you, but I'm scared you'll go nuts or something."

"Mr. Counter. You know I would never touch you. You've been great to me. I say cruel things to you sometimes but I don't mean them. You know that."

"I'm not sure I do. But here goes." Mr. Counter took a deep breath and gulped. "There's every chance I'm actually your dad," he mumbled.

"You mean, my real dad? You mean I've been talking in my head to the wrong fuckn bloke all this time? I sat with some stranger holding his hand, helping him to die? And all this time you're my real dad, and not, not, that fuckn alky I thought was my Dad?"

Mr. Counter looked down, then gradually raised his eyes to look at me. He was embarrassed, that's what he was. Kate would be proud of me perceiving that. I wasn't going to make it easy for him though.

"I wouldn't quite put it like that. But yes, that's what it was," he admitted.

"You fuckn shithead asshole! You let me go on like that, even get stuck into the booze so I would keep on thinking he was my Dad, when all the time you were the bloke behind the scenes pulling the strings?"

"Your dad and me. We were best friends even when he married your mum, and I never touched her all those years. And we stayed best friends all those years."

"You expect me to believe that?"

"You can ask your mum."

"Fuck her!"

"I don't think you mean that. If you reached out to her, I think she'd come and see you."

"How do you really know I'm yours?"

"You got my blood type, which is rare and neither she or your Dad had it."

I found myself staring at him, trying to figure out if I looked like him or not.

"But the wavy, curly brown hair? You don't have that?"

"I do, but I keep it cut down to a crew cut, always have. And now it's got a bit of grey in it too."

"OK. Now I get it. My mum. She fell for your hair. That's what the sheilas like, don't they?"

"I don't know, James. I don't know."

"So, did Dad, I mean, did whoever he was, know I was your kid?"

"No. We never told him. He would have been devastated. He thought the world of you, wanted the best for you. But the booze got in the way."

Mr. Counter stood up with his arms folded. I knew what he wanted. I slowly rose and we both waited for something to happen. But it was Mr. Counter who moved first. He came around the table with his arms stretched out. "All these years," he said, "I've never hugged you, not even when you were little. But I wanted to so badly." The tears in his eyes, they just about made me collapse. He really meant it. It was all true. I could hear Kate telling me that this was the big moment, that I should go forward and hug him too.

And I did.

*

Connie and Vi sat across from each other in the living room. The blinds on each side were drawn, the lace curtains at the front pulled together, allowing a fractured view to the street. Connie had got out her best china and was placing the cups and saucers on the lace covered coffee table. Vi sat upright, clad in a dull green dress, plain, decorated with a small brooch that Eddie had given her so many years ago, her black leather handbag sitting in her lap. Connie had got out her best china for the occasion for it felt like there was something to celebrate, the past absorbed to the present, a feeling that lost baggage had at last been found. The light clinking of the china as she poured the tea invoked comforting memories of past cups of tea, a little milk, no sugar, and a tea strainer.

"He'll be here in twenty minutes or so," said Connie.

"Shall I get some biscuits?" asked Vi.

"I doubt he'll want any. Beer drinkers, you know."

"I suppose so." Vi sat uncomfortably on the edge of the sofa. "Connie?" she said, "I've never thanked you for taking me in, not properly."

"You know that's not necessary. You're my sister and I love you, and it wasn't your fault that your husband turned out how he did."

"But I did choose him, and it should have been Eddie."

"We don't need to go over all that again. What we have to do now is try to get James to understand."

"He was a lovely little boy, you know, Connie."

"Yes, I know."

"I should never have left him."

"You had no choice. It would have killed you if you'd stayed. We both know that. And he would have hated you all the more, because you were the bad one that was always having to tell him what to do."

"I suppose you're right. But leaving him with that drunk. Maybe he hates me more for it."

"No, Vi! No! The life his father led him into, then Eddie too…"

"I know I blamed Eddie, but he tried to save James, I see that now. James would have been out of control without Eddie after his father died."

"Well, you know what I think about that. Eddie was thinking of himself first. He just wanted the boy with him. But we can't go over all that again. We had it out with Eddie last time. What's done is done."

"I suppose so."

They both fell into an awkward silence. Connie sipped her tea, looking out at her sister over her tea cup. Vi looked into her cup. There were no tea leaves, no fortune to be told. They waited in silence until at last the lumbering Humber pulled up in front of the house. Eddie came to the door.

"Eddie, we're almost ready. Come in for a cuppa," smiled Connie as she opened the door.

"I won't stay, thanks. Got the missus in the car."

Connie peered into the car, beckoning Mrs. Counter who wound down the window, her hat getting in the way as she put her head out to reply.

"Oh, we won't stay, thank you. Eddie has a lot of work to do at the pub."

"Oh, please. Just for a few secs, stretch your legs and all that."

Mrs. Counter smiled, the heavy powdered nose crimping a little, "Oh all right then. I'll just come in for a quickie and a visit to the loo."

Two more cups of tea were poured and they all sat in silence, comforted by the clinking of china and sipping of tea.

There were no biscuits and the ride back in the lumbering Humber down to Geelong took forever in a silence not golden, instead coloured by the dark grey of the You Yangs.

*

The brat was sleeping in the corner of the kitchen, curled up like a dog. There was a rope tied around her ankle and the other end tied to the tap in the kitchen sink. The brat's foot looked blue and there were red marks around her ankle where she had strained against the rope, trying to get loose. Flo sat in her usual place at the laminex table, smoking her Garricks. She wasn't staring into nothing though. She was reading her bible, reading it out loud:

"…when the overwhelming whip passes through it will not come to us…"

The screen door bursts open and Tank's big body stands over the brat. "What the fuckn hell are you doing?" he yells.

Flo continues:

"… for we have made lies our refuge, and in falsehood we have taken shelter…"

Tank grabs her bible and flings it across the kitchen. "You stupid fuckn bitch!" he screams, "look at the brat's fuckn foot. It's gone blue, you're gunna cripple her!"

"You should fuckn talk!"

Tank leans down to undo the rope, but just as he does, the brat wakes up and screeches in a high-pitched voice and grabs at Tank's face, scratching his cheeks, and blood starts oozing out and trickling down to his mouth.

"Serves you fuckn right," says Flo, "…whoever sheds the blood of man, by man shall his blood be shed…"

Tank loosens the rope and detaches it from the tap. Then with the knotted end, he whips it down on the table. The brat screeches some more, and Flo's eyelids flicker a little. She takes a draw of her Garrick and steels herself. Tank grabs the brat and whips the knotted rope down hard on the table, this just missing Flo's hand as she flicked the ash of her cigarette into the ashtray.

"Go on, then. Get it out of you. You can do all you want. I deserve it, I know. And I'll leave it to the Lord to deal with you, because only He knows just how much you deserve."

Tank's arm freezes above his head, he has the brat in a headlock with his other arm, her jaw clamped shut so she can't scream. Flo wants to be beaten, and he wants to do it, but because she wants him to he won't. He throws the rope into the kitchen sink and turns to go back out, still holding the brat who scratches and pulls trying to get out of the headlock.

"That's right. Run away!" mutters Flo.

"What did you fuckn say?"

"You heard."

"Fuck you!" But he did not leave.

"Are you going to let that boy hang for what you did?" cried Flo.

"Did what?"

"Oh Lord! Give me patience to deal with this idiot!" she calls, looking up to the fly-spotted ceiling. "You killed, her, didn't you? On one of your visits. You gave her money then you killed her."

"What kind of a bloke do you think I am, you fuckn whore?"

"Nah, she's the whore and that's what you like. In one of your fits of rage you fucked her and killed her with a beer bottle, of all the fuckn disgusting things."

"I wasn't even there that night."

"Yair, that's what you say. But the Brat, she saw you there. You was there with the boy, what's his name?"

"Chooka. But I wasn't there, for Christ sake."

"She saw you, blood all down your front. That's what she told me."

"Where's Linda, then. She must have been there too if the Brat was there. She'll tell you I wasn't there."

"You went there after we came back from the hospital. You was steamed up. I know. I told you not to go."

"You fuckn did not."

"I told Jesus to stop you. I prayed hard to stop you."

"Did the brat say anything to the cops?"

"Yair, except that she said she saw Chooka."

"So she didn't see me then?"

"So you was there?"

"Fuck you! Are you a fuckn detective now?"

"Linda said the cops got the brat scared and she just said the first name that came into her head. Because you know, she likes that boy."

"The fuckn shit of a kid, just like her fuckn mother. I'll talk sense into this fuckn little shit." He tightens the headlock. The brat squirms.

"Yair, I s'pose this is your idea of talking to her? You fuckn murdering bastard!"

Tank clenched his fists, the brat bit his hand, but he didn't feel it. Flo's eyes flickered just a little. Maybe she had taunted him enough, maybe this time he would finish her off with a big blow to her little head, or maybe he'd just throttle her. She imagined the pleasure in his face as he did it. But she glanced across to the kitchen door and behold, saw that God had arranged things on cue. Linda came in, calling out for the brat. And she was followed by Iris. The son of God had delivered his message in no uncertain terms. For it was through Iris that Jesus had risen.

*

"Come on, mate, it's time to meet her majesty," said the cop. He opened the cell door, it wasn't really a cell, just a door, and a room with no bars, just a tiny window way up high looking out to Geringhap street, at least that's the direction I thought. I had no way of knowing at the time. I got up off the bunk, ran my fingers through my hair then the cop took me tightly by the arm and led me out and up several flights of stairs, until we came to a big polished wooden door that he opened with a big key and pushed me through. The courtroom looked huge to me, but I think that was because there was hardly anyone there, just The Preacher on one side and Mr. Counter and my lawyer on the other side. I peered into the gloom of the ceiling and all round, the smell of polished wood hanging over everything, the dark colours adding to the gloom. Way up high I saw a very white face of an old lady, full of wrinkles and a huge head of white hair, wisps of it dyed the colour of tea. The cop gave me a nudge. "You better bow to her, if you don't want to get on her wrong side."

"Who the hell's she?"

"Her honour, Justice of the Peace Grace McShearn."

I don't know if I bowed or not. I didn't know what was going on. The cop put me in the dock and I just stood there, feeling like a dope. But at least I was up higher and could look out over the courtroom where I saw Kate and Grimesy sitting in the back row. I waved and smiled a big grin, it was so good to see them. But they just put on little smiles. Her honour stared down at me. I s'pose she didn't like me smiling. She banged her gavel.

A bloke stood up and went on and on about what case I was and the charges laid against me and on and on. He sat down and then The Preacher stood up, stretching himself up and up to make himself look seven foot tall. And he held his head back, just like the white cockies do when they're cracking a gum nut, his nose the biggest beak of all.

"Your honour," he said, "I am Senior Constable Gregory Pope, prosecuting this case on behalf of her Majesty the Queen's Royal Victorian Police Force, your honour, with the deepest respect and responsibility."

Her honour sat motionless. Said nothing, peering out over her rimless spectacles. The Preacher coughed and continued.

"The crown charges that on Sunday, February 10, 1957, at approximately 1.00 a.m. one James Henderson, the accused, did unlawfully enter the residence of one Millicent Flattery of 25 North Shore Rd. and in a drunken fit of rage did batter said woman to death with a beer bottle and did defile her body in unspeakable ways. The charge is murder in the first degree. This despicable young hooligan went to this residence with the thorough and complete and only intent of defiling this woman and murdering her in revenge for the wrongs he claimed she had done to him."

Her Honour looked down, the top of her head barely visible from the courtroom below, writing notes, and spoke without looking up.

"And what do you have to say for yourself, young man?"

Gees, I didn't even realize she was talking to me. I just stood there looking dumb, waiting for the Preacher to keep on droning on, but he sat down.

"Young man?" The cop came up behind me and gave me a nudge. I was about to speak when the lawyer beside Mr. Counter stood up.

"He pleads, not guilty, your Honour," at which The Preacher jumped up.

"Your Honour," he complained, "on behalf of her Majesty the Queen, I object to this intervention. This hooligan has already confessed to the murder, I have it in writing here, in the notes I made." He opened his bible and pulled out the notes where he always kept them.

I was about to answer "yes" but the lawyer jumped up and said, "If it please your Honour, the confession so-called was obtained under duress. Nor is it signed by the defendant, your honour."

"I think I did it, your highness," I blurted.

The Preacher jumped up and with a great flourish of his long arms he announced, "I rest my case."

"This case is remanded for trial, the date to be set forthwith, in the superior court of Geelong. Next case," announced the Justice of the Peace, still not looking up.

The cop led me out of the courtroom, but as we went down the stairs he said, "you want to go to the toilet? They're moving you to the Geelong gaol to await trial, and I've heard that there's no toilets in the cells, just buckets."

*

Thank goodness, they took my clothes. I must have been wearing them for a week, without a bath or shower. I needed a shave and a haircut too, which they took care of as soon as they'd showered me with a hose and gave me a kind of jump-suit, I think they call them, like overalls. They were dark green. The guards were nice enough and this one guard who had a little Errol Flynn like moustache took me by the arm and led me out of the reception and into the prison. It was a shock, I tell you. The tiers of cells, all iron bars everywhere, steel steps and catwalks, enough to scare the shit out of anyone. Looked like they'd imported the whole thing from a James Cagney movie set. Of course, it was built a long time before that. The guard led me past a row of cells on the ground floor, a few blokes sitting or walking around their cells, muttering to themselves, some of them sticking their arms through the bars trying to touch me, but the guard gave them a little bang on the knuckles with his truncheon. We came to an empty cell, the door open. "Cell 45," said the guard, "this will be your home for a year or two. Make sure you read the rules, especially the one about putting your bucket out. If you don't, you'll be the one that's collecting the buckets." He gave me a little push, slammed the door behind me and locked it with a couple of big keys.

The cot didn't look too bad and the cell was kind of little, but then it was bigger than the doorway to the Victorian archives. At least it was a roof over my head. Prison cells are supposed to be horrible things because they take away your liberty, so they say. But it wasn't how I felt that day. A prison in designed to lock you up and keep you in. But it's also designed to keep people out and away from you. And right now, that's what I wanted, to be alone. I lay on the cot, my head resting on my hands. My mind was blank, I wanted sleep and it came to me.

*

I know it seems a bit stupid, but when I awoke the next morning, must have been before they go around and get you all up, the first thing I had to do was sit on the bucket. Shit! Really! How could a bloke live like this, the fuckn stink and the bucket, you can't sit on it anyway. When I finished my business, and put the bucket out where it was supposed to go, I lay back on my cot and decided that prison wasn't a good place and that I'd rather kill myself than have to go through this every day. So, when the guard came to get me because I had a visitor, I was happy, and hoped it was the lawyer that Mr. Counter had got me.

But it wasn't a lawyer that was waiting for me in the visiting room, it was half a lawyer, Grimesy! As soon as I saw him, I was so happy, I tried to run to him and give him a hug, but the guard grabbed me and said, "no touching! I'm the only bloke that's allowed to touch!" So we sat down across from each other at a heavy old wooden table, made by one of the convicts, no doubt.

"Howyergoin' mate?" asked Grimesy trying to hold back a grin.

"How's it look?" I growled, holding back my own grin.

Grimesy didn't beat about the bush. "Why the hell did you say you did it?" he asked, frowning at me.

"I was just telling the truth. I said I think I did it, but I didn't say I did it."

"You stupid bastard. You played into the Preacher's hands."

"Anyway, I've come to my senses this morning. I don't want to spend the rest of my life in here."

"What are you saying? You want to hang?"

"Shit no! Of course I don't"

"Well, that's what everyone's talking about. The Geelong Addy's doing a big job on you. Front page, all about sex and violence. They've made you out like the green tent murderer."

"Fuckn what?"

"The green tent murderer, a bloke called Owen McQueeney. He was in the cell you're in, cell 45, right?"

"Yair, that's what the gaoler said."

"He was hanged just down the road from here on October 20, 1858."

"Shit! But he must have done something really bad."

"Yes, shot a pretty woman with two little kids and she was holding the baby in her arms when he shot her right through the eye."

"And they're saying I'm like that?"

"Yes, but with all the sex, Millie being a prostitute, and then our little seminar in your professor's flat." Grimesy grinned in spite of himself. "You should have seen the headlines in the Sun and the Addy. The Preacher was in his element."

"That bible-bashing fuckn bastard."

Grimesy suddenly changed the subject. "Kate couldn't make it this morning."

"Oh, shit. Gees, I miss her."

"No doubt you do. She had tutes all day and demonstration cases to attend to with her students at Royal Melbourne."

"So can you get me out?"

"Gees, James. I'm not exactly here as your lawyer. Still doing my articles. But that's why I'm here."

"What then?"

"The firm I'm doing my articles with. They're interested in your case. It's such high publicity, they think they can do pretty well out of it."

"Yair? Nice of them to think of me."

"I know. But they've got some really good contacts. They know what to do and who to talk to, if you see what I mean. Better than these Geelong solicitors whose only experience is collecting their fees when people buy and sell their houses."

"So, I have to fire my lawyer, the one that Mr. Counter got?"

"No. I already did it for you."

"Shit! Thanks a lot!"

"No, really. I talked with Mr. Counter and it's all OK. His solicitor will tag along with my lot."

"What do I have to do?"

"Everything I tell you, exactly. And the first thing is to renounce your supposed confession. I've already talked briefly with The Preacher. He wasn't too pleased. I thought he was going to have Dopey sit on me, as a matter of fact."

"Shit, what a couple of fuckn losers."

"They're winners right now, with all the publicity they're getting."

"So how do I take back my confession?"

"I want you first to sign this. It's a statement retracting your confession. You can swear it in front of the gaoler here, hand on the bible."

"Shouldn't it be in front of a solicitor or something?"

"Yes. But it will do for now. Just something to scare the shit out of the Preacher."

I did as I was told and the gaoler took me back to cell 45. I couldn't understand why there were so few convicts and why it was so quiet. The gaoler said that it wasn't a real prison any more. Something about a practice prison and it being kind of like a hospital.

"You mean I'm here because I'm sick in the head?"

"I don't know," he said, "I'm only the gaoler. But I tell you, I'd be sick in the head too if I had a doctor like the one you've got."

"What do you mean? I don't have a psychiatrist."

"That's what you say. She's gorgeous. I never saw such legs."

"You saw her?"

"On the front page of *The Sun*! Yair. Doctor Kate they called her."

*

That night I couldn't sleep. After that shit in the bucket, everything had become crystal clear. I was having such a good time at the uni, I wasn't going to let that Preacher take it away from me. And as well, it looked like Iris was alive! If only she'd come and visit me. We could make up. Oh my God! If only she were here right now!

I heard the clanking of keys and I peered through the bars to see who was coming down the catwalk. The lights were dim, there was the sound of a couple of blokes snoring in their cells.

Soon out of the gloom there appeared, as if in a scary movie, two huge bodies. They were too big for the gaoler or the other guards. Then in horror, the light in my cell came on and I saw standing at the bars of my cell, The Preacher and Dopey. The Preacher stood taller than ever before, his bible held high above his head, almost hitting the pipes that ran across the ceiling. And Dopey, with a dopey grin, rattled the keys as loud as he could, then opened my cell door.

"So this is cell 45," he said, as I cringed towards the back of the cell, "the correct number if I may say so, sir?"

"Indeed, it is God's will," replied the Preacher. "And now it will be his doing to make sure that justice is done in the name of her Majesty's police force and the good people of Norlane."

The Preacher had to duck his head to enter the cell. He held his bible out to me.

"Take this in your filthy hand, you villain, and say after me…"

I grabbed the bible and threw it hard against the wall. It fell to the floor, loose pages coming apart, fluttering slowly behind it. I crouched down in the corner of my cell, expecting a battering. But it didn't come. Instead, the Preacher dropped to his knees, scrambling like an insect, trying to gather up the loose pages., muttering, his head and nose stretched out, "oh Lord, what violent creature is this, splattering your Word against the wall, defiling it on the filthy floor of his prison cell, upon which who knows what filth has been laid?" He stood up, clutching the loose pages, trying to insert them into their places in the bible which he clasped too tightly in his other hand.

"Constable," said the Preacher, now sitting precariously on his haunches, "move yourself forward in such a way that you may, in consequence, retrieve this disgusting filth of a person so that he may receive the truth through the bible."

Dopey waved his truncheon in the air and stepped forward. "Up we get, now, or I'll have to help you up with this," he said, pointing the truncheon at me.

"Leave me alone!" I whimpered, "I'm innocent! Fuckn innocent!"

"Take the bible, you nasty sinner, take it!" demanded The Preacher, "and in it you will find your confession, written down carefully according to her Majesty's code of conduct for her Royal Constabulary! Read it and sign it and swear by Almighty God that it is the truth!"

I thought for a moment that I might retreat under the bed, but there was no room and the bed was firmly attached to the floor all the way around. There was nowhere to go but lie down flat, and that I did, calling out, "I am innocent of all charges! I never made a confession! It's all lies!"

"Are you accusing me, the messenger of Jesus Christ himself, of untruthfulnesses?" The Preacher's eyes narrowed, a snarl twisted his thin lips, and his beak nose twitched. "Constable!" he ordered, "it is time for the laying on of hands. Do so, in the name of the Queen!" He stood up and stepped back to the cell door, hands on his hips, bible carefully inserted into his inner pocket.

Dopey dropped his truncheon on to the cot then stooped down, his short beefy arms reaching around his rotund torso. "All right you evil bastard," he said, his cheeks looking like they were full of a minimum of chips, "this is where you meet your maker, in the senior constable here."

He grabbed me by the back of my collar and the seat of my pants and hurled me across the cell where I landed at the Preacher's feet in a crumpled heap. I curled up expecting the bastard to put the boot into me, and he did, right into me guts. But it didn't hurt as much as I expected, in fact I felt some of the old fire coming back into me. My cheeks and ears were pulsing with blood. I was on fire. I rolled with the kick, from a size 16 boot I'd say, then made a grab for the truncheon lying on the cot. Dopey was too slow to stop me, and before they knew it, I'd thrust the truncheon right into the Preacher's balls. I heard a huge wheezing intake of air as he inhaled and held his breath in pain. But he didn't yell. He bit his lip till it bled, and grabbed his bible in his both hands and pressed it into his groin. "May God in his mercy help me!" he cried.

Dopey wrenched the truncheon out of my hand, kneed me under the chin knocking me backwards, then lunged forward, all his weight on his knees pressing down on my chest. The air burst out of my lungs, I gasped for air. This time, it was the end, no hang man would be needed.

But the Preacher saved me. "Rise my good constable," he cried, "rise and allow this evil man the opportunity to face the hang man as must all sinners who have done despicable acts as he."

Dopey lifted his knees and stood unsteadily, using his truncheon as a support. I leaned back on the cot, huffing and coughing, my eyes closed.

"Look carefully, my son!" droned the Preacher in his familiar baritone voice, "thou shalt sign the retraction of the retraction of the confession." He thrust the bible with the written retraction wedged inside it into my face. I took it and stared at it. Dopey handed me a pen. The Preacher continued, "sign it my boy, and thou shalt be forgiven your heinous crime once you are hanged."

"Amen," said Dopey.

"Perhaps he needs a little more help to put pen to paper," said The Preacher to Dopey, nudging his elbow.

"Oh, yes, right sir!"

"Oh, and yes. incontrovertibly, unless you sign this, I will be charging you with assaulting an officer of the Royal Cons-tabulary," said the Preacher, rubbing his balls.

I took the pen and wrote in my very worst scrawl:

"*Futete*"

*

I don't know how many days went by, I never felt so helpless, except when I was sleeping in the doorways trying to find Iris. They wouldn't let me phone anyone. All I could do was sit in cell 45. I asked for my kit bag of exercise books, but they said I couldn't have them because they were evidence according to the Preacher. I was waiting for them to come back and beat me up again, but so far, nothing. The stupid bastards probably hadn't even looked at it. I just asked for a pencil and paper, but they wouldn't give that to me either.

I was so happy when at last I had a visitor, Mr. Counter, and when I got to the meeting room I saw that he had my stuck-up auntie with him as well. Mr. Counter strode up to give me a hug, but the gaoler stopped him. "No touching," he proclaimed.

"We're trying to get you out on bail," said Mr. Counter. Your mates from Melbourne are pulling some strings, I think. But that's not why we're here."

I sat down opposite them, auntie sitting apart, leaving an empty seat between her and Mr. Counter.

"Who's the empty chair for?" I asked.

"Your mum was going to be here," said Mr. Counter.

"Gees! Dad!" I blurted out, and I put my head between my hands. Mr. Counter was taken aback, as was auntie.

"Yair, too bad he wasn't here," said Mr. Counter.

"No, I meant…"

"I know what you meant, Jimmy."

"Hello Jimmy," said auntie.

"G'day," I said, still with my head in my hands, ruffling through my hair.

"Your mum couldn't come," said auntie.

"Why not?" I asked, lifting my head, looking at auntie and then Mr. Counter.

Mr. Counter opened his mouth to answer, but auntie kept at it. "She's had a stroke and she's in hospital," she said.

"A stroke? What's that?" I asked, feeling foolish because I didn't have a clue.

"It was a big one, and she can't talk, probably will not make it more than a few days," said Mr. Counter.

"A blood vessel has burst in her brain," added auntie.

Well, who was I going to talk to? I started muttering to my Dad, but stopped because it wasn't my dad and I know it doesn't matter because he's dead and so if he is or wasn't my Dad, I can still talk to him, can't I?

"We're going to see her after we leave here. The hospital's just down the road from here."

"Yair, I know all about that hospital. I was there when Iris..."

"I know. Speaking of which, you wouldn't happen to have the clothes you wore that night?"

"What night?"

"The night you're supposed to have killed Millie."

"Maybe. I s'pose Abbie washed them."

"They had blood all down the front, Spuds said, right?"

"Yair. That's what I remember he said and what he told the Preacher too. Why?"

"Because your mate Grimes says that maybe the blood was from when you were cradling Iris in your arms that night."

"Gees, Mr. Counter, I mean Dad, I mean..."

"It's all right. Why don't you just call me Eddie?" my new Dad said with a smile.

"Gees, Mr. Counter, Dad, I dunno. I'm all mixed up, you know? I'm buggered if I know what's what."

Auntie shifted in her seat. She wanted to go, I could see it. She never had much patience. That's one of the reasons I didn't ever want to go live with her. Fancy living with an old spinster, for Christ sake. A cranky old bitch, that's what she'd be.

"I'll ask Abbie to look for the clothes. They were your good Fletchers and shirt that my wife bought you, weren't they?"

Auntie shifted in her seat again.

"But Abbie always washed my clothes and put them away all nice and pressed. She really liked doing that," I said.

"Anyway, it won't hurt to ask."

"Can you ask Grimesy to do something else for me?"

"Of course."

"Could he bring me my Latin books and other uni stuff so I can keep up with my uni work? And get the solicitor or whatever he's called to make the bastards here let me read and write in my cell? They won't even let me have a pencil or paper, except to wipe my ass. Sorry, excuse me auntie."

"I'll do what I can. I have to wait until he shows up at the pub, because I don't have a phone number for him. But I do for your Melbourne solicitor, so I will phone him too."

"We should be going," said auntie, "I'm very worried about…"

I just sat there and said nothing. I couldn't think what to say. I mean, was I supposed to be all broken up about a mother who walked out on me and me Dad, except he wasn't me dad. Shit, it's all fucked up. Iris? Are you there somewhere? Iris? I really need to talk to you, and I need one of them big wet kisses, you know?

*

I spent that night thinking about Iris, imagining she showed up in my cell and we went at it just like we used to. It seems like years ago since my Latin exam. Trouble was, though, it always ended up a nightmare as I lived that horrible night over again when her life bled away all over the bed.

The next morning, right on cue, good old Grimesy and the solicitor showed up with not only my uni books but my kit bag of exercise books as well. So now, I could be quite happy in my cell. Except, of course, for the bucket business. So the first thing I did was write a letter to the Addy complaining about the bucket and pointing out that this was 1957 and there was such a thing as a sewer in Geelong, wasn't there?

And now that I had time to think a bit, I realized that I hadn't met any other prisoners. That I was in solitary confinement which was supposed to be a horrible part of being locked up in gaol. But I liked being on my own, didn't I Dad?—whichever of you wants to listen—I liked it. I was used to it. That was my problem, according to Iris. It's what made her get mad at me, my always wanting to be left alone, even by her when I'd had my fill. "You're just using me up," she'd say, "like all men, like me mum says. Once you've fucked me, ya leave me." And I'd say, "who's your mum?" And she'd get up and slap me and say, "fuck you, it's none of your business." Course, I thought I knew who my Dad was. How wrong could you be? Shit, Iris will laugh when she finds out that my dad was not my Dad.

And then I had another visitor. As the gaoler led me out of my cell, I was sure that this time it had to be Iris. It just had to be. But when I got near to the meeting room, I could hear screeching and yelling and I knew that it was not Iris. Unless, of course she'd come with Linda, because there was no mistaking that ear-splitting scream of her brat. On cue, the little vixen zoomed out the door of the meeting room and ran down the passageway, a gaoler chasing after her yelling, "you're not allowed down there, come back here!" and the brat bangs into my gaoler and kicks him in the shins and he yelps and swears and joins the chase.

And there she was, Little Linda sitting there over in the corner of the waiting room. She was all dressed up, though, and looked even pretty, I'd say, not so worn out, and dressed in clothes that even I could see were nice and new and must have cost her a penny.

"Gees, Linda, what happened to you? You look great!"

"Fuckn thanks for the compliment, you shit!" she laughed.

"No worries!" I say as I plonk myself down in front of her. "Thanks for coming to see me."

"Yair, well I wouldn't have, but Iris made me."

"Iris?" I said, my ears going red. "Iris? She's not dead, then? It's not just a rumour?"

"Nah. She's alive and kicking, that's for sure. In fact, she's living with me."

"What's new about that? Didn't you all live with your mum and dad and Iris when she felt like it?"

"Yair, sort of, though Iris always said she didn't live there."

"Yair?"

"And by the way. Flo is not me mother."

"Who is, then?" I asked, don't know why, because I didn't really care, did I?

"Millie."

"No kidding? That fuckn…"

"You better not say it."

"So you've come to see me, even though I murdered your mum?"

"Yair, because that's what the stupid brat said you did."

"She saw me murder Millie?"

"Nah. She told The Preacher that she saw you coming out of her house that night, blood all down you."

"Shit. Linda. I can't remember anything about that night, and I don't remember being in that house."

"It's my house now," she said with a cocky smile.

"Yair? How come?"

"Because I was Millie's daughter and we worked together, and she left it to me in her will along with everything else."

"She had money enough to leave stuff to you? She owned the house fair and square?"

"Yair."

"Fucking hell!"

I sat and thought a while. I could hear the running and yelling going on outside the meeting room, the gaolers still trying to catch the brat. Linda was obviously having fun. I sat quiet because I couldn't think of exactly what to say next. Tank, her dad, was Millie's best customer! So, would Linda step into the breach? Shit, it was too much. And then with Tank and Flo being brother and sister. Linda puts her hand out and squeezes mine. Her fingers are decked out with rings and her wrists with bangles. She smiles sweetly, something I'd never seen her do before. In fact, I think she was sober. "I know all about Iris and I suppose you do too," she said.

"Only what Flo told me that night at the hospital when Iris was dying.

"That Tank and Flo are brother and sister and that Iris is their daughter?"

"Yair. That's it."

"That's only the half of it."

"What else could there be?"

"Well, you know how she won't sleep in one place for very long? She goes off, escapes through windows, you must know that."

"Yair, but I thought she did that at the pub because she didn't want anyone to catch us at it."

"Maybe a bit of that. But she does that at Tank and Flo's too. They most of the time have never known where she was right from when she was little, like my brat out there."

"You mean she kept running away?"

"Yair, especially at night. She'd sleep who knows where."

"But what about school?"

"She never went to school. Tank and Flo were so fucked up about it, they didn't want anyone to find out that she was their daughter. She was born at home, and they kept her locked in her bedroom till I dunno when. After she got old enough, she started slipping out her bedroom window and sneaking into other peoples' houses, wandering around the neighbourhood. They never registered her birth so they couldn't send her to school, could they?"

"Fuckn shit!"

"I don't think she can read or write, But I'm not sure about that. I never saw Tank or Flo teaching her. I s'pose she might have taught herself. The only thing Iris can do, I'd guess, is recite Flo's fuckn bible off by heart."

I looked at Linda in astonishment. I was so thankful for her telling me all this. I squeezed her hands back and drew her towards me.

"I can't tell you how much all this means to me, Linda. I nearly went crazy trying to find her and was convinced that she was dead, because I couldn't find any trace of her anywhere and I went to the Victorian archives and never found anything and then came to the conclusion one night when I was full of booze and out of my mind that she never existed at all and that I'd imagined the whole thing."

"Yair, well. She'll be fuckn cross with me for telling you all this."

"Can I ask you something else?"

"Go on then."

"Does Iris help you out in the business? Did she work for Millie?"

Linda grinned. The noise of the brat suddenly came louder. "Not as far as I know. Course, now you know what she was like, there's every chance she slept at Millie's on and off, but she slept in lots of people's places and most of them never knew it."

"Yair, it's not the sleeping I'm worried about, bugger you."

"You fuckn men. You want each woman all to yourselves, but then you go off and fuck everyone you can. What do they call youse? You know the word, don't you, now that you're a uni student?"

"Hypocrites?"

"Yair. Fuckn hypocrites, that's what you are. Fuckn hypocrites."

At that moment, the brat screeched to a halt at our table and punched me in the stomach. It was her way of saying hello because she liked me.

"G'day brat," I say.

Linda grabs her hand and holds on tight. "Ya didn't see Chooka there at Millie's did ya?"

"Fuck no!" she yelled and ran off, running around the meeting room, tipping over as many chairs as she could. Then she comes back. She's got a crumpled up piece of paper in her hand.

"Who did you see, then?"

"Tank of course. I told the fuckn Preacher that lots of times."

"You did?" I asked.

The brat punched me again and threw the piece of crumpled paper at me. "Yair," she said, "and I gave him a good kick too." Off she went again, tripping up the chairs, then returned. It was like a game.

"Who else did you see?" I asked.

"Only Tank. But he's always there." She had yet another piece of paper, squeezed into a ball and threw it in my face.

"Fuckn little brat!" I complained, grabbing the paper and putting it in my pocket. The gaoler would use it as an excuse to give me bucket duty if I left any mess behind.

Linda grabbed the brat. "Gotta go. Got a very important appointment at the pub with a couple of beers."

"Yair," I said, "sorry I won't be there to serve you. Can you get Iris to come?"

"You know what she's like. Nobody, except maybe you, can get her to do anything."

I handed her a note. "Would you please give her this?"

"But what if she can't read it?"

Then you'll have to read it to her."

The note read:

Ovid loves you.

"What the fuckn hell's that supposed to mean?" she asks, staring at the note.

"Don't tell me you can't read either."

"Fuck you!" she cried as she crumpled it up and threw it back at me.

The brat grabbed it off the floor and stuck it in her mouth.

"You fuckn little shit!" I yelled and grabbed her arm.

"Hey asshole!" yelled Linda, "leave me little brat alone! Gaoler! Gaoler!"

The gaoler rushed over and grabbed me by the scruff of the neck and pushed me away and I fell over a chair and slid to the floor. "Get up you fuckn murderer!" he ordered with great satisfaction, "you're going to solitary for this!"

Since I was already in solitary I didn't think that would matter. I sullenly gave myself up to him and Linda laughed as I was led away.

I wasn't taken back to my cell. Instead the gaoler led me down a long catwalk, past many cells, a few of which had inmates, and they all stuck their arms through the bars and whistled at me like I was a sheila. We reached the end of the passageway and entered a small windowless room. "On your knees," ordered the gaoler. I saw that look on his face. It was the same as Dr. Pulcher's.

And when he was done, he said, "Now masturbate into this cup."

"What? You fuckn pervert!"

The gaoler brandished his truncheon. Ya want a dose of this?" he threatened.

I did what I was told. Kate was wrong. There is such a thing as a bad orgasm.

*

The bastards wouldn't let me out to go to my mother's funeral. Poor mum. What a life she had first with my Dad or whatever he was, and then living with that bitter body auntie Connie. I know I should have gone with her that day she walked out on us. I know I should have. My Dad, I mean Mr. Counter, he should have made me. But he didn't. I suppose it would have been awful for him too, seeing me go away and live with my mum, and knowing it was probably the last he'd see of me. But there you go, who knows what might have happened? And I never would have met up with Iris, and shit, I wouldn't want to be without that to think of, and I do go over those amazing few hours we had after my Latin exam, every night I relive them, every night.

So now I'm sitting in my cell 45, waiting for something to happen, sitting on that fucking stinking bucket, and the days go by. I no longer have so many visitors coming to see me. My gaoler taunts me, tells me that none of them care about me, and why would they, because they've got their own lives to worry about, don't they? I've changed my tactics with him. I don't swear at him anymore, because that's what he wants. He likes to see my ears and cheeks go red. So I just sit on my cot, reading through my old notebooks. Thank goodness Grimesy managed to get them back from the Preacher. And I've been expecting the Preacher to come and try to break me open. Ever since I talked to the brat, I was sure that he'd come because it was obvious to me that he didn't have a case. Who the hell would believe anything that the brat said in court? They'd never be able to get her to stay still for long enough to answer a question. Besides, Mr. Counter had dug out my old clothes that I had on that horrible night that Iris died (that's still how I think of it), and got a mate of his in the police forensics lab in Melbourne to look for any remnants of blood and he found some. It wasn't Millie's according to Dad. Apparently, Linda had produced a piece of the blood-stained sheet from Millie's bed.

The only one who came regularly was Mr. Counter, I mean, my Dad. It got that way, though that I wished he wouldn't come because we ran out of things to say, once he'd given me a run-down of the usual goings-on at the pub, told what little news there was on my case and that the Preacher and Dopey showed up at the pub at six o'clock every night just like they always did. And the Preacher never said anything about me and even when Dad asked him why wasn't he dropping the case, the Preacher kept saying that it was out of his hands now and nobody could figure out what that meant.

And still no Iris. I pleaded with Mr. Counter to find her and bring her to me but he said he couldn't force her to come, could he? And besides, he only got fleeting glimpses of her, she was still occasionally sleeping in my room, and Little Linda said she was sometimes at home and sometimes at Millie's, now Linda's, and who knows where else she slept.

The trouble with gaolers is that they don't know when to stop. Once they get you doing what they want, they get off on the bullying and they can't resist beating the shit out of you. So at night when there was nothing to do or think about except bodily functions, I began to plan my revenge, or properly, an action that would put my gaoler out of action. He had changed himself on to a deep night shift, no doubt so he could get access to me without anyone knowing. He'd come into my cell and I'd have to perform or get beaten, and more and more it was both. Now, what I'm about to tell you is absolutely disgusting, but you have to under-stand the situation I was in. It was unbearable, having to do what he made me do. It was my only course of action. Any inmate worth his salt can acquire a knife and that applies to yours truly. I had originally considered biting off his you-know-what, but even I thought that way too disgusting. The thought of it. No, I couldn't do it.

The faint sound of Johnny Ray singing "Walkin' in the Rain" wafted in from some bloke's radio. Funny, I never much listened to the radio and couldn't give a shit about the top songs. But there was something about that song and Johnny Ray's kind of lost voice. It took me back to when I was looking for Iris that cold night in Melbourne, going from doorway to doorway, shivering from the drizzle that wouldn't let up. I started to hum along with it as I sharpened my knife on the bluestone wall of my cell.

*

The next morning, I was taken from my cell and led to the interrogation room where awaited none other than the Preacher and standing by the door was Dopey. My right hand was bandaged from a cut I had received last night, but the Preacher paid no heed to that. Instead as soon as I entered, he stood up as tall as he could in his usual way and pronounced, "I have a few more questions for you, young man, in my capacity of Queen's Counsel, which may be of individual consequence to you."

"Where's my fuckn lawyer, your majesty?"

"There is no need of that at this stage."

"What fuckn stage is that, your majesty?"

"We have new evidence," he said, his beak stuck up in the air, "evidence that is absolutely substantial and incontrovertible in consequence."

"Yes, what's that?" I asked, feeling all cheeky because it looked like I had got away with my gaoler's foreskin.

"We found a match between your semen and semen found in Millicent Flattery's vaginal orifice."

"It's a fuckn lie! You put it there, you fuckn bunch of shit-heads!"

"I am her Majesty's representative. I do not lie."

"Yair? Well you better get specimens from half of Norlane because that's whose left their marks in Millie's post box!"

Dopey grunted and shifted from one foot to the other. "He's got a point there," he mumbled.

The Preacher took off his hat and banged it on the table. "I'll have none of that!" he barked, spittle spraying out of his parrot-like mouth, set between rapidly reddening cheeks. And the spittle was directed at Dopey, chagrined and frightened. For a moment, I thought the Preacher was going to hit him with his bible, which was raised well above his head poised to strike.

"Yair, well this has got nothing to do with me," and I got up to leave.

At that moment, though, the door flew open and in ran the brat, chased by Linda, Grimesy running behind, and further behind, I am sure to this day, as I tried to look past Dopey who was trying to block the door, I caught a glimpse of Iris peaking around Grimesy from afar, her slender little body looking all of 14 years old and no more. But Dopey managed to slam the door shut behind Grimesy so we were all enclosed in the tiny interrogation room with the brat running the show. She did her usual stunt of throwing over the chairs and this was enough to cause The Preacher to almost burst in frustration. He reared up, holding his bible aloft, looking at it, I suppose hoping it would tell him what to do. I know what he wanted to do, he wanted to swat the brat with his bible like he was swatting a fly. She then jumped up on the table, Linda standing there, smiling proudly, and jumped up and down making a terrible din and pointing at The Preacher. "He's the one! He's the one!" she chanted in time with her jumps, "he's the one! He's the one! And so is he!" And she pointed to Dopey.

"The one what?" asked Grimesy, almost speechless.

"At Mil-l-lie's, at Mill-l-lie's!" she chanted.

"And that's all?" persisted Grimesy. I was wishing he'd let up.

"And Tank, Tank!!"

"And anyone else?"

"And Chook-a! And Chook-a!" she said pointing to me.

"And anyone else?"

"Mum-m-y! Mum-m-y!" she said pointing at Linda.

The brat suddenly tired of jumping, climbed off the table and went running out the door and down the passage with Dopey chasing her.

"So, either it was a gang bang, or she's lying. The only way to determine this would be to get a sample of semen from all persons named, except of course Linda," said Grimesy, clearly enjoying himself.

The Preacher gathered up his papers, plonked his hat on his head and departed, his tail between his legs, if you could imagine a giraffe doing that. We all followed and I could almost have walked out of the gaol with them, except that the gaoler on duty at the front just caught sight of me in time. I wasn't trying to escape, though. I was looking for Iris.

*

A couple of days went by, I'm not sure how many. I was in a kind of frenzy, a "manic state" as Kate would say. I sat in the corner of my cell and did all my uni work that I could, kept up with the Caesar translations and all the rest. I couldn't hardly sleep, in fact it got like I couldn't tell whether I was awake or asleep. I started walking up and down the cell. I walked round and round my cot, reciting Tacitus and even bits of Ovid. Sweat poured down my sides, my shirt stuck to my back. I began to peel off my clothes, trying to cool down. I would close my eyes, but it seemed like I was still seeing the cell and I walked round and round my cot without bumping into anything. I was convinced I had a kind of x-ray vision. I ran my fingers through my hair, my beautiful brown wavy air that was now dank with sweat. I rubbed my eyes and opened them, and then I gasped at what I saw. Iris stood before me, her slender little body swaying as though in a forest of trees bending in a cool breeze. Her sweet thin lips sparkled with the wetness I cherished. "Iris! My Love! You're alive!"

"Of course, I am, stupid," she said, standing across the other side of my cot.

"Oh Iris! I've waited for you for so long!"

I extended my arms and she jumped lightly onto the cot and let me take her into my arms. Oh God, Dads, Ovid and whoever else is listening! Words fail me! What can I say other than I must let myself be taken away, pulled down into an abyss of love, lust, her wet lips I feel cooling, sliding all over. My body melts at her touch. I see the mist in her adorable sheep's eyes that envelope and reduce me to little more than an insect scurrying here and there, hoping, searching for love.

*

It takes a long time to wake up from love. And when I did, Iris was gone, the cell door locked. I called for the gaoler, but no one came. I called again threatening to empty my bucket through the bars of my cell. A new gaoler marched up. He opened the cell door. "You have a visitor," he said.

"What time is it?" I asked.

"Eight a.m., Monday"

"Monday?"

"Yair. You've been out to it for a day or two. We were starting to get a bit worried. Pack up your things. You're leaving us."

I felt like I'd just come off a real bender. The saliva was caked solid in my mouth, my hair stuck to my fingers when I ran them through it. I hadn't shaved for I don't know how long and my beard itched like hell and I couldn't stop myself from rubbing it between my fingers.

"Can't I get cleaned up?"

"Where you going to do that? The bathrooms are reserved for the staff, you know that. Come on. Get going."

I stuffed everything I could into my kit bag and trudged on behind him. He never looked behind. I could have stayed there and he wouldn't have known. We came through the turnstile and entered the passageway to the reception. The gaoler pulled me into a room where I had to sign for my belongings, all of which I forgot I had. But the first thing I noticed was the red packet of my Craven A's. And my lighter that someone had given me, or maybe I never had one. Who knows?

"Sign here," he says.

And I was out in the street before I knew it, the sun tearing at my eyes. Without thinking I dropped to my knees, head in my hands, eyes covered.

"What are ya fuckn-a doing down-a there?" comes a voice. The voice I knew right away. It was my old mate Spuds. I looked up, barely making him out against the glaring blue sky of Geelong. I felt his beefy hand under my arm as he pulled me up, then he gave me a bit of a shake. "Ya all right-o mate? Ya look like shit."

"Shit and fuckn hell, Spuds! What the buggery are you doing here?"

"Had to drop-a by and visit an old mate in the clink for beating up his missus. Too much-a grappa, I think. Heard they was-a dropping all the charges against ya, so I told Eddie I'd pick you up. Here, this'll bring ya back-a to life."

He hands me his bottle of grappa.

"Shit and fuckn hell, Spuds! I can't drink that. I'd have to go into training for a week. Let's go and have a beer instead. There's a pub just across the road, isn't there?"

"Yair. I think ya mean-a the Vic-a, Victoria hotel. We can go there if ya like. They're a bit stuck-uppa for me, though."

I look across the road and I see Swampy's truck. "You still working for Swampy?" I ask.

"Off and on. Not-a much time to work after we have a few beers."

"Is Swampy at the pub now?"

"Where else?"

"Then let's go. It'll be like old times."

*

We never made it to the pub, at least not right away. I looked across Gheringhap street and thought I saw someone in Swampy's truck.

"I thought you said Swampy was at the pub?"

"He is."

"Then who's that in the truck?"

"Fuck! Someone's-a stealing the fuckn wreck. Who'd want-a do that? Fuckn bastardi!"

We ran across the road, me struggling to carry my kitbag full of my notebooks. Spuds threw open the door and then stepped back, his jaw dropped half a foot. "Shit and bloody hell!" he cries. I looked past him and there, sitting in the middle of the front seat, was Iris.

"G'day," she grinned.

"Well, bugger me!" was all I could say, and followed it up with, "oh! Shit in Heaven!"

"Aren't you going to give me a kiss?" she says, still with a big grin.

"Where do ya want it?" jokes Spuds.

"Get the fuck out of the way," I splutter, dropping my kitbag and pushing into the cabin. Those wet kisses, they're what I've dreamed of so many lonely nights in gaol.

"Oh, Iris, I thought you were dead!"

"Too bad, huh?"

"Fuck, Iris! You haven't changed one little bit!"

"Yair, and you have, so I've heard."

"What do you mean?" By now I was kissing her all over and she's pulling away.

"You stink!" she says.

"Yair, that's right, he smells like a shit-house," says Spuds.

"Fuck off!" I snarl.

"He's right. No more kisses till ya clean yourself up. Didn't the gaol have any water?"

"Just a bucket."

*

I never thought of myself as a hero, just the opposite. I'd had time to mull over my life when I was in gaol and it wasn't too good. I started to feel sorry for myself and came to the conclusion that I'd had a hard life and was dealt a rotten hand. The trouble with sitting alone for too long in a little cell is that you can't stop yourself from going over and over the things that you did and didn't do. Thinking up ways not to blame yourself for your current circumstances requires a lot of talking to yourself, and then having to answer your own talk. If you don't blame yourself then you blame others, isn't that right? Someone has to have the blame heaped on them. I started to wonder how old people manage this, because they have a lot more memories than I have, so how would they get through it all? They've had a lot more time to do things they were sorry for, haven't they? And this got me to thinking about my Dads, yes, my drunken dad and my real dad (so he says). My drunken Dad must have suffered something terrible because of all the things he did to my mother and to me, not that he beat us much, but more that he started out with such great promise with a great job down at the Phosphate company, but pissed it all away with the booze. And I could see now that the booze does one wonderful thing for a bloke, it gets rid of all those relentless self-blaming thoughts and without guilt or any other complication, lays the blame on everyone else, or doesn't even let you think in terms of blame at all. You just live your life in a comfortable fog, only now and again reminded of the impossible situation one is in, which is that the booze demands that you spend all your time and money on it, and eventually you run out of both so if you have a good friend or family, they'll take care of you while you drink yourself into an unconscious state, never to wake up, and an alcoholic stupor, no matter what it looks like from the outside, as far as the drunk is concerned—and believe me I know even though I'm so young—wraps up your mind in a blanket and won't let it think beyond the craving, there's no room for guilt or blame. So I came to the conclusion in gaol that I did the right thing by my alcoholic Dad sitting with him, holding his hand, helping him move on. And I saw clearly that he didn't care one hoot for me and I had no right to expect it.

As for my other Dad, my real Dad, so called, things seemed to me to be a lot more complicated. Mr. Counter, I mean Dad, came and saw me in gaol almost every day. Always, I felt guilty after he left and always I blamed myself for all the awful, ungrateful things I had done to him, even without meaning it. We would sit there, staring around the meeting room, looking for things to say. He'd ask me about the gaol, if they were treating me all right, and of course I'd say everything was fine, which it was, well except for that small incident with my gaoler and of course the bucket business. I liked being on my own, but I didn't tell him that. And I'd ask how things were at the pub and he'd tell me this or that about the characters who'd come in, and whether this or that barman was pilfering cigarettes. He told me of Sugar now promoted to being the manager of the pub so that took a lot of work off Dad's hands, and I said that was good, and Sugar deserved it and I was sure he would do a good job. One thing I know he really wanted to ask me but didn't. He wanted to ask me if I really did kill Millie, just between the two of us. He wanted me to tell him man to man that I didn't do it. But he did not ask and I did not offer.

I did once try to talk about Mum to him, but he got so emotional about it, I stopped. He almost cried, actually, he pretty much did cry, and I said how really sorry I was how it had all turned out, and that I deeply regretted not getting the chance to see her again and start a new life as her son. But to be honest, I didn't really believe what I was saying, and I think that Dad felt it. So that made things worse. Seeing Mr. Counter cry over her, my mother, the wife he could not have, and look at me with so much love in his heart, I just couldn't bear the responsibility of taking it on. And afterwards in my solitary gaol cell, I cried quietly too, I cried for the Mum who I had rejected and for the Dad whose love I could not absorb.

I carried all of this with me and my kitbag as Spuds ushered us into the old bar, the greasy canvas still hanging in the doorway. And when we entered, a roar spontaneously rose from the crowd, blokes calling out, "Good-on-yer mate" and lots of joking abuse. I immediately grabbed Iris and held her to me, because I knew that she should not be there. And she clung to me too, completely overcome. Because I tell you, all those blokes screaming and yelling, and a woman, well a girl, in the bar, that was enough to start a riot!

I could see behind the crowd, Sugar peeking out from the bar. He was pouring a couple of pots and beckoned to me. Then Mr. Counter appeared behind him and Sugar moved away. We made our way through the crowd until everyone suddenly went quiet. Mr. Counter poured a lemon squash for Iris, thinking that she was not old enough to drink and he was probably right, but I grinned to myself, there's no way anyone could prove it!

A loud, deep raucous gravelly voice snapped through the silence. It was Swampy. He raised his pot high above the crowd and announced:

"Haw! Haw! To the best mate we have who beat the fuckn coppers and now he's got the best sheila in Norlane!"

"Here! Here!" chanted the crowd. And we all downed our drinks, even Mr. Counter from behind the bar, breaking his number one rule.

It was a bit hard getting out of the bar. Swampy and Spuds especially wanted to kick on, as usual. But Mr. Counter, Dad, shouted the bar and everyone was happy while me and Iris sneaked out the back and met him in the kitchen. Abbie was there, all smiles.

"Here's your bacon and eggs," she smiled, "and your room is all just like it used to be." She glanced a little warily at Iris. "And this must be Iris?" Her big teeth sparkled with her great smile.

"Yair, this is Iris," and I turned to her, grinning, "Iris meet Abbie my best friend."

"Servant, more like," Abbie joked.

Iris put out a limp hand and they shook. I looked around for Mrs. Counter but she wasn't there.

"Where's Nipper?" I asked.

"Ah well, it was very sad. He broke off his chain and scaled the fence, we reckon, and ran straight across the Melbourne road and a car ran him over. It was the busy footy traffic coming back from Melbourne."

"Too bad. But I always knew he'd have a violent death."

Iris squeezed my hand. She remembered that time with Nipper. But I was remembering something else. We sat down to eat our bacon and eggs, gulp down some tea.

Mr. Counter came in with my kitbag. "You left this in the bar," he said.

"Gees, thanks, I don't what I'd do if I lost it."

"Yes, I know."

Then Abbie chimed in. "Your clothes and everything are all in your room. And there's a towel there for you and I'll put another one there for Iris." She looked coyly at Iris, then to me. "You could do with a wash," she said.

"There she goes," I said to Iris, "she's like the mother I never had." And immediately I said that I knew I shouldn't have.

"Get settled in, son, and later today we'll talk about what you want to do."

"O.K. Dad," I said.

We got back to my old room and slammed the door shut.

"He's your dad?" she asked, "I thought your dad drank himself to death?"

"Yair, he did. It's a long story. But I got to hit the shower, don't I?"

"You do," she said, planting wet kisses on my forehead, the only place where there was no hair.

*

I'm sitting in the vestibule of auntie Connie's house, my books on the lace covered table. The light is dim and I peer through the lace draped window at the squalls whirling around outside, blowing old scotch thistles down the road. The first winter chill is here and light rain gently taps against the window and iron roof above. My uni books are strewn on the floor beside me. I can hear auntie Connie fiddling around in the kitchen.

The day I got sprung from gaol and returned to the pub, I'm trying hard to forget. I can't bear thinking about it but my mind keeps swirling around like the wind outside, sweeping up my thoughts, going around and around, obsessive thoughts, as Kate would call them. I'm at a loss to understand why things turned out the way they did, especially when I spent many hours, day and night, dreaming about Iris and me getting back together, repeating those magic moments after my Latin exam. And when I rushed out of the shower, a towel loosely draped around my body and barged into my room, and readied myself to pounce on her, lying there, on my bed, flat on her back, her hands behind her head, her hair, I now noticed, cropped short like it was the first day we met. I had planned to leap on the bed and get to work on her. But I don't know why, I thought she'd be there, lying there, naked waiting for me. But she was completely clothed and she looked at me, sort of past me with those grey disconnected eyes. For one horrible moment, I imagined her at Millie's, running from room to room, satisfying her customers. I dropped my towel and stood before her. Maybe that would be enough to bring her back. And there was plenty to look at, I can tell you. And she did glance at me, and she did hold out her arms, inviting me in. And I did approach slowly, and lay down beside her. I gently unbuttoned her little floral dress to expose her neat, still small and round tits, and tried to gently pull it off. I wanted her naked. She didn't help me in this task. Instead, I had to push her over to get at the buttons at back, had to put my hands up under her dress to pull off her panties. But at last, I had her naked, lying flat on her back. I cocked my leg over her and sat back, looking down, pleased with what I saw. She smiled and put her hands up to ruffle my wavy brown hair that needed trimming. I ran my hands through her firmly cropped hair and that was enough to send me off. I started at it, but I could see that her heart was not in it. She was going through the motions. Me, I was of course, going for it. But it was all pure sensation, my mind running in another direction. I rose up on my knees. She grabbed me and pulled me forward, guided me into her tits and it was there that I let it all out.

I sat back on my haunches, stunned, I don't know what kind of expression I must have had on my face. And then she laughed, looking down at my deposit, of which there was a lot. Maybe because of what happened she doesn't let anyone inside her any more. She's just too scared. Yet she didn't look scared. She looked amused, or something like that.

"What's going on?" I said, talking as much to myself as to her.

"Gees, I don't know," she said.

"Are you scared to do it now?"

"Maybe."

"Well, are you?"

"I don't think so. But you were just the same, weren't you?"

"Well, it's sex, isn't it? Like a friend of mine said, there's no bad orgasms."

"Except I didn't have one, did I?"

"Nah, so what's going on?"

"And who's your friend, by the way?"

"Just someone I met at uni."

Iris scowled like I'd seen her when she talked to Tank, "You asshole, you've been fucking uni girls while I was dying."

"It's not like that," I complained.

She put her fingers between her tits, scraped up some of my deposit and then stuck her fingers into my mouth.

"Oh shit and fuckn hell, Iris, what the fuck are you doing?" I screamed trying to spit it all out.

"So you're still the asshole you always were," she said, this time with a smirk.

"I spent months looking for you, Iris. I couldn't find you. It drove me crazy. I thought you were dead.."

"Yair, not crazy enough," she grinned, just as I was about to climb off her.

"You can ask my uni friends," I said.

"So, are ya going to give me an orgasm or not?" she asked with a big smile, the one that I liked.

*

I couldn't concentrate, so I put on my old school jacket and stepped outside into the cold wind and the rain that had died down to a drizzle. I walked into the open paddock beside auntie Connie's, picking my way through the big scotch thistles, some of them as high as my waist. They said there were lots of tiger snakes in among the old grey rocks, but they wouldn't be out in this weather anyway. I found a large rock covered in hard greeny-grey lichen and sat down, feeling the wet seep through my pants. The wind blew red dust from the roadside into my face and I covered it with my hands. They were building commission houses on this land too. I could see in the distance the half-built houses and hear the hammering of nails.

That first month at uni was gone, well gone. I had nowhere else to stay except here, and life was glum, as glum as it could be, because auntie Connie was a bitter old lady who never had a fuck in her whole life and she lived in a little house in this desert of a place that soon would be surrounded by a desert of commission houses. I knew as soon as Iris left, which she always did, a fact that I had conveniently forgotten—I knew that my life in Norlane was untenable. I woke up that morning and the window was open and Iris was gone, just like always. Where she had gone, nobody knew. She lived a life of fleeting moments. Like a ghost, she appeared here and there, disappearing for days in a row, reappearing somewhere else. For heaven's sake, she could just as easily emerge from one of these rabbit burrows in amongst the old rocks. I knew that I had no future with her, nor she with me. And now I couldn't understand why I had been so obsessed with finding her. I should have gone on with my new life, an exciting and amazing uni life, and forgot about her. I nearly did, mind you. But I didn't, did I?

So here I am, stuck with old auntie Connie, poor thing. She's nice enough to me, but we just don't have anything to say to each other. I don't know what she does all day. She never goes out. Her groceries are all delivered every week. She watches TV in her room. And now she's got me. Kate won't take me in. I think she's done with me. I don't know about Grimesy. Maybe he's still doing her. Who knows? I heard that Dr. Pulcher's seminars were still going, though, but I dared not show up to one. Anyway, you had to be invited, and I wasn't expecting Dr. Pulcher to do that any time soon, was I?

I walk to Yarraville station every morning and take the train to Flinders Street and then I walk to the uni. They're long walks but I like them. I practice my Latin poetry on the way, and I talk to the homeless blokes all along Swanston Street. I have come to the conclusion, well it's not really a conclusion, that maybe Dr. Knappenberger was right. Maybe I don't belong there. I'm still struggling to catch up with all the work and I'm not getting very good marks with my essays and assignments. In fact, it looks like I could fail, even in Latin. The other students, I haven't seen what marks they're getting, but going by the tutes, they're a lot better than I am. They say that it's the final exams that count, so when they come, quite a few months away yet, I'll have to make a super human effort to get through them. They're like the matric exams only multiplied by I don't know how much.

*

One morning I was working really hard on forgetting Iris. She'd been in my head a lot, so as I walked to the Yarraville station, I started singing hymns to myself, the ones I'd learned in Sunday school what seemed like eons ago. I kept at it, all the way to the station, the train, and then Flinders street where the homeless buggers were hanging around the station and in the doorways on the way up Swanston Street. I had to work really hard at remembering some of them, but after a few days, they came to me easily, and I sang away, no noise mind you, I didn't want people looking at me thinking I was a religious freak. Then, as I walked up Swanston Street, shivering like buggery from the drizzle and cold wind, I found myself standing in front of the Church of Christ, a tiny little church nestled beneath a big office building, its tiny turrets sticking up like they were giving it the finger. I was singing *Onward Christian Soldiers* and just finishing the last verse and then to my favourite chorus that I would sing over and over again:

Onward, Christian soldiers,
Marching as to war,
With the cross of Jesus,
Going on before!

I pushed at the old red door, but it was locked. And I don't know why until this day, I started banging on the door and kept at it until my knuckles were sore. And then, just as I was up to *Marching as to war*, the door creaked open and a bloke with a pale, very smooth face, kind of like a much younger version of Dr. Pulcher, poked his head out.

"The Church is closed to tourists," he said.

"I'm not a tourist," I said, "I'm a uni student."

"So, come back when we are open for service."

And suddenly I blurted out, and to this day I just can't understand where it came from, "I want to talk with Jesus!"

The bloke looked me up and down and saw a Latin book in my hands. Yes, that's right. I'd given up on my kitbag and now just carried my books in my hands, like the other uni students do.

"All right," he said, "but just for a moment, mind. We don't want any tramps coming in here."

I slipped inside and made my way straight to the front. I'd only been in one other church ever, and that was the little Baptist church behind the hall where I went to Sunday school and did my matric exams. That was a simple little church made of wood panelling and frames, weatherboard on the outside, painted cream. This church was made of stone, of course, much older, but it was just as simple inside, except for the pews that were all really heavy and polished, and the wood floor just the same. The walls were painted white, and the long and thin stained-glass windows pretty simple, disappointing because there were no scenes from the bible, just floral designs mostly. I sat in the front pew, and my eyes came to rest on a tiny crucifix nailed to the wall above the small wooden altar. But instead of Jesus talking to me, it was Flo, for God's sake. I'd lost control of my head. Gees, I really needed Kate.

I looked around me and was relieved to see that Flo was definitely not in the church, only the bloke who let me in. He was standing at the back of the church with his arms folded. And then I broke out in song, the song of Sunday school:

Jesus loves me this I know
For the bible tells me so –

My voice floated through the dark ceiling beams exploding against the slate roof, showering the entire church with pearls of song. At that very moment, I felt, like they say, born again, my childhood innocence resurrected. There was only one witness, the stranger, the bloke who had let me in. Except, when I looked around, he was gone. I continued my song:

Little ones to Him belong,
They are weak but He is strong.

I dropped my books on the floor and ripped the clothes off my body. "This is who I am! Take me Jesus!" I raised my hands, stretching my body as high as it would let me, standing on tip toe, reaching, reaching for the sky, almost yelling:

Yes, Jesus loves me!
Yes, Jesus loves me!
Yes, Jesus loves me!
The Bible tells me so.

For a very brief moment, I felt free, free of my life and all the troubles of the past. Was this what they called absolution? Did I hear him call my name? Naked, I ran forward and grabbed at the crucifix, unable to reach it.

And then I looked down and I saw I was truly naked. And I thought of Kate. What was this? How could I stand starkers before Christ himself? Embarrassed, I dropped down on my haunches, hugging myself tightly. Ashamed, it was, as if I'd exposed myself in front of everyone I'd ever known. If they knew what I'd just done, they'd never let me live it down. The only person who'd understand, it pained me to admit, was Flo, that sad sinner from my other world. I crawled back to the pew and gathered up my books. One of them was Plato's Republic. I gripped it so hard I almost wrenched it in two. If the other students in my Philosophy tute saw me now, gees, I'd be the laughing stock. Plato couldn't talk to Jesus, could he, Dad or Dads?

Father, whoever you are, can you forgive me?

11. Little boy lost

They were dry sobs, like trying to vomit up some awful thing inside his head, but it wouldn't come out. James screamed as loud as he could to get it out, but to no avail, though it did stop the sobs. The echo of the scream reverberated throughout the empty church. "Oh! Lord!" The words reverberated in his head, He opened his eyes and saw the little crucifix looking down at him, and he reflexively turned his eyes downward, where he saw two large shoes, brown suede hush puppies they were. And in them stood a large man, dressed in a crumpled open neck shirt, blue that reminded him of his old school shirt, tucked into well pressed gabardine Fletcher Jones pants, fawn, matching the hush puppies.

"My son," said the Pastor in a kindly voice, "let me help you." He leaned down showing his round face, wisps of fair hair tinged with red, combed across his bald head, a smile like that of Jesus curing the sick and dying.

"I'm not your son!" James yelled, "I'm nobody's son!" He leaped up from his haunches, a cat like leap, and tore the crucifix from the wall, lunged at the Pastor intending to pour out his rage and beat him to a pulp. Rage is a blinding force that, while endowing its owner with amazing strength beyond his ordinary capacity, also deprives its owner of its safety, not to mention reason. The Pastor was twice as big as the small, stocky James who attacked him without method or technique. The Pastor simply grabbed the wrist of the offending arm that held the crucifix, a vice-like grip that reminded James even through his rage, of Grecko's championship fists.

"Now I think you had better put your clothes on," said the Pastor in a calming voice, tightening his grip so much that it caused James to purse those thin lips of his, lips that were now trying to stop a scream of pain from coming out. He looked down at himself, suddenly feeling the vulnerability of nakedness. The Pastor sensed as much and slowly let go of his arm, carefully took the crucifix from his hand that quickly went limp, a movement that allowed James reflexively to cover himself with his hands. He stooped forward, aware of his pale buttocks baring themselves to the rest of the church, and of this calm man who stared at him with such kindness, it almost repulsed him. For he had never experienced such kindness in his life, or so he thought. Not even from his mother whom he now hardly remembered, not even from his new father, so-called, who when he helped him did so with a stern manner, always demanding something of him in return, always telling him what he could not do.

*

"What are you studying at the university?" asked the Pastor as he gathered up James's books.

"I'm not."

"What do you mean? Why are you carrying all these books then?"

"I've decided to quit."

"You mean, just now, this very minute?" The Pastor frowned, his lips bunched together as his cheeks stiffened.

"Yes. Right now, This very minute."

"But why? You look like an intelligent young man."

"I don't belong there."

"What brought this on? Let's sit down here and talk about it." The Pastor took James, now fully dressed, by a loose dangling arm that showed no strength at all, and ushered him into a pew.

"The professor told me so. I don't belong there."

"But all these books you have. Looks like you are engaged and reading."

"The Latin is too hard for me. I thought I was good, but I can't do it like they say I have to. And I can't keep up with the classes and I make a fool of myself in the tutorials."

"Where are you from, may I ask?"

"Yair, well that's it, isn't it?"

"What do you mean?"

"The professor, that German one they have, he asked me what high school I went to and when I said Geelong, he tossed my assignment back at me and told me I didn't belong at Melbourne uni."

"Oh, I've heard of that professor. He's an infamous bully. You shouldn't take any notice of him."

The Pastor still had the crucifix in his hand.

"I don't care. Anyway, he's right. There's a lot of other stuff I could tell you."

"Your father? I heard you calling out."

"I don't have a father. Not a real one, anyway."

"What do you mean?"

"He's dead. Or I thought he was."

"What?"

James's ears were now a bright red, his whole face and hands pulsing with the hot blood of rage. The Pastor calmly put his very large hand over James's clenched fist, the knuckles white, yearning to pound into something.

"Forget it. I shouldn't be telling you all this stuff. I've been in gaol too. I have to go."

James stood up and slowly pulled his fist out from under the Pastor's hand.

"My son," said the Pastor, "don't leave now. You're not up to it, and I wouldn't want you to make a hasty decision of some kind. Let's go out back to my office where we can have a longer talk in private and you can tell me more of what ails you. After all, you didn't come in here for nothing, son."

"I told you, don't call me son," James growled, his ears reddening yet again.

"Sorry! Sorry! My mistake. Come on out back and let's talk it over."

James slumped back down to the pew. He turned and looked hard into the Pastor's kind face, The slight curl of his lips, not quite a smile, but compassionate; his eyes squinting, red-tinged eye lashes, blue eyes scrutinizing his face, offering help.

"Come on." The Pastor stood up and returned the crucifix to its place on the wall above the small altar. James stayed in the pew, slumped forward, then leaned down to pick up his books. "You are a fine looking young man," observed the Pastor, standing at the end of the row, his big hands grasping the backs of the pews, "you have a whole world in front of you, a wonderful life ahead of you. It will be what you make of it." James stood up, hugging his books to his chest, holding Plato in his hand. He edged sideways along the pew, towards the Pastor. "That's the way. I'm sure we can work all this out. And if I can't help, I know others who can provide you with the counselling that you need. I know a lot of people at the university. There is a fine chaplain there."

James stopped and looked at him quizzically. "I'm not going to any chaplain. I don't believe in any of that shit, anyway."

"And what kind of shit is that?" The Pastor then spoke in soft, measured tones. "You are in the Church of Christ. You knelt before a crucifix. You have faith, young man, or you would not be here."

"Then why am I reading this, then?" cried James, thrusting his Plato into the Pastor's chest, "he didn't believe in God."

"God created Plato and many others like him. He wanted you to learn to think for yourself, to understand how wonderful and complex life is and can be. Besides, I think he did believe in God in his own way."

"That's not what my lecturer says."

"University lecturers these days lack faith, unfortunately. But you, young man, I can see that you can think for yourself and that you do have faith."

"How to you know that? Only I can know that."

"You are here, aren't you? In God's church. You stripped naked before Christ the son of God. You exposed yourself to him. What more convincing act of faith can there be?"

James stared at the Pastor's blue eyes, wide open, clearly excited. His enthusiasm was catching. Tears welled up in his own brown eyes. "I don't even know you. You don't know me, what I've done," he said.

"I don't need to. I can see it plainly in your eyes." The Pastor reached out with both arms, James clung to his books, but found himself edging forward, getting close enough for the Pastor to embrace him.

And that is what the Pastor did. He hugged James to him, the books jammed between them up against James's chest. "The Lord is with you," whispered the Pastor, "know that he will be with you no matter what."

James felt a kind of mild delirium as he found himself snuggling his head into the Pastor's shoulder, feeling the warmth of his neck against his cheek. He would have stayed there for he knew not how long. He felt safe, even saved. But the Pastor gently pushed him away and stepped back from the pews into the aisle of the church. "Go, young man, go out into the world, do good and enjoy God's blessings."

James stood, holding his books, full of hope. Yes, he could do it. He would go out in the world. He was young. Fit. Strong. Able. Jesus brought him here, now he would take him wherever he went. He stepped towards the door of the church. The bright light of Swanston Street awaited him in the world outside. "I don't even know your name," he said.

"I am Donald Ming, Pastor of the Church of Christ, and I am very pleased to meet you."

"Gees, Mr. Ming. I'm sorry for smashing your crucifix. I'll come back and pay you for the damage."

"Don't worry. But do come back and let me know how you are doing. Of course, you are very welcome at our Sunday services and our youth meetings every Tuesday evenings."

"OK. Thank you. I promise I will come back. I walk up here every day to uni and back." He hurried to the door, once again ready to take on the world.

"You didn't tell me your name."

"James."

"James what?"

"James Henderson."

"A nice English name."

"I'm not a catholic, if that's what you're asking."

"Didn't have to ask."

James turned to leave, but then looked back. "You don't look Chinese," he said, "with a name like that, I mean."

"My great grandmother was an Irish Scot who came out for the gold rush in 1850 or thereabouts and met her Chinese husband on the gold fields."

"Oh," said James, not imagining how such circumstances could have arisen. He pulled the big door open and nodded good bye to his new-found mentor, even smiling as he left. He stepped out into Swanston street, the rain clouds gone, the late morning sun shining down, full of hope. He stood in the shadow of the big door at the top of the steps. "I have the world at my feet," he said to himself, aping the Pastor. The cool morning breeze of summer gently caressed his thick head of hair. He shook his head and sat down on the steps, his books in his lap. The breeze caught Plato's Republic, rhythmically turning the pages. He watched them until they stopped and his eyes came to rest on one passage:

Slowly, his eyes adjust to the light of the sun. First he can only see shadows. Gradually he can see the reflections of people and things in water and then later see the people and things themselves. Eventually, he is able to look at the stars and moon at night until finally he can look upon the sun itself.

He looked up at the sun, raising his hand to shield his eyes. What lay beyond?

*

The late morning sun warmed his forehead, dazzled his eyes. Clenching his books, he shifted into the shade of the big cone shaped doorway at the top of the steps. "I have the world at my feet," he again repeated to himself, thinking how he felt that day he bounded down the steps of the Baptist church after his Latin exam and into the arms of Iris. The warming breeze gently caressed his hair. He shook his head enjoying the breeze and felt a whiff of freedom, the pages of Plato's republic zipping further forward, but he paid no notice. He squinted across the street into the sun. People walked up and down, busy lives, going who knows where. He looked up Swanston Street towards the university and was immediately brought back to earth. He put his books beside him and buried his head in his hands. What was it to be? Here he was, on his way to the uni, not wanting to go, convinced that he was destined to fail. But the Pastor's encouragement had deeply affected him. Nobody had quite spoken to him like that ever. It was advice, but advice given in kindness and compassion. All the advice he ever got from his "father" was given with a touch of resentment, always hard edged, always conditional. Do this, or you'll be sorry. Not like the Pastor. Look to the future, youth is on your side, was what he said.

I'm young, I can do something with my life. There's a lifetime of hope ahead. And if I don't go on up the street to the uni, where will I go? Back "home" into my dreary little room in auntie Connie's house in Yarraville, its lace curtains keeping out the sun, living in the bedroom that was my mother's? I lie there on the lumpy bed, the window wide open every night, hoping that Iris will sneak in. But she's gone again, and will never come back. And auntie Connie hovers over me, smothers me. It's like being smothered in Plato's cave. The Pastor is right. I have to look forward, go out into the world, make something of my life. I've been stuck in a cave far too long. I was imprisoned in that old pub and all those stupid people, now I'm imprisoned in the cave of the past, auntie Connie reminding me with every cup of tea and biscuits, of how my mother supposedly loved me. And if she did why did she leave me, sitting there with my dad, who wasn't my dad, helping him on his way to his disgusting end. And what lay ahead? Failure assured at the uni, a fascist professor and a poofda Latin teacher self-proclaimed mentor and pervert.

James stirred, clutched his books and walked slowly down the old bluestone steps. He looked up the street and walked towards the university. Then he saw, across the street a soldier standing on the corner, stopping people as they walked by, handing out pamphlets. He sauntered to the corner and crossed by the lights. The soldier saw him approach and immediately walked part the way across the street to meet him.

"Have you registered for the draft?" he asked.

"What draft?"

"The war, Vietnam," said the soldier, amused.

"Oh, yair, I forgot," grinned James, "I was going to."

"How old are you?"

"Nineteen, going on 20," James lied.

"You have to register when you're twenty, you know."

"I know that. But anyway, I might enlist before that. Go over and kill a few Japs, you know," grinned James.

The soldier looked at him, puzzled, even more amused. "Japs aren't in this war. It's Vietcong we have to kill this time."

"Viet-who?"

"Vietcong. Thinking of joining up? Here's a pamphlet to give you some information. It's a great life. You'll have an exciting adventure, and at the same time make a man of yourself, get out in the world, and of course, you're serving your country, doing what every great Aussie does who loves his country. Keeping the commies out of here."

James took the pamphlet, shook the soldier's hand. "Goodonya mate," he grinned. He wedged the pamphlet into *The Republic* and sauntered on towards the university. He had walked up to the next set of traffic lights, when he stopped, managed to tuck his books under his arm, then pulled out the pamphlet to see what it said. The front showed a picture of a helicopter landing in a clearing in the middle of the jungle. Young musclebound men with great smiling faces were leaping down, running forward into the jungle. He unfolded the brochure and there before him was a large group of happy, very youthful faces of nineteen-year-olds, just like himself, all dressed in military uniform, slouch hats, some even with arms round each other. The captions read:

Make friends for life, go to war for your country, save us from communist peril. Sign up for three years, get a big bonus at the end, and help towards your further education.

Now, one could say that James, at this moment, was vulnerable and confused. He had just ripped off all his clothes in a church and tore down a crucifix. He was lucky that the Pastor had not called the police, because with his record of arrest, he could easily have ended up in the Collins Street police lock-up. He returned the pamphlet to its place in *The Republic* and stood at the corner, to an observer, looking lost. But he was not lost, he was thinking. Thinking not all that clearly, maybe, but coming to a conclusion that his choices, bearable choices, were few. Failure at the uni was certain. He had tried to keep up, and especially devastating was the struggle with his favourite class in high school, Latin. The fact was, he just wasn't smart enough, not as smart as all the others, who spoke English like the pommies, who came from fancy private schools. It hurt him deeply that he could not measure up, not like back at the pub where they all thought he was a genius. The old bastard professor Knappenberger was right. The uni was no place for him.

James looked back at the soldier, old enough to be his father, still handing out his pamphlets, engaging in jolly chit-chat with passers-by, snapping back at the occasional uni student who gave him anti-war cheek. He looked up and grinned when he saw James approaching. "Don't tell me," he said, "you want a draft registration card. Well I'm sorry, I don't have them. You get them at the post office. Anyway, you should have received one in the mail by now."

James looked the soldier in the eye. "I don't need one," he said, "I want to sign up."

"Mate! You're a uni student aren't you?"

"Yair, but I'm done with it."

"Young fellow, you've come to the right place, and I can tell you, you'll never regret it."

"OK. So, what do I do?"

"Come on inside and we'll do the paper work. Of course, you'll have to pass the basic medical first. But by the look of you, you're just the fit and wiry young bloke we want, a good match for the Vietcong bastards hiding away in their tunnels like ferrets."

"All right then. I'll sign up for a year and see how it goes," said James confidently.

The soldier laughed. "A year? Not likely. The minimum is three years. We spend half the first year training you."

"Then I suppose it has to be three years." James sat down on the one chair available, dropping his books on the bare steel desk, all the furniture painted with khaki army style colours. The soldier sat at his side of the desk, pulled open a drawer and withdrew a stack of application forms. He looked up and scrutinized the stack of books. "So, you're doing Latin and Plato?" he said. "You must be sick of it. All words and no action. You've come to the right place." He leafed through the stack of forms. Here's all the forms you need. Just fill them out, mainly all you need to do is write in your full name, date of birth, address and names of your next of kin. Then sign at the bottom there and you're signed up, pending medical and administrative approval."

"Administrative approval? What's that?"

"You know, the higher-ups. The ones that's been to uni. They'll give you some tests to make sure you can read and write and do a bit of arithmetic. I don't really know what they do, to tell you the truth. I'm just a lowly corporal, and that's where I like to be."

James leaned back on the chair. "And will they send me to Vietnam?"

"Depends, mate. You look like a pretty fit and sprite young bloke. You'd be great at dodging bullets in the jungle, I reckon," said the corporal with a grin. His forty-year-old face lit up with a big smile that reached the entire width of his face, showing a bunch of crooked yellowish teeth. The furrows from the edges of his mouth ran all the way up to his eyes that slanted slightly inwards, mischievously squinting out from under his low brow. James looked back at him, pen in hand.

"I just sign here?" he asked.

"Yep! And then I'll help you fill in the rest of the form."

"And then what?"

"You wait until you get your call-up, and then you get your medical and start your training all on the same day."

"Where do they do the training? Puckapunyal?"

"Depends. It might start there, but you'll end up at the jungle training base in North Queensland."

"You been to Vietnam?"

"Nah. Too old now. Hurt me leg anyway, can't do combat any more. Did some time in Malaya, though. They were the best days of my life, that's what. Found myself a Malayan beauty too and brought her back here. These Asian women, they treat their men, well, I'd best not tell you anymore. It's for you to find out. Sign the form and let's get on with it!"

James stared into the corporal's face, a grey face, his dark beard showing, even though there were signs that he had recently shaved. It sounded like bar talk to him, like he'd heard lots of times in his days at the old pub. He leaned forward, gripping the pen tightly, holding it above the place on the form where it said signature. "Here goes!" he said.

"Press hard," urged the soldier, "it has to make three copies underneath."

James pressed hard, and began the down stroke of the "J." But as he did so, a big fist clamped over his hand, causing the stroke to go off across the page.

"Stop! Do you know what you're doing?"

James looked up, shocked and angry. It was the Pastor.

"What the fuck are you doing here? Let go of me!" James growled.

"My son! You're signing your life away!"

"I told you, you're not my father! Asshole!"

"I'm not letting you sign that," said the Pastor, his figure towering above both James and the soldier sitting at his desk, meekly looking on. "Corporal, or whatever you are. This boy is not in a proper mental state to make such an important decision."

"And who are you to say so?" asked the soldier, gaining his composure, "the kid is over eighteen he's got a right to do what he wants."

"First of all, he's just a kid. Second of all, he had what I'd call a mental breakdown fifteen minutes ago inside my church."

The corporal stood up, the metal chair scraping against the concrete floor. "Is that right, James? That's your name, isn't it? I'm having trouble reading it upside down."

James tried to pull his hand from the pastor's grip. The pastor laid his other hand on James's shoulder. "You must not do this," he said calmly, then he let go and cried, "thou shalt not kill!"

The soldier grabbed a handful of pamphlets from his desk. "I'm having no part of this," he grumbled and walked out.

*

James was late for his Phil 1 lecture. The old door creaked when he opened it to peek in. The lecturer was down at the lectern, droning on as usual, one eye on his lecture notes and the other on the clock half way up the wall at the side of the lecture hall. James tip-toed in and slid into a seat in the top row at back. The lecturer's voice barely carried to the back, where he sat alone. There were some twenty other students scattered about the hall, built like a theatre, seats for some three hundred students. There were supposed to be that many in the class, and on the first day of class there probably were. But the crazy system was that you could buy a copy of the lecturer's notes for a shilling from the philosophy department secretary, or get a free copy from another student who had taken the course before. So, reasoned James, there was no point in going to the lectures unless it was a way of making you learn the material, especially because the lecturer read out his notes word for word, stopping exactly on the dot when the clock showed that the lecture time was up, and he'd even stop in mid-sentence.

James looked up at the clock. There were exactly ten minutes of the lecture left.

I don't know why I'm here. That bastard of a pastor, pushing me out the door and up Swanston street, past the corporal still handing out pamphlets. Who did he think he was? My father? I felt like a little kid who didn't want to go to school.

Of course, I hadn't read the lecture notes and had no idea at what point the lecture was at. The other students I met in the philosophy tutorials told me that you didn't need to know what's in the notes. Just get a hold of previous years' exam questions and swat up answers to them. They were often repeated, and if you were lucky you would have prepared answers to the questions that showed up on the final exam. But it's only a few weeks till the exams and I haven't done anything to study for them. I know I should have. But I just haven't been able to make myself do it. I just go to uni and hang around the café, drink loads of shitty coffee, watch the smart bastards playing snooker or poker in the student union, maybe read Farrago. I'd even walk across to the Ballieau library and watch all the conchies working away. But I couldn't make myself do anything.

Then came the Latin tutorial. I wasn't ready for it, I don't know why I bothered to go. That smart Iris look-alike with long hair, she could do everything, and the smug tutor Lepidus, his public-school tongue preening his thick lips like a Pomeranian, salivated every time she opened her mouth. He always read out the Latin for her to translate:

"Similis est haruspicum responsio omnisque opinabilis divinatio; coniectura enim nititur, ultra quam progredi non potest. Ea fallit fortasse non numquam, sed tamen ad veritatem saepissime dirigit; est enim ab omni aeternitate repetita, in qua, cum paene innumerabiliter res eodem modo evenirent isdem signis antegressis, ars est effecta eadem saepe animadvertendo ac notando."

I looked around the class, the other students all with their heads down, trying to figure out what sentence they would have to translate when their turn came. I always tried not to sit next to her so I wouldn't have to follow her. But this time I came in late and had to sit in the only vacant chair that was next to hers. She had lips too, voluptuous lips, that's what I'd say; full, bright red, reminding me of Kate. I twisted around as if to speak to her, my eyes straining to get a look at her full lips. She smiled as she spoke, tossing her head back, smart bitch that she was:

"So, it is with the responses of soothsayers, and, indeed, with every sort of divination whose deductions are merely probable; for divination of that kind depends on inference and beyond inference it cannot go. It sometimes misleads perhaps, but none the less in most cases it guides us to the truth..."

"Thank you, Miss Robinson. Well done!" drooled the tutor. "Continue Mr. Henderson."

My eyes were now staring vacantly in his general direction. All I saw was a blur of the small thin window that opened out on to the green lawn beside the library. I stared at the book, not even knowing what page I should be looking at.

"Mr. Henderson? Do you have the right page? It's page twenty-five, in case you haven't yet found your way."

I remained silent, sweat running down my sides and no doubt showing in beads on my forehead.

"Mr. Henderson?"

I gripped the book with both hands, dropped my head, in a silly and hopeless way, as though the tauter my body, the better the chance of translating the passage. My lips were pursed shut, my teeth clenched so tight. "I, I," I stuttered.

"You know, Mr. Henderson, divination may well apply in your case. I think I can safely predict that you will fail this course if you do not do the required amount of preparation for the class," he said sarcastically. The bastard never did like me, right from the first day of class when I said fuck or something and never knew I'd said it.

"Fuck you, and fuck the rest of you," I muttered, throwing *De Divinatione* on the floor. I stood up pushing over the chair and left, calling over my shoulder as I went, "I'm not playing your game anymore."

Who knows what they said after I slammed the door. I knew what I had to do, now. Find Kate. Those lips had awakened me.

*

James squatted on the lawn and squinted at the Ballieau. The autumn sun warmed his face as it sat perched above the glass building. He turned and lay down flat, his books strewn around him. This was the very spot where Kate had roused him, that first day he had made it to the uni. He had not heard from her since that last time he stayed in her flat and serviced her like the hungry dog that he was. And Grimesy had never mentioned her to him at all, even when he was in gaol. Of course, there was no reason why he should not contact her, but the truth was he had never thought much of her once she stopped the sex. He had never thought of what they had as a relationship. More like an unstated deal, out of which he got much more than did she, or at least that was what he thought. That was his trouble. He just did not think much about anything or anyone. He took things as they came, did things without thinking. He had always been like that, impetuous, and, until Kate came along, basically out of control. It was his bad temper, that's what his mother always said and so did both his dads he guessed, but they never told him so to his face. Mr. Counter even seemed to like his "standing up for himself" as he called it when he got into fights at the pub. Kate had taken him in tow, taught him how to control himself, that was what made their relationship so special. Not like Iris who just reacted to him in fits and tempers, just the way he reacted to her. But unlike him, her solution was to just run off and leave him. A free spirit, that's what she was and always will be, thought James. Not like Kate. She always seemed to know what was coming next, always seemed to have a plan for herself and for him when he showed up. She was so calm, so sensible, and so good to him. Better than a loving mother. No telling him what he had to do, no threats of what would happen to him if he didn't do what he was told. A warm, though somewhat detached mother, who just knew how to quietly and calmly get him to do everything she wanted. Of course, it helped that pretty much everything she wanted, he did too. But she wanted it in a certain way, with certain flourishes, she shaped him, that's what she did. Not control, but sharing, nudging, caressing.

He rolled over and stared into the sun, his hand shading his eyes. It was just now dropping below the Ballieau. Someone walked past and for a moment he thought it was Kate. But no. He twisted his head around to look across at the Law School building. Maybe Grimesy would be there. He would know where Kate was. Maybe he was still getting it on with her. He had not heard much from him either, never heard from anyone because he was stuck out there in Yarraville with his aunt and her lace curtains and the scotch thistles in the paddocks outside his window. He struggled up and made his way across the lawn, past the library on to Royal Parade, crossed at the lights on Grattan street, and made his way up Royal Parade to Kate's flat. He was standing at her door when he remembered that he had left his books lying on the grass. But no matter. They could stay there, he muttered to himself.

The flat was on the ground floor of an old two story red brick building, set in a hollow square, ringed by poorly kept low cypress hedges. Dust and dirt from the busy road swirled around as he approached the door. He knocked, but the noise of the knock was overwhelmed by the clanking noise of a tram running down Royal Parade. There was no answer. He was about to knock again when someone appeared at the doorway of the flat across the square and called out, "there's no one there, been empty for a couple of months!"

James turned and walked away. He had better go back and collect his books, if they were still there. But on a whim, he decided to drop in at the pub on the corner just up the road. Maybe Grimesy would be there. They used to have a few beers there and sometimes that poofda professor would show up too. Though it was a bit too early, almost five o'clock. Grimesy would probably be buried in his law books or whatever he did, doing his articles they called it.

He entered the public bar and immediately felt at home, the pungent smell of smoke and beer, the noisy chatter of the blokes. "I'll have a pot," he said, as he dropped two shillings on the bar counter.

"Right-o mate," said the barman.

He took one sip, licked the foam from his lips as he had done countless times, and stared blankly across the bar counter at the picture of Queen Elizabeth propped up in between rows of liquor bottles. And then he felt a light touch on the back of his neck, fingers rubbing his hair. Blood ran to his cheeks and ears and he grabbed at his neck as though to shoo off a mosquito. The mosquito was too quick for him and in its place another hand, slender, long nailed hand, smelling of a familiar hand cream, grabbed his hand and pulled it away. And there, as he turned, was Kate, grinning in all her incredible splendour, garbed in a striking black dress, a deep V to show her cleavage, shoulder-less, knee-less, a mini dress like no other.

"What brings you here?" she asked. "Buy me a beer?"

"Gees, Kate. Been looking for you. Just came from your flat."

"Gave that up a while ago. Not there anymore," she said, smiling, her head held back, conveying the sense of distance James had learned to accept. She was never "his" not that he wanted her to be, after all he shared her with Grimesy, or to be more precise she shared *him* with Grimesy.

"Another pot," called James, "that all right, Kate?"

"A shandy would be better," she called to the barman "if you don't mind."

"Shandy? What's with you?" James asked with a frown.

"It's a bit early. Don't drink like I used to. So now you've found me, I hope you're not looking for what's gone long ago," she pondered defensively.

"No, no. Nothing like that. Need your advice."

"Got yourself in trouble again?" Kate grinned, squeezing his arm for effect.

"Well, sort of."

"Well, out with it!"

"I left my books lying on the grass in front of the Baillieu," he blurted, feeling stupid immediately he said it.

"James! That's all? Are you in some kind of trouble?"

"No, not like that. I haven't done anything stupid, well not that kind of stupid, though I did leave my books behind."

"So why don't you go back and get them? When did you leave them there?"

"Just now, just before I went looking for you."

"James, come on then. Get it off your chest. Out with it."

"In my Latin tute this morning, I…"

But Kate was looking past him to the door of the pub. James followed her gaze and there he saw against the bright light of Royal Parade, the silhouette of none other than professor Pulcher.

"Look who's here!" cried Kate, clearly a little nervous, and with good reason.

"Hello darling," purred Pulcher, "everything all right?" He looked fleetingly at James, then back to her, then stepped briskly forward and kissed her full on the lips and she responded in kind, a glint in her eye as she saw James gaping over his shoulder.

"Claude, love, you remember James here? Your favourite student from the recent past?"

Pulcher turned to James. His woolly eyebrows raised and lips pushed forward into a smirk. He frowned. "Oh, yes, of course," he said, speaking as though James were not there, "this is the one who nearly got us locked up, the one that killed that wretch of prostitute."

Kate took a deep breath and quickly grabbed at James's right fist which she knew would be coiled, clenched ready to strike. "James was cleared of all that, weren't you James?" she said, squeezing his fist and nudging her foot forward to press on his toe as well. Pulcher stepped back a little, cringing, as though he expected to be hit.

"You fuckn poofda shit!" he cried, his fist straining against Kate's grasp,

"James, now, these things happen you know. Calm down." Kate looked back at Pulcher and smiled, "James is going through a bit of a crisis right now. I'm sure he didn't mean that."

"I think I'll leave now while you two sort this out. I'll be waiting in the car, Kate," he said and turned and left.

Another piece of James's world had crumbled. He looked pitifully at Kate, eyes watering, trying not to burst into tears, embarrassed that this was so. He even wanted to slap Kate herself. Instead he blurted out, "so what about Grimesy, then?"

Now it was Kate's turn to be upset. This little upstart, she thought. How dare he, after all she had done for him, or to him was maybe more accurate. "I don't think that's any of your business," she said with a smile that could kill.

James pulled his hand free of her grasp. "I think I'd better go too. He grabbed his beer and gulped it down, then banged the glass back on the counter.

"Jimmy," she implored using the name she always used with him in bed, "you have to understand. Dr. Pulcher and I got married a few months ago. He's my husband."

James stared blankly at her gorgeous eyes and those lips he had so much enjoyed. And to think that Pulcher, that lecherous poofda now owned them. "You're fuckn crazy," he cried, "and by the way my name's Chooka." He made to leave, but Kate pulled him back, determined to make him understand. In a nostalgic way, she actually loved him. He was such a dear boy, so lovable, so raw.

"I'm not that young anymore," she said. "Don't you understand? Women like me, we have to think of the future, our livelihood. Claude is rich, he'll take care of me and my children."

"But he's a poofda, how will you have kids? He'll fuck you up the wrong way,"

"Jimmy, don't be a shit. Listen to what you're saying. After all, you gave yourself up to him too, for the same reason. Money and a place at university, your future."

James sniffed and let go of Kate's hand. There was no reply to this. He suddenly truly understood his situation. He had no future with these people. He wasn't going back for his books. Uni was no place for him. Yet again, Knappenberger was right. How many times would this have to happen before he believed it? Then he did what he thought he would never do. He turned his back on Kate, that voluptuous beauty of old, and swore that he would wipe any memory of her out of his mind.

12. Things we dare not tell

James lay on his mother's old bed, waiting. It was now several weeks since he signed up. Each day he got up around lunch time, showered, sat at the kitchen table and ate the eggs and bacon auntie Connie had cooked for him at nine o'clock. Each day he would stare at the cold eggs and bacon and the cold cup of tea. And each time he would get up, switch on the electric kettle, put the plate of eggs and bacon under the grill to warm them up, singeing them just how he liked them, then warm up his cup of tea, mostly milk anyway, with boiling water from the kettle.

Barely a word was spoken, Auntie Connie stayed in the front room, staring through the lace curtains, and reading her E.V. Timms novels. She didn't know what to talk to him about, and he didn't care to make it easy for her. After the eggs, he would shower, gather up a few of his books and set out pretending he was going to the university, mumbling "bye aunty," as he quickly slipped out the door. They had nothing to say to each other, thought James, indulging in self-deception that had become a habit of mind. The fact was he did not want to talk to her in case he let it slip out that he had signed up for military service and would be most likely going off to Vietnam. If she knew, she would immediately tell Mr. Counter who would then see to it that it all got reversed. Mr. Counter was an antiwar type, he knew, just like his old Dad.

Or maybe it's more accurate to say that they were only antiwar in their own lives, or for their mates who didn't want to go. Of course, they were glad we won World War 2, but those blokes—remember Bomber, the bloke whose arm I broke? And his brothers, a nasty bunch, but they were right, weren't they? Dad and dad—not sure which is which—were just selfish, that's what they were. Let the other blokes, blokes like me now, go out and

254

risk their lives while they stayed at home having a good time, working in so-called essential services. What a joke.

A cool breeze wafted in through the open window, always open, always ready for Iris. James could hear the scotch thistles scraping against each other as they bent in the breeze. "One day, she'll show, but she'd better hurry up. I mightn't make it back from Vietnam," he grinned to himself.

And as he grinned, he rolled over in his bed, buried his head in his pillow, lay on his belly, stretching, wriggling, hoping for Iris.

And then she came.

*

When young men, boys really, get together, so James knew, but came to find out even more so, they are capable of anything, most of all unmitigated destruction, accompanied by constant laughter. Jungle training proved to be a taxing, strength draining experience, but it did what it was supposed to do for the army: hardened these young men. "You come in as boys and you leave as men," their drill sergeant said when he welcomed them. And when they left, the sergeant said it again, but added, "and thank goodness, because the Vietcong eat boys for dessert." At Kokoda barracks, somewhere in north Queensland,, James learned all the necessary skills for surviving and killing, hand to hand combat, shooting with several different kinds of weapons, and the special skills of jungle warfare. And what the recruitment corporal had said turned out to be true. James's small, stocky size and his agility made him a prime candidate for leading small parties into the jungle around the Mekong Delta.

James felt confident, even ebullient, when they boarded the cargo plane, and sat in the sparse seats on their way to Saigon. He had excelled at training, even though it was hell at first being ordered around by a bully. But he was good at just about every-thing they made him do, and best of all, he wasn't making a fool of himself like he did at the uni. Here, all the other blokes were just like him. They were all equals, all looking out for a good time, adventure, and, of course what the recruitment corporal had promised him, looking forward to beautiful Asian women who would care for all their needs.

Except that they never got to Saigon. They landed at the base of operations in Nui Dat, near the Mekong Delta and some distance from Saigon, as he found out later. The base was only half built when he got there, and found that his job was to help clear out the people from the surrounding villages so the base

could be secured. They were going to move the villagers—
"relocate" them—the commander said, for their own safety. None
of them wanted to go, leave their homes and houses they had
inhabited for many generations.

*

We were all about the same age. We yearned for two things, sex
and violence, which I discovered amounted to the same thing. We
were so fit, had so much energy, there was no stopping us. The
platoon commanders, most of them from private schools and
university types, they knew that's what we wanted, and they
played on it. Kept lecturing us about respecting the local
villagers, they were "on our side," but we never believed them.
We knew from what other blokes had told us that you couldn't
trust anyone, kids included. The Vietcong were all over the place
and they'd kill you as quick as look at you. That's what. So, our
section, eight of us in all, would move into a village, go from
house to house, herd the poor buggers out and march them away
to another place that had these temporary prefab houses in a
jungle clearing. We did this every day for a month or more, I
suppose. But me and my mates had a deal. Each day one of us
would take it in turns of hanging back in the village as we herded
its people out. We'd look over the women, and depending on our
predilections, the bloke who hung back would select who he wanted.
There were no rules. You could choose whoever you wanted. I
always went for the young ones, the ones that looked like Iris. But
you'd be surprised about the predilections of some of my mates. It
wasn't long before I got tired of it, mainly because you felt you
could not take your time, enjoy the pleasures, not like it was with
Iris. It was a quick job most of the time, you had to slap them
around a bit, try to shut them up,

My mates gradually got the same way, and it was then that we
did unspeakable things that I dare not put on paper. We were, after
all, a pretty close bunch of blokes. We saw each other shit and
piss, we showered in the same showers, we slept in the same
dingy hut, so it wasn't long before we started ganging up on the
best of the girls, and the ones that resisted the most, we held
down for each other. We'd have been court-martialled if our
commanders found out, but there was no way they could find out.
If some villager tried to run on to the base to rat us out, they would
be shot before they got through the checkpoint. Besides, we often
justified what we did by accusing the girls of working for the Vietcong. They were the enemy after all and as far as we were concerned

we could do anything we liked to them. Of course, none of us had ever heard of the Geneva convention. I know, I know. They weren't supposed to be the enemy, we were in South Vietnam after all, they were supposed to be on our side. But none of us believed it.

It wasn't long before we got sick of the gang rapes too. The time floated by, the routine bullying of the villagers became just that, routine, no feeling for them at all. Just getting the job done. It seemed like years, but was only months, and the villages had been cleared out and the perimeter around our base was pronounced secure. More new recruits started to arrive, and we seasoned jungle men showed them the ropes, but by then, there weren't many young girls left. And we had heard that the Americans were trying a new strategy against the Vietcong, securing each village systematically, going through each village, rooting out any Vietcong suspects, and isolating the villages from Vietcong intrusion. Nobody believed it would work, and it was obvious why it wouldn't. All villagers looked the same to us, they were all Vietcong as far as we were concerned. So, when we were given the job to move into a village to round up suspects, we mostly just picked out the men who were about the same ages as ourselves and assumed that they would be in the Vietcong. And that's where a lot more unspeakable things happened. We devised various tortures that I still have nightmares about. And we all agreed, being really close mates, that each of us would take it in turns of doing it, because it soon became clear that a couple of us were much more into torture than the rest of us, and we thought that the best way to keep the lid on things so we didn't end up in a court-martial, was to spread the torture around.

*

As their commanders lecture them, young men, when they are carousing together, must be constantly reminded in war that it is dangerous and they could be killed at any time. It seems such an obvious thing, but was especially true for those whose mission it was to secure the villages of Vietcong. There were mine fields in many places, the constant threat of booby traps, many ingeniously constructed. And given their camaraderie it was a wonder that none of James's tight little group had been wounded, let alone killed. That is, until now.

James lay on his cot, the heat rising from the concrete floor of the infirmary, the canvas tent above sagging from the tropical rain, the humid air too thick to breathe. He coughed and choked, felt a terrible pain in his leg, no it was a numbness, not pain, of maybe both. As he had noticed in those he had tortured, the pain seemed to lose its effects. But not with James. He had given up trying to remember what had happened. The medics had stoked him full of drugs anyway. The drugs, he supposed them to be morphine, are way better than the booze, he mused. If only he could breathe. The suffocation brought him close to delirium, He drifted off, back somewhere, back where he was safe and secure. Talking to his Dad again. His Dad who was dying, no, dead.

Do you remember Dad? I'm feeling really close to you right now. Maybe I'm dying too? I look up from collecting glasses and there she is, right beside me. She's got this hair that looks like it was rinsed in mud from the Barwon river. Her face is all red and wrinkled up. You'd reckon it'd slipped down into her neck, that's how awful it was. Her left eye was all red and runny, and her right eye was hidden behind a swollen lump of blue flesh. And she's standing there, a blood-orange ribbon tied round her head, and she's got this dirty yellow dress that looks like a North wind blew it on her like a piece of newspaper slapped against a tree. What was her name again, dad? That's right, Bella.

"Two beers quick," she says.

Dad, you remember her, don't you? She picked blokes up in the bar, blokes she reckoned had some dough. You must remember her. She was the only woman I ever saw come into the old bar.

"There you are Bella. Now what the hell happened?" says Mr. Counter, dad, I mean. Oh shit. Dad, did you know?

James groans and stirs in his cot. A medic comes by, "you all right, son?"

"I'm not your son."

"Soldier, that's no way to talk to your dope source," jokes the medic.

Bella takes a few long sips of beer, licks her lips, and says, "shit, I picked a good one this time!"

"Yair?"

"He threw his leg at me. That's what he did!"

"He what?"

"His wooden leg. He took it off and threw it at me! Got me fair in the fuckn eye, here. See it?"

We could see it all right, Dad, couldn't we? You could hardly miss it. Then she tells us the story. She picked up this bloke with the wooden leg because she felt sorry for him, and as well, he had won a hundred quid on the races that day. Besides, she reckoned she could manage a bloke with a wooden leg and not get bashed up like the others did to her all the time. So she helped him spend his winnings on a bit of grog, then took him home for tea. They get home and they drink more booze and they go off to bed. And she says to him, "take off your leg, it'll get in the way."

And he wouldn't do it. He wouldn't take it off.

"The dirty bastard!" she says, "it was good enough for me to take me pants off, so it was good enough for him to take off his leg!"

He says no and Bella says she kept nagging away at him to take it off and then she kind of fell asleep. Next thing she knows, she's half asleep, half awake and feels this tickling, burn on her ass. He's trying to wake her up by burning her with his cigarette!

"I believe it but thousands wouldn't," says Mr. Counter, I mean Dad number two, or maybe it should be number one. I don't know. What the fuck!

And next thing Bella says, "yair well, take a look! No panties!"

She turns around and lifts her dress over her head! And we all see the proof! The bloke had burnt his initials on her fat cheeks! So, she gets him to take his leg off and he does and throws it at her and it hits her in the eye. She grabs it and beats the shit out of him and then smashes it up. And without his leg he can't do nothing to her. She orders him out of the house, and the last she saw was him hopping down the street using the front fences to prop himself up.

And then she plonks the leg on the bar counter, all patched up with sticky tape, and tells Mr. Counter, Dad one, to give it to the poor bloke when he comes in next. And I bet the leg's still there, hanging on the wall just below the picture of the Queen.

James heard the medic's voice again. "I'm giving you another shot to calm your down. You're tossing and turning all over the place, talking to your father, who's not here of course. It's PTSD. It will pass."

"Doctor?" called James.

"What is it?"

"Have I lost my leg?"

"No, it's mostly all there."

"Fuck! Mostly?"

"There's a big hole in your thigh, the tendons were smashed a bit. But we can stitch you up OK and when you get back home, they'll make you good as new."

"I'm going home?"

"That's right. When the next flight shows up."

"But I don't have a home…"

"Sleep, rest. That's what you need. Worry about other stuff later."

The morphine kicked in once again. James mumbled and fell into his dream world again, or was it just another place where he could indulge his sickness and talk to his dads over and over?

*

Dad, you're sitting on your stool in your corner of the old bar. I think we're dying together, you know that? No, you don't have to grab me like that, I know you're there. Ouch! Don't pull me. I know, you're trying to protect me, but I'm old enough to take care of myself. What's that Dad? I should stay out of the Snake Pit, stop pulling me. Who? Shotgun Sally Doolan?

Boy! What a great hunk of fat she was. She comes into the Snake Pit and says, "I'm sick of the three ins." Remember? She was married to one of these two brothers and lived with them both. We all reckoned she might as well be married to them both. No one could figure out which one she was married to anyway. They were little blokes and she bossed them round, bashed them up at least once a week. One of them always had a black eye. I think they called her "Shotgun" because she had a shotgun wedding,

She always looks real sick and tired of everything. And she orders her usual, that awful yellow stuff, got egg in it, what was it called? That's right Advocaat. No wonder she was so big. Drinking those horrible things. And the barmen. They hated mixing them. She orders it and says again, "I'm sick, I yam. I'm sick of the three ins."

And Mr. Counter says to her, "and what might they be?"

And she says, "Sick of smoke-in, drink-in and root-in!"

Then she just quaffs down that yellow stuff and grabs one of her blokes by the ear and says, "we're going home, you little bugger. And where's your brother?"

They reckon she did them both at once. I was just a kid then, and I believed it, even though I had no idea what it entailed. But after my tour of duty here, I know it's more than possible because me and my mates have done it and more. Unspeakable things I tell you, Dads, both of you. You'd be amazed. And jealous too, even if you wouldn't admit it. Well, maybe not you, Mr. Counter, Dad number two now.

James felt strong hands grab him and lift his weight on to a stretcher. He heard the vague drum of the old DC9's props. The medic yelled in his ear. "Home! You're going home!"

Dad, the number one Dad, the one that's dead, the only one I can talk to. I'll tell you everything. All the unspeakable things. And only you will know.

13. The way I treated father

"James?"

"My name's Chooka."

"It says James here on your record. See? James Henderson, Blue Platoon. The jolly fellow, freckled face, carefully combed reddish fair hair, a small wave coiffed in front. Just like the Beaver's hair in *Leave it to Beaver.*

James struggled to open his eyes. Morphine persists long after it has been injected. It's the eyes that go first and that come back last.

"Open your eyes, you mug!"

"Fuck off!"

"Sounds like you're coming back to life, the old Chooka I knew!"

Chooka struggled to open his eyes, felt vague aches down below. One leg raised above the other, perched on a large soft pillow.

"Your Dad sent me. He couldn't get away."

"Which fuckn one? I've got two you know."

"What kind of bullshit is that? The drugs are talking. Wake up and look at me, you bugger."

"Two. There's the dead one and the live one."

"Stop putting it on, Chooka. Open your eyes."

Chooka felt around down below. He spread his hand out carefully and took a very large handful of softness, jiggled it around. It all was there. "They took me leg off, didn't they?"

"Chooka. Open your eyes. It's me!"

"My fuckn leg! They cut it off! I'll have a wooden leg, just like the poor bugger at the pub."

"Chooka! You're all there, although I'm not sure if you're all there inside that silly head of yours. Wake up! Bugger you! Your dad sent me. He's got you a job."

"I'm in the army. I don't need a job. Fuck off!"

"Jimmy, mate, it's Grimesy. Paul Grimes. Come on!"

"Grimesy? Shit! I don't believe it? Where are we? How'd you get here?"

Chooka opened his eyes, his large lids fluttering over the almond shaped eyes that Kate and Iris so loved. He let go the handful and extended his hand from under the covers. Grimesy took it and squeezed it hard. "You're in the Royal Melbourne Hospital, the one just down the road from where you and me and Kate used to get it on. That make you feel better?"

"Gees, Grimesy. I'm sorry. I should have known. It's the morphine or whatever it is they give you."

"Are you in pain?"

"Nah, nothing to speak of."

"Your Dad asked me to pop in. He's on his way up here. He thought it would be good if I came in first."

"Why? What's happened?"

"Your auntie Connie. She kicked it."

"Yair? What happened?"

"They found her in the kitchen. Heart attack, they think. Happened a week ago."

"Too bad. He sent you here to tell me that? I mean, it's not like she was my mother, not that it would have made any difference anyway."

"Jimmy. We don't want to talk about that. And I don't think your dad wanted to either."

"You mean Mr. Counter. I don't know if he's my dad or not. He says so. I don't know."

"I think he probably is, after all he's told me. Anyway, you might as well go along with it. He's a good bloke."

"Yair, he's all right I suppose. He's helped me a lot, but he keeps interfering with my life."

"That's what fathers do, isn't it?"

"You're beginning to sound like Kate. Has she been talking to you?"

"No. Haven't seen her in ages."

"She got married didn't she?"

"So I heard. And good luck to her. She did it with that silly old bugger Pulcher. What a laugh! Lots of money though, and he has a great house. I saw it when I went to the wedding."

"You were at the wedding? How come she didn't invite me?"

"You were in Vietnam."

"'But I saw her before I went to Vietnam."

"Really? Well, that must be because they officially got married a few months before they actually had the wedding. But I don't know, Jimmy. It doesn't matter, does it? You wouldn't have gone to the wedding anyway, would you?"

"S'pose not. I don't know."

"You heard anything of Iris?"

"No. You still carrying a torch for her?"

"She's all I ever had, really. I got nothing else. Except my army mates, and that's good. I tell you, these Asian women…"

"You better stop there, Jimmy."

"It's Chooka."

"Yes, Jimmy, I know. But I've always called you Jimmy, and it's staying that way."

"So, what's Mr. Counter got lined up for me this time?"

"A job."

"I'm not going back to the old pub. For one. Two, I'm staying in the army."

"I'm told you'll be discharged after you get out of here. You're no good to them any more with one and a half legs."

"What? They told you that?"

"Not exactly, but it's what they meant. You'll get a decent pension and a scholarship to the uni if you want it."

"Fuck the uni. It's not the place for me."

"That's what we all thought."

"Who's that then?"

"Me and your dad, and I talked with Kate too. And there was a Pastor too, some bloke from the Church of Christ on Swanston street. He was really upset. Reckoned you were tricked into signing up by some recruitment officer."

"So I'm just supposed to do what you all have decided for me?"

"We're trying to help you. Jimmy. You've had a rough trot."

"Well I don't want to be helped. I'll find myself a job."

"It's head barman at the Newmarket Hotel."

Chooka turned away and winced as he pulled on the muscles of his wounded leg, and quickly rolled back again to face Grimesy. "Newmarket? That's near the stockyards, isn't it?"

"Yes. A great place. Famous footballers go there and I hear a lot of racing blokes. Bookies too. Near Flemington racecourse. Sounds like just the place for you."

"So you say. I'm tired. Need to sleep. I don't know, Grimesy. You're a good bloke, and Mr. Counter, Dad, he means well."

Chooka's voice trailed off.

"I'll be back," said Grimesy, "and your Dad will be with me."

*

The pain of life descended on James when he finally woke up, the morphine no longer an option, an ache pulsing deep inside his thigh, and worse, the revolving thoughts in his head, feeling like a pressure cooker, the pain behind his eyes almost unbearable. It was on this day that Grimesy appeared again, accompanied by Mr. Counter. The nurse had just informed him that he had better pull himself together because he would be going down to rehab this morning for the first of two weeks of physical therapy. James stared at her, a woman in her forties, a thick smoker's voice reminding him of Flo, the stupid bitch.

"Come on, luv, get yourself sitting up, now. No slouching around in bed," croaked the nurse with a grin, rearranging the pillow behind his head, pushing him forward. "Come on now, sit up, up we get!"

"Up you, nurse. My head's exploding. I can't get up."

"Come along now. I'll get you an aspirin. Now help me, get yourself sitting up. Or you won't get your medal!"

"Medal?"

"Don't you returned servicemen always get medals for being brave?" she quipped.

"Yair? I suppose so," mumbled James as he made an effort to pull himself up in bed and sit up against the extra cushion the nurse had placed behind him.

James could not know that outside the hospital there was a noisy group of demonstrators, waving antiwar placards, reciting in unison, "Make love, not war! Make love, not war!" walking round and round in a large circle in front of the Royal Melbourne Hospital entrance. Their numbers had begun with just a few early in the morning, but were rapidly growing. Word had got out that there was a special wing of the hospital that housed wounded vets from Vietnam. He might get a medal or two. But there would be no thanks for having served in a very unpopular war. The huge peace march of many thousands down Swanston street had happened while he was in Vietnam.

"All right, now. There you are. All bright and handsome for your visitors," announced the nurse.

"Visitors?"

"I'll get them now. And I'll bring back an aspirin too."

*

The nurse, closely followed by Grimesy and Mr. Counter, returned with a small glass of water and an aspirin in her hand. "Here you are, take it. Your visitors are allowed fifteen minutes only, then you have to go to rehab."

"You're as bad as my army sergeant," complained James with a grin.

Grimesy stood back, pressing Mr. Counter forward. "Here's your dad, Jimmy. I told you he'd be with me this time."

Mr. Counter put out his hand and James feebly raised his. It may have looked feeble, but it wasn't because he had no strength. It was because he had no will, still unsure whether Eddie Counter was his real father, and even if he were, whether he should treat him as such. Grimesy guessed the problem. "He's your real dad," he said, "we had the hospital do a blood test. You have the same blood type, and besides you look like each other, don't you?"

Eddie. Eyes watering, grasped James's limp hand. "Jimmy, you really are mine, you are my son."

But James responded mechanically, "I might be your son but I'm not yours." He looked him right in the eye, still belligerent.

"Sorry! Sorry! That's not what I meant. Call me Eddie if you can't call me Dad. Come on Jimmy, let's try to get off to a fresh start."

"Kind of hard, isn't it? I mean, I probably killed a prostitute, failed uni, did unspeakable things in Vietnam," James cried as he let his head fall back on the pillow. He closed his eyes and waited for the aspirin to numb his pain.

Eddie leaned forward. "Grimesy tells me you were injured, got a buggered-up leg?"

"It's going to be OK, they said." James opened his eyes and looked once again straight into Eddie's eyes that squinted back at him from under a furrowed brow.

"You stayed with your old dad, though, didn't you? You stuck by him. That's something to be proud of," Eddie responded.

"Except that the two of you tricked me and he wasn't really my dad."

"But what matters is that you did the right thing, Jimmy, isn't that right? You did the right thing, just as you bravely did the right thing and fought for your country in Vietnam. You're a straight arrow and good person, in spite of yourself, Jimmy, and I'm proud to have you as my son."

James squeezed his eyes shut. His leg hurt and the headache pounded away on his left side. He wasn't ready yet to acknowledge Mr. Counter as his real Dad. "Heard of Iris?" he asked, eyes still clamped shut.

Eddie wanted to say, haven't you got over her yet? It's time you did. But he folded his tongue against his teeth and said nothing. The silence caused James to open his eyes and asked again. "Iris? What's she doing?"

"We haven't seen her for a long time at the pub," answered Eddie with a sigh.

"You want me to have a look for her?" asked Grimesy trying to be helpful, knowing of course, that looking for Iris was a lost cause. And James, of all people, knew that.

"No. I was just wondering. I missed her in Vietnam."

"Sure, you did," said Grimesy with a smirk.

"No, not like that, shit-head," grumbled James doing his best to hold back a grin.

Eddie grabbed the moment, the first time the small glimmer of a smile appeared.

"I've got you a job, if you want it," he said.

"Job? I'm not going back to that shit-hole you call a pub," growled James.

"Jimmy, I told you yesterday," said Grimesy, it's not the old pub."

"Oh? Gees, sorry. I forgot. Must be the drugs. Where was it?"

"I have a mate who's the licensee at the Newmarket pub. You can start there as soon as you're able to get about. And what's more, you can stay in Connie's old house in Yarraville. You know she died, of course."

"Yair? About time. She might just as well be dead as sitting there staring at the lace curtains all day."

"Shit, Jimmy! Haven't you got a nice thing to say about anyone, even after they're dead?" said Grimesy impatiently.

James turned his head away. Now even his mate Grimesy with whom he'd shared a lot of good times, was getting at him. He tried to bury his head in the pillow.

"She left you her house," said Eddie.

"She what?" Jimmy sat up suddenly awake.

"She left you her house in her will. It's yours, but it will cost money to maintain, and you have to pay the rates and things like that."

"But I don't want to live there. I couldn't live there. Sleeping in mum's old bed, the lace curtains, those scotch thistles. Anyway, it's too far from Newmarket."

"Well, you'll have to decide what you want to do. I'll take care of the house until you are well. But then it's up to you what you do with it."

The nurse suddenly appeared, banging the door open as she trounced in. "Time, gentlemen, please! We have to go to rehab, don't we Jimmy boy?"

14. Before we were married

The Newmarket hotel was a small step above the old Corio Shire pub even though it was probably much older. Painted in a sickly cream over brick just like the Corio Shire, but two stories high, it looked like two buildings, their steeply gabled roofs joined together, one half of it, probably the first part of the pub had a crenelated front, a protruding cornice over two narrow windows on the second story, the ground floor composed almost entirely of large windows. The second, larger part of the building was all stucco at the ground level, set back further from the footpath, shaded by a large portico supported by wooden columns, rather worse for wear, decorated with cheap wrought iron at the corners of the where the columns met the eaves. From across the Geelong road, one could see, set way back, a lone tall chimney, rising above the big sign that said "NEWMARKET HOTEL" in large blue and white letters, colours meant to convey the North Melbourne football team. Across the footpath from the one door that opened to the public bar rose a very tall utility pole, its typical crucifix-like shape supporting buzzing electric wires upon which sat, perennially, swarms of seagulls and cantankerous magpies that came to rest after feasting on the scraps and remains of slaughtered animals from the abattoirs one block away.

*

James had a spacious room up the stairs and at the back of the pub, much bigger than the one he had at the old Corio Shire. The licensee, Frank Highlands, his new boss, was a short, stout jovial bloke, who dressed like it was the last century, resplendent in a dark pinstripe double breasted suit, a fob pocket, and even a pocket watch on a chain. And when he walked, he swaggered in the way that some stout people do, his arms almost horizontal and his legs apart to keep his balance. Whenever someone spoke to him, especially if they asked him a question, no matter what it was, he had a habit of pulling out his watch to check the time.

James took a liking to him instantly and enjoyed bantering with him back and forth, even though it appeared to him that he was head barman in name only. There were maybe a half-dozen barmen including a few part timers for the rush hours, but they were all treated exactly the same, none was more senior to any other. James was happy with this arrangement, at least for the time being. He just wanted to be part of the blokes, do his job, have a few beers afterwards, have a few laughs, and everything would be all right. Nothing to worry about.

He reached under the bed and pulled out his old kit bag. He opened it with difficulty, the latch was stuck. The old bag had seen many traumas. He leafed through random notebooks, not caring to examine them closely. There was an empty notebook which he pulled out and looked around for a pencil. He had a mind to put down some of the things he'd done in the army. But he had no pencil and besides, there were unspeakable things, things that could not be put down in writing, that was for sure. But the notebooks reminded him of the old days at the Corio Shire pub, the fun he had hanging out in the public bar, they were great times. And there was Iris, in her prime at thirteen years old, oh how he missed her.

In this pub, though, there was an even bigger contrast between the public bar and the saloon bar compared to the old Corio Shire. The rough and ready blokes that came into the public bar were a lot like the blokes at the Corio Shire, though a lot of them smelled a bit because of their jobs at the abattoirs across the road. But the saloon bar, that was something else. The price of the booze was a lot higher and they served fancier drinks, drinks that James had no idea how to mix. And the blokes that came in there were all dressed to the nines, ties, sparkling white shirts with cufflinks, suits and swanky sports jackets, and a lot of the younger blokes with crew cut hair styles. Many of them had tall, expensively dressed women hanging on their arms, sparkling jewellery hanging from their ears and necks. This was not a place for James, but his boss insisted that he get experience in all parts of the pub. So, on this day, he grudgingly tended bar, putting on his best manners, talking like they did at the university.

In the corner of the saloon bar which, unusual for a pub of any kind, had tables and chairs to sit on as well as the few stools drawn up to the bar, James noticed a bloke sitting at a table in the far corner, counting money, placing it in piles, a thick notebook at his elbow, in which his lady friend, dressed like a secretary, her hair coiffed high and extreme like fairy floss, wrote as he dictated to her. When he saw James looking at him, he nudged his secretary who quickly grabbed the two empty glasses in front of them and approached the bar. James kept peering at her partner who continued to count money.

"Two soda waters, please," she asked.

"Don't I know you?" called James, looking over her shoulder at her bloke.

"He's my boss," she whispered, "and he doesn't like to be asked questions."

"Two soda waters coming up. That's twenty cents. I'll bring them over to you."

"My boss will pay you," she said.

"Looks like he could afford it," grinned James. He poured the soda waters and, managing just a slight limp, carried them to the table. "Here you go," he said, "two soda waters."

The bloke looked up briefly and said, "put it on my tab."

"What tab is that?"

"The one they keep under the bar by the sink."

James leaned on the table and looked more closely. "Now I remember. You're Skeeter, aren't you? Don't you remember me? I used to be your runner at the old Corio Shire."

"You got the wrong bloke, mate. Corio Shire? Never been there."

"I was just a kid. You ran a book behind the back fence near the dunny. You taught me the hand signs. Look, I can still do them." James stood back and waved his hands and arms, signing with fingers. "And I remember that one time when the cops chased you across the paddock and you ate the betting slips."

The money-counter looked at him with a smirk.

"Maybe..."

James extended his hand. "Chooka they call me, I was Harry Henderson's kid."

"Pleased to meet you Chooka. I'm Studs Mackerel, gambler supreme."

"You don't remember me?"

"Not today. But maybe tomorrow," said Studs with an air of mystery.

"Well, I remember you as Skeeter and that's what I'm going to call you."

"Call me what you like, so long as you have money to bet with."

At that moment, Chooka's boss waddled into the bar.

"G'day Slim," called the gambler.

"Still counting your ill-gotten gains?" grinned Frank. "Have you met my new head barman?"

"We just met."

"I used to work for him," announced James.

"No kidding? If I'd known that, I wouldn't have taken you on!"

"Now, now Frank. Ease up, or I'll call in a couple of debts you owe me," said the gambler. "Anyway, he's mistaken. I never been anywhere near the Corio Shire pub. Been coming here for years, you know that."

"If that's what you say," intervened James. No doubt you've got good reasons to lie about it, he thought.

"James! Meet Studs, Studs Mackerel. The best bookie in Melbourne and easily the finest gambler in Australia!"

"Yair. We met. I remember he was a great bookie."

"Do you follow the ponies?" asked Frank.

"Nah, not really. I liked working for the bookie though at the old Corio Shire. Very exciting and a lot of fun outsmarting the stupid cops. I was only a kid though."

"Tut! Tut! We don't talk about the Queen's finest like that around here. Never know who's listening," warned his boss, "isn't that right, Studs?"

But Studs was busy dictating numbers to his secretary. Frank tilted his head in the direction of the public bar, and James followed him there, where his eyes immediately came to rest on a large, contorted frame, lounging over the bar.

"Gees, if it isn't Swampy!" cried James.

"Haw! Haw! Ya love me so much ya followed me here to the meat market? Haw! Haw!!"

"Eddie told me you was here, haw, haw. He told me to look after you, so that's what I'm doing."

"You came all the way up here to do that?"

"Nah. It's the cattle sales over at Flemington. I come here every few months."

"Are you staying here, then, in the pub?"

"Fuck no! I wouldn't spend one minute more than I have to in this haw, haw, noisy dump of a fuckn city. Got me truck outside. Soon as I'm done, it's back to the farm."

Chances were, though, that Swampy would be sleeping in his truck.

*

Swampy stood at the bar with his drinking mate, half his size, just as filthy, an oily face that oozed sweat at his temples, yellow dried saliva at the corners of his mouth, large hands a deep colour of reddish brown as though they had been baked in the sun, his face the same colour. They called him Banger for obvious reasons; he was the head slaughterer at the abattoirs. And he smelled like it too.

"Go on, Swampy, you won't get married. You aint got wot's needed to do it!" Banger grinned, pushing his glass forward. "Fill her up, and do Swampy's too."

James complied, expertly pouring the perfect beer, an exact quarter inch of head in a fresh glass.

"Hey, sonny, not a fresh glass, don't you know the head's better in a used glass?" Banger growled.

"Sorry mate, but it's new health rules. We're not allowed to fill used glasses. Has to be a new glass every time," replied James as he raked in the money and went to the till.

"What's this shit? You gotta be fuckn kidding me!" whined Banger.

"Rules is the rules," said James with a smile, proud of his bad grammar, then to change the subject, "so what's Swampy not got?"

"Haw! Haw!" chuckled Swampy. "Wot ya mean, aint got wot's needed?"

"You haven't got one. Bessy bit it orf."

"Haw! Haw! Haw! Ya bastard. Haw! I got the biggest y'ever seen!"

"Bull shit, Swampy. If you've got one, it's too small, I bet!"

"Yair? Who'er you to fuckn talk? Betcha ain't got much neither."

"Bigger'n yours, I bet."

"Yair? Bet mine's bigger."

Swampy looked him up and down and reckoned he could win because Banger was short and stocky, whereas he was over six feet tall with long legs and fingers.

"Betcha?" says Banger.

"Yair. Betcha five fuckn beers."

"Yer sure?" asked Banger, a big smirk on his face.

"Yair, c'mon, who's got a ruler?"

James produced a ruler. Swampy licked his moustache and rubbed his leg with his toe.

"Right ya bastard, fuckn whip it out! Haw! Haw!" chuckled Swampy.

"You first. You made the bet."

"Awright, ya bastard, if you're fuckn scared."

Swampy unbuttoned his fly, his fingers go in then flip it out holding it between his thumb and finger. He stretches it out as far as he can.

"There y'are, ten fuckn inches. Beat that!"

"Shit! Not bad Swampy! But you should see mine."

Banger reached into his kit bag and pulled out a blood-stained newspaper parcel.

"Well? Haw! Haw! C'mon, let's see it. How long?"

Banger undid his fly and then holding his parcel down near the place, suddenly flipped out a long, thick, blood-stained black thing which was that of a horse! "I win," he bragged, prancing around, flipping it up and down like he was shaking off the drips. "Mine's longer than yours!"

Swampy made those deep donkey noises of his and wiped his nose on his sleeve.

"Ya fuckn bastard! Fuckn bastards all of you!" he yelled with a big grin. He grabbed Banger by his dirty blood-stained shirt collar and pulled him towards him. Then he bent down and placed a big kiss on his cheek, his large moustache prickling Banger's nose as he did so. Banger shrieked and pulled away, dropping his parcel. Everyone in the bar cried out in unison, "Oh fuckn shit!" And Banger added, when he had managed to compose himself, "What a fuckn prick!"

James lined up five glasses. "You want them all at once?" he asked with a grin.

*

"I hear you and Kate parted ways," said James.

Grimesy stared at James across the wide Saloon Bar counter, an amused look on his well-scrubbed, closely shaven face and said, "I told her to fuck off."

James was grudgingly working the Saloon bar. It looked like that was where he was going to be stuck for some time. He disliked it. Didn't like the smart-ass bastards that came in there, reminded him too much of the uni. No doubt that's why Frank wanted him in there. At least he was mostly on his own so was his own boss, except when the part-timers came in for rush hours.

"I suppose I should have warned you," said Grimesy, sipping a beer that James pushed across to him. "But I thought you weren't in too good a shape to take it."

"Are you still fucking her?" asked James as he wiped off the counter.

"I asked her to marry me, would you believe it?" said Grimesy.

"Bull shit!"

"Just kidding."

James looked up and flipped the damp wash cloth at him. "No, you're not."

"She was doing Pulcher all that time, in between you and me, would you believe that?"

"Not then, but now I do. That two-timing bitch."

"Take it easy James. We did pretty well with her, didn't we?"

"We did, I admit it. She taught me just about everything I know."

"And you knew fuck all back then, you poor little Norlane boy!" quipped Grimesy.

"Fuckn grammar school poofda!" retorted James.

"I'll take another pot, and put up another one as well. I'm expecting a mate to show up any minute."

"You've got a mate? I thought I was your only friend."

"Very funny. Think you're a big man now that you've been to Vietnam and fucked all those Asian beauties."

"I fought for you and the rest of you smart bastards and I've got the scars to prove it!"

Grimesy looked away towards the small door that opened to Geelong Road.

"By the way," said James, "I need to talk to you about my house."

"The one you inherited from your auntie in Yarraville?"

"Yair. I'm going to sell it."

"Really? Did you check with Eddie first?"

"It's none of his business, is it?"

"Why don't you want to live there? It's not that far from here."

"It's a shit-hole. Those fuckn wild scotch thistles and the lace curtains."

"But there'll be new houses all around there soon, so there'll be no more thistles."

"Anyway, I like it here. More action. More to do."

Grimesy grabbed James's busy hand that held the wash cloth. "You're up to something, aren't you?"

James looked Grimesy in the eye. "I just want to be my own boss," he replied. "Don't you want to be your own boss?"

"Are you kidding? I'm a young lawyer in a law firm! I've got bosses everywhere I look!"

James pulled his hand away. "Yair, I suppose so. Sorry about that. You ought to do something about it."

"I am."

"Like what?"

"I'm getting older and so are my bosses. Soon, they'll be too old, and I'll be ready to take their place. Anyway, you should hold off on your house until…"

James moved down the counter to serve other customers. He glanced up at the door and saw it open, the glare of Geelong Road hit his eyes and against that glare he saw what he could not believe, almost dropped the glass he was filling at the tap. He carefully looked down at the glass and placed it in front of the customer, grabbed the edges of the counter with both his hands to steady himself. His injured leg shot pains up into his thigh and crotch.

"James!" called Grimesy. "I told you I was meeting someone!"

And there he stood at the bar, flanked on one side by Eddie Counter, and the other by Iris. James mechanically took the customer's money and rang it up in the till. Then he stood, gaping at Iris, both hands gripping the bar counter, his knuckles white, his arms shaking. He tried to speak but nothing came.

"Where's the service here?" called Eddie, "three pots please!"

"Just a dry ginger for me," whispered Iris.

"Never mind, I'll serve them!" called a voice from behind. It was Frank swaggering in from the public bar. He looked at his pocket watch, then filled two glasses. "Go on, James, go around and say hello to your Dad and you haven't introduced me to that lovely little thing he has in tow."

Eddie spoke up. "G'day Frank. Meet Iris, an old friend of the family, especially James. And I believe you're met Paul Grimes here."

"Pleased to meet you all. How are things going down at the Corio Shire, Eddie?"

"Just the same. Getting ready for 10 o'clock closing hours. How about you?"

"Yair, going to be a bugger. They're making it hard for us poor publicans to make a living."

"That's for sure."

Iris stood mute, looking down, her hands clasped together, fingers nervously rubbing her knuckles, almost embarrassed to be there. It had taken a lot of coaxing, if not a little force, to get her here. Eddie had the window of James's old bedroom nailed shut after she slipped in one night. Everyone had collaborated to catch her. Like chasing a rabbit. But, like a trapped animal, she had suddenly dropped all resistance, bared her throat, allowed herself to be taken, cleaned up in the bathroom by Abbie and dressed in nice new clothes that Linda had bought her. "Tell little Jimmy that I've missed him and I hope you bring him back home with you," said Abbie with her big toothy smile. Iris did not answer, as was her usual way. Abbie understood. She had been with Iris when she went through her bad times and good times with Jimmy. Mr. Counter and Jimmy's mate Grimesy had been very insistent that she not let Iris out of her sight for one second. But Iris made only one feeble effort at Jimmy's bedroom window. Abbie suspected that Iris was not really serious about running off.

James just stared. Although still short, Iris was no longer thin and child-like. Her body had filled out, breasts full, almost buxom, a welcome feature that James had missed, having spent himself entirely on the skinny shapeless bodies of Vietcong girls. It's true that often they reminded him of Iris, but that was when she was a girl. Now, he could see that she was a woman. Abbie had applied just a hint of rouge on her cheeks, hiding that emaciated pale face that had haunted James ever since that terrible time he searched for her all over Melbourne and Albert Park. And her lips, the seagull wings that he always adored, were touched up with a pale but strong pink.

*

James had just joined Iris at the bar when the Saloon door flew open and in walked Studs Mackerel with his entourage, his secretary on his arm, her hair exactly the same, coiffed to the roof.

"James, better clear Studs's table for him," nodded Frank. A customer sat at Studs's table, not knowing that it was unofficially reserved. James asked him to move and bought him a beer to make up for the nuisance.

"Who wants in on the biggest deal of the century?" proclaimed Studs as he sat down at his table, his thick notebook in front of him, his secretary sharpening her pencil with an electric sharpener. A group of men, well dressed in sports coats, hush puppy shoes, shirts and ties gathered around him.

James sidled up beside Iris whose eyes had followed his limping figure coming towards him. In rehab he had learned to cover his limp pretty well, but he had to work on it and at times like now when he was excited to see Iris, he paid it no attention. He grabbed Iris's dry ginger and handed it to her, then took his beer and raised it high, an invitation for her to clink her glass to his. Grimesy and Eddie raised their glasses and Grimesy, never lost for words, said with a big grin, "To the happy couple!" Iris took a tiny sip and looked at James with that aggressive glint in her eyes, her mouth puckered forward and a slight frown. This wasn't going to be easy, thought James, but then nothing with Iris ever was.

They had one round of drinks until Frank looked over and said, "James, it's five o'clock, you better get behind here. It's getting busy." He turned to Iris. "Apologies young miss, but your bloke has to earn his keep."

"Yair, I've been telling him that for years," quipped Iris cracking her first real smile.

James was so surprised, never had he heard Iris joke in this way, that he downed his beer and slipped his arm around her, pulled her to him and kissed her square on her seagull lips. "Welcome home, love!" he whispered. "At last I've found you." Iris almost dropped her dry ginger. Memories of their childhood trysts came flooding back. Against her immediate inclination, she allowed her body to be pulled against his as she placed her dry ginger, still full, on the bar.

"Come one, James. Let's go! The customers are waiting!" called Frank, turning to Iris, "you are welcome to stay at the Newmarket Hotel, my dear."

"I'll get her stuff," said Grimesy, "where's the accommodation entrance?"

"It's around the corner, and up the stairs. Put her in number six, it's the biggest room in the hotel, and the one next to James."

Iris gently pulled herself free of James's hug. She wanted to say, "maybe you should ask me if I want to stay," but did not. She was in James's hands now, in a strange place, with no idea where it was. And the room was upstairs. There'd be no climbing out the window. James returned behind the bar, watching Iris trail after Grimesy. Eddie managed to lightly grab his arm as he limped past. "I'm proud of you son," he said, "I know this is what you've always wanted. Make the best of her, mate." James paused and smiled ever so slightly, but enough to satisfy Eddie. He nodded, and moved on. The wonderful thing as far as Eddie was concerned was that James let him call him 'son'. He waved to Frank.

"Going so soon?" called Frank.

"Got a pub to run!"

But he did not return that day to the Corio Shire pub. Eddie had decided that he would stay away when the new closing time clicked in, let Sugar deal with it all. Sugar, poor bloke, he had turned out to be a very good manager. Eddie let him run the place pretty much as he wanted. It was more important for him to accompany Iris and Grimes to Melbourne, and at last add the final touch to get James settled. James had always pined for Iris. Now he would at last get his wish. There would be no more excuses. And Iris seemed to have grown up a lot, mainly because, he suspected, she had lived with Linda in her house of business for some time now, with only occasional disappearances, and those to sneak into James's old room, as far as he could tell from what Abbie told him.

*

James worked feverishly in the Saloon bar. It was packed full of customers celebrating the end of 6 o'clock closing. It was auspicious that it was on this very day Iris had returned, James thought. The bar was the noisiest he had seen it in his few weeks working at the Newmarket. It wasn't just the end of 6 o'clock closing though. It was also because Studs was up to one of his deals, had most of his clients in a kind of frenzy. And this would go on for several days, leading up to the grand final of the football between Collingwood and St. Kilda. Each of them had, today, won their semifinal match. Studs had taken bets on those games too. Both of their wins were expected, so the payouts were not all that great, Studs had no doubt made out quite well. The surprising thing was that he was already taking bets on the grand final and blokes were falling over themselves to place their bets on one or the other, this even before Studs announced the odds.

It was 9.30 and some customers were beginning to leave, having realized that 10 o'clock was a very late time to keep drinking, their money was running out, and they were very drunk as well, not having slowed down their drinking, keeping at it as though the 6 o'clock swill was now the 10 o'clock swill. Frank had approached Studs and asked him to finish up, and Studs did so.

"Gentlemen," announced Studs, "It's time to go home. My secretary here is getting tired, she needs her beauty sleep! We'll be open for business tomorrow at lunch time. See you all then. And I'll have odds on the Grand Final you will not be able to resist!"

"Time! Gentlemen, please!" called Frank. "We'll see you tomorrow after 10.00 am."

James turned to serve one last customer then all of a sudden, Iris was standing beside him. "Thought you might need some help," she said with a tiny smile. She grabbed a dish cloth and began to wipe down the bar.

"Gees, thanks Sweetie," whispered James, putting his head close to hers, "you know women aren't supposed to be in the Saloon Bar or any bar really." He glanced quickly across to Frank who was busy saying good bye to Studs.

"You think I don't know that? You think I grew up in Toorak or something?"

"I was just joking. I love that you're here."

The last customer left and Frank went to lock the door. He called out to James.

"Check the bar and the Ladies Lounge will you James? Make sure they're all locked."

"OK Frank." James took Iris by the hand. "Come on and I'll introduce you to the other barmen and you can have a look at the Ladies Lounge."

"What for?" Iris asked.

"Never know, you might want to work there, wait on the tables or something."

To James's surprise, Iris did not resist. But then, you could never be sure what was going on inside her head. She herself didn't even know that.

"Who's that Studs bloke?" she asked. "He acts like he owns this place."

"He acts like that everywhere. I've known him for years. He used to be the bookie at the old Corio Shire pub. I kept nit for him and sometimes I was his runner."

"Runner?"

"Yair. He took the bets around the back of the pub just behind the dunny. I'd collect the bets and run back and place them for the blokes. I was just a kid then."

"So was I."

James led the way into the public bar where a few stragglers were still trying to empty the last dregs. And to his horror, there was a cop standing in the middle of the bar, bible held aloft. He gripped Iris's hand, and she, his.

"Shit!" murmured Iris, "is that who I think it is?"

"I'm not going in there," said James. He squeezed Iris's hand and pulled her back into the Saloon bar. He called to Frank. "There's a cop in the other bar. I'm not going in there, if you don't mind."

Frank smiled. "Oh, that will be the Preacher. Don't worry about him. He's harmless."

"Not to me he isn't. He destroyed my life, or nearly did."

"It's true," said Iris.

"Well I think you'd better tell me all about it one day. If it's that bad, leave it and I'll do the rounds of the bars.

"Thank you, Mr. Highlands," said James. He poured himself a beer and one for Iris, then led the way out of the bar, upstairs and to his room. "Come on," he said, let's get you settled into your new home.

15. Beware of them who have money to lend

Iris's room had two chairs as well as a bed, so they went there. James sat on the bed and handed her a beer.

"You know I don't drink that piss," she said.

"Oh, right. I just thought that you might have come to it, living with Linda and all. Has her little brat been tamed yet?"

Iris sat on the bed beside him as he placed the beers on the small bedside table. "I helped her keep her books, counted her money."

"But you can't read."

"Can now, sort of. Taught myself. Linda got me started, and I got the hang of it pretty soon."

"And her clients?"

"Fuck you! Fuckn men, it's all you think of!"

"Sweetie!"

"Do you have to call me that? I'm not sweet, am I? Never have been."

"Shit, Iris. You are a sweetie to me, and that's all that counts."

James reached for her, she felt new, not like any girl he'd held. No longer a girl, a taut solid body. He longed to run his hands over those curves. She sat, stiff. Unresponsive. He turned his head to her lips, ran his fingers lightly over them, lips in full bloom, but now clenched shut. She was not ready. Whatever she had been through in Linda's house, he didn't want to imagine, but could not stop himself. It made no difference any way. He wanted a piece of her, that's what. It had been a long time. And he pursed his own lips in an effort to put away those despicable thoughts.

Iris gently pulled away. "So, who is that Skeeter bloke? You were going to tell me."

James reached for his beer and took a couple of gulps. He got up off the bed and sat on the old leather chair, cradling his beer in both hands.

"Back in the old Corio Shire, they called him Skeeter because he buzzed round the blokes like a mosquito. You had to be careful or he'd bite you for a few quid and a lot more. I was his errand boy. He bragged that he'd only ever worked four days in his life, He reckoned he worked just long enough to slip over and do his back in and go on workers comp. He was always spending dough. He'd come in to the pub every morning at nine, soon as it opened, and drink till twelve then he'd take home a pie for lunch and have a snooze and be back at four and drink till closing at six. And on Saturday nights he'd buy half a dozen bottles of beer and a bottle of plonk to tide him over the Sunday."

"He was always on the take, though. He used to run a raffle. Mr. Counter wasn't too keen about it because he said it was against the law, but Skeeter talked him into it, saying it was for charity. He was a smooth talker, was Skeeter. He could talk anyone into anything. And the prizes were pretty good. He started out raffling chickens and ducks at a bob a ticket, and I sold them for him while I did my rounds picking up glasses. This worked great until a bloke that won the raffle claimed the chook as his own! Skeeter'd been pinching them from blokes' chicken coops!"

"But that never stopped him. He raffled radios and TVs. Of course, everyone knew he was pinching them, but nobody cared as long as it wasn't their own stuff that was pinched. Then Mr. Counter noticed that the same stuff kept being raffled. Turned out that the raffles were drawn in secret, and that Skeeter picked out a few mates to always win and for a small cut, they'd give their prize back to him each week!"

"And you worked for this bloke?" said Iris, unimpressed. But James talked on, he was on a roll.

"He was the smartest bookie too. He never wrote anything down, kept all the bets in his head. He reckoned if there was nothing written down then the cops couldn't get any evidence to do him in. And it was true, too. The cops knew what he was doing and besides some of them made a few quid off him themselves. A cop shows up and says to Skeeter, 'I'll have a quid straight out on the favourite in the last-race.' He wouldn't hand over any dough. If the horse lost, then nothing happened, but if it won, the cop comes around the back of the fence to pick up the winnings."

"Then those other cops came down from Melbourne. The flying squad they called them. They were a pack of bastards, They showed up every month and demanded a twenty quid fine from Skeeter, and if he didn't pay up, they'd make like they were going to take him in on some trumped up charge. He paid them for a while, but you know what cops are like. They wanted more and more and pretty soon poor Skeeter told them to get stuffed, and took off like a kangaroo across the paddock, chewing up the betting tickets and swallowing them as he ran. By the time they caught him there was no evidence, but that didn't stop them, did it? Nah. They charged him with loitering, creating a public nuisance, abusing a police officer and resisting arrest. And in court they told all sorts of terrible lies about him, how he beats his wife, threatened them with a knife and stuff like that, so the JP gave him thirty days in the clink. That didn't worry Skeeter one bit. He could make even the lousiest deal seem good. He said the only thing he missed in gaol was his regular few beers, but otherwise he didn't have to work, and what's more he got free meals."

Iris looked around the room. "How could you trust a bloke like him?" she asked in a matter of fact way.

"He always paid me pretty well. I had no complaints. But Mr. Counter put his foot down and wouldn't let him do any more gambling in the pub. The cops got to him, I'm sure of that now. But it didn't stop Skeeter coming up with other scams."

"Like what?"

"Gees, Iris. What do you care?"

"You're just the fuckn same, aren't you? All you want is to do me. Your head is just one big prick!"

"And you haven't changed either, it seems," observed James coldly.

They both looked away, their eyes resting on the small window above the bed. Then their eyes met, each anticipating what the other would say.

"Don't say it," said Iris.

"It's a long way down from the window, if that's what you're thinking."

"I don't do that anymore."

"Yair, right. So why are you here then?"

"Not to climb in and out of windows, if that's what you mean."

"Why, then?"

"What else did Skeeter get up to? One thing I know. He never showed up at Linda's, or I would have heard about it. And just about everyone from that pub did, you know."

James leaned forward and extended his hand. She took it. "I'm trying to be good," he said. "I've been through a lot."

Iris ignored his plea for pity. "You're obviously taken with this Skeeter bloke. If he means so much to you, I want to know what it is about him that's got you in."

"I'm not taken with him."

"Is it because now he's rich?"

"Iris!"

"Come on, you're jealous. You'd like to be just like him," chided Iris.

"He went to gaol, you know, as did I. I don't want to go back there."

"But?"

"All right. I'll tell you more. gaol gave Skeeter time to think up another even better scam. When he came out, he went straight back to his old drinking routine at the pub and he got friendly with the postie and milkie. Mr. Counter kept a close eye on him but never saw him take any bets. But he had lots of dough and Mr. Counter was sure that something was going on. And it was. I knew all about it."

"Skeeter got the milkies to leave betting cards—place cards they called them—when they delivered the milk in the morning to people's houses, along with any money they won with the previous bet. Then later the postie would collect the card and the money that was bet. He never got caught all the time I was working for him. Only trouble was I lost a lot of dough because I wasn't running bets."

"So that's it?" asked Iris.

"That's enough isn't it? The bastard pretends he doesn't know me."

"Who wouldn't?" she joked.

It was her invitation. James leaned forward from his chair, and pushed his head into her robust breast. She leaned forward and ran her hands through his still abundant wavy hair. He reflexively lifted his head, and tossed his hair back in the way that had endeared him to her when they first met. "Remember the time on the grass in the old burned out building?" he said as he lifted her on to the bed, wincing when his injured leg got in the way.

"Oh poor darling! Your war wound!" whispered Iris, "let's make it better."

*

"St. Kilda hasn't got a chance," said Frank as he poured a beer for himself and Studs. He and Studs often had a quiet beer on a Saturday morning just before Studs went off to the races for the day. He let Studs into the Saloon bar early, before it opened at 11.00 am.

"How would you know?" asked Studs as he leaned his elbow on the bar, a foot resting on the railing below.

"Because I know the doctor who attends the St. Kilda team. He says they're not up to it."

"You mean Phil the dill?" laughed Studs.

"Yair. You know him too?

"Of course. I know everyone. He thinks they aren't fit enough?"

"Won't be able to go the distance. Says they carouse too much, they're drunk every Friday night. What team could win if half them are playing with hangovers?"

"Hmm. What if Collingwood was in worse shape?"

"What do you mean?"

"Just saying. What if a few of their top players got sick?"

"Studs. Don't go there. You're not thinking of…"

"No! No! I would never think of such a thing."

"That's good to hear. The Grand Final. I mean, it would be a travesty. It's sacred! You can't fiddle with something like that."

"No of course not. But I just have an inkling about this. I think I'll offer good odds on St. Kilda to win. Besides Collingwood is the favourite."

"No doubt about that." Frank eyed Studs suspiciously. "You're not going to…"

"Of course not. You know me…"

"That's the trouble, I do."

At that moment James appeared at the entrance. "Everything's open, Frank. We're right to go for the day."

"Thanks, James."

"Hey, Chooka! Come over here. I remember you now," called Studs. "It was a while ago. Sorry I forgot. I was busy taking bets."

"No worries, Skeeter."

"It's Studs, you bugger!"

"Oops! Sorry. Studs. Pleased to meet you again. And for me, it's James. They don't call me Chooka around here. What you got cooking? I know you always have something going."

"As a matter of fact, how would you like to do a little job for me?"

"Wait a minute, Studs. He's my head barman," warned Frank.

"I know, I know. And a good one too I hear. Trained by one of the best at the old Corio Shire."

"How's Iris?" asked Frank, trying to change the subject.

"She's great, Frank. She's keen to help out or something. Could we try her out in the Ladies Lounge?"

"Doing what?"

"She could wait on the tables."

"We don't serve them. I don't want to start that. Too much trouble."

"Then something else?"

"Can she add up?" said Studs slyly.

"Yair. She's great with numbers. Kept the books for her sister's business."

"You need someone in the office, don't you Frank? Count the money, make it tally with the tills. Who's doing that right now?"

"I was going to have James do it. I've been doing it up to now."

"Gees, Frank. I wouldn't want to take on something like that on my own. It would be great if Iris could help out."

"It will mean you'll have to be up and out of bed and ready to start work at 8.00 am. Count the money, check out the stock and there's a lot more to do. The beer pipes have to be flushed out every week. Orders to place with suppliers. Could you and Iris do that?"

"Gee, that would be great, Frank. It will make Iris so happy."

"Are you sure you want to have your missus at your elbow every minute of the day?" asked Studs with a mischievous grin.

"We're not married," said James. "Not yet, anyway."

Studs and Frank looked at each other, amused. Neither of them had had much luck with their wives, of which there had been many.

"OK. We'll give it a go," said Frank as he emptied his glass and washed it under the counter. "But Studs, I don't want him getting mixed up in any of your scams."

"I wouldn't dream of it," smiled Studs as Frank looked at his watch and swaggered away to check out the rest of the premises before opening.

"Now, young man," said Studs as he turned to James. "Can I buy you a beer?"

"Thanks Studs," but I'm on duty. Not allowed to drink with the customers unless Frank says so."

"Suit yourself. Just one thing, though. I'd strongly advise that you put as much money as you can get a hold of on St. Kilda to win the grand final on Saturday."

James grinned a big grin. "That's Skeeter talking!"

"Not a bit of it. Skeeter was small time."

"Who's taking bets on the footy?"

"Me of course! You can lay it with me."

"But if you're sure St. Kilda will win, why would you take my bet?"

"Because Collingwood is the favourite. Everyone will bet on them."

"What odds are you offering?"

"For you, my new colleague, five to one."

"And on Collingwood?"

"Two to one."

"I'll have to think about it."

"Sure. But don't delay too long. The odds may change. You know where to find me, right here at my corner table."

*

Eddie couldn't believe what he was hearing. Sugar handed Eddie the phone, but when he went to take it, Sugar's hand didn't let go. Tell-tale beads of sweat appeared on his bald head and he licked his lips with a loose tongue. "It's your son," he said with his usual smirk.

"Sugar, give me the phone, damn you!" He wrenched it away from him, and Sugar's eyes stared blankly over his shoulder. "Get Sugar a biscuit!" he yelled out to the kitchen. Sugar had fallen to the floor, his arms and legs flailing, banging the unwashed linoleum floor. His foot booted Eddie in the shins and Eddie unthinkingly kicked him back. "Quick, he's going to kill himself!"

"Dad? Eddie? What's going on?" came the distant voice on the phone.

"Jimmy? Oh, sorry. Sugar, the silly bugger, is having one of his diabetic fits and just kicked me in the shins."

"Well kick him back!" mocked James."

The cook appeared with an Anzac biscuit, crumbled it up in her hand and stuffed it into Sugar's mouth while one of the other barmen held him down and stuck the wooden spoon in his mouth that the cook kept especially for these occasions. Eddie turned away and held the phone tightly to his ear.

"James, nice of you to call. How are you doing? The leg coming along OK?"

"Yes, Dad. Sorry I didn't get a chance to say good-bye to you when you left last Saturday."

"I had to hurry back to the pub. These new long hours, you know. We're having a hard time getting used to them. Never know whether the customers will stay around after six or not."

"Yair, I know what you mean, Dad."

"And has Iris settled in OK?"

"Yair, she's beaut, Dad. I'm hoping Mr. Highlands will give her a bit of work to do."

There was a pause. Eddie waited. What was coming? Jimmy only called him when he wanted something. They never did chit-chat anyway.

"Dad? You still there?"

"Right here, Jimmy. Looks like Sugar is coming out of it."

"Too bad," said James, quickly regretting it, "I mean, poor bugger."

Eddie waited again. The pause was a little longer this time.

"Dad?"

"What is it you want, son?"

Jimmy bristled. That word again, but he clenched his teeth and screwed up his cheeks.

"You must have plenty of money. This long distance call will cost you some," quipped Eddie.

"Funny you should mention money."

"Uh, oh. Out with it, Jimmy."

"I was wondering if you could loan me a thousand dollars."

"What?" Eddie held the phone away from his face and stared into the mouthpiece.

"A thousand? What for? You going to buy a house?"

"Not yet. But there's auntie Connie's house that's mine, right? So you could loan me the money and if I don't pay it back you can take it as a share of the house."

"I don't think so, son. What do you want the money for? Have you been gambling?"

"No, Dad, no! You know I don't gamble... unless it's on a sure thing of course."

"Tell me what it's for."

"It's to help Iris get on her feet. She wants to start a cleaning business."

"A cleaning business? But she wouldn't have a clue how to do it and where to get customers."

"She's real smart, you know. Just because she didn't go to school. And she can read now, too."

"Why don't you save up and loan her the money? Why don't the two of you get married, anyway?"

"Don't start on that, please Dad. You know we don't believe in it. And you ought to know why, oughtn't you?" Jimmy retorted, then immediately wanting to take it back.

Eddie could imagine the smart-ass look on Jimmy's face. "We all know what she's like, Jimmy. She'll just as likely take off through your window and take the thousand dollars with her."

"She's grown up, Dad. She's not a kid any more, and neither am I, and the window is on the second floor so she can't jump out of it anyway," he blurted.

Eddie paused once more. He closed his eyes tightly as if it would help him to say what he knew he was about to say but didn't want to. The little bugger! "All right. I'll send you a check, but I want it paid back in three months."

"Gee, thanks Dad. We'll pay it back sooner than that. Iris is a great worker, you know. And don't send us a check. We're going to drive down and pick up the cash, if you don't mind."

"Drive? You drive? Whose car?"

"Yair, Dad. That's one of the things I learnt in the army. Learnt how to smash up lots of trucks and jeeps."

"You've got your license?"

"Yair," he lied, "they had a special program for army blokes."

"All right then. When are you coming down?"

"Tomorrow. It's my day off. Mr. Highland's lending me his car."

"It will be great to see you, Jimmy. Iris will be coming too?"

"Yair, but I haven't told her yet. Bye, Dad. See you tomorrow."

"OK, son. Drive safely now."

*

Iris didn't like cars, she had hardly been in one. She refused to sit in the front beside James and sat curled up in a little ball on the back seat of Frank's lumbering Humber. Frank had been reticent to lend it to him, but in the end, relented, especially after Studs spoke up and vouched for Jimmy.

"Do you know where to go?" asked Iris, her voice thin with fear.

"Of course, I do. Just straight down the Geelong road."

"Why are you going back there? It's good riddance, that's what I say. Let's not go, and take a ride somewhere else."

"Iris, I can't do that. I promised I'd go down to see Eddie and the other blokes, if they're still working there."

"You mean that weirdo Sugar?"

"Yair, right! I'll give him another punch on the fuckn nose if he gets in our way, that's what!"

"What have you got against him? What'd he do to you? We're going down there just so you can punch a weirdo?"

"Iris, love. Cut it out will you? Anyway, don't you want to see your mum and sister?"

"Fuck them all," she mumbled.

"OK. Sorry. But Linda's all right isn't she? And I wonder if that little brat is still running around like crazy."

"She was helping out in the business."

"Business? No! You mean…"

"Not that. She's too young, but nearly old enough, says Linda. She just cleans the house and tidies the beds."

"Does she go to school yet?"

"I don't know, I don't think so. But Linda says she will send her, poor little kid. I'm glad I never had to go."

"Yair? You would have learned to read and write, though."

"I've learned enough of it from Linda. And I do the sums as well for her business."

"You mean count the money?"

"More than that, don't you know anything about running a business?"

"Nah, s'pose not."

The Humber stopped at the traffic lights where Yarraville Road met the Geelong road. James pointed to the left. "You see that little house with the low brick fence and the vacant lot beside it with all them scotch thistles?"

"What about it?"

"That's our house. Auntie Connie's old house that she left to me."

"So why aren't we living there, then?"

"Because the windows open too easily and you would run away too often," he joked.

"Ha! Ha!" Iris sat up and stared down the street. The lights turned green and the Humber lumbered forward. "But really. It would be better there and we could make it into our nice little home."

"And get married?"

Iris did not answer. She nestled back onto her corner of the seat, pushing against the door.

*

They arrived at the Corio Shire pub. James turned the Humber into the car park, and parked beside the old cypress tree. He grinned to himself as he remembered the corpse that was, and Dopey trying to find it. Those were great days, never to return he supposed. They got out of the car and James locked it carefully, according to Frank's seriously delivered instructions. Iris stood beside him, her arm linked to his. Unusual for her, thought James. "We'll go in the back way," he said.

"You mean, you want to kick that dog up the ass again?" quipped Iris.

"Yair, that would be a laugh, wouldn't it? But Eddie told me they lost him. He got loose and ran across the Melbourne road and some bloke ran over him. Serve the little bastard right, anyway."

James led Iris towards the back gate and was about to open it when he felt a bony hand clutch his shoulder, the fingers with long nails digging into his skin.

"Do not enter that place of evil!" croaked a hoarse, witch's voice.

They both turned to see who it was, though both already knew who it had to be.

"Flo! You stupid fuckn bitch! Take your fingers off me!" growled James. He wasn't beyond giving her a smack across that wizened nicotine stained mouth of hers.

"And the Lord said, do not partake of the evil drink."

"Bull shit, Flo. He did not. Please fuck off," ordered James.

"Don't talk to my mother like that!" cried Iris as she pulled at his arm. "She might be a witch, but she's my mother."

"Oh yair, right. You want me to smack her one for you, after all she's done to you?"

"Jimmy! Don't!"

James was not sure whether Iris meant it or not. There was no love lost between the two of them. And he was not sure whether Iris knew the circumstances of her birth that Flo had revealed to him that terrible night at the Geelong Hospital.

Flo let go of James and turned to face Iris, her nose almost touching hers, her smoky breath causing Iris to grimace. She took Iris's head in her hands, squeezing her cheeks. She then pulled her towards her and kissed her on her forehead. Iris let out a squeal of horror. Then Flo pushed her back and, still holding her head, pronounced in a screaming hoarse voice, "the devil lives inside the putrid innards of this boy! Leave him now while you can! The devil will play with you like a kitten with a mouse, he will taste your charms, then he will kill you like he did our dear sweet Millie!"

Iris shook herself free and recoiled in horror. But no sooner had she gotten free than she saw James poised, wound tightly, ready to spring like a tiger, his fists clenched as hard as cricket balls.

"No! Jimmy! No! Don't do it! It's what she wants! Jimmy, don't!"

James wanted to knock her block off, that's what. He grabbed the loose collar of her blouse and was about to strike her an unholy blow, when he felt a familiar hand grip his arm from behind.

"Take it easy, mate," said Grecko, we don't want another corpse in the car park do we?"

James turned to see Grecko smiling, tall, solid, steady, like he always was. The adrenalin suddenly washed away, he relaxed his grip of Flo's collar, and his arms went limp. "Gees, Grecko. You're a sight for sore eyes. You saved me!"

"That's what I'm here for, mate."

"And he saved Flo too," put in Iris. She pulled at James's arm. "Come on. Let's get back in the car and go home. This placed brings out the worst of you."

"I have to see Eddie to finish our business."

"I know, mate, and here it is," said Grecko, handing James an envelope.

"Gees, thanks Grecko. But I better go in and thank him."

"You can, but it's probably better that you don't go in. Sugar is there and he's the manager now. Things could get a bit nasty."

"I'll take that," said Iris as she snatched the envelope out of James's hand. "What's in it anyway?"

James tried to snatch it back.

"OK, kids. I'll leave you to it, but I think you had better get in the car if you're going to fight over it."

At this moment, they remembered Flo. She had dropped down on her knees, under the cypress tree, her gnarled hands clasped together, praying. James thought he saw the hulk of Tank, her husband-brother-father of Iris, fast approaching. "I think we'd better go," he said to Iris. He grabbed her hand and pulled her into the front seat of the Humber beside him. The car was still running. Grecko slammed the door behind them and they drove off. "We came all this way just for this?" asked Iris as she peaked inside the envelope.

"It's a thousand dollars," said James proudly, "and soon it will be five times that amount."

"Jimmy, what are you up to?" asked Iris, worried.

"You'll see," said James.

They spoke no more, Iris now comfortably sitting in the front seat, staring out the window. James imagining what he will do with the winnings.

*

They lay in James's bed, James well satisfied on many accounts.

"So why didn't you stay at the uni?" asked Iris.

"I don't want to talk about it."

"Why not? You're always complaining that I don't talk."

"That's different."

"Bull shit."

"OK. So you really want to know?"

"I wouldn't ask you if I didn't."

"I wasn't good enough."

"Why not?"

"Just like you couldn't read when I first met you…"

"But now I can."

"Yair, but I went to Geelong High School where they didn't teach me anything, so when I got to uni I couldn't do half the stuff. I was a big deal in my Latin class at High School. But at uni, all the other conchie private school kids were way better than me."

"So you gave up?"

"Sort of."

"You should go back."

"I can't. Because I flunked out."

"Won't they let you try again?"

"Nah. I did my dash. Besides I shouldn't have been there in the first place. That's what one bastard professor said, and he was right."

"Yair? What was it like, then?"

"I just didn't feel like I belonged there, you know?"

"Shit! I feel like that everywhere," said Iris, half joking.

"Yair, I know. I think that's why I love you so much."

Iris took her eyes off the window through which she had been gazing wistfully and said, "you really mean that?"

"We found each other when I fell into your arms the day of my Latin exam."

"But you passed that exam, didn't you?"

"Yair, but I shouldn't have. There's ways to kind of fake it."

"Fake? You mean cheat?"

"No, not really. I mean fake it. And the trouble was I felt like a fake walking around the uni pretending I was a uni student like the rest of them but I wasn't."

"But you were good enough to get accepted into the uni weren't you? I don't know. Can anyone just show up and go there?"

"Not really. Let's not talk about it anymore? I want to be with blokes like my own kind. And it's pubs where my kind hang out. It's that simple."

"And what about me?"

"You're my kind too, that's for sure," said James with a grin. He pulled Iris to him and they held each other so tightly they were one.

They lay together, dozing until James leaned over and switched on the radio. The grand final would be almost over by now. They could hear the yells and screams of the bar crowd as they watched the match. It must be close, mumbled James to himself.

"What's that sweetie?"

"So now I'm sweet?"

*

"And with seconds to go, the scores are level, it looks like this match will be a draw," announced he commentator.

"Shit!" cried James. "They can't do that!"

"Can't do what?"

"Saint Kilda has to win. Studs said so!"

"You bet on the Grand Final?"

"What do you think I got the thousand dollars for?"

Iris roughly pushed him away and jumped off the bed. "You stupid shit! Studs is a crook! And you shouldn't gamble anyway."

"Studs said it was a sure thing. He's got it fixed, that's what he said."

"And oh!" cries the commentator, as loud screams come from the bar, "with one minute to go Barry Breen has collected the ball from a scrimmage, throws it on his boot and it dribbles in for a point! The scores are now Collingwood 10.13, 73 and Saint Kilda 10.14, 74."

"You see?" said James, now sitting on the side of the bed, trying to grab Iris's hands. "We're going to be rich!"

"Jimmy, love. Don't you see what Studs is up to? He's pulling you in."

"He's a good mate," Iris. I've known him since I was a kid. He always treated me right."

Iris let herself be drawn back down to the bed. She ran her hand through his tussled hair like she always did. It calmed her, and it usually calmed him as well. "If we're going to live together we are going to have to share ourselves, I mean really share, don't you think? Remember that time we ran away from the pub and we were going to grow vegetables and sell them at the side of the road?"

James blinked and grabbed her hand, pulled it down to his mouth and kissed those beautiful slender fingers. Her hands were the most graceful thing about her. "We were just kids then," he whispered.

"Yair, but we truly gave ourselves to each other, didn't we?"

"Gees, Iris. I dunno. I never thought about anything like that."

"Well it's time you did."

"Gees, Iris. Maybe you should go to uni you're so smart."

Iris squeezed his nose between her thumb and forefinger. "You're a bastard, you know that?"

"We both are," grinned James, possibly the first time he had joked about his uncertain origin, but also only now realizing that maybe Iris did not know about hers.

Iris stared out the window. She bit her bottom lip. "I know who my mother and father are, unfortunately," she said wistfully.

James pinched her cheek with his rough hand and kissed her lightly on her fluttering lips. A seagull landed on the rusting corrugated iron roof just outside the window and wailed for something to eat. "Come on!" he said, let's go down and collect the winnings!"

"Let's not," purred Iris, "let's share our winnings right here. We're worth more than a thousand dollars."

*

Most of the bar were Collingwood supporters. A few fights erupted over the loss, St. Kilda fans sneaking away quickly to find a St. Kilda-friendly pub, James emerged looking sleepy, as did Iris. Frank gave them a fierce look. They were supposed to have been in the bar long before to cater for the big crowd of heavy drinkers.

"You two, get into the saloon bar. There's going to be some heavy drinking now till closing."

"Right Frank. Sorry, we lost track of the time, and then got distracted listening to the footy."

Yair. OK. You're supposed to be the Saloon bar manager. Now do your job," growled Frank as he waddled away, looking at his watch.

"We close at ten, right?" asked James.

"Right. So get to it."

"What about dinner?"

"What about it?"

Frank stared at them both. Iris squeezed Jimmy's hand. "I'll take care of it," she said, "we'll grab a pie or something as we go."

"And later on, Studs and I want to talk to you, Jimmy," said Frank.

"Oh, you mean my winnings?" said James, excitedly.

"That and more. You're a game young bloke, that's for sure," said Frank and he waddled away into the public bar, slapping customers lightly on their backs, buying them a drink here and there.

People were not yet used to the late closing hours. Most of the customers stayed around till six and then started to drift away. There was no six o'clock swill any more. Jimmy missed it, the mad excitement and shrill din of the drinkers calling for more rounds of drink, glasses clattering, money hitting the counter, the ring, ring, ring of the old cash register. By seven o'clock there were only a few customers still in the bar so Iris went off to get a couple of meat pies from the kitchen. And when she returned, she found Jimmy, Studs and Frank huddled in the corner around Studs's table.

"Here's your thousand and another two thousand for your big win," said Studs as he thumped three wads of notes on the table in front of James who reflexively grabbed at them. Frank leaned forward over his paunch and slapped Jimmy's hand. "Aren't you going to count them?" he asked with a smirk.

"I trust Studs," said Jimmy, "I've known him since I was a kid, and he never gypped me for a penny."

"Well, that's saying something. Better not let the blokes in the bar hear that or it will ruin Studs's reputation!" joked Frank.

"What are you going to do with the money?" asked Studs. "It's a lot of dough."

"I dunno. Might buy a car. See what Iris wants to do."

"I can tell you what Iris will want to do, I know women," said Frank.

"You ought to, you've been through enough wives," joked Studs.

Iris arrived with the pies. "One for Jimmy and one for me. Do you blokes want anything?"

"No thanks, I don't eat while I'm doing business," said Studs with an air of self-importance.

"I'll have something after the pub closes," said Frank.

James, always hungry, gulped down the pie.

"Don't you want sauce?" joked Iris.

"Too late."

"So now..." said Studs, looking around the bar.

"We've got business," said Frank staring down at the cash sitting in front of James.

"What about giving the money to Iris and she can take it away and count it and no doubt she'll have some ideas about spending it," joked Frank.

James looked up at Iris who stood at his elbow.

"Good idea!" she said with a big smile as she leaned over to collect the three piles of cash.

"Hey! Wait a minute! They're my winnings!" grinned James.

"You could spend it on a wedding," said Frank, half seriously.

Iris pocketed the money and walked away.. "Thanks a lot Frank," she said with a grin. James sat quietly

"I love weddings," said Frank.

"That's why you've had so many of them," quipped Studs, "now let's get down to business."

"What business? I'll let you two go to it then," said James.

"No, stay," said Studs, "you're welcome to join us, isn't that right Frank?"

"Absolutely. You've shown that you're a gutsy gambler, James. With your help, we can make even more money," said Frank.

"But I'm happy with what I made."

"How would you like to make many thousands more, and I mean *many* thousands?" whispered Studs looking around the bar as though there were people trying to hear what he was about to say.

"Gees, maybe. Iris and me, we're happy with what we've got."

"And your auntie's house? Does Iris want that?"

"Yair, she does, but I told her I'm going to sell it. I couldn't live there. Too many horrible memories."

"Eddie says it's just a little house anyway and there's tiger snakes all around the scotch thistles next door."

"Did you tell her that?" asked Frank.

"No."

"What the two of you need is a nice big house in Footscray or even Flemington near here, with a nice garden, big rooms where you can relax, and an outside where you can have a beer or two, and a garage for your new car."

"And bedrooms for the kids you'll have," added Studs.

"Shit! We're happy just working here in the pub and living upstairs. We don't want for much," said James.

"Well, as much as I'd like to be sure you'll always be here working for me, wouldn't you like to have enough money that you could go out on your own, be your own boss?" asked Frank.

James was about to answer, though he wasn't sure what he would say, when he felt a heavy presence behind him. A large hand grabbed him by the back of his neck and pushed his head down to the table. Another large hand banged a dog-eared bible on the table.

*

"Preacher, fuck you!" cried Studs, "what do you think you're doing?"

"Are you not aware that you are in consequence cohabiting with a known murderer?"

"What?" called Frank, incredulous.

"Come on Preacher," snarled Studs, "he never did it and you know it."

James stayed still, his head buried under his arms. The Preacher lightened his grip.

"Don't think you'll get away with it, you disgusting little bastard, and I know that's what you are, don't think I don't know it."

"Fuck you!" mumbled James, the sound muffled under his arms.

"What did you say, child of sin, the devil himself?" cried the Preacher, loud enough for all to hear, even as far away as in the public bar.

"Preacher, sir, let him go," said Frank, a smile always on his face, but this time his eyebrows sloping inward, pleading. "I will vouch for him. He is in my employ."

"More fool you! The devil's handyman that's what you are!"

"Right. So, if you don't mind, sir, we would like to close up the pub. It's a quarter to ten."

"I'll take a beer and a whiskey," demanded the Preacher, "and make it quick before the pub closes."

Frank waddled back a little and looked at his watch. "Senior constable, you know damn well that I cannot serve a policeman alcohol while he is in uniform. You yourself have told me that, many times, isn't that right?"

"Give him a fuckn beer," muttered Studs, "anything to get rid of him."

"What blasphemy did I hear, Mr. Mackerel? I've a good mind to take you in."

"Give him a beer," muttered James joining in the chorus.

At that moment Iris, who had been busying herself behind the bar counter, appeared with a tray on which were a large pot of

beer and a double whiskey. "At your service, constable," she said
with an exaggerated smile.

"It's senior constable, miss." He scooped up the whiskey and
downed it in one gulp. He then took the pot of beer, replaced it
with his hat, quaffed down the beer, then replaced his hat with the
empty glass. He let go of James's neck, stepped back and said,
"Good evening, gentlemen and ladies, snatched up his bible,
loose pages still sticking out of it, and left.

*

Studs looked furtively around once again. Clearly, he was waiting
for Iris to leave and this she did, giving James a slightly cross
look.

"Now, James, this is what Frank and me are planning, and we
think you have earned your place in our team."

"I don't know, Studs. I mean…"

"You haven't heard what it is yet."

"I know. But Iris. I don't think she likes me gambling."

"It's not gambling. Gambling is when you don't know what the
outcome will be. This is investing. We know what the outcome
will be, just like we knew St. Kilda would win."

"You really knew that?"

"Of course! I only bet on a sure thing, and I cut you in as a big
favour to Frank."

"But how?"

"The footy timekeeper is a friend of mine. He wasn't going to
sound the siren until St. Kilda were in front."

"But that could have been a long time, if at all. What if Collingwood was way in front in the last quarter?"

"We had taken steps to make sure that did not happen."

"Like what?"

"I think it's best if you don't know, James, just in case the cops
start to snoop around," said Frank. "Don't want you to get caught up
in anything, given your, well, past dealings with the likes of the
Preacher."

"So, what's the plan then?"

"We know already what horse will win the Melbourne cup."

"You do?" Come on. Nobody could predict that and be so sure."

"Well, let's put it another way. We know for sure what horse
will *not* win the Melbourne Cup."

"And that is?"

"Galilee, the favourite."

"And how do you know that?"

"Can't tell you, unless we are sure that you are with us and will help us make sure of the outcome."

"OK, I'm in."

"Well, not quite. You have to put up some money, of course. There will be a few people to pay off, some expensive bills to pay."

"How much?"

"More than you've got."

"And how much are you blokes putting in?"

"Well I can't put anything in because I'm the bookie, and it would be illegal for me to do it. I'd lose my license."

"I've promised $20,000," muttered Frank.

"But that's how much my house in Yarraville is worth."

"Who told you that?"

"My Dad, Eddie."

"Are you in or not?" asked Studs, looking towards the door.

"The Preacher coming back?" asked Frank.

"No. My secretary, she should be here soon. She takes care of all the paperwork. If you want to put up your house instead of the money, that's OK. She's a justice of the peace, so she can take an affidavit or whatever it's called, to confirm that you've put up the dough."

"I'd better ask Iris. I need to think about it."

"I can tell you now, Jimmy, I mean James, if you ask Iris, she'll say no, but you probably already know that," said Studs.

James looked across to Iris who was busy washing glasses. "Anyway, what's the use of knowing what horse will not win? How can I make money on that? Don't I need to know what horse will win?"

"Smart bloke you've got here, Frank!"

"That's what his Dad, Eddie always said."

"It would be stupid if I told you before you came in, wouldn't it? I mean, you'd have the information and then it would be very likely that you'd blab it around to others, even though you would know that it was against your interest to do so."

"How do you mean?"

"The more people that know it, the more who will bet on it, then the odds would go down. It's that simple."

*

It was closing time. Frank waddled over to the saloon bar door. He was about to close it when Dolly pushed past him, her hips that Frank knew so well, pressing on his belly. Dolly was her

name, according to Studs who had named her because she always
looked like a doll, especially her hair. Frank was much taken with
her, they all knew that, and she returned the favours at times.
Studs used her as a kind of bargaining chip with Frank when he
wanted to do something that Frank might not like. And his cup
caper was one of them.

"Why, Mr. Highlands. How nice of you to open the door for
me!"

"Always my pleasure, Miss," answered Frank, bowing to the
extent his belly would allow it. "Unfortunately, I have to ask you
both to leave now, as there's a cop snooping around and I don't
want to get nabbed." He looked nervously at his watch. "The
Preacher is a nasty piece of work, as we all know."

"This will only take a couple of minutes," said Studs, staring
at Frank and nodding towards the bar where Iris was still washing
glasses. Dolly took her place nestled beside Studs.

"Dolly, you met Jimmy, I mean James, Henderson, here didn't
you?" said Studs.

"G'day love," she said, her bright red lips flashing her well-
practiced smile. "Nice hair you've got there."

"Hey Iris, Jimmy and me will finish up the Saloon Bar. Could
you give them a hand in the public bar? There's a good girl,"
called Frank, looking at his watch.

"Hello Iris!" called Dolly. "The rude buggers wouldn't bother
to introduce me to you. We girls have to stick together, you know."

"Pleased to meet you, Dolly. I'll go. I know when I'm not wanted,"
answered Iris with a slight grin.

"All right then. Let's get down to business," said Studs. "Did
you bring the papers?"

"All here Mr. Mackerel." Dolly pulled out some papers typed
with carbon copies still attached. "All he has to do is sign on the
dotted line, right here."

"There you go! You see what a great secretary she is?" said Studs,
pushing the papers across to James.

"What are these for?" James asked.

Frank, always careful, quietly left the little group and began
cleaning up the bar counter, putting glasses away, even sweeping
the floor. He wanted to be able to say that he never knew what
was going on.

"Don't worry love," said Dolly, "they're just to make sure we all
remember what we agreed on, that right Mr. Mackerel?"

"Exactly. So now, you have the three thousand you won on the Grand final."

"Two thousand, one thousand I owe Eddie."

"Oh, right. I forgot about that. Do you want to put the two thousand down on Light Fingers to win?"

"Light who?"

"Light Fingers. It's the name of the horse that's going to win the Melbourne cup in a few weeks."

"You said you weren't going to tell me."

"Yair, I know. But I've decided I can trust you, now that you know just about everything."

"Just about? What do you mean?"

"Well, there's a little something that we need your help with to make absolutely sure that Light Fingers wins."

"What's that?"

"Well, it's best I don't tell you in front of Dolly. I don't want to involve her in anything that might muck up her being a Justice of the Peace."

"She can leave, then. Can't she? And I'll sign the papers later."

"Trouble is that she has to witness you sign the paper, so she can legally put her JP stamp on it and sign it herself."

"Gees, I don't know Mr. Mackerel…"

"Studs to you, mate. You're one of us now."

"I better read this before I sign it, anyway. That's what they always told me in the army."

"Go ahead then. I'd suggest that you keep the two thousand winnings, or maybe give them to Iris to keep her happy. Then you can write me an IUO for whatever amount you want to place on Light Fingers."

"What are the odds going to be?"

"So long as nobody else sniffs it out, it will be astronomical, about 35 to 1."

"Gees, Studs! Are you sure?"

"Sure as Dolly is sitting beside me right now."

On cue, Dolly called out to Frank, "Hey Frankie, love, aren't you going to get me a little drinkie?"

"Can't. It's after hours," grinned Frank, already mixing her a brandy and dry ginger, her favourite. He waddled over and handed it to her, his belly grazing the table as he leaned over and gave her a light kiss on her forehead, his nose getting a whiff of the scent of a hairdresser.

"Thank you, luvvy," she said with coy exaggeration.

James peered closely at the document. It simply said:

I promise to pay Studs Mackerel $......... *within one week after the 1966 Melbourne Cup race and guarantee my house at 842 Geelong Road as surety in the event that I do not make such payment.*

Signed ....

James Henderson.

Witnessed by:..............

Justice of the Peace

"Just put in the amount you want to bet, luvvy," urged Dolly, then sign it at the bottom."

But I can't put up the whole house, that would mean I'd be betting $20,000," complained James.

"You're right, of course, James. You always were a smart little bugger," said Studs. "Then how much do you want to put up?"

"I was just going to use my Grand Final winnings."

"Yair, makes sense. But from what I know of your little Iris, she won't let you."

"You're right there."

"Tell you what. Dolly will just cross out the house part, and just leave it as a simple IOU. And I'll trust you to come up with the money, say within three weeks after the race. That would give you time to sell the house to raise the money in the very unlikely event that Light Fingers doesn't win."

Without waiting for James's response, Dolly pulled the paper back and went to cross out the part that referred to the house as surety.

"You're absolutely sure that Light Fingers will win?"

"As sure as you're sitting there now. It's guaranteed. This is just a small formality."

"You'll pay me all my winnings, and just keep the part I'm borrowing from you?"

"Right. Simple as that. Your house is only there in case Light Fingers has a heart attack or something. And God save us all if that happens, which it won't."

"Horses don't have heart attacks, do they Mr. Mackerel?"

"Of course not, Dolly my dear, it was just an example."

James stared at the document. Dolly handed him a ballpoint pen.

"It's a sure thing?"

"Absolutely!"

"If it's not, I'll kill you Studs, and you won't get the house anyway," said James, looking Studs in the eye, then added for effect, "you know I've fought in Vietnam."

"I know, I know. It's a sure thing."

"All right then, so long as we understand each other."

James took the pen and wrote in $25,000.

"Press hard," urged Dolly, "we have to have it in duplicate."

James signed the form and pushed it back to Dolly who ceremoniously reached into her gold-sequined handbag for her JP stamp and pad, banged it on the ink pad, then with a flourish, signed on the dotted line, *Dolly Mackerel*.

"You two are married?" asked James, incredulous.

"Not really. It's just a legal formality," said Studs with a smirk. Dolly pretended not to hear.

"Now here's your part, the last thing that we have to do, and it all depends on you."

"What's that?"

"Galilee's trainer drinks here every Friday night and most Saturdays."

"Buy him a few beers and make friends with him. Anyway, he's also a mate of Swampy's, who I know you know pretty well."

"Yair, so what?"

"Take this."

Studs nudged Dolly who rummaged in her handbag and finally retrieved a small medicine bottle. He shook it and held it up to the light. "You see this?" he said, "it's our ticket to Heaven!"

"Oooh! Take me with you," crooned Dolly.

"Dolly. I think you should leave right now. This is between only James and me. It's better all round that nobody else knows any of this."

"OK. Mr. Mackerel. I'm very professional." She gathered up the papers, pen and stamp and left.

"You'll have to go out the back door. Go through the kitchen." Studs pointed.

"What's in it?" asked James.

"You don't need to know that either."

"You want to poison the fuckn horse?"

"I wouldn't call it that. Just make him a little sleepy at the right time."

"But how can we get the horse to take it?"

"We don't. We get the trainer to give it to him."

"Make friends with him, so you can visit the horse a lot, people get used to seeing you there. Take Iris along. Women love horses, don't they?"

"Studs, this is crazy."

"And crazy not to do it. We'll be as rich as kings!"

"I'm not gunna do it."

"You just signed an IUO."

"Then tear it up."

"James, be sensible, be the smart bloke I know."

"Find someone else to drug the horse. That wasn't part of the deal."

"Tell you what. Think about it for a day. I will put off laying bets for twenty four hours."

"But you've got the bet, haven't you?"

"Are you kidding? You gave me an IUO. That's just to cover my placing the bets with different bookies over the next few weeks. You can't place a huge bet with one bookie on one horse to win. It will look suspicious, especially if the horse wins. I have to lay the bets slowly and carefully choose the bookies, including in other states. Got to spread the bets out, that way it won't affect the odds too much, and we'll get a great return on our investment."

"You're going to lay out your own money?"

"On your behalf, James, my boy. On your behalf."

"I need to think about it."

"Take a day, but promise me one thing."

"Yair?"

"Don't tell Iris. I can tell you now, mate, I know women. And if you tell her, all bets are off. She'll go ape-shit."

James stirred in his seat. He wanted badly to punch Studs hard, right between his furtive eyes. Studs sensed it. "Look, Jimmy, James, or whatever. Tell you what. I'll get Dolly to draw up the papers so you and Iris can get married. I'm pretty sure that she could even marry the two of you, unless you want a church wedding."

James's eyes lit up. "You've given me a great idea!"

"What's that?"

"We can get married on Swampy's farm, have our honeymoon there as well, and Spuds can be best man!"

"Me? What? I don't think so."

"Not you, Studs. My old dago mate Spuds. We worked together on Swampy's farm."

"Oh, I think I remember him. The big muscly dark bloke, hair as black as coal. Always drinking with Swampy."

"That's him. Can you loan me $200?"

"But you just won $2,000 off me."

"Iris has that. I want to buy her a ring, and can't really ask her for that money, if you see what I mean."

"Tell you what, mate. Here's $200 Consider it a wedding gift from me to you both."

"Gees, Studs. I didn't think you had it in you. You're such a good bloke."

Studs raised his glass, still full. "To relationships," he said, "you and me and you and Iris."

16. She married the man behind

"I took you on, and then your sweetheart Iris, as a big favour to Eddie, I hope you know that," said Frank. He was sitting with James, Iris and Dolly in Studs's corner.

"Well, I hope you're satisfied," said James, trying to control his sarcasm. "I think it's worked out pretty good."

Iris wanted to say, "yair especially as you don't pay me," but James was holding her hand tightly under the table, trying to tell her something, probably to keep her mouth shut.

"So, what's going on?" asked Iris, openly belligerent. "What's this meeting about, Mr. Highlands? And what's Dolly doing here anyway? We just closed up the pub and she shouldn't be here after hours."

James squeezed her hand and turned to look at her. "I asked for the meeting," he said.

Dolly flashed her red-lipped smile and touched her mountain of hair lightly with her fingers. She produced her gold sequined hand-bag and took out a pen and a typewritten document. "Let's get started," she said looking around the table.

"I thought all we had to do was sign some forms or something," said James.

"What's going on?" asked Iris, pulling her hand away from James.

"I've been meaning to tell you but I didn't get around to it But I do have something for you," said James.

"What?" Iris flopped back in her chair, flabbergasted. James had placed a gold ring on the table and she blurted out, "what's *she* doing here?" obviously referring to Dolly.

"I'm here to marry you," said Dolly, her smile now etched deeply in her face, seemingly never to stop.

"What? Jimmy, what the fuck are you up to?" was the best that Iris could say.

"Dolly is a JP and she has the forms and I think all we have to do is sign them with a witness, and that's why Frank is here."

"And the ring?"

"Well it's for you, of course."

"You could have told me, or asked me…"

"Well, you've been wanting me to do it for a while now, haven't you?"

"Yes, but, shit Jimmy. You're a fuckn stupid piece of work!"

"I know. But I do love you, you know that."

"And these two knew about it before I did?"

"Well, I thought it would be a great surprise, and there's another one coming."

"Surprise? What about considering me? How I'd feel when you sprung this on me? I feel like I've being traded like one of the sheep over at the stockyards."

James looked Iris in the eyes, those light grey eyes, the ones he likened to a sheep those years ago when they first came together. And boy, did they come together then, he thought. He picked up the ring and twiddled it in his fingers.

"Look, you two, are you going to sign this form or not? I've got other clients to meet after this," said Dolly through her smile.

"Iris love, please, I beg you!"

"What was the other surprise?"

"We're having our wedding and our honeymoon at Swampy's farm and we'll camp out on Spuds's potato patch, just like we dreamed of."

Iris now was speechless. The trouble was that she couldn't have thought of a better place for their wedding or their honeymoon. It touched her deeply that he had thought of it. But it was his not asking her that made her angry. And for the first time in her life, she swallowed it. She forced a meek little smile and put out her ring finger. "You can put it on if you like," she said sweetly, almost with a smile, the corners of her mouth twitching.

As usual, James had no idea what he had done. "I'm not supposed to put it on you until the wedding," he said.

"What if it doesn't fit?" she said.

"Gees, I didn't think of that."

"You don't think of a lot of things," thought Iris.

James slid the ring on to her finger and it seemed to fit.

"It's a perfect fit!" she proclaimed. And she turned to kiss James lightly on his blushing cheek.

Dolly pushed the form to James. "Sign here, and Iris, you sign next to him there," she said pointing with the pen. "And Mr. Highlands, you sign there where it says 'witness'."

"That's it?" asked James. "Now we're married?"

"You will be, as soon as I sign it and stamp it with my JP stamp," said Dolly as she rummaged in her bag for the pad and stamp. She banged the stamp down hard with a flourish and applied her signature. "I now pronounce you man and wife."

"Now you can move in together," joked Frank.

"We could do with a bigger room," said Iris.

"So could I," said Frank, "but this is an old pub and there isn't one."

"And when is the wedding?" asked Dolly as she got up to go.

"Don't know. We haven't set the date yet. Has to be before the Melbourne Cup, though."

"Make it a Sunday," said Frank, "when the pub's closed, then you won't have to take a day off work."

"Have a wonderful wedding, all of you," Dolly said, her big smile even bigger, "I'll let myself out through the kitchen, right?"

*

Iris shivered. It was cold. There was a real chill in the October air and it was much colder once they got to Swampy's farm. The cypress hedge that ran along one side of the property up to the old barn, blocked the wind a little, but truth be told, the chill of the Tasman sea couldn't be stopped. She snuggled up to James to keep warm. He had once again borrowed Frank's fancy Humber, ugly lump of a car it was. She basically had no clothes to speak of, had never really thought about getting dressed up, not ever. All she had on were her work clothes, a soiled old white blouse and a pair of black slacks she had picked up from somewhere, found them lying around the pub. She glanced across at James who was a good match. He had on just what he usually wore when he was tending bar. Anyway, they were going to camp for their honeymoon, so what was the point of getting dressed up?

Frank had been a bit doubtful about letting James take the Humber. He was a city man and had no idea about farms, thinking they were all in the outback, desolate and dusty, like he had seen in the movies. He had heard that there were foot-deep potholes that you couldn't see until you hit them. And all that dust, it would get into the lovely clean engine of his Humber. "Go slow!" he had ordered, "I don't want you banging up the front end. These Humbers cost an arm and a leg to fix."

For once in his life, James did what he was told. He did go slow, too slow for Iris who was now getting impatient. They had turned off the Bacchus Marsh road ten minutes ago, on to the gravel track that led up to Swampy's farm house.

"Can't you go a bit faster?" asked Iris, her teeth chattering with the cold.

"I promised Frank I'd be careful."

"There's no potholes as I can see," said Iris. "Does this car have a heater?"

"Frank said you can't see them, so I have to go slow."

"Jimmy, I'm freezing!"

"Gees, sorry sweetie. I think it has a heater but I don't know how to switch it on. Anyway, it has to be only a couple of minutes more. I think the farm's over the next rise. That little shed there, is where Spuds keeps his tools."

James pointed, but Iris didn't look. She snuggled into him, burying her head in his lap. He stroked her head and rubbed her neck lightly.

"You better put two hands on the wheel," she whispered.

"Look! Look!" cried James, gently pushing Iris away, "it's Swampy's!"

The gravel road wound up the rise to the old farm house, its rusting red corrugated roof hiding behind a couple of old gum trees, dwarfed by the old barn, its timber walls with gaping holes where the wind had lifted off the planks, and rusted roof looking too heavy for the walls that leaned precariously to one side.

"The barn's just like Swampy," grinned James, "leaning in all directions, a wonder that it can stand up."

Iris sat up. "Is that Spuds' old Ford ute?"

"Yep! And there he is helping Swampy on his old horse."

Swampy, already very drunk, sat on Bessy, a horse that had borne him to the old Corio Shire pub so many times and suffered many indignities into the bargain, slowly plodded down the track to meet them. Iris started to giggle, forgetting how cold she was. There was Swampy, dressed in his celebratory garb that all the locals at the pub knew well, very formal attire, striped pants, tails, white vest, starched collar, a large flourishing bow tie. He pulled the horse to a stop and raised his top hat. "Welcome to the Swampy Paradise Hotel! Haw Haw!" he crowed in his gravelly voice.

James poked his head out the window. "G'day Swampy! Lead the way!"

The horse ambled back up the track, and it took all James's driving skill not to run them down.

A small group of excited people stood at the barn entrance. It had no door of course. But the person Iris was most excited to see was Little Linda, her big sister (though smaller than Iris), and her brat daughter hanging on to her hand.

"Is that the brat?" asked James as he pulled the car to a halt.

"She's got a name you know," said Iris as she struggled to open the car door.

"Gees, sorry. I've forgotten. I always called her the brat."

"They're all dressed up!" said Iris.

"Well, it's a wedding."

"But look at us! We're dressed like tramps!"

"Come on Iris, you worry too much. Nobody cares."

"Well, I do. It's our wedding."

"It's just an excuse for a booze-up."

"That's all it is?" cried Iris, "it's our wedding!" Tears were already in her eyes.

"Shit! Iris, I didn't mean it that way."

Right then, as if sent from Heaven, Linda opened the car door and grabbed Iris by the hand, pulled her to her and gave her the biggest hug. "Come on luv, I've got just the stuff for you." She pulled her along, Iris on one hand, little brat on the other, and they ran to the farm house where Swampy's sister, still in jodhpurs, stood at the door.

"Watch out for the whip!" yelled James, then he looked across to the small group of people standing at the barn entrance. Spuds bounded over. "Chooka me old-a mate!" he said, holding out his hand, "congratulations!"

"Gees, thanks Spuds. Thanks for letting us camp in your potato patch."

"Not many potatoes there now. Struth, you look as old as-a me. Must-a been-a Vietnam!"

"Yair, well…"

"Yair, yair. OK. I know. I had-a the war too." Spuds looked down, embarrassed to have raised the issue."

"Where's the booze?" asked James.

"It's on-a the way…" He looked back down the track to a dust cloud. Here it-a comes now!"

A second Humber appeared in the dust, driven a little faster than James had driven. It pulled up right beside the other, so now there was one black and one white, the white being Eddie's, who stepped out and strode towards James.

"Booze bus at your service," he said, holding out his hand.

James did not take his hand. Instead, he looked up and into Eddie's aging face, dark eyes like his own, impenetrable, tufts of grey eyebrows, strands of greying hair combed over a rapidly balding scalp. "Dad!" he simply called, feeling a wash of emotion rise from his toes to his eyes, and he opened both arms and drew him into a hug, his nose nestling against Eddie's neck. He managed to hold back the tears, but he need not have. For Eddie at last felt like the father that never was. Jimmy, like Jesus, had opened his heart to him.

"James, my son. I have always loved you," Eddie said to himself.

For the rest, there is little need to describe the wedding. Everyone got very drunk, they consumed a barrel of beer that Eddie had kindly provided, and who knows how much red wine that Swampy had produced from his secret cellar (not a cellar exactly, just a hole dug in the floor of the barn). There wasn't really a ceremony, no presiding preacher or anyone else making a speech and declaring them man and wife. It was all taken for granted. Finally, Iris had had enough and declared the wedding over, time for them to run off on their honeymoon. She grabbed James's hand and pulled him away. He had broken his promise to her, one extracted too easily she knew that he would break it. He got blind drunk, something that a former alcoholic should never do. But she was not so sober herself, having for the first time, pretty much, taken a few sips of the red. They staggered together toward the black Humber to which Spuds had attached strings of potatoes to the aerial and to the back bumper.

"I'd betta drive you," Spuds said.

But Swampy intervened. He had been relatively quiet most the time, but drinking heavily as usual. "No drinking and driving!" he drawled, "Haw! Haw!" He led Bessy out of the barn and grabbed Iris by her midriff. "Up you go," he called and hoisted her onto the horse who remained calm, being used to all kinds of abuse.

Iris screamed and laughed at the same time. Her head was dizzy from the wine, but she held on tightly to the horse's mane.

"You next!" Swampy called to James grabbing him by the arm. "Up you go!" and with Spuds helping, they hoisted Jimmy on to Bessy, cosily tucked in behind Iris. They were both suddenly very frightened. It looked a long way down to the ground. What if Bessy decided she didn't want them on her back? Eddie stepped forward, worried and sober.

"What about our camping stuff? We can't sleep out at Spud's place without a tent, it's too cold," cried Iris.

James hugged her to him with both arms. He was frightened of falling off. And then it began to rain.

"Swampy!" yelled Eddie in exasperation, "take them inside the barn. They can't camp out in this weather." He gave Swampy a hard slap on his back as though to wake him up.

"Aw! Haw! Haw!" drawled Swampy, "come on Bess old girl, let's take the lovers in."

He slapped Bessy on her backside and she neighed loudly, stamped her feet, and Jimmy held on to Iris for grim death. Iris wanted something solid to hang on to, so she let go of Bessy's mane and reached back to hold James. Disaster was afoot. But the long-suffering Bessy calmed down and moved in a very slow walk towards the barn. Swampy took up the loose reins that hung down and led her into a corner of the barn where bales of hay were stored.

"Please let us down," pleaded Iris.

"Me too, if you don't mind Swampy, you fuckn shit-head!"

"Haw! Haw!" answered Swampy and made as though he was about to give Bessy another slap. And he would have except that Linda grabbed Swampy's arm and rubbed herself against his long legs. The brat, at the same time, was running between the horse's legs, making her a little nervous.

"Be nice!" purred Linda. "Pat Bessy like you know how," she said with a slight smirk. "Hey! Brat! Come here to mummy. We don't want the horsey to kick you, do we?" she called, managing to reach under Bessy and pull her out from under.

"I want to ride the horse!" screamed the brat.

"She's still the fuckn same," mumbled James.

"You should talk," quipped Iris as Eddie reach up and helped her down.

"You can manage yourself," he said to James.

Suddenly, all was quiet. Spuds had found a soft spot on a couple of sheep skins and was fast asleep on the oily shearing platform. Hearing the harsh call of his sister, Swampy led Bessy out of the barn and did not return. Linda held the brat to her, holding her head and forcing it on to her belly so her screams were muffled. Eddie stood, hands on hips wondering what was next.

"We'll have our honeymoon right here in the barn," said James. "We can make ourselves a little cubby over there behind the hay stacks."

Iris looked up at him, holding his hand. He was such a baby at heart, she told herself. She shouldn't get angry at him. Besides, it was what she especially loved about him. Who else in their right mind would suggest to his newly married wife that they sleep on a bed of hay?

Eddie looked from one to the other. "Well, I think I'd better go, unless you two want anything else?"

"No. Dad. We're all set, aren't we Iris luv?"

"Yep. We are."

"Linda, would you two like a lift home?"

"Thanks Eddie. That would be nice. I have a lot of business to attend to, and the brat here has to get up for school in the morning."

*

In the space of a month after their wedding, the newlyweds had managed to set themselves up pretty well at the Newmarket pub. Frank had agreed to have a door put in connecting their two rooms and Iris had made one of the rooms into a nice little sitting room, turning James's bed into a couch with cushions she had found down at the Op Shop in Footscray and keeping her room with her single bed in which they slept. Both rooms had old windows that were jammed shut, but after a lot of effort, Iris had managed to loosen them and had them opening and closing smoothly. James had refused to help, looking on her enterprise as part of her "weird thing for windows" as he called it. Both windows looked out over the steeply gabled corrugated iron roof, and a tall red brick chimney that rose up from the kitchen below.

"Jimmy, look," said Iris as she stuck her head out the window and looked towards the Geelong Road, "there's the stockyards over there." On a still day, when there wasn't much traffic, they could hear the bleating of the sheep and wailing of the cattle as they were led to slaughter.

The day before the Melbourne Cup was a Monday so James and Iris had the day off in lieu of working Saturdays and of course Cup Day itself would be a big working day at the pub. To the extent that it had ever been possible, Iris was happy as she lay in her bed, James beside her, lightly snoring, lying on his stomach, one arm draped over her shapely body, her silk nightdress bunched up around her waist. "Her bed" was still a very new idea to her; she had slept in so many other beds and often not on beds at all, most of her young life. She looked at James, her husband, and twiddled one of his curls around her finger. She turned to him, propping up her head on her hand. She could not explain why she always ended up with him given that he was such a silly boy and didn't seem to know what he wanted to do. Maybe it was because, like her, he was never really happy either. "It's because we don't know what to do with ourselves so we just naturally come together. God brought us together that day of Jimmy's Latin exam," she smiled to herself. "Maybe Flo was right. God told us all what to do and punished us if we didn't do it." She wondered if maybe she should go to church, seek out Flo. But she quickly pursed her lips at the thought. Jimmy had told her how Flo had held him up and cursed him at the Corio Shire Pub that day he went down to get the loan from Eddie. Flo's not God's messenger. She couldn't be. The devil's, more like it. She rubbed her hand against the hair on the back of his neck, just the way he liked to rub her hair when she kept it short like a boy's.

"I know you're awake," she said.

James rolled to his side to face her. "It's early isn't it? Let me sleep. Got a big day tomorrow."

"Let's go off somewhere and have a picnic," she said, "look outside, it's a beautiful sunny spring day."

"Can't. Have to go down to the racecourse."

"What? You? Are you a horse thief now?" Iris joked, tickling him under the arm.

"Nah, it's something I have to do for Frank and Studs. I said I would."

"And what's that?" Iris was immediately suspicious. Anything to do with that loathsome Studs was suspect.

"Nothing special. Just have to check something out for them."

"We could take some sandwiches and have a picnic at the racecourse, look over the horses the day before the cup, when there's no crowds. That would be fun, wouldn't it?"

"I s'pose. But it's probably best if you don't come."

Iris pushed herself up and sat astride his naked body. She leaned down, her hands on his shoulders and dug her nails into his skin. "What's going on?" she asked, eyes sparkling, looking for a fight.

"Ouch, stop!" cried James, pulling at her hands, wriggling and twisting to throw her off.

Iris resisted, pushing down on him, wriggling to resist his wriggling and before either of them knew it they were entwined as lovers will be, the savage resistance transformed into an ecstasy matching the day of the Latin exam.

*

They lay back, just fitting side by side on the narrow bed. James reached for a cigarette. Iris grabbed the packet. "You'll end up like Flo!" she said, crossly.

"So what?"

"So what? She's a hag and a witch! And the smokes will kill her."

"So what?"

"All right if you want to be a smart-ass!" Iris opened the packet and pulled out a smoke. They were Camels. She lit one then blew the smoke in his face. Jimmy pretended to choke then grabbed her hand and wrenched the cigarette away. He took a deep draw, held it for as long as he could then slowly let it out, blowing smoke rings. Iris rolled back and slipped on a dressing gown. "OK," she said, "I'm going for a shower. And then we're going for a picnic at the racecourse."

"No, we're not," answered James, cheekily.

"We are. Unless you tell me what Studs and Frank have got you doing. You don't have to do everything they tell you, you know."

"It's nothing."

"Liar!"

"I said it's nothing. And I'm not a liar."

"It's about that money you won off Studs, isn't it?"

"The two thousand? I won it fair and square."

"Right. But that Studs. He never loses. Bookies are the ones who take bets on the sure thing that the blokes who place their bets will lose."

"So now you're an expert on gambling?"

"What are you up to?"

"It's nothing. I'm just going down to see Galilee's trainer. He drinks in the public bar and I've got to know him. He's a really good bloke, and really smart with horses. He said I could come down and he'd show me around. That's all."

"You said you were checking something out for Studs and Frank."

"I'm doing that too."

Iris picked up a towel and moved towards the door; then hesitated. "You've placed a bet on the Cup haven't you? How much?"

James looked away. He rubbed his tongue against his teeth, trying to stop himself from saying what he knew he was about to say. "I put a bet on Light Fingers to win."

Iris dropped the towel and stood belligerently with her hands on her hips. "Don't tell me. Studs talked you into betting the two thousand you won from him. Because if you did, it's too bad because I've spent it all."

"What? What on? Stuff we need for when we move into our house in Yarraville."

"Iris! No! You know I can't live there. It will drive me mad!"

"It will be completely different with me there, won't it? And besides, by the time I'm finished with it, it will be like a new house."

"But..."

"You have, haven't you? You've bet the lot on the cup. You stupid bastard. They've conned you!"

"I'm not stupid!"

"The whole lot? You bet the whole lot? And what if the nag loses?"

"It won't lose."

"Without the money to fix up the house, there's no point in moving in there. You might as well have bet the whole house!"

James rolled off the bed and looked out the window. He slowly turned and stepped towards her. "Iris, luv..."

"Oh no! Oh no!" Iris put both hands to her mouth, as if trying to stop the words from coming out. "You really have bet the whole house!"

"It's a sure thing, Iris. We'll make thousands. We'll be set for the rest of our lives!"

"That's it! You've done it this time. I'm getting out of here!" She ran to the window, thrust it open and slid out on to the roof.

"Iris, come back! You can't go anywhere. The roof's too high! You'll kill yourself!"

The roof sloped steeply down past the chimney to the Geelong road. Iris had to let go of the window-sill and began to slide towards the road. She grabbed at the chimney to stop the slide. James climbed through the window and reached for her, but she had slid too far. To make things worse, he had no clothes on, and his bare feet caught on the old rusty nails that held on the roof.

"Go back, you silly bugger!" called Iris, trying to hold back a grin, aware of the spectacle of a naked man chasing her over a tin roof.

James did as he was told and climbed back in. He was putting on clothes and shoes so he could get back out and haul Iris in, when there was a knock at the door. "Is everything all right?" came a querulous voice.

"Everything's fine!" called James.

"Is someone on the roof?" called Frank nervously.

"It's just Iris, having one of her tantrums. She'll get over it."

"I heard that, you asshole!" yelled Iris. "I'm getting out of here, I tell you. This is it!"

Frank nervously looked at his watch. "She's going to jump off the roof?" cried Frank. "Stop her, James. She'll kill herself!"

"I tried to pull her back in but she wouldn't come. It's hard to pull her up the slope. The roof's too steep."

A nervous man at the best of times, Frank looked at his watch again and ran down stairs to call for help. The first thing he thought of was to call the cops.

*

A faint drizzle descended on the roof. The heat of her anger gone, now Iris felt cold. She tried to wrap herself in her dressing gown, curled up in a ball pressing against the chimney. She looked out towards the Geelong Road and pursed her lips, pushing her tongue against her cheeks. What was she doing? More importantly, what did she want? She thought of coming back in, but now she was frightened she would slip down the roof and fall off. James put one leg out the window, trying to find a footing. Maybe once he saves me, he'll wake up to himself and see what a stupid drip he is. He's all I've got anyway and all I'll ever have because who else would bother with a street bugger like me, who doesn't even know who she is and doesn't even have a birth certificate, and who would be homeless except for James? she said to herself. All I have besides him is big sister Linda, living in her brothel— that's what it is, not a guest house like she always says. The blokes that go there, including my own stinking bully of a father, are loathsome, ugly, foul animals, all of them. At least Jimmy can be nice, especially as I can get him to do what I want a lot of the time, but then he lets the other blokes take advantage of him. I have to go back in. I have to stop this window thing. I couldn't help it. I just had to get out of there and now I'm stuck. Iris looked across to James and held out her hand.

He stepped gingerly on to the roof. Now it was slippery from the light rain. He heard the siren of a fire truck in the distance and glanced out to the Geelong Road. There was a cop car approaching as well. Iris clung to an old brick in the chimney and tried to stand up, but her foot began to slip and she sat down again, simpering. "Jimmy, I'm sorry, I'm sorry. I don't care what you've done," she sobbed.

"Hang on a minute. I'm coming. Silly Frank has called the cops, I think."

Iris closed her eyes tight. She was too frightened to look down. The cop car screeched to a halt outside the pub and out clambered none other than the Preacher, his beak nose observable even from the roof. "It's the fuckn Preacher," growled James, "that's all we want!"

"Who?" snivelled Iris.

"The Preacher, the bastard. The one that railroaded me, that made me confess to killing Millie."

"Stay away from him, then. He'll try to do you in," cried Iris.

"He'd better stay away from you, or I'll fuckn kill him."

The fire engine pulled up and in short time the top of a ladder clanked against the roof just below the chimney. The Preacher pushed the fireman away and began climbing, his long limbs appearing to hang off in all directions, like a spider climbing up a web. "Hang on there, miss. I'll be there to get you in a moment," he shouted, managing at the same time to wave his bible in the air.

"Don't you touch her!" yelled James, "you hear me?"

The Preacher's capped head appeared at the edge of the roof, his beak nose almost touching the rung of the ladder as he pulled himself up. "Of course, it would be you, you murdering scum, son of the devil!" announced the Preacher.

"Stay away! We don't need you! Stay away! Leave us alone!" cried Iris.

"Looks like the Lord has spoken. Your little girl here, the one you defiled when she was just twelve years old, don't think I don't know all about you, is in a spot of trouble."

"Please officer, we're all right," simpered Iris.

"It doesn't look that way to me, in consequence. What did he do, try to rape you?" he snarled. The Preacher was now standing on the top rung of the ladder and looking for a foothold. Seeing the roof was so slippery, he lay flat against the sloping roof and stretched himself up, one foot pushing against the rung of the ladder, his long arms and legs stretched up, as he extended a hand to Iris, the hand in which he held his bible. "The Holy Book will save you, my dear. Just lean down and grab it, and I'll help you down."

"Don't you fuckn touch her!" warned James, his ears red, cheeks ablaze. "And that bible, you fuckn bastard, it'll mark your end!"

Iris glanced quickly at James. She knew he was on the verge of losing it. "Jimmy! Don't!" she called, "please, love, go back inside. She tried to stand, but quickly sat down against the chimney, her bottom now slowly slipping down towards the Preacher, the roof nails digging into her, stinging as they tore the flesh.

"Do not, I inform you, Mr. Henderson, interfere in official police business," announced the Preacher in his deep, officious voice.

"Your fuckn bible, it's missing pages, did you know that?" growled James.

"The bible will save your little girl, Mr. Henderson, you scum."

"Pages 121 and 122, they're fuckn missing, aren't they?"

The Preacher looked up at James and sneered, "The bible will save your little girl's life, in consequence, and you will be charged with aggravated assault and abusing an officer of the Queen's constabulary."

"Jimmy! Go back! Stay there!" cried Iris.

But it was too late. James threw himself forward, head first, the most foolish action that one could possibly take given the steep slope. It was all that the Preacher could do to lift up his bible and try to deflect James's flying body. But it was of little use. James knocked the bible and arm aside and landed on the Preacher's head, squashing his big beak nose into the tin roof. Bright red blood poured into the roof, but worse, to keep his balance, the Preacher had pushed too hard against the ladder and it slid away, now leaving him dangling over the eve, his legs flailing away looking for a footing of which there was none. James, miraculously, some would say, had managed to twist himself into a position that allowed the foot of his good leg to find a footing in the gutter, so he ended up lying on his side, able to push up and sit, even if precariously, on the edge of the roof and watch the Preacher hanging, flailing, blood still pouring out of his nose.

"I never killed Millie!" cried James, "you hear me?" his voice deep and very, very serious. "But I know who did, don't I?

"Get me off here!" called the Preacher, give me a hand! That's an official police order!"

"I'll give you a hand all right!"

"Jimmy! Don't! Jimmy!" called Iris.

"How about a foot instead?" Jimmy jabbed at the Preacher's hand with the foot of his bad leg, so it wasn't quite strong enough to dislodge him.

"Jimmy! Stop! Jimmy!" Iris sobbed. She let go of the chimney and began to slide towards the Preacher who craned his head up with considerable difficulty.

"Miss! Don't! Stay where you are."

And at that moment a ladder once again clanked against the roof and a fireman called out, "Constable! There's the ladder. Kick your left leg across and you'll find it!"

But it was all too late. James pushed himself across, using the gutter for leverage and with both hands, grabbed the Preacher's shoulders and pushed. The Preacher's flailing legs did not help. He lost any hold he had on the roof and slid off, James toppling down on top of him. In a split second a blinding light flashed before his eyes and he looked down, and saw to his horror, Millie lying dead on her bed, the Preacher, naked and snarling, thrusting a big knife again and again into her lifeless body. Another blinding flash of light and his suspension in time collapsed as they landed with a thud on the concrete path below, the Preacher on his back, and James landing with a sickening thud full on the Preacher's chest. Bright pink foam oozed out of the Preacher's bird-like mouth and beak. James lay flat out on top of him, staring into the his eyes that appeared to be fogging over.

"My bible!" wheezed the Preacher, hardly able to move his lips, "psalm 23!"

"Fuck your bible!" snarled James, "you killed her, didn't you? You killed Millie! The brat gave me those pages. She was there and so was your bible."

The Preacher's eyes looked dead, but his lids fluttered and lips quivered. James pressed down on his chest as though to stand up. He heard something crack and guessed that it was one of the Preacher's ribs.

"You fucked Millie and then you killed her, you fuckn creep! I saw you!"

The Preacher's body suddenly shook and his mouth opened wide gasping for air. "Bible...psalm..."

James rolled off the Preacher's quivering body, reached for the Preacher's battered bible and threw it away. You want psalm 23? Then here it is!" he snarled as he kneeled on the Preacher's chest and recited what he could remember from Sunday school:

"The Lord is my shepherd; I shall not want. He maketh me to lie down in green pastures: he leadeth me beside the still waters. Yea, though I walk through the valley of the shadow of death..."

The Preacher's body convulsed, his head dropped to the side, tongue protruding through his bloody lips.

Iris looked down in horror. A fireman had already reached her and was helping her down the ladder. Frank was peeping out the front door of the pub, too timid to get any closer. The Preacher's young constable-in-training stood holding the ladder, frozen with fright. "Is he dead?" he asked.

"Better call an ambulance," said James, seeing Frank at the pub door.

"I'll call it in," said the young constable, as the fireman and Iris came off the ladder.

"What have you done?" whispered Iris as she clung to James, trying to stop whimpering.

"Nothing. it was an accident, wasn't it? We just lost our footing and fell down. He was unlucky I fell on top of him."

Iris stared down at the lifeless body of the Preacher. It did not look quite so big as it did when he was standing. "Are you hurt?" she asked, hugging him close to her.

"I think I'm OK. Scratched my hands on a few nails, that's all. How about you?"

"The same. I'm cold."

"Let's get cleaned up. We can still make it to Flemington."

Iris held tightly to his arm. "I don't think so," she said, "not after all this."

"All what?"

"James. The Preacher. Looks like he's dead and you're acting like it was nothing."

"It's good fuckn riddance as far as I'm concerned."

"He's a cop. They won't let it go."

"He killed Millie, you know that?"

"What? When did you find that out?"

"I saw him do it. Just now. I saw it with my own eyes."

Iris stopped and pulled on his arm. "Jimmy, you didn't actually see him do it, did you?"

"I had a vision. But I also knew as soon as I opened up those bits of crumpled paper the brat threw at me that day when they came to the gaol to see me."

"I don't get it."

"When I got back to my cell I opened up the balls of paper and they were two pages out of the Preacher's bible. The brat found them in Millie's bedroom, I bet. How else could she have got them?"

They reached the pub door where Frank stood, holding a couple of blankets.

"What the hell happened?" asked Frank, nervously looking at his watch as an ambulance siren sounded in the distance.

"It's nothing to worry about. We had a bit of an accident getting Iris off the roof."

"The Preacher doesn't look too good, He's not moving and the fireman has put a blanket over his body, like he's dead."

"Yeh. Too bad," mumbled James as he pushed past, dragging Iris with him.

"James, you can't leave. You have to go back out there. The cops will be all over you."

"I have to get to Flemington, don't I Frank?"

"Under the circumstances," said Frank, fingering his watch chain, "I think we'd better call it off."

"What?"

"James, you heard me. I'll talk to Studs."

"So you are up to something. What is it?"

"Nothing, really. I just bet the house on Light Fingers," said James, trying to laugh as he said it, winking at Frank.

"You're not joking, are you?" cried Iris, digging her fingernails into his arm. "It's true. You really did bet the whole house."

"It wasn't quite like that,' said Frank.

"What was it like, then?" asked Iris, getting angry again. She turned to James, digging her fingernails into his flesh even more. "Did you sign anything? Did you?"

James looked away and stepped back outside to watch the ambulance come to a halt and the medic approach the Preacher.

"He did," interceded Frank, but it's nothing. We can un-sign it, I'm sure. I'll talk with Dolly."

"Dolly? What does that stupid bitch have to do with it?"

"She's not so stupid," said James, biting his tongue as soon as he said it. "She's Studs's legal assistant."

"She's a solicitor?" asked Iris in disbelief.

"No, a Justice of the Peace and she takes care of all of Studs's financial and social arrangements, if you see what I mean."

"She's a prostitute and a JP? You've got to be kidding."

"Shssh. Keep your voice down," pleaded Frank.

The young constable approached them cap in hand. "Mr. James Henderson, that's your full name, sir?"

"So what?"

"Headquarters has informed me that I have to bring you in for questioning. It appears that the senior constable has passed away."

"And you want to blame it on me?"

"They just want to ask you some questions, sir, for the record. It's standard procedure when someone dies under abnormal circumstances."

"Go fuck yourself." James turned his back on the young constable and stepped back inside the pub. "I'm going back to bed," he mumbled.

"Then I'll have to arrest you," called the constable, as he followed James into the pub. Iris waited for Frank to stop him from entering, but true to his timid character, he did not. So Iris stepped in.

"I don't think you can go in unless you have a warrant," she said, having no idea what a warrant was.

"I'll need you to come down to the HQ as well, miss," he replied. "You were a witness, weren't you?"

"I don't talk to coppers," answered Iris. "If you want to question me, talk to my lawyer."

Frank shifted nervously and coughed. "You have a lawyer?" he whispered loudly.

"Of course, I do. Doesn't everyone?"

The constable took out his pad and biro. "And who might you be, miss?"

"My name's Iris."

"And your last name?"

"I don't have one."

"Everyone has a last name."

"I don't and even if I did I wouldn't tell you."

Frank pulled out his watch and said, "we better go inside. Jimmy doesn't look so good. He might be hurt because of the fall."

The constable went to grab Iris, but she gave him such a threatening look that he withdrew his hand. He turned back to the police car. The ambulance and fire engine were well gone. "You'll be hearing from me," he called back over his shoulder.

Iris ran upstairs to the bedroom. James had climbed into bed, fully clothed. There was blood on the pillow. She gently pushed his head from side to side looking for a gash and found none. His eyes were clamped shut. "Wake up, you bugger," she said. She lifted his head forward and found a lot of blood at the top of his head. But there were no cuts or gashes that she could find.

James stirred. "The blood's the Preacher's," he said, eyes still closed. "It's where I butted his beak with my head when I shoved him off the roof."

"Jimmy! Shut up! You did no such thing!" Iris looked round quickly to see whether Frank had followed her into the room. But he had not. He had gone to phone the doctor.

*

Studs took up his usual place at the table in the corner of the saloon bar. Dolly sat beside him in all her sequined splendour, ruled notebook in hand, numbers and figures carefully entered beside names, all neatly laid out in columns. On the floor between each of their chairs was an open kitbag in which there were piles of money, packaged in various amounts of twenties, fifties and hundreds, each held together with rubber bands.

"No more bets," called Studs, "the cup will be starting any minute. Many customers, some even from the public bar, were hanging around expecting to collect their winnings as soon as the cup was run. Expectations were very high because most bettors had bet on Light Fingers to win, having heard the rumour that it was a sure thing, that a fix had been put in.

James stayed in bed refusing to get up, recovering from his fall, so he said, though he felt no soreness anywhere on his body. He was, rather, distraught, even despondent. The argument with Iris had set off a sequence of events, a sequence that was controlled by a kind of destiny that reminded him of his time in Vietnam. And the Cup, the worry about the Cup. If Galilee won… He tried not to think about it, but it weighed on him like a sack of potatoes. In fact, when Iris tried to rouse him, he couldn't bear to look at her, hid under the sheets. His belly had that shrinking empty feeling. He wanted to throw up, but there was nothing there. And, scarily, he found himself feeling around under the bed for a bottle of plonk or whiskey or anything. A relapse; he was on the edge. The wedding binge had opened the door and it had not closed. He squeezed his eyes and cursed Frank. It was all his fault!

Frank had played a pivotal role, oblivious of his part. Had he not panicked and called the cops, had it been some other cop than the Preacher who came, things would have turned out differently. Now, there was an impending calamity, Frank just felt it, his nerves frayed so badly that he had, most unusual for him, taken to drinking brandies with his customers on the other side of the bar, buying them drinks and receiving grateful slaps on the back for doing it. He also eyed Studs with a certain amount of resentment and fear, harbouring a gnawing feeling that Studs had taken him for a ride as well as James. Studs appeared too jolly. He stood to lose lots of money if Galilee won, assuming that he had bet on Light Fingers using Jimmy's IOU as a guarantee as he said he would, laying out his own cash with several bookies, assuming that he would never need to turn Jimmy's house into cash. Light Fingers was a sure thing, though, wasn't it? He knew the fix was in. Jimmy was supposed to have made sure of that.

Frank bought customers drinks. None of them admitted that they had bet on Light Fingers, after all they did not want others to know it, or the odds would drop. And besides if the cops got wind of it they might start poking around. Each time he bought a customer a drink and downed a brandy himself, Frank glared across to Studs and managed to catch his eye every now and again. Studs appeared not to notice and cheerfully dealt with his clients, every now and again, sliding his arm around Dolly and pulling her to him, each time Dolly complaining that she couldn't write properly in the notebook when he pulled her so.

When the Melbourne Cup finally came on, James was still in bed. Iris had tried to rouse him, pull him out of bed, but he would not budge, just nestled down under the covers, flat on his belly. "Here!" she said, "take the tranny and listen to your stupid horse race. I'm going back down to do your work for you." She dropped the transistor radio on to the bed and left.

And work she did. There was one other barman working the saloon bar. She took over. Washed the glasses, reorganized the shelves, served customers, said nice things to them, which they appreciated. Her presence in the Saloon bar transformed the place, thought Frank, as he watched her work. Everyone said you couldn't have a woman work the bar. They were dead wrong. At least as far as Iris was concerned. She's better than her hubby, smiled Frank to himself. He looked at his watch; James had still not shown up. He was about to ask Iris where he was when the Cup came on the television and everything stopped while the race was run. He looked around him and guessed that everyone in the bar had a bet on a horse. Studs would make a lot of money today, so long as the right horse lost, Frank grinned to himself.

Light Fingers did not win. The favourite Galilee won by a neck. The Saloon bar erupted with yells and angry cries, and foul abuse delivered at the television set, fists shaking in the air. Then an uneasy silence. A few customers sidled up to Studs's corner with their tickets. They had bet on Light Fingers for a place. They got a little money back. A slightly larger number of blokes, smiling and looking cocky, who had bet on Galilee, looking around them at the losers in the bar, a look saying, "I told you so," fronted up to Studs and received their winnings.

"You can put it on the next race," Studs recited over and over.

But the winners didn't really feel like winners. They quietly slipped out of the bar, bought a couple of bottles and went home to drink in peace.

17. He barracks for his boy no more

"When you joined the army, I thought you'd make something of yourself," said Eddie.

"You sound just like my father," said James, unable to look Eddie in the eye.

"I am your father."

"I know. You're just like he was before he hit the booze."

"What are you going to do?"

"Kill myself."

"It's no joke, Jimmy. You shouldn't talk like that."

"You asked for it," muttered James, burrowing down under the covers where he had been for the last two days.

Eddie looked across to Iris. In a frantic phone call she had pleaded with him until he finally agreed to drive up to see if he could talk James out of his slump, as she had called it.

"I can't get him out of bed and Frank said he's going to fire him if he does not come down for work tomorrow."

"What is it? Is it about the money he borrowed from me? If that's all it is, forget it."

"I'm sorry, Mr. Counter, Dad, I mean. I spent a lot of it on fixing up the Yarraville house."

"I don't think any of this is your fault."

"It is. If I hadn't jumped out the window..."

"But Frank said something to me about the house?"

Iris sniffed, trying to hold back a tear. "Studs, you know him?"

"Skeeter, you mean, that's what he called himself down at Norlane."

"That's him. He tricked Jimmy into betting our house on the Melbourne Cup."

"What?"

"The stupid bugger. He ought to kill himself, if you ask me! Was Frank in on all this?"

"I think so, but he says he wasn't, that Studs scammed him as well."

"Have you gone to the police? They know all about him, you know. They'll have him locked up in no time."

"But there's the IOU. He claims he now owns the house unless he gets paid all the money he laid out on James's behalf."

"How much?"

"Frank said $20,000."

"I don't know what I can do, except call the police."

"But you can't. They're already sniffing around, reckon they are going to lay charges against James for killing The Preacher."

"You said he didn't, though."

"It's all my fault. If I hadn't climbed out on to the roof. I was so angry with him though. He'd bet our house! The stupid bastard.!"

"So, he did kill the Preacher?"

"It was an accident. But the cops, you know what they are, and there's this detective Striker, he's been talking to Frank and Studs, and he's been trying to question me, but I made myself scarce."

"Jimmy! Jimmy! Wake up! Are you listening to all this?" Eddie grabbed what looked like Jimmy's shoulder and shook him. "Come on! Out you get!" He beckoned to Iris and they both grabbed the covers and ripped them off the bed, leaving James stark naked, curled up into a ball. "Where are his clothes?" Iris rummaged in a drawer and threw some clothes on to the bed.

They had managed now to reduce James to a helpless, pitiful state. He began to whimper, even sob, something that Iris had never seen before. It reduced her to tears as well. "Oh, my sweetie! I'm sorry!" She threw herself on the bed and tried to cuddle him. She lay beside him, hugging his curved back, her chin pressing on his shoulder, kissing his neck. "Mr. Counter, I think you had better go," she said, twisting her head to look at him, tears trickling down her cheeks.

"I see. What you both need is a lawyer. I'll phone Grimesy."

*

"He's still in bed?" asked Grimesy, incredulous.

"It's been three days." Iris looked down, then glanced at Grimesy, wishing he were Jimmy, standing confidently in his dark striped suit, and Geelong football club tie.

"He must be hungry."

"I took him cups of tea, that's all. I'm scared he'll hit the booze again."

"Can you get him out of this hole?"

"I already have, I think," grinned Grimesy.

"You've told the cops to fuck off, then?"

"Tut! Tut" We mustn't speak ill of the dead," he joked.

"I mean…"

"I know what you mean. Now is your boss around?"

"Frank Highlands, you mean?"

"He's the licensee of this place, right?"

"Yair. I'll get him. I think he's in the kitchen having lunch."

"I'll sit over here, is that all right?" Grimesy pointed to Studs's table.

"I s'pose so. It's where Studs usually sits."

"Good. He should be here any minute. I already spoke with him."

"I'll get Frank." Iris left, just as the Saloon door opened and in walked Studs, Dolly hanging on his arm, her lipstick smudged, eyes red-rimmed, her hair coiffed up even higher than usual.

Grimesy stood, smiling. "Thank you both for coming. Have a seat."

Studs sat at the table, pulling Dolly with him. His mouth was drawn down at the corners, he sniffed and wrinkled his nose.

"The IUO. Would you hand it over, please?"

Studs elbowed Dolly in the ribs. "Give it to him," he muttered. Dolly made a great show of opening her sequined bag, searching as though she could not find it.

"Come on, you fuckn bitch, give it to him," growled Studs.

"Now, Miss…"

"Dolly."

"Dolly who?"

"Just Dolly."

Grimesy turned a page of his legal notepad. "That's not enough, Miss Dolly. I must have your full name. The law requires it," said Grimesy. There was no such law, of course.

"Doris Farmer, J.P." she answered as she retrieved the IOU.

Grimesy perused the note. "I see your JP stamp. Could I see your JP certificate, please?"

"Oh, I don't have it with me, Mister what'sya name."

"Grimes, Paul Grimes, and I'm Jimmy's solicitor. "Miss Farmer. I have checked the records. You are not a JP and never have been. It's a fake stamp, am I not correct?"

Studs squirmed in his seat. It was times like these that he always had one very strong urge, and that was to run away. He did it with the cops down at Norlane and the Corio Shire pub, and he would do it again now. He made a grab for the IOU, but Grimesy snatched it away just in time. "You don't need to run, Mr. Mackerel. I'm not the police."

"You're just as fuckn bad," growled Studs as he jumped up, pulling Dolly with him.

"You acknowledge that this IUO is worthless?"

Dolly clung to the table, Studs trying to pull her away.

"And if you beat her again, I'll call the cops," warned Grimesy.

"It was a fair deal. I laid out thousands of dollars for that little snot. I have a right to collect it from him."

"What evidence do you have of that?"

"Dolly, show him the betting slips."

"What slips?" she asked, confused. "I've just got my record book." She looked across at Grimesy. "I'm Mr. Mackerel's accountant, you know," she said proudly, still gripping the table, her brightly painted nails scratching the surface.

"Shut up, you silly bitch!" cried Studs. "Give me that book!" He tried to pull it away but Dolly held tight, scratching his hands with her long nails.

"Here, Mr. Grimes, it's all in here."

She threw it across the table and Grimesy deftly caught it. It was the final straw for Studs. Time to run. And he did, leaving Dolly holding the bag as it were.

Dolly produced a small mirror and makeup case from her bag and began to touch herself up. She fixed the smear of her lipstick, and carefully pushed her mountain of hair into place. "I have to go to the toilet," she said apologetically.

"By all means," said Grimesy, leaning back in his chair. He did not expect to see her again.

At this moment Frank, who had watched the proceedings from the doorway to the kitchen, emerged, fidgeting with his watch, He waddled across the Saloon bar, and stood looking down at Grimesy. He nervously tried to lick off a brown smudge of gravy that clung to the corner of his mouth. "You must be Paul Grimes?" he asked.

"I am indeed. Pleased to meet you. James has told me what a great publican you are."

"What do you want from me? I see that you have settled everything with Studs, that cunning bastard."

"This IOU. You were the witness to this? I see your signature." Grimesy waved the note at him.

"Yes, I did it to humour Studs. I always try to keep my customers happy, even if they are a nuisance."

"So, you agree that this was a complete scam and that you have no part of it?"

"Absolutely. Why would I want to do anything that would get one of my employees into trouble?"

"Indeed. Why would you?"

"Well I mean, I just thought it was a joke. You know, customers in a pub like this. They're always playing jokes on each other. Aussie sense of humour, you know." Frank forced a grin in an effort to make the obvious foolishness of what he was saying more convincing.

"Sure. All in good fun. So now I'm going to keep this note and will file it away in my office drawer and it will never be seen again."

"So everything's honky dory now with Jimmy? You've saved his house?"

"It's like none of this happened, though, I tell you, you could have lost your liquor license if this had got out."

Frank shifted uneasily on his feet. "Yair, I know that, Mr. Grimes. I know that." He turned to see Iris standing right by him, then looked back at Grimesy. "Iris and James will be OK here for as long as I'm licensee," he said.

"That's very good to hear. And now I'd better go up and see James. What do you think Iris?"

They were about to go upstairs together when a tall, slender, dapper young man, dressed in a tightly buttoned double breasted grey suit stepped into the bar.

"Is the licensee around?" he asked.

"That's me," answered Frank.

"Detective Striker, C.I.D. I'd like to speak with you and also one of your employees, James Henderson."

"About what?"

Iris moved towards the door.

"Stay right here, miss," ordered Striker, "I'm investigating the death of a police officer who I understand fell off the roof of this establishment while trying to rescue a young lady and I'm guessing that the young lady is you?" He nodded at Iris.

Frank looked at his watch and coughed nervously. "James is upstairs in bed, recovering from the accident. He's been in shock ever since it happened."

"I'd like to speak with him none the less."

"You can try, but he won't speak to any of us, he's so upset."

"Perhaps you should come back at another time," said Grimesy.

"And you are?" asked Striker in his most officious manner.

"Paul Grimes, solicitor, of Grimes and Buttersmith. Here's my card."

*

Things might have turned out differently had Flo not entered the Saloon bar at that very moment.

She stood at the door and took a long draw of her cigarette. Her grey eyes, grey face and loose hanging cheeks were the epitome of death. It was in her eyes, her raking smoker's cough, and her skeleton frame, thin flesh covering the bones beneath.

"Where is he? Where is the devil?" she sneered.

"Mum!" cried Iris. "For Christ sake!"

"Look at you! You disgusting piece of trash!" Flo looked up, as though seeing right through the old stamped tin roof of the bar, up to Heaven itself, her hands clasped together. "Oh God! Damn her soul! Damn them both!" she cried, dropping to her knees. "Lead me to him! The devil must be vanquished!"

"Take care of your mother," ordered Striker, agog at such a display of what he considered insanity.

"You mind your own business," said Iris, stepping towards Flo.

"Mister Highlands. You are the licensee. Escort this woman out of the bar," ordered Striker.

Frank looked at his watch. But remained rooted to the spot. Then he swayed from side to side and suddenly found himself mumbling, "The bedroom is that way, through the kitchen and up the stairs."

Striker took one step towards the kitchen when the door from the street flew open revealing Tank's silhouette, his huge body, a gorilla framed in the doorway. "Flo! Ya silly bugger, come on, get up!" He grabbed her by the hair, hair that was wound up and held by a hair net and started to drag her out. Flo clawed at his hands,

"Slaves to the devil, all of you!" she screamed.

"Let her go!" ordered Striker, "in the name of Her Majesty's police!"

"Fuck you and fuck her Majesty. She's my wife and I'll do what I like!"

Striker stepped forward. Flo was now hanging grimly on to Tank's wrists. Striker took another step forward, reaching out to grab Tank's arm. Iris took the opportunity to sneak away and run upstairs to warn James. Tank let go of Flo and she flopped to the floor. He then swung a haymaker at Striker, his huge fist connecting with Striker's square, closely shaven jaw. Striker collapsed in a pile. Flo scrambled up and staggered towards the kitchen, gaining speed as she went, looking for James. Tank lumbered after her, but she was nimble and managed to keep just ahead. And then they heard the most horrible scream, thin and piercing. It was Iris's thin sharp voice. "Oh God! Help! He's hung himself!"

Frank, with difficulty, stepped over Striker's prone body and half ran half skipped to the kitchen, leading the way up the stairs. Tank followed, taking the stairs two at a time, his huge bulk slowing him down. Striker stirred and was now on his knees, spewing blood and saliva on the floor. Iris stood at the stop of the stairs, her hands to her mouth, screaming. Frank was first in the room and saw James, naked, hanging from the ceiling, a belt twisted around his neck and tied to the light cord. Tank pushed Frank aside and grabbed James by the legs, lifting him up to relieve the weight. The legs felt warm to his cheek. It was likely James was still alive. "Someone undo the belt or get something to cut him down" he growled.

"Leave him alone!" cried Flo, "It's God's work! He's sending him to Hell where he belongs!"

"Shut up you stupid bitch!" screamed Iris, tears streaming down her cheeks. She clutched Flo's shoulders with both hands and shook her so hard, it was a wonder that Flo's neck didn't snap. "It's your fault! It's all your fault!" She looked around the room and added, "and mine too," and kept shaking and shaking.

"Iris, you better let her go. You're hurting her," wheezed Frank.

At that moment, Striker appeared at the door, butcher's knife in hand. He staggered in, pushing Iris and Flo aside, and stepped up on the chair that James must have used to launch himself. Tank's legs were getting tired and he was swaying back and forth. He would have to let go any second. "Hang on," said Striker, "I think I can undo the belt." He dropped the knife to the floor and fiddled with the belt buckle.

"Come on! Hurry! I can't hold him much longer!"

At last, the belt came loose and Tank took the full weight of the body, falling forward, and James landed with a thump on the bed. Iris jumped on the bed, pulled the belt away from his neck, and lay close to him, hugging his naked body. "I'll keep him warm," she sobbed.

Frank grabbed the bed sheet and covered them both. "Is he still alive?" he asked meekly.

"I don't know, I don't know!" sobbed Iris.

*

Iris took over James's job as head barman of the Saloon bar. Frank was most impressed with her work, she was so dependable, so thorough. The glasses had never been so clean, the entire Saloon bar spotless. And the customers, contrary to all dire predictions that a woman could never tend a bar in an Australian pub, were most appreciative, and amazingly well behaved and respectful. For a while, blokes would come into the bar just to experience the spectacle of a woman barman. But there were no snide jokes about women in bars, only polite please-and-thank-you's. For her part, Iris had found her place, she thought. She enjoyed the bar routine, the cleaning and preparing more than anything else, but now that the customers had got used to her, enjoyed their company too. The regulars came in each day, she had their drinks ready, learned their names, they smiled, occasionally told her of their troubles. And gradually, some of them began to bring in their lady friends or even wives, something everyone had predicted would never happen.

And now, she was well settled in her house at Yarraville. She had decided in the end to keep the lace curtains and enjoyed sitting at the little table with the lace tablecloth that auntie Connie probably made, sipping a cup of tea in the early mornings, watching the cars go by on the Geelong Road. Later in the day there would be hammering and sawing as the builders got to work on the new Commission house next door. It would be good to have neighbours to replace the nests of tiger snakes that hid away among the scotch thistles and rough old rocks covered in lichen. James would be pleased with that, she thought with satisfaction.

*

On some days Flo would catch the train up to Footscray and stay for a day or two. They had come to an unstated arrangement, which was basically to observe and appreciate a silence between them, Flo having learned to keep her mouth shut, never to proselytize with Iris. If she could talk to her, she would tell her daughter, born in such terrible sin, that she had prayed so hard to Jesus who in the end had appeared to her one morning as she was stubbing out a cigarette at her kitchen table. He did not speak, but she heard Him, His faint image appearing in the steam of her kettle that sat on the gas stove boiling and whistling. He had forgiven Iris for she knew not what she had done by being born. He held out his hand to Flo, His thumb bent across his palm, the fingers slightly curled up as though He were beckoning to her. Foolishly, she had, through habit, reached for her Garrick cigarette box and held it out to Him. "You are a foolish woman," he said, "she is your life, made in your image, go to her, comfort her, forgive her the sin that you put upon her." The image became clearer and with it, Flo weaker. She wanted to stand before Him, but knew that she must not stand, but kneel. She felt all the life drain from her body, slid off her old chrome chair and fell listless to the floor, like a drunk slides away under the table. The table obstructed her view of the kettle which whistled loudly. Jesus had departed. Had Tank been there, he would have abused her, "what the fuckn hell are you doing under the fuckn table?" Or maybe he would have supposed she had kicked it, thought Flo. Either way, she had no need to worry. Tank had got three years for assaulting a police officer and was languishing away in the Geelong gaol. Good riddance to him. She could lie here under the table and die in peace, in her own kitchen, which was her life anyway.

When she awoke, she knew she was not in Heaven or Hell, but still under her table. She scrambled out, looked for her cigarettes and threw them into the fire of the kitchen stove. Jesus had spoken and this was her answer. She quickly packed a small bag, walked down to the station and caught the train to Footscray and she was sitting on the front step of Iris's house when Iris got home from work. Both of them, without thinking at all, ran to each other and hugged in silence. Iris did not ask what had happened, Flo seemed so genuinely happy to be with her. Occasionally on weekends, Linda and the brat came with her, only now the brat wasn't ever called the brat, but Sylvy or her full name Sylvia when she was naughty, which now was not that often. Linda had started her at school and to everyone's amazement, she learned to read in no time and loved going to school. Iris looked forward to her visits and enjoyed reading books along with her. When Flo went off to church, Linda regaled Iris with stories of her clients, many of whom Iris could remember, some of whom she had probably slept in their house when she was as free as the wind, she liked to say, the wind of "window."

*

On Monday, her day off, Iris would take the train into Flinders Street, do a little shopping, then catch the tram up to Pentridge. She searched for things to take James, but always, if she happened to buy something for him, he rejected it. He wanted for nothing, he insisted. All he wanted was her, and she, he could not have. Grimesy had done his best to get him off. Striker had charged James with murder, which Grimesy managed to beat, but the secondary charge of manslaughter had stuck. The image of an upright moral preacher being squashed to death by an uncouth ill-tempered youth was too much for the jury. Grimesy tried to convince the jury that James was suffering from severe mental trauma from his tour of duty in Vietnam, but this hurt rather than helped, because the Vietnam war was not popular, many of those returning from military service spurned and derided. And his attempted suicide was viewed paradoxically by the jury as something that he had brought on himself. In the end, the judge sentenced James to ten years in the notorious Pentridge prison, with mandatory psychotherapy for the first year, eligible for parole at the Governor's pleasure. During the trial and for some time afterwards at Pentridge, James was placed on suicide watch, but gradually this surveillance loosened as it became apparent that James had quieted down and adjusted well to the routines of prison life. He had his own cell, not that much smaller than the rooms he had slept in over the years, his room at the old Corio Shire was smaller, he thought, the one at the Newmarket not much bigger, and if you counted Iris into it, smaller. It was just Iris that he missed, but even there, as he thought about the years they had been together, he wondered whether they really did love each other like they said. It was mainly sex, after all, followed maybe by a bit of love, but really, what was it? He was starved of it in prison, for there was no love there, it was just rough sex if you were so inclined and wanted it. And now he did not want it. It came with too many complications and come to think of it, when he was with Iris, it too came with endless complications. So, he had settled down to a kind of happiness with himself, alone in his cell, taking his food with regularity, writing in his note-book, although that had tapered off too. There didn't seem any point to it. The first few months or so, when Iris came to visit, they talked a lot. He insisted on giving her the house, which at first, she resisted, firmly stating that owning a house and living in it went against her whole way of life. It would make her into something that she was not. But James would not listen. He insisted on signing over the deed to her. Grimesy had strongly objected, pointing out that, among other things, it would be considered a sale so there would be stamp duty and all kinds of expenses to pay, and could Iris afford it anyway? She would have to borrow money to pay for the transfer. And who knows? With good behaviour, argued Grimesy, he might get out on parole within a couple of years. Then he might have nowhere to go. What then?

*

Iris would remember forever the day they met in prison and James signed over the deed. Grimesy made one last attempt to stop him, charging that it was tantamount to committing suicide. She saw James's tell-tale anger rise up, his ears and cheeks bright red. "Then fuck off," he said to Grimesy, "I don't need you or the house."

Iris reached over, grabbed Jimmy's hand and said, "Jimmy, sweetie, don't say that. Grimesy has been such a good friend." She took the deed and looked at Grimesy, then back to James. "I promise I will look after it, and it will be there for you when you get out."

Grimesy took both their hands. "All I want is what's best for you both," he said with a faint smile, then added with a bigger smile, "talking as a friend, not as your lawyer."

James squeezed Grimesy's hand hard. "Have you told Eddie?" he asked. Eddie had not come near him ever since the Newmarket incident.

"I have. He was none too pleased. After all, he passed the house on to you."

"Fuck him!"

"You don't mean that. He's done a lot for you, I'm sure you appreciate it."

"You're starting to sound like one of my fathers," mumbled James.

"I promise I'll keep in touch with him," said Iris.

The fact was, Eddie had given up on James. It seemed that every time he did something to help him, he messed it all up, got himself into big trouble. Giving him the house just created an opportunity for James to show how messed up he was. Betting it on a horse! For God's sake! The boy has no sense. He was a danger to himself and others, that was what the judge had said when he delivered his sentence, and he had to agree. And marrying that hopeless little cunt Iris who didn't know who or where she was a lot of the time, what kind of future could you expect? It was a very sad circumstance. He had gone to the wedding in an effort to show his support, but it was such a ramshackle affair, he

came away disgusted and decided for his own peace of mind, to give up on them, sever all ties. Maybe he just didn't know how to be a good father. He thought he had done everything he could to help him, to make up for the lost years. Maybe he did too much.

"Me too," said Grimesy.

The prison guard hovered above them. Time was up. James wanted dearly to hug Iris, but hugging was not allowed. There were no tears in his eyes, though. His whole body was stiff with resolve. He would take his punishment like a man and enjoy his days and months of solitude. As he walked back to the cell, he muttered, "well Dad, wherever you are, this is where you've put me. Being here will be just like sitting on your old stool at the pub."

"What's that, son?" asked the guard, quite a bit older than James, probably near retirement.

"I'm not your son," answered James, grinning at the guard as he was let into his cell. And as the key turned in the lock, he lay down on the stiff mattress, his hands behind his head, thinking of the life that awaited him. The past now was well and truly over, from here in his cell, in his solitude, he could create his future, which, given the space of his cell, he knew rested entirely within himself. He must not allow the past to dictate his future.

*

That I accidentally on purpose killed an asshole like the Preacher was probably something I should be punished for, but the bastard deserved it, especially as he and I knew—and we are the only ones besides the brat— that he had killed Millie in a horrible murder. At least my murder was an accident. His was a disgusting horror of a killing. And then to try to get me hanged for it. That was the end. The bastard I hope is roasting in hell right now for his filthy crime. Poor Millie. OK, so the Preacher had a family, or so they said. Don't know how anyone could put up with him or would even acknowledge him as a relative, he was such an asshole. Anyway, what's done is done and I can't bring him back. I don't have anything to make up for, although I would, if they brought them in, apologize to his family, if he has any, and tell them that I'm sorry. They wouldn't believe me, though, would they? I mean, how else can I convince them I am sorry except by suffering here in prison for ten years? And how can that make them feel any better? It doesn't bring the Preacher back, does it? All it does is remind them of the so-called crime. The only way they can forgive me is to forget that the crime ever happened, and how is that at all possible? I could get on my knees, lash myself with a whip, even cut off my fingers before them, but that would not bring the Preacher back, would it? It would only cause them to remember the so-called crime all over again and demand more punishment for me. Even if they tortured me until I died, would that erase the so-called crime?" I'd say it would etch the so-called crime into their brains, so they would never forget and never forgive. Anyway, if they're good Christians, they should love me as well as forgive me. It's all impossible.

The December sun beamed its limitless energy through the small barred window of his cell. He quickly dismissed any thought of Iris climbing through it. Instead, he reached for one of the three books he had managed to keep in his cell, Plato's Republic, the Bible and Ovid's Love Poems. All three books reminded him of his past failures. The day he signed up for the army was a clear sign of failure in his opinion, given that he was injured and did nothing at all to stop the atrocities of which he was a part. His ridiculous idea that he was a star Latin student, so gullible, so easily taken in by that poofda professor Pulcher. I should have beaten the shit out of him when I had the chance. Those uni people. Grimesy was the only good bloke among them. And don't talk to me about Kate, that slut. And the bible, what use was it? Look at Flo, the poor stupid woman, getting beaten up by Tank every other day. Why did Jesus allow that? Dad? Are you listening to me? But I tell you Dad, I'm not dwelling on the past, I'm going to read and read these three books and by the time they let me out I'll know them off by heart. I'll recite every page. It's an endless future, Dad, don't you see? Are you there?

James closed his eyes and allowed his body to relax. "I'm serving Time, Dad. Time. Here, I'm suspended in it. You're doing the same thing, where you are, just like you did when you sat on your bar stool, spoke to no one. Just sipped your beer and plonk, no thoughts, just a simple feeling of satisfaction, nothing to think about, nothing to look forward to except where the next lot of booze will come from. A life at peace with itself. Don't you think Dad? Dad?

James rolled off his bed and kneeled beside it. He stared up at the small barred window, the sun's rays striking his face. "Dad? Can't you answer me just this once?" He called, his hands clasped together in the manner of prayer.

A voice inside his head boomed, "son! Save yourself!" He clasped his head in his hands as though he had a terrible headache and cried, "I'm not your son!" and threw himself on his bed, burying his head in the pillow, crying inconsolably, his whole body convulsing with sobs. And then, against his will, a memory penetrated his sobs; he remembered the Preacher in his dying moments calling for his bible, and he, James, of all people, reciting psalm 23, "The Lord is my Shepherd," he said to himself, and said it over and over again, until he fell peacefully into a deep sleep, from which he hoped he would not awaken.

*

The next morning, or more like midday, he awoke in a sweat. The unrelenting summer sun pierced through the bars and filled his cell with an oppressive, overbearing heat. Faint noises of traffic wafted in on the breeze, carrying the high-pitched voices of children. Embarrassed, he awoke to thoughts of Kate.

Iris, I know you're there. I'm sorry for everything, truly I am. I did everything for you I always said, and I'm sorry. I did it all for myself now I see. I didn't know. I never thought at all. I drank too much. I gave it up. I did God's work, though. I killed that devil The Preacher, I know the Lord will forgive me, for I did his work for him. Presumptuous I know. You probably don't know that word, Iris my love. Never mind. I'll keep talking to you. You're the only one left for me now. Tell Flo I love her too, though I haven't much room in my heart left for anyone else, but you. I will serve out my time and every day pray to you. I'm used to not having you. I know you're happy alone and apart from me. I brought only misery on you. And you risked your sweet little life on me. I look forward to my full ten years, praying for you every day, why shorten it? The longer I am here the more time I will have to pray for you.

The guard appeared with a lunch tray in hand.

At Jimmy's insistence, Grimesy had petitioned for his time to be served in solitary confinement, with exercise in the common yard for only 30 minutes every Monday. He received all his meals in his cell. He had become convinced that his own company was the only company that could be trusted. For was it not clear that, when he lived with others, he inevitably got into trouble? The sensible thing to do was to be alone. It did not stop him from thinking of others and in that way their lives were part of his. Maybe it would take all of ten years of thinking alone with himself, his memories of others, and his favourite books, to come to terms with his past life. Thinking is a way of making amends, saying sorry a million times over, it surely will work. He looked at the lunch tray and did not feel in the least bit hungry.

He rolled off his cot and began to do push-ups. He had never exercised in his life, except when forced to in the army. It just seemed like something that he had to do. He was unable to do many and quickly the sweat poured in great streams from his neck, armpits and everywhere else. He reached to the lunch tray and drank the cup of water. Then turned the tray back.

Each day the guard would come by, find the cup empty, but most of the food untouched. And each day James did more and more push-ups, now counting them and writing the tally on the wall. At this rate, the entire wall would be full in ten years. As he grew thinner, his mind grew clearer, or more precisely, uncluttered. He refused visitors, viewing them as a distraction from his single-minded pursuit of redemption. Soon, his mind was free of most all memories, he had successfully starved them out. So that he would not forget Iris, he counted his push-ups in Irises ("one-Iris, two Iris,"). She would stay with him for as long as he lived, and he with her even after that, he was sure.

*

The heat wave passed and for a while the sun stopped shining through his cell window. His daily routine had come to him naturally. Read, sleep, exercise, water, sleep, read, sleep, exercise, water, sleep. So immersed was he in this routine that one day began to blend in with another, night into day, day into night. It was not a rhythm of light and darkness, but a trance-like state of enlightenment. He counted his push-ups with difficulty, stopped trying to think and found this to be incredibly liberating. Free of thought, his body became a haven of peace. His mind had become his body. James was now beyond knowing. Redemption was not something that you could achieve through good deeds or confessions. It had to be felt, it had to descend on one. All one could do was to prepare the body to accept it when redemption came down.

When the sun finally appeared again through the bars of his cell, his eyes remained shut, yet he saw every sunbeam. But on this morning, he did not roll off his cot, and did not begin his push-ups. He heard his mother call, or was it Iris? He called out, but his lips did not move, no sound entered his cell. He reached for his cup of water, but no hand or arm moved.

The water in the cup had run over.

THE END

Other fiction by Colin Heston

9/11 Two.
It's politics as usual when criminologist Maciver tries to thwart a terrorist drone tack on New York City. Harrow and Heston Publishers. 2016.. E-book and paperback. Amazon

The Tommie Felon Show and other outrageous stories.
A collection of stories ranging from the absurd to the improbable, with a cynical twist. Harrow and Heston Publishers. 2017. E-book and paperback, Amazon.

About the Author

Colin Heston is the pen name of a criminologist of international repute. He has written nonfiction books on the history of punishment and torture, edited a four volume encyclopedia on *Crime and Punishment around the World,* and regularly contributes to a variety of criminology and criminal justice periodicals. His next novel, *Ferry to Williamstown*, a subcultural murder mystery set in Williamstown Australia, will be released early in 2019. He is currently putting the finishing touches to his next nonfiction book, *Civilization and Barbarism.*

HARROW AND HESTON
PUBLISHERS

Australia,
New York & Philadelphia